ANTELOPES

A Modern Gulliver's Travels

By
David Rich

Also by David Rich:

Sail the World? – An Absurdly True Story, Prequel to RV the World

Myths of the Tribe - When Religion and Ethics Diverge

Scribes of the Tribe - The Great Thinkers on Religion and Ethics

The ISIS Affair - Putting the Fun Back in Fundamentalism

Table of Contents

1

"Where are we?" The plane was dark, with no aisle lights, and the air was smoky, with a bright metallic taste.

Mack elbowed Lucas, sprawled out in the next seat. Lucas had a purple welt across his forehead, and his orange-red hair looked a mess, draping his face like Raggedy Andy, and difficult to make out in the dark. He didn't respond to the elbow.

Mack and Lucas were Arizona Lottery employees, chaperoning eighteen newly minted millionaires in first class to Carnival in Rio. They'd taken off from Caracas at three a.m., on the third leg of their flight. But now it was dead quiet, except for a loud whack in the back, followed by a lighter thump, repeated endlessly. There were no alarms, no cabin crew, and it was freezing cold.

Mack felt his forehead, finding a lump the size of a peach pit. "It smells like an electrical fire," he said, coughing. He looked closely at Lucas's pale face and bloodshot eyes. Probably in shock.

Lucas struggled to sit up. "Where's my big book? You know the one I mean." He looked around. "I'm worried now, mate." He shook his head as though he were dizzy.

"Your millions-of-quotes book? Forget the unimportant stuff and find our hats. We have to look good when we're rescued. Full uniform, you know." Mack brushed a hand over his head, obviously feeling muddled.

"Unimportant to you, not me. Me mum gave me that book."

Mack rolled his eyes. "Haven't seen it. Don't know where it is. Don't care." He felt as languid as silk, floating with no particular place to go.

1

Lucas looked so pole-axed that Mack felt sorry for him. "You might have dropped it on the floor and it slid somewhere when we…apparently crashed. There's been a lot going on."

Someone pounded on Mack's shoulder with more force than necessary. "Ah, Mrs. Sherman. You can lay off now."

Courtney Sherman, one of the eighteen winners, was as round as a cement mixer and twice as strong. Her hair looked like a wig, every strand the same flat black, and she wore a purple blouse under the straps of overalls she'd sown into a long denim skirt. She was looking forward to Carnival as a chance to convert sinners.

She leaned into Mack's face. "Call me Courtney."

"Just a second. I've got a problem here." He turned back to Lucas. "Forget your big book. You couldn't read in all this smoke anyway. And quotes are silly stuff."

"Indeed," said Lucas. "And I quote. 'Be careful; with quotations you can damn anything.'"

"Yeah, and who said that?" demanded Mack.

"Who knows? I don't."

"You remember the quotes but you don't remember who said it? That's bizarre."

Mack grimaced as Courtney bellowed. "You two listen up. Now's the time to say our prayers. Ask the Lord Almighty to spare us, deliver us from this predicament. You're supposed to be taking care of us and you haven't done a thing."

Lucas said, "Cut the religious claptrap—"

Mack held up a hand. "No, Lucas. Let Courtney be." Mack turned to face Courtney, who reminded him of his mother. "I appreciate your concern, but the Arizona Lottery doesn't take sides on religion. But I'd be happy to pray with you while Lucas assists the survivors."

"That's a firm negatory," she snapped. "Lucas must also give thanks that we're alive. Then we can tend to the others."

"We have to check the cockpit, ma'am," said Mack before turning to whisper at Lucas, "Don't trash poor Courtney, you hear?" Then he continued as if he hadn't interrupted himself. "We'll come back and pray if you'd like."

Courtney stood next to Mack with her hands pressed together, clogging the aisle. "Pray first. Time for clear thoughts and clean actions. And a mighty dose of prayer."

Mack sighed, clasping his hands. "Dear Lord, keep us safe in our time of need. And help us get out of whatever mess we're in. Amen." He put his hands down. "Now, Courtney, we need to help the living. You could check out the whack-thump noise in the back, see what's causing that."

Courtney shook Mack's shoulder. "Something's really wrong in back."

Mack unsnapped his seatbelt like he hadn't thought of it before. "I haven't seen the cabin crew since before the crash."

Lucas frowned. "I don't want to read it. But I want to make sure it's still around. From me mum, you know."

"Stop about the book already. Besides, you're in America, now. Well, South America, I suppose."

"Always was an American. Me mum says so. Even if Immigration doesn't agree. Airplanes have always been trouble." Lucas eyes were out of focus. He looked like an oversized kid.

"Get up." Mack unsnapped Lucas's belt, whipping the cloth cap with the seal of the Arizona Lottery from his back pocket and setting it on his head. He turned to Lucas. "Put your cap on."

"Okay." Lucas jumped up and slapped on his own cap. Lucas stood inches shorter than Courtney. Mack towered over both of them.

Mack said, "We'd better check the cockpit, see what's going on up there. That's where the flight attendants went, before we…landed."

Courtney groaned. "We should all pray and then get everyone out of here. Something might blow up, like ourselves."

"Spoken like a true leader yourself," said Mack. "So why aren't you helping the others? I'm sure Ellen is."

"Who can deal with this mess?" She pointed at the back.

The cloud of green smoke smelled poisonous and the seats were cock-eyed. Crazy Peter, the wild blond guy, had barfed on the seat in front of him, purging the drinks they drank with abandon in first class from Phoenix to Miami to Caracas.

Mack sighed. "This is our job, Courtney. So, let's find the crew."

"Before whatever happened, they went up front, into the cockpit." Lucas pointed.

"Yeah, I know that. Something funny with the cockpit door." It was curved forty-five degrees, making the padding look like the inside of an egg. "Let's check it out."

Courtney vehemently shook her head. "But what about the others? We should attend to them first. And don't you find the whack-thump noise rather worrisome?"

Mack waved away the smoke and gently took Courtney's arm, the size of an eight-by-eight, steering her toward the nearest seat. He patted her shoulder. "You have to get out of the way so we can make sure everyone's okay. Help Ellen or stay put until we need you,"

Just then Lucas ran by, ramming the cockpit door with his shoulder. "Oh, sheissarino." He ricocheted backward, fluttering fingers padded with blisters. "Little hot up there. The outside door is the first priority, eh?"

"Whoa, the outside door it is." Mack gave the circular lock a mighty twist, colossal tug, and magnificent jolt. Nothing.

"There's a lock on these things. Right over here, on the underside of the doohickey." Lucas clicked something, and with his left pointer finger twirled the handle, which slid into a groove. The door opened a crack and a torrent of wind tore Lucas's cap off, pasting it against the opposite bulkhead. Lucas was right behind it, spread-eagled. The cockpit door turned pink in the hurricane of air.

Mack yelled, "Everyone out. No time left to screw around." He shoved the door closed, watching Lucas collapse off the wall. "Fine acting."

"I'll deploy the chute." Lucas punched at indentations, buttons, and whatever seemed handy. Still no chute. "Might be a big drop." He pushed the door open a few inches and peered outside. The wind spread his bushy hair into a fantail. "I can't see a damn thing in the dark. Could be a real worry, mate."

"Brilliant. Get a big flashlight, a torch, and let's see how it looks out there."

"Here you go, young man." Courtney shoved a flashlight in Mack's face. "Anything else I can do to help, let me know." She added, "I'll pray for you both," and bowed her head.

"Sure thing, Courtney." Mack elbowed Lucas out of the way and aimed the flashlight through the crack, the wind so strong it seemed to blow the light back inside. Mack grimaced as he stared down, wind whipping his face. "About a ten-foot drop. Not that far."

"Amen." Courtney raised her head and swept toward the door.

"Wait a minute, Courtney." Mack held up an arm, but she ignored it, kicking the door open and plopping down in the doorway. The plane gave a shudder and the whack-thump stopped for a second as the wind became a tornado inside the cabin.

Courtney jumped out and crunched on the ground with a splash. At her unearthly screech, Mack shined the flash down. "Are you okay, Courtney?"

"That's a hearty negativo, son." She leaned on ham-like legs, wallowing in a mud puddle as the wind blew her into the shape of a forty-five-degree butterball.

"Okay. Who's next?" asked Mack as another millionaire walked up.

"Ready, sir," said James Dean. "But I need my hat. I'm uncomfortable without it, naked, like an undressed deer in season."

"I can identify with that. You help Courtney out of the puddle and we'll look for your hat, and our formal ones too."

During the nationally broadcast lottery drawing, James had imitated his namesake from an old movie called *Giant* and the performance had gone viral. They had to find their official hats because Mack considered them critical to establishing credentials with the locals.

Mack poked James, who jumped cleanly out the door, fortunately landing clear of Courtney.

5

Mack flashed the light on James, who walked in a precarious tilt around Courtney, trying to see which way she was facing. She looked pretty much the same from any direction.

"Next," said Mack as Lucas pushed two large bundles in his face. "What's this?"

"Supplies. We need more liquor and pillows, blankets, food, and water too."

"We have to get our people off first, and then worry about necessities." Mack crushed the gray cap into his back pocket.

"I'm next," yelled Ef. Everyone knew Ef. He'd collared them all, trying to sell property on the furthest outskirts of Phoenix, where it might grow in a millennium. He was jumping up and down like an elevator, similar to his shoes. "Gotta get someone on the ground with management skills. Someone has to organize this disaster." Ef selling himself long.

"Ladies and children first," said Lucas. "Or can I interest you in desert scrub, hold the utilities?"

"Just trying to help." Ef stood on his tiptoes. "Aim the flashlight so I know where to jump."

"Go ahead." Lucas bobbed the light over the little group below. Ef grasped the edge with his hands, hanging indecisively. Lucas stepped on his fingers.

"Aheeeee—" Ef plummeted into the puddle. He faced off with Courtney as she ransacked the bundles of supplies James had failed to guard.

"Whoosh." The door to the cockpit flared and the other dozen plus millionaires, along with Mack and Lucas, jumped out the door. They fled the puddle to the shelter of strangely shaped rocks. Lucas and Mack adjusted their uniforms and slapped on the cloth garrison hats the airline had made them wear instead of their formal hats. The airline didn't want them mistaken for someone important like a pilot.

Light flickered from the door of the plane, subsiding, then expanding. Mack pushed Lucas. "Get back up there and see what's happening."

"Go yourself." Lucas clicked the rapidly dimming flashlight on the scene around them. Blond Peter was trying to rollick and roll as if party mode still ruled. But he couldn't compete with the vicious wind. He ran down like a wind-up toy with a tired spring, and his good buddy Chuck was nowhere to be seen. The two of them had celebrated on the flight like Siamese twins. Only seventeen lottery millionaires were left.

Ef was organizing, but it was difficult to tell what. Ellen consoled the bereaved, which included everyone. And Mack stood in awe, distracted by Ellen.

Courtney lectured James that alcohol was not allowed in their new residence, though no one had a clue where that residence was. But it definitely wasn't Rio.

The rest milled around, awaiting Mack's orders, surrounded by hundreds of pinnacles, boulders, and glistening puddles of water that smelled like rotten fruit.

Mack held up his arms. "Listen up. We don't know what caused the crash, but the plane could catch fire at any moment. Lucas will take you to safer ground. Lucas, show the kind people where to go.

"Then I need volunteers to go back on the plane to find available supplies and see whether there are other survivors. We'll try getting to the luggage before the plane explodes or burns." The gangway above them belched a single puff of smoke. "Now men, we're going back in. Volunteers?"

Lucas shone the light on the faces around him. Zero to none volunteered. "You'll have to call the names of volunteers."

Mack said, "Mr. Peter Vittorio, Mr. James Dean, Mr. Roy Jacobowitz, and Mr. Barry McCafferty. Front and center, report for duty." He motioned Lucas to turn the spotlight on the plane as irresistible Ellen stalked forward.

She said, "Now look here, Mr. Steward."

Mack practically stuttered. "I'm not a steward. I'm simply irresistible, make that irresponsible. What I mean is, for some unfathomable reason, I'm responsible for your welfare. So, take care of these poor souls while we try to gather food and look for other survivors."

"No siree, your list of *volunteers* is sexist. You have no women at all. You must include me. Or," Ellen indicated Molly and Betty, "at least one of us."

7

The others looked elsewhere as Nick, the Serbian Orthodox priest said, "'Adam was deceived by Eve, not Eve by Adam—it is right that he whom that woman induced to sin should assume the guide lest he fall again through feminine instability.'"

Lucas turned the light on Ellen as she, completely out of character, forwarded a finger signal at Nick.

Mack's heart melted at the sight of Ellen in the harsh light, her filmy blouse caressing the curves above her swirly linen skirt. Then a corner of the plane caught his eye and he understood the whack-thump. "Shine it over there."

A collective gasp escaped the group as the pale light traced the outline of the small part of the plane's rear they could see. They had *landed* on the edge of a sheer cliff, breaking off the rear two-thirds of the plane. A strip of metal held the back thumping against the cliff face. It wouldn't last long.

Ellen put a hand to her throat. "That's the coach section. They're doomed unless we save them."

Mack sighed. "We'll do our best. You continue tending the only flock we know is still among the living."

Lucas swung the torch toward the gangway as the whack-thump intensified.

"Well, Okay. Anything to avoid feminine instability." Ellen helped gather the rest of the group as the men circled Mack.

Mack said, "We'll rescue everyone we can. Then gather food, water, and blankets, and find a way into the luggage compartment. It's going to be chilly, wherever it is we're at."

"Going to be, hell." Lucas shivered. "It's already colder than the outback in a blizzard."

They shivered as the gale tore at their clothes, and queued up behind Mack and Lucas.

Mack stared, trying to decide whether the light came from the glowing cockpit.

"Looks like a reflection," said Lucas.

"We'll boost you up so you can make sure."

"Boost me how? It must be fifteen feet straight up."

"It's more like ten or twelve. I need athletic volunteers. James, Barry, and Roy."

"Yeah, and what about me?" Peter illustrated his athletic ability by executing a half-assed cartwheel.

"You did better when you won the lottery."

Peter glanced at Roy. "Guess I've gone downhill since."

"James, Barry, and Roy. Make a pyramid so Lucas can climb into the plane. We've got to stop screwing around. We don't have enough food or blankets, and someone might be alive in coach."

James and Barry hit the ground, side by side, and big clunky Roy climbed on their backs. They shook in the wind as Lucas scrambled over their backs onto Roy. Lucas clutched the door frame.

"Gotta get you in shape, sailor. You're not doing too good."

Lucas pulled himself up. "We may have five minutes. The cockpit door is black, and the whack-thump has changed." It had sped up, as if the equilibrium had shifted.

Lucas raced around the smoky front section, ripping off curtains. He tied five together and looped them around the seat nearest the door. "Come on up, guys. And hurry because it's getting hotter up here."

The entire group made it, standing in the doorway staring, none venturing forward. "To the rear," said Lucas.

The others looked at Mack, who pointed. "To the rear."

They tiptoed until they stood next to the whack-thump, which was receding. Mack ripped the curtains from the doorway, revealing the glow of a false dawn.

"Good view, eh?" Lucas stared.

Mack could make out faint terrain, which must have been a vertical mile below them. The light was too dim to see.

"Down there." Lucas pointed and everyone peered over the edge, looking at the mass in the bottom of economy class. It was so dark no one could see the bottom, whack-thumping away.

"The tail may pull the plane over." Mack beckoned them away from the precipice. "Get as much food and blankets as you can and let's get out of here. Maybe the luggage is in the level part of the plane."

"Chuck might be down there," said Peter.

9

Lucas said, "We have to see if there's anyone left to rescue." At their incredulous he said, "Someone could be alive."

Everyone stared except Lucas, who said, "Come on, gentlemen. Where's your compassion?"

"I agree," said Peter. "Chuck has to be down there. I can't think of where he would have gone, otherwise."

Mack nodded. "You're right, so let's do it. We'd never forgive ourselves if we didn't."

Lucas was pale. "Yeah, if there's any of us left to forgive. But then, it was my idea. Not to worry."

Mack gestured to hurry up. "Grab as many curtains as you can and we'll loop them together." In a few seconds they'd made a lumpy gray rope, Peter on his stomach feeding it over the edge, into the void.

"Just there. Flip it this way." Lucas jerked it to the left, snaking the end onto the mass below. "Where's the light? Shine it down there."

Roy found a halogen light, which Mack aimed below. He flicked the switch on, and just as rapidly off. "Enough of that. You saw the carnage. No one survived."

"Yeah." Lucas untied and dropped the end of the loop as he hopped up. "Got to get all the supplies we can find."

"Don't forget my hat," said James.

"Don't worry. We'll take everything important." Mack walked down the aisle, flipping open overhead bins. "Toss the stuff out and we'll ransack the galley."

"Hey, look at this." Barry brandished a fire ax. "This might come in handy."

"Toss it with the rest and let's get a move on. You guys hit the galley. Take everything you can grab and don't worry about what's what. Time's getting short."

"Amen to that," said Lucas.

"And look what I found. Our dress hats." Mack whipped his on and tossed the other to Lucas, the hat changing Lucas into an authority figure in his gray pinstripe suit, the regulation uniform for the chaperones of the new millionaires. "AL," the logo of the Arizona Lottery, was embroidered like scrambled eggs on a pilot-style hat.

"Lookin' good." Mack flipped the hat over his bald spot. "But we have to get moving. Toss that stuff down. Good job. Where'd you get that great coil of rope? There must be several hundred feet."

Within minutes they'd vaulted out of the plane, moving piles toward the rest of the group.

"Front and center." Mack beckoned them together. "We've gotten everything we can find. Now, same volunteers to look for the luggage compartment."

"Any survivors?" Nick held pale Mary tight.

"We're it. Now the luggage."

"That's a big negatory, Mr. Mack," said Courtney. "You have no moral leadership. I've once again had to cull legions of liquor from your leavings." She gestured at jagged miniature booze bottles lined up like fractured crystal.

Mack looked her up and down, from brown brogans to the mud covering the bottom of her tent-like dress. "Actually, a pository, Courtney. If you're running out of things to do, you can help Miss Ellen here." Mack avoided staring at Ellen. "You can join our expedition if you'd like."

"No. I'll stay here and do housewifey things. You big brawny men go ahead and keep us poor damsels safe from distress. We're counting on you."

"If I knew you better, I'd think that was sarcastic."

Ellen turned her back. "No need to know me better, sir."

Mack grabbed the fire ax. "They loaded the luggage on the other side. Same group, Roy, Barry, Peter, and James." Mack led them between spiky rocks and around a dimly seen granite pinnacle that hid the nose of the plane. The glow of false dawn would turn to sunrise in a few minutes.

"My god, look at that," gasped Lucas. "There's a fancy face on top of the hill. You ever seen anything like it?"

"Luggage first." Mack brandished the ax like a Viking. They staggered around the towering pinnacle and ducked in front of the plane, partly sheltered from the wind. Benny and Peter gushed noteworthy obscenities at the end of the procession.

"Stop." Mack held up a hand. His neck prickled like he was in a haunted house.

Lucas fingered the side of the plane. "The luggage compartment might be here." The wind seemed to be dying.

"I'll get it." Mack swung the ax with all his might. It ricocheted, almost smacking him in the forehead. "Whew. We'll have less of that," dropping the ax. He looked over their entourage. Peter was a flake and James would be lost without his hat. Roy was an eternal pessimist, but he was rough and ready, a big, amiable, and perpetually fucked up sailor who couldn't stand being called a yachtsman. And Barry, ex-Tennessee state trooper, retired as a private eye in Sun City West. "What do you think, Roy?"

Roy said what he always said, dramatic and simple. He slashed the air with his hand. "Everything's going downhill."

"Thought so. Take this." Mack handed the ax to Barry. "Bust in the side of the plane. That might be the luggage compartment."

"Yes, sir, Mr. Mack." Barry grabbed the ax and slammed it against the seam. The ax bit into the crack before spinning through the air, bouncing off rocks like a pebble off water, disappearing into the curious vegetation they could begin to see around them.

"Enough of that," said Lucas. "Let's see what's on top of the hill."

Barry said, "No. Let's find the ax, put it back together, and try again. It's light enough to find it now."

"You're overruled," yelled Lucas as they followed Mack around the crumpled nose of the plane. Barry was last seen rummaging in the foliage.

Mack climbed around the blackened windshield of the plane, trying to peer through the glass, but he couldn't see a thing. "So, where and what was the big deal you saw, anyway?"

"Further around, on top of the rocky knob. The one with the—wow. There's a big gold umbrella beside it—" They caught a gleam of the rising sun on a golden statue towering above a canopy that must have knocked over by the plane.

Ef, the shyster real estate salesman, sidled over. "I hope we didn't ruin anything important." He salivated as he dashed to touch the statue. "It must be worth a fortune." He wiped a

12

hand across the highest part he could reach. "What is it, anyway?"

He stepped back, which they all did in unison, taking in the grandeur of the golden figure.

"Well, it looks like that big old stag in Bambi, when he reared up during the forest fire? That old movie, you remember, eh?" Lucas couldn't understand the lack of reaction.

"You just wiped his dick," said Mack.

Ef jumped back and looked the golden thing up, down, and sideways. "I didn't know he was standing on his hind legs or I would've been more careful. I don't want to touch nothing like that, even if it's golden."

Barry ran up, excited. "I found the ax." He looked up at the towering statue and tucked the ax in his back pocket.

Lucas cocked his head. "So, what do you think it is?"

"Classic sculpture in metal precioso," said Madison, the new millionaire poet. "Make a fortune fabuloso. Inspired it me and also thee, I see."

The group had fallen silent, wondering what the bloody hell this thing could be, way out in the boondocks. They were beyond where civilization could pretend to exist, outside the United States of America.

Barry scanned it. "I, for one, like it a lot. It has a certain flavor."

"And the flavor is gold. We're rich." Ef rubbed his hands.

Mack shook his head. "You're already rich. This is not the frosting on your cake. The statue seems sinister to me."

Roy was sober. "Everything's going downhill. And we should too." The blazing lip of the sun was about to appear on fluted rock spirals at the edge of a vast mesa.

Strange creatures of the night seemed to float in the ether at that exact spot, shimmering through a hazy fog.

James said, "It's not a horse. It's like a big poodle, except for the horns, all dressed up to go to market. I particularly like the little shoes."

Roy squinted, then pointed. "There's more than just this statue." For the first time in his life, Roy was stricken sober.

13

"Bloody hell." Lucas was stunned. "Let's get back to the group. We have to protect them or something."

"Oh, for Chrissakes," said Mack. "It's a bunch of aliens that look like the statue. We need a plan." It hit him that he was mistaken. Human history boiled down to this second, with no time to make a plan.

"Jumping Josephat. They're like blimey kangaroos. A second ago, they were a mile away and now they're practically on top of us."

"They gallop nicely on their hind legs." Benny, the new millionaire horseman, was in awe. "Saw off the horns, get rid of the funny clothes. They'd win going away."

"We're going away." Mack straightened his hat and signaled Lucas to do the same. But it was too late.

2

Lord, the ruckus, and the dust. The apparitions darted around like whirling dervishes, especially the little ones, making the humans dazed and confused, unable to keep up with what was happening. By the time Mack stopped speaking, they were surrounded.

The statue was twenty feet tall, towering above them on a three-foot pedestal of white quartz veined with gold, representing a superman of this particular species. A Greek sculptor would have been proud of its bulging muscles, extended calf, and sleek limbs. The eyes were bewitching, staring down with emerald clarity. The antlers were miniature, as if full size would have been ostentatious. It was an idealized version of the creatures.

The creatures were not as impressive as the giant statue, yet more remarkable. Some sported charming racks of horns while others were hornless, dressed in autumn tones, and svelte for their height. Not one was overweight, though all were tall, compared to the humans. Their faces were gentle yet eloquent, and one had crossed eyes. The eyes were velvety and huge, emerald green like the statue. The most amazing part was their tiny feet, the size of a quarter. Honest to god, they couldn't walk under ordinary laws of physics. How could they cover territory like they did?

Three extra-large creatures wore maroon and silver tunics like Caesar or Nehru, flanked by Legionnaire soldiers. Garish but effective in identifying the power brokers.

The hundreds of juveniles lacked the *savoir-faire* of their elders. They skittered like drops of fat on a red-hot skillet, dashing between the humans as if they didn't matter. They wore

15

baggy shorts and skimpy tunics with funny little hats on backward. Some had dyed their hair blue or purple. Others wore rings imbedded in shimmery golden flesh. They kicked up clouds of dust, bringing on coughing spells and black oaths by the new millionaires, making them feel lucky they were still alive.

Lucas shivered. "What's that smell?"

Mack blinked, flustered. "Maybe all kids stink, no matter the species."

Except for shaking like leaves, Lucas and Mack looked good in their suits, silk cravats, and formal Arizona Lottery hats. Mack gathered his courage but still felt like a fool when he raised his hand.

"We come in peace. In fact, we didn't mean to come at all. But you can see we had no option." Mack pointed at the plane, going for the sympathy angle. "We'd appreciate it if you'd contact the United States government and let them know where we are. Then we can get out of your hair."

The creatures either didn't comprehend or weren't interested, staring with limpid green eyes.

Lucas said, "'I am ashamed to think how easily we capitulate to badges and names, to large societies and dead institutions.'"

"Lucas, your quotes worry me more than these close-mouthed aliens. These particular institutions are far from dead, and besides—"

The closest of the three leaders raised his hand, or tiny split hoof with bone-like fingers. Breathless, the humans waited for their first communication with aliens.

And boy was it loud, sounding like "WHISTLE, BURP, FART." Thus, it went through endless variations, the farting verbal and fortunately unscented.

Mack shook his head at Lucas. "We lost the big lottery in the sky. We should've stayed home, you with your new bride, and me paying child support instead of fighting my ex. Shoot my ass and hang it over the fireplace but keep a piece as a memento of my monumental stupidity. Baby-sitting lottery winners. A fine job for a supposed adult. What's your excuse?"

16

"My goodness, aren't they cute?" trilled Ellen. "They're the most adorable creatures on earth, don't you think?"

"This is really scary shit," said Peter. "For a second, I thought I'd gotten some bad stuff, but you see them too. And hell no, they're not cute. They're obnoxious. Especially the little speedy shits."

"The aliens are way too tall to be cute," said Mack. Ellen glared at him as if he were a moron, and he wondered whether he might be.

Lucas quoted, "'We men have made god in our own image. I think that horses, lions, oxen, too, had they but hands would make their gods like them. Horse-gods for horses, oxen-gods for oxen.'"

"What the hell *are* they?" said Billy K., screwing up his freckled face like he'd eaten a box of green ants.

Mack focused on Billy K., the most down-home guy in the group. "Reckon they're pronghorns, or something like that," Mack falling into Billy K. lingo. They'd admired his homespun humor on the night of the big lottery drawing.

"Don't think so," said Barry. "They look more like impala, like in South Africa."

"The smaller horns mean they aren't caribou," said Benny. "I've seen caribou with racks so big they can't get their heads off the ground. And they aren't horses, but they sure are gorgeous."

"They kind of look like antelopes, though rather different," said James, shoving his hat to the back of his head, careful not to uncover his bald spot.

"Antelopes it is," said Mack. "So, that's official."

The fancily dressed Big Three approached the millionaires, making the humans look pathetic in their ordinary attire, which except for Lucas and Mack, was decorated with splotches of mud.

Nick, the Serbian priest, had a big goofy grin like he couldn't grasp the enormity of the situation, clutching Mary protectively.

The three important antelopes stepped onto a three-tiered Olympic-style podium. The top guy did a fabulous series of what sounded like "snarfle, whipple, fartle." Then a

17

colorfully dressed legion of spiffy antelope soldiers marched up, wearing maroon and silver tunics with matching capes. The uniforms were so sharp Italians must have tailored them.

Mack called to them as they pranced by. "Hey, where you going?"

"Look at those guys," said Lucas. "They're hipping and hopping like kangaroos. Got to be related. Maybe they're from Oz."

"Yeah, in unison and perfect goose-step. But what the holy hell are they doing with the plane?"

"Nothing. Whoops." Lucas gasped.

With no ceremony at all, the five troopers unfolded tiny gadgets into multifanged instruments thirty feet long, twisting the prongs to fashion gigantic forks.

Lucas's hand shook as he pointed. "They're sticking them under the nose of the plane."

"Yeah, and now they're doing the funny language bit."

The soldiers counted down with whistle, fart, and burp, levering the elaborate pitchforks like a fulcrum. The nose of the plane pitched up and free from the huge rock at the base of the golden statue, sliding off the mesa into thin air. It arched and swooped like a toy plane with a broken back, floating drunkenly toward the floor of the river valley far below, landing with a poof of dust. Too far away for the sound to reach them, their last connection with the past, destroyed.

"Rest in Peace," said Reg, a Catholic brother and the most erudite of the new millionaires. Lucas rubbed teary eyes, and even Peter seemed sober. Ellen, Courtney, and Nick recited prayers, like they were trying to outdo each other. Courtney won the competition, hands down.

"Amen," said Courtney, and that put an end to the mourning.

Lucas quoted, "'Pray. To ask that the laws of the universe be annulled in behalf of a single petitioner confessedly unworthy.'" He added softly to Mack, "Mark my words. This could get out of hand."

Mack whispered back, "I told you about— Ohmigod." The young antelopes went nuts, worse than before. Dozens tiptoed up to humans and made insane faces, sticking out funny triangular tongues. Finally, the second Big Guy held up a hoof and stopped them cold.

The five Legionnaires grabbed the twenty-foot-high umbrella that must have sheltered the golden statue before the plane knocked it over.

"Pretty cool, eh?" Lucas whistled as the maroon and silver-clad soldiers twirled the humongous umbrella. They anchored, nudged upward, and raised the huge canopy to the vertical.

Mack said, "Looks like the marines on Iwo Jima."

When the golden umbrella was secure, three saluted while the other two buffed with long cloths, like spit polishing the statue for dress inspection.

Lucas whistled. "Impressive, but the natives don't look that friendly. Enough to make you worry, eh?"

The antelopes looked ominous during the entire operation, dark frowns sweeping the crowd like a wave. The golden statue rivaled the rising sun, at which the two polishers saluted and bowed their heads, and in a heartbeat the entire alien assembly did the same. After a frozen twenty seconds, the aliens opened their eyes. The spiffily dressed Legionnaires surrounded the humans, placing micro-thin loops of an evanescent material around the neck of each. Each human except Lucas and Mack.

"Go away, scat," screeched Ellen, the most moderate of the lot.

"Negatory," yelled Courtney. She wrenched away from her captors and stretched the loop near the breaking point. "These godless idolatrous creatures have done got my goat and I'm not going to put up with it anymore." She wrenched her ample body away and the loop followed it faithfully, yanking her back as if by magic. "Whoa." Courtney was surprised, so she did it again.

"Watch that woman," said Mack. "She could be the death of us all."

Lucas shook his head. "Watching her won't do much good, and besides, I'm sick of watching her. And I have a quote to commemorate the golden statue. 'If we assume that man actually resembles God, then we are forced into the impossible theory that God is a coward, an idiot, and a blunderer.' What do you think of that one? Pretty good, eh!"

"I'm up to here with your quotes. I should have stayed home and found a better job and a proper girlfriend."

"Geez, I told you about Nance. You made a smart-aleck remark, that she sounded like a he."

"I have my eye on a lady from church." Mack folded his hands as if in prayer.

On the fourteenth boomerang stretch by Courtney, the loop snapped, launching her like a heavier-than-average marshmallow into the center of her fellow humans.

She practically smothered Nick, bounced off Mary, and bowled over Ef, who collapsed without a murmur. Courtney came to rest, wind-milling her arms with her face wedged in Barry's left armpit. When Barry lifted his arm to push her away, Courtney grabbed the ax in Barry's back pocket, ripped it out, and ran screaming up the hill toward the golden statue.

Courtney chanted as she waved the ax over her head. "Dear God, kill the infidels. Reduce the idolaters to rubble; Dear God, kill the infidels. Reduce the idolaters to rubble."

By the time the antelopes understood what she was up to, Courtney had rammed her ample body halfway up the umbrella pole, chopping at the statue.

"Get her," yelled Mack. He glanced at the Big Guys and wished he hadn't. The third Big Guy gestured for the Legionnaires and they reached Courtney in a swoop and a leap. But not before she'd taken a whack where Ef had touched the golden statue, slivering off enough gold to gild an airplane. Two antlers and the golden dick lay in the dirt.

The antelopes were enraged as the Legionnaires bound Courtney and dragged her back to the humans. The padding was too tight. Courtney's face turned purple.

The juveniles were replaced by skittish elders as seven-foot-tall antelopes cut rapidly through their midst, brushing against them as if tempted to trample. Dust swirled and the humans coughed their lungs out.

Ellen said, "Now cut that out. Have you no decency?"

"Cough, hack," said Lucas. "She suspects an antelope of molesting her. Strange woman."

Mack coughed. "At least they're leaving the two of us alone."

"It feels like we're about to be sacrificed."

A single Legionnaire appeared with a cushion held high over his head, sinking to his knees in front of the three Big Guys, lowering the cushion for inspection. On it lay two golden horns and a large golden dick.

The Big Guys thundered their outrage, screaming gibberish at the bedraggled humans.

Mack felt sick because Courtney was his personal responsibility, and she was obviously choking to death. Mack bowed to the three Big Guys and squeezed his throat, pantomiming strangulation. He almost choked himself senseless while bowing and nodding toward Courtney where she'd collapsed in the dust, motionless.

The three Big Guys stepped off the three-tiered podium, which the podium-bearers toted next to Lucas and Mack, who stared as the three Big Guys stepped back onto their places of esteem. Snarfle, ear wiggle stuff, dance with little feet. Then a heartfelt fartissimo before the rioting dust cloud of antelopes slowed to a blur.

Mack looked out the corner of his eye at Lucas. "We'll salute in unison. One, two, three," and they snapped a crisp one. Their fingers bounced off the bills of their caps like waffles shot from a toaster.

The three Big Guys did something like a salute back and stepped off the podium. They marched up to Mack and Lucas, offering horny hands. Lucas and Mack shook heartily, working their way through the three big shots. Mack again pointed at Courtney, who occasionally twitched. The ranking Big Guy gave a chirp and two Legionnaires propped Courtney on her feet, loosening her bonds.

Courtney jerked to life and harangued everyone in sight. "Oh, ye of little faith, worshiping idols. Repent! Yeah! Repent right this instant! Yeah!"

A Legionnaire swooped up to Courtney and smacked a horny fist on top of her woolly head. She collapsed in stages, her knees buckling and waist jerking sideways as she fell in a heap.

Lucas and Mack were shocked but Courtney shook her head, bounded to her feet, jerked her neck like a marionette, and rejoined the group, unusually silent.

Mack bowed his head toward the big three and shrugged. They bowed back as Legionnaires scurried around, falling in behind Lucas and Mack. The three Big Guys about-faced and headed off, with the humans straggling behind.

By doubling the length of their stride, Lucas and Mack managed to keep up with the three Big Guys. They marched under a camouflaged covering extending to the horizon as the rising sun showed them exactly where they were, though they hadn't the vaguest idea where that could be.

"Venezuela or Brazil?" asked Mack.

"Could be Borneo," said Lucas. "I've never heard of towering mesas like this, stretching over the horizon. There are rows of them and it's a very long way down. They're like giants from another planet."

Reg pointed at a broad river in the far distance. "Venezuela, south of the Orinoco River, which might be what we see out there. We're on a tepui. They're so remote that almost none have been explored, except by helicopter. I read about them in *National Geographic*. The sides are too steep and the shrubbery too dense to get through with a chainsaw. Arthur Conan Doyle wrote a book set on these tepuis, *The Lost World*."

Mack shook his head in wonder. "The antelopes must have been here a long time. They could be as advanced as we are."

"How advanced are we?" asked Reg.

He turned to look at Reg behind him, a balding Falstaff gone to seed. The double length stride made Mack miss a gigantic step. He tripped and catapulted into the Big Guy in front of him, and it was lights out.

**

Mack woke up staring at something high and white like a ceiling, unless it was low and white like a bandage. He rubbed a hand over his face. No compresses. The room was entirely white but it wasn't empty. His visitor looked like one of the three Big Guys, maybe Big Guy Number Two.

The Big Guy stood and made the biggest variety of discordant sounds ever heard by mankind. Mack held up a hand and swung his feet over the side of whatever he was laying on. It looked like a vivisection slab.

"Apology accepted. Where are my people?"

The Big Guy sighted along a prominent nose with bewitching green eyes. He looked fabulous in a maroon and silver tunic over stark white pants, towering next to the ceiling. The Big Guy took Mack's wrist and propelled him toward the brilliant white wall, which opened at their approach. They entered the lowest level of a cavernous auditorium jam-packed with antelopes. Even with thousands of antelopes it was relatively peaceful without juveniles, ignoring the cacophony of verbal belches, farts, and snorts.

Screens encircled the huge auditorium on three levels. Each screen was lined with curlicues like Arabic and globs like splatters of bird poop. The top row of screens showed a slide show of colorfully dressed antelopes, hundreds standing in long lines.

The Big Guy led Mack to a long high table on the main floor. Several antelopes and the other humans sat on one side. The table reached just under the humans' chins.

"Whoa, guys. Excellent to see you again. I hope I haven't missed anything."

"Nothing we understand," said Lucas. "But in your absence, I was brilliant, which should merit an exceptional performance rating this fiscal year. I need the money, not being a millionaire myself. At least Marylyn needs the money."

"So, she should stop saving money at I. Magnums sales. What the hell's going on?"

"Your guess equals mine. They herded us in here after you tried to deck one of their leaders. What came over you, anyway?"

"Tripped. Made a mistake. I forgave myself."

"If only we could do the same. Look what you've gotten us into. I realize diplomacy is the art of saying 'nice doggie' while looking for a big rock. But who wouldn't be worried about this turn of events?"

Mack looked at the three circles of monitors. "I don't see anything ominous. What do you think is so terrible?"

"We're captives. They've stuck handcuffs on everyone, except you and me. That's what's going on. Do you have attention deficit disorder?"

"It's more than that. Look up there?" Mack pointed. "What do you make of the screens on top? I'm impressed they have TV, but that may be a sign of intellectual inferiority. Ask yourself why a whole population would line up on TV. It's elementary, dear Lucas. It's either a quiz show or they're voting. I'd guess voting."

"And what is it they're voting for or against, dear Mack?"

"Haven't a clue. We'd ask the Big Guys, if we could understand each other, but it surely has to do with us. Did you notice the antelopes are dressed in different colors on the three levels?"

Lucas peered. "You're right, for a change, but only half right. They're not only dressed differently, they're different skin colors. We've got our buddies, the golden antelopes on the bottom screens, but the other two are weirded out colors. Dark ones in the middle and awfully pale ones on top."

"The dark ones are ebony black, say ermine, and the white ones are washed out like ivory. So, we have the golden kind plus ermine and ivory antelopes."

"Nice," said Lucas. "Goldies, Ermies, and Ivies. Kind of has a ring to it."

"Wait a cotton-pickin' minute," yelled Ef down the table. "We won the big bucks but we're in chains while you're free as kings. You're not looking out for our interests first, which is what you're supposed to do. So, get us out of these things. We deserve more than two wimps."

"Oh, pot and kettle, I'd reckon," said Lucas. "Who scooped the rock off your head, mate?"

"We're ready to go home." Courtney yelled from the other end of the table. "You entice us on a bogus trip and now leave us to the mercy of heathen aliens. The Arizona Lottery will have your scalps for this, and we'll have the scalps of the Arizona Lottery."

24

"Hush your mouth, Courtney. We had no worries until you attacked the golden statue. It's your fault we're in a pickle."

"I'm in no pickle. As you can see, they removed my protective clothing. It gives me the shivers now. I might have fallen when I climbed the big umbrella. I've done my best to get these heathens on the right track and deep down they probably appreciate it. I'll continue until my dying breath. I'm free as a bird."

A buzzard, thought Mack. "Do you suppose what's going on has anything to do with your abuse of their hospitality? Trying to chop up a statue of their God. And what is that around your wrists, Mrs. Free-as-a-bird?"

"Hospitality? You jest. My backsliding son is more hospitable than these turkeys. Not much else to compare them to, I'd say." She pulled her wrists off the table. Out of sight, out of mind.

"Hey, Mack," said Peter. "Check out the tassels they're wearing. Outasight, and the curious hats around their little horns. Cool, eh?"

Mack looked to see sexy antelope strippers wearing tassels, but spotted nary a one. Peter meant a group with golden skullcaps fitted around embryonic horns. "Yeah, they're cute." They were holding small objects and rolling on the floor, moving prominent lips. "Real cute."

"Hey, Mack," said Billy K. "Check with your buddies and see if they have postcards. We could write the folks back home."

"Why not?" said Ellen. "Writing postcards would keep our minds off the worries Mr. Lucas keeps reminding us about. Reg says we're close to the highest waterfall in the world. They might have some real nice cards."

"We can't write postcards with our hands in cuffs," said James. "Or they wouldn't be legible. But they probably don't have postcards. Who'd they send them to?"

"Maybe their Ermie or Ivie cousins," said Lucas. "But I doubt they have a postal service. There doesn't seem a way to deliver mail around here."

"Stop fantasizing," said Mack. "We have to figure out what's going on and get the hell out of here"

25

"Hear, hear," said Benny. "First rational thing I've heard since the crash. So, what's the plan?"

"We'll reveal that when the time is right." Mack failed to stare Benny down.

Benny chuckled. "Give us a hint of the direction your great plan is headed. That would whet our appetites and raise our confidence."

"It's contingent on what happens in the next hour or so."

"So, as soon as we see which way the Goldies jump, we decide which way wc jump."

Roy flashed an uneasy smile. "Everything's going downhill." His singsong voice dropped, accompanied by the usual descending hand motion.

That put a damper on things before Billy K. said, "I have a plan. Now don't you all go looking at me like that. I didn't say it was a wonderful plan, or a good plan. It's just a plan. We might as well try it because an hour or so from now might be too late. I didn't like the looks on some of these mugs."

"What do you propose?" said James, fiddling with his hat.

"We run right up those stairs to where we came in and then we leave. See what happens. I mean, they haven't said we couldn't."

"They haven't said anything we could understand," said Ef. "We've had no communication at all."

Mack knew Ef would be pitching desert land to the Goldies if he figured out how. "They understand us. We just don't understand them. Does anyone else have that feeling?"

"I do," said Reg. "The one over there is listening to us. He has an ear cocked in our direction." Reg stuck a finger under his left elbow and pointed at a tall Legionnaire standing at attention. The Legionnaire's face was turned toward them instead of forward like his compatriots. "And the Big Guys, as Mack calls them. They seem familiar with our lingo, and a lot of others are too."

"How the hell could that be?" said Peter. "They're a bunch of aliens stuck up here since all eternity, no contact with anyone."

"Where'd they get their tellies?" said Lucas. "The monitors don't say Sony or Motorola. I'll bet they understand satellite television and have been eavesdropping on us for ages. Well, since we had television and radio, anyway."

"One of them said hi to me," said Ellen, and blushed at their stares. "Wasn't anything, really. He was just being friendly."

"He actually said hi, and it was a he?" said Mack. "That's strange. Did he say it with a whistle, a burp, or a fart kind of thing?"

"Said it straight out, like *hi*. Though it was a little like a whistle. I didn't want to encourage him so I didn't say hi back."

"Anyone else see this happen?" said Lucas.

Mack sat there like a bowl of jelly, trying not to think of an alien mucking about with Ellen.

Ellen scowled. "What do you mean? Don't you believe me?"

"Of course, we believe you," said Lucas. "But someone else might have a different take on it. What he did before or afterwards. What he meant by *hi*."

"What part of *hi* don't you understand?" said Ellen. "It was perfectly innocent."

"No way it was innocent. If they understand English, we have no secrets and no way to get away," said James. "And we need to escape asap."

"That was a really dumb plan, Billy K.," said Ef. "Half of us couldn't run up those stairs. They're way too steep and the antelopes are a hundred times faster than we are."

"But they might not care. That could make them real slow."

"Then why are we tied up, except for Mack and Lucas? Assuming we got out of the building, where would we go? Slide down the side of this mile-high mesa?"

"Enough already. We got important company," said Mack. It looked like the number two Big Guy again, with flanking Legionnaires.

The Big Guy bowed curtly. "Honk, snort, sniffle."

27

New dialogue, thought Mack, bowing back. "How may we serve your eminence? Any little thing you'd like, such as giving you Courtney in exchange for letting the rest of us go?"

"I heard that," bellowed Courtney. "You should be horsewhipped—"

"It was a joke, Courtney. Perhaps a bad joke but still a joke."

The Big Guy said nothing, sweeping a long arm in a circle and pointing at the monitors.

"Yeah," said Lucas. "What's that about?" The humans followed the gesture and stared at the monitors. None of the tiers showed golden or any other kind of antelopes. The screens were filled with squiggles and blotches like a kindergartner's doodles.

"You don't happen to have a translator handy, do you?" said Mack. "We'd like to know what's going on."

Big Guy Number Two had a wisp of a smile on his face. "Sniffle, snort, honk."

"Everyone's leaving," yelled Benny. They stared as the auditorium emptied in seconds, the stairs whisking hundreds of golden antelopes out invisible doors at the top.

The Legionnaires stood at attention. At a nod from the Big Guy, they released the handcuffs and substituted wire loops around the humans' waists.

As they were separated into three groups, Ef demanded, "What the hell's going on?" His shoes squeaked as he was propelled into a group with Billy K., James, Benny, Nick, and Mary.

"What exactly do you have in mind?" asked Lucas, as he was herded into the same group, though without restraints. Lucas tried to dodge the antelope doing the corralling, resulting in a comic dance. Everyone watched as Lucas tried to out-broken-field-run a master, finding it impossible to outmaneuver an antelope.

"You win." Lucas stepped back with his new group. "What's next?"

"We've been split into three groups, for what purpose we should know soon," said Mack. "It looks like I'm stuck with you guys." Courtney, Peter, Madison, Roy, Ellen, and Barry.

Not too bad, thought Mack, with minor or major exceptions. "Hi, Ellen."

She practically spat. "Big help you are. A failed leader, doing nothing."

"I beg your pardon, Madame Ellen. Do you have a better plan? Right now, I want to avoid anyone getting beat up."

"You're a wuss. There's no sign they'd harm us."

A Legionnaire slapped a heavy handcuff on Courtney's left wrist, pulling it behind her back, then snapped a matching handcuff on her right wrist. The enormous connecting chain pulled her arms toward the floor, where she stood in martyr mode, raising her eyes to the heavens, or at least up, moving her lips. She was either in great pain or an imitation of great pain as sweat ran down her face like rain.

Mack stepped forward and pointed to Courtney's handcuffs, pantomiming taking them off. The Big Guy sternly shook his head, nodding at the Legionnaires who herded the three groups up the moving stairs. The first group consisted of Reg as leader, with the quieter millionaires, Fats, Rudd, Molly, Betty, and Arturo. Lucas headed the second group. The last was Mack's.

They whisked up the fast-moving stairs and outside under the camouflage canopy. On the left sat a teardrop-shaped shell the size of a VW van, so black it glistened. On the right sat a large white egg painted with loopy scallops, shimmering like a hologram. Six Ermine and five Ivory antelopes guarded the teardrop vehicles. Four of both were heavily armed, wearing side holsters the size of a Swiss Army knife. Two Ermies dressed in rainbow colors, along with a single balding Ivie, who seemed absent-minded and not really interested, were stiffly shaking hands with Goldie Big Guy Number Two. They displayed no cordiality and little diplomacy. The Ermines were overtly hostile, jerking their hooves away almost before the handshakes began.

The Golden antelope guards marched Lucas's group to the black bubble where the number two Big Guy stopped them. He placed a stick pin with a black head in Lucas's collar, almost skewering Lucas as he jerked away. The Big Guy waved the group toward the Ermine vehicle and placed a similar pin in

Mack's collar. The Ermine vehicle opened high gull-wings and the Ermie guards escorted Lucas and his group inside. Everyone waved and yelled lustily at their departing acquaintances. Mack could hear every word Lucas was saying.

"You bugger. Quit pushing. Let Nick and Mary sit together. They are married, you know. And Ef, leave that stuff alone. Let's keep a low profile until we know what's going on." Mack could hear Benny complain, Billy K.'s jokes, and James' imitation of himself.

Mack said, "Do you read me Lucas? If you do, say something intelligent. Maybe the separation is only temporary." Mack heard a gulp and then Lucas's voice

"So, they gave us mics. Pretty cool, eh?"

"Combination mic and receiver. Better than Dick Tracy, I'd say."

"Who's that?"

"Never mind. But at least we can keep in touch, figure a way out of this mess. Do you think Ellen was right, that we've been wusses?"

"Ellen was right," said Ellen. "Though I hope you aren't that far gone and started talking to yourselves."

"The Big Guy gave us mics and receivers. They're packed together in this little bitty thing," said Mack, pointing at his collar. "Pretty cool, eh? But what about the Ivies group?"

Mack took off after Big Guy Number Two as he handed the third group over to the Ivies. "Hey, Senor. Could we get one of those pins for—"

Before Mack finished the sentence, the Big Guy flourished a pin and pinned it on Reg's collar.

Mack yelled at Reg's disappearing back, "It's a mic and receiver. So, we can keep in touch—"

The gull-wings on the Ivory coach closed over Fats, Rudd, Molly, Betty, Arturo, and Reg, with no time for protests or goodbyes. Reg's group, the Ivies, included Rudd complaining about such a dumb bunch and Fats mumbling that putting up with Rudd would save him a packet of reincarnations and earn him super karma. Molly and Betty wondered whether Betty's deceased husband could see her now, and Arturo was,

30

as usual, saying nothing. Mack tuned them out and realized that doing so tuned him into Lucas's group.

Mack looked down at his collar, cross-eyed as he tried to see what made it so sophisticated. He didn't want to mess around and lose contact with the others.

The Ermine and Ivory vehicles disappeared with a "whoosh," Mack and his group staring where they'd been a second before. The only evidence was two silvery ovals.

Mack edged over to take a closer look before a spiffy Legionnaire headed him off. The silvery ovals were tubes that looked like railroad tracks receding to infinity inside. Mack guessed pneumatic tubes.

Mack whispered into his pin-mic, "Where you at now?"

There was no answer. Mack thought a few seconds and then visualized Lucas and group. "Where you at, Lucas?"

"Don't know but it looks pretty much like where we left you. Tons of humongous boulders, rocks as high as an elephant's eye. Except all the antelopes are black. Make that Ermine. It's a beautiful black like that shiny volcanic stuff, not the pumice junk with holes in it."

"You mean obsidian?"

"Yeah, that's it. We have a huge reception committee and the crowd is interesting, to say the least. There must be a festival. Flowers are everywhere, everyone's dressed up, and, Christ, you should see their Big Guys. They are really Big Guys, a foot taller than your Big Guys. And pouty. They don't look friendly. I have to go since I'm the spokesman." Pride overwhelmed his accent.

"Pretty good for an Aussie, leading a delegation on our first contact with Ermie aliens. Your Big Guys are bigger than my Big Guys. Indeed. Keep in touch and I'll see what's going on with Reg."

Mack thought about Reg. "You there Reg? How's it going?"

Reg came back immediately. "Rather calm here, compared to the Goldies. I like the Ivies. They're relaxed with no agenda to speak of. It's like being on vacation, and best of all, they fed us first thing. At least we think it's food. It looks

31

and smells good and doesn't taste bad, though it's not what we're used to."

"No hamburgers and hotdogs, eh?"

"Not even a TV dinner, or plates with little compartments. It's mounds of different colored mashed potatoes like whipped cream. But more substantial than either. Though the fluorescent color is a bit off-putting. How about you and Mack?"

"You're making me hungry. Our first move will be a hunger strike. How's Fats and Molly and Betty; oh, yeah, and Fats?"

"You seem to have forgotten Rudd, who's as diplomatic as ever. He's complaining about the color of the food. The rest are as happy as I've seen them."

"Oops, they're moving us. But go ahead." The Legionnaires led them to an impenetrable stack of boulders, nonchalantly walking through as they opened like hidden doors. They were in a small room with human-sized chairs, a long table, and real doors lining one side of the room. Fragrant bouillon-sized chunks were stacked in five pyramids, colors ranging from boring beige and glittery gold to forest green, orangutan orange, and baby-poop yellow. Three Legionnaires stood at one end of the table and indicated the humans should eat. A lone Legionnaire opened a barred door on the side of the room.

Reg continued, "I think we're having a religious ceremony. Only a guess. They're quite different from the Goldies. None of the on-the-floor stuff, flopping around. These guys stand and bob, holding a round bolster. And they dress completely different from the Goldies. They wear ties. Can you believe it? Actual ties, like you see at home. Long ones and bow ties."

"I'll let you go now. We have a crisis. They locked Courtney behind bars. I'm sure you can hear her screaming."

3

Courtney was in a frenzy, banging her head against thick rubber bars that bulged with every whack, the screaming worse than needles under fingernails.

Mack ran to Courtney and mimed for the guards to open the door and remove the shackles. The closest Legionnaire tried to open the door but with the insane screaming, couldn't concentrate. He tripped against Mack, knocking him against the table of food. Platters of colorful cubes slid onto the floor in slow motion, covering Mack's face in goop.

"Sorry about that." Mack licked off a couple of cubes. Better than two days of airline food.

"Hey, save some of that for us, you big pig," said Peter.

The guard jumped up as if he were expecting an attack, throwing Mack against the bars of Courtney's cell, where Mack felt like he'd stuck his head in a jet engine.

Mack yelled at Courtney, "SHUT THE FUCK UP."

She stopped, staring at Mack.

"Please. I'll try getting you out, or at least get the cuffs off you."

"I'm happy to die for Jesus, but I would like to eat first. And you should have your mouth washed out with lye!" She harrumphed and resumed screaming.

Mack motioned at the guard. "Get the cuffs off her and give her something to eat. That should do it."

The guard stood with horny fingers stuck in his ears. The other Legionnaires had disappeared.

Ellen reached between the bars and caressed Courtney's face until the wails subsided.

The men stood stupefied as the guard removed his fingers from his ears. To their amazement, he opened Courtney's cell and stripped the manacles from her wrists. But when she tried to walk out, he closed the door in her face.

"Sorry about that Courtney," said Mack as everyone scooped chunks of food off the shiny floor.

Peter slurped the green stuff. "Not bad. Tastes like avocado."

Ellen nibbled the yellow. "I like this." No one mentioned its exact shade.

Mack took a handful of mixed colors. "Here, Courtney."

Courtney spit. "You can call me Mrs. Sherman. God rest Mr. Sherman's soul."

Mack felt sympathy for Mr. Sherman's soul. "If that's what you prefer, ma'am. It's Courtney from here on out." He again offered colorful cubes.

Courtney grumped, "That looks terrible, you haven't washed your hands, and it's Mrs. Sherman. Can't you get anything right?"

"If you're hungry you'll eat. I doubt we'll see different food in the future. Are you considering a diet?"

"I can lose weight but you'll always be ugly," sniffed Courtney.

"Was that another blankety-blank quote? I'm sick up to here but you give me a yell if you change your mind about eating."

"I like the brown cubes." Barry scrunched his face. "Tastes like venison."

Mack laughed. "I wouldn't call it that if I were you. The antelopes may be against cannibalism."

"Don't be silly." Ellen shook her curls. "They're probably not even related. They seem more like us than real antelopes."

"Not a thing I'd like to say," said Madison. "But then I'd like to make your day. They're better lookin' when they're cookin'. Taller, leaner, faster, smarter."

"They're not better looking," scoffed Peter. "Our women are much prettier. Of course, I can't tell which are females since the antelopes dress the same, except for Big Guys

34

and Legionnaires. But the commoners look alike. Can't tell who's what."

Mack stared at Peter, amazed he had a thought unrelated to partying, women, booze, or drugs. Then he realized it had to do with women, and was interrupted by a squawk on the collar pin.

"Come in Mack. Big news."

"Yo, Lucas. What's up?"

"Found a buddy. And most of them speak English. They picked it up from satellite, radio and telly. Also, Spanish and Portuguese."

Mack frowned. "Then why are they playing games?"

"It's the Goldies who're playing games. The Ermies don't play games, or at least they say they don't. It's nice to get the inside scoop."

"You hope it's the inside scoop. Who's your new friend?" Mack took a bite
of the food, wrinkling his nose.

"The guy in charge of food. Crazy food."

"The Goldies food is also weird."

"The Ermies whip their food for religious reasons, and the three antelope religions are completely different. My new Ermie friend gave me a brochure. The pamphlet's sketchy on the Ivies' religion, which the Ermies say is strange. Of course, the Goldie religion is something else, too, according to the Ermies. I always thought religion was BS, but this stuff is real interesting."

"What about the new friend? He seems a good influence. You sound unworried."

"He's a great admirer of Hollywood. Yak, yak, yak, talks nonstop. Mostly about his personal life, which is a yelp. This is one crazy society, maybe worse than the one we left. And you were right about the tellies in the Goldie auditorium. They were voting, and you almost got it right about what for."

"Spare me the suspense." The rest crowded around Mack's collar.

"A heresy trial with the death penalty for you know who— The one who chopped up their holy statue."

"Praise the lord. I'm a'goin' home." Courtney fell on her knees, sending a tremor through the room. She repeated the refrain over and over, thanking the Baptist god for the privilege of dying. "I'm a'goin' home. I'm a'goin' home."

"I heard that and she nailed it. They all voted, the Goldies, Ermies, and Ivies. Anyone voting against trying Courtney for heresy, which carries the death penalty, condoned the desecration of their own god. They're all more or less monotheistic, I think. The little pamphlet isn't clear."

"How do they execute her if she's found guilty?"

"I don't know that part. Maybe they'll take a hatchet to her like she did the Goldie god, called Radnicharra. The Ermies consider Radnicharra a silly god. I may have gotten the names mixed up. This makes them bitter enemies."

"Well, religion can be tricky."

Ellen disagreed. "Religion is about loving your neighbors. Everything else is fake religion."

"You mean anything outside of Roman Catholicism?" Mack asked.

"Not at all. The Church is ecumenical. We welcome all who believe in one God."

"Jesus Christ!" said Barry. "Has the pope gone that far? Back in Tennessee he seemed mighty down on other religions. Especially Jews and Protestants, and maybe other ones too. I don't know much about it myself and I can't say I give a good Goddamn."

Ellen shuddered. "Blasphemy."

Courtney interrupted her prayer of thanksgiving. "You should all have your mouths washed out with lye. You're bad examples, nigh unto evil."

As if on cue, Lucas said, "'Nor is it you alone who knows what it is to be evil, I am he who knew what it is to be evil, I too knitted the old knot of contrariety. Blabb'd, blush'd, resented, lied, stole, grudg'd. Had guile, anger, lust, hot wished I dared not speak. Was wayward, vain, greedy, shallow—'"

Mack interrupted, "Enough already."

"No, no, let him finish," said Madison. "Never diminish poetry."

36

Lucas continued, ""—shallow, sly, cowardly, malignant, The wolf, the snake, the hog, not wanting in me, The cheating look, the frivolous word, the adulterous wish, not wanting. Refusals, hates, postponements, meanness, laziness, none of these wanting, Was one with the rest, the days and haps of the rest.' Pretty cool, eh?"

Peter shrugged. "Doesn't sound evil to me. It sounds pretty normal, like most everyone. Not evil at all."

"That's the point," said Ellen. "Without religion you're adrift, Peter. Being adrift is evil."

"So, I got another one for you," said Lucas over Mack's groan. "'Morality is simply the attitude we adopt toward people whom we personally dislike.' I thought Ellen might appreciate that. Or not."

Ellen shook a finger at the mic. "That's silly. I like you all. I only dislike your cavalier attitude toward religion."

"There you have it," said Mack. "I like the part Ellen said about Catholics accepting everyone who believes in one god. That might make antelopes the same as Catholics." Mack danced around like he was witty.

A new voice piped up on Mack's collar mic. "Very interesting. The Ivies are also unique."

"Hey, Reg. I'd love to know what's going on but maybe we should cool it on the air. They gave us mics for a reason. It could be so they can track what we're up to."

Lucas voice crackled over the mic. "So what? We've got no choice, unless we use lingo the antelopes don't understand. Otherwise we can't keep in touch."

"Good idea. From now on we'll be cryptic, though cryptic isn't really us."

"You're both a couple of degrees east of rational," said Reg.

"We're here to entertain you," said Lucas. "What should we know about the Ivies?"

Reg said, "Maybe I misspoke. I find religion fascinating, enchanting even. At least my own. The Ivies are an interesting mix of religions we're familiar with. They dress up like Protestants used to, in suits and ties. Ivies pray toward the Goldies' tepui, which has a magic stone like the Muslims in

Mecca. They're required to lead a perfect life, which Judaism used to do. They outlaw outside television except CNN for the political elite. Ivies have a humdinger network of their own, very pious. Daily prayers are praise for their god. They don't ask for things like the Goldies and Ermies."

Mack said, "Why don't they kick us off the tepui so we don't bother them anymore, bygones forgotten?"

"They were voting on other things too," said Lucas. "If we thought about it, it's obvious what they're most afraid of."

Barry frowned. "Yeah, what's that? It's not obvious to me." He turned to the Legionnaire standing in the middle of the room, listening to everything. "How about more chow?"

The guard dropped the handcuffs as an invisible door slid open. A waiter entered with heaping platters of colorful cubes and a large pitcher. The guard cobbled the broken table leg together, and the waiter slid the platter and pitcher onto the table. The humans rushed the feast, chomping and slurping. Cherry lemonade was served in gargantuan cups and declared scrumptious. Ellen carried a plate to Courtney.

"The vote gives us a trump card," said Lucas. "They're more afraid of us than we are of them. After a millennium, they've finally been discovered. Can you imagine the impact of that? After thousands of years, or however long they've been up here, they're outed."

Mack summarized, "So, the vote whether to try Courtney for heresy passed on all three tepuis. Anything on whether there's a trial and if so, how long it'll take?"

Reg said, "I'll check."

"What else besides voting to divide us into three groups?"

"Well, one question was whether to help us return home," said Reg. "The Ermies and Ivies voted to divide us up while the Goldies voted no. The Goldies were outnumbered, but they all voted to imprison us so we don't blow their cover."

Mack said, "We'll promise not to blow their cover if they help us get back. That should be our first strategy."

"Right," said Lucas. "But they're not dumb. Someone would rat them out. Think about who we're dealing with, from Rudd the rat to Peter the party boy."

Mack said, "Better lay off character assassination. I'm getting dirty looks from Peter."

Lucas sounded like he was smiling. "I doubt few of us, after a few drinks, could resist bragging about a scrape with seven-foot aliens."

"Gotcha," said Mack. "But we have to try—"

"I sort of did," said Lucas. "I asked Badsr, that's the guy I liaison with, if he'd help us get back to civilization, and he said no problem if it were up to the Ermies. But the Goldies refused. Even if we promised on their respective holy books not to talk. Poor Courtney."

"Why so?"

"They execute by boiling oil, deep fat frying. The Goldies, I mean. It's part of their religious tradition for dealing with heretics. A high calorie *auto de fe*."

Mack clenched his fists. "I hate it when you know more than I do."

"You don't have a chance because the Goldies are secretive. They won't admit they understand English, much less provide a translator. The Goldie Big Guys are fluent in English."

"That's what I heard too," said Reg. "Of course, the Ivies, Ermies, and Goldies hate each other. Nothing one says about the others is believable. So, it's hard to tell what's true and what's twaddle."

Mack pondered. "Is anyone looking for the missing plane, making a rescue attempt?"

"Well, they'd have to be?" said Lucas. "No plane has ever disappeared without a search. Me mum married a guy who flies the big birds. He says they have homing devices in the black boxes, easy to find with GPS. Rescuers should be on their way right now."

"So, all we got to do is sit tight and keep Courtney out of boiling oil."

"I would appreciate that," yelled Courtney from her barred room.

"What made you change your mind? A minute ago, you were celebrating martyrdom."

"I prayed for guidance and he answered my prayers. Dying for a bunch of aliens adds no stars to my crown. They're not even human. Not in the image of my Lord and Savior."

"No brown nose quality there, eh?" said Lucas

"Hey," said Reg. "Be kind. The lady's doing the best she can."

"There's something in what you say." Mack wondered about Courtney's star-spangled crown. It almost sounded like superstition, which had never occurred to him before. "Are you happy, sitting on your butt, waiting for a rescue? The flight recorder is a mile below the tepui. Why would they look on top? How long will it take them to realize we're missing from a wreck that fell thousands of feet? Someone may be on the way, but not to the top of the tepui. And none of us have the vaguest idea which way you went."

Reg said, "That's a reasonable objection to sitting on our thumbs. We're getting baths and mine is next, so sayonara and adios."

"Me too," said Lucas. "Adiosing, that is. The Ermies are putting on a culture program and they're proud as partridges." Lucas clicked off.

"Peacocks," said Mack. The guard was sound asleep, propped next to Courtney's door. The group sat stuffing their faces in human-sized chairs, which must have intended for juvenile antelopes. The lemonade was obviously alcoholic. Only Mack and Courtney were sober, a fate Mack felt he should avoid as he filled a tumbler of the frothy red potion.

"Which nobody can deny," sang Peter.

Mack laughed. "You're as intelligible as a Goldie. But at least everyone is happier than usual."

"We're feeling fine." Ellen swayed like a swizzle stick.

Madison sang "When Irish Eyes are Shining," as his shined brightly, alternating with Barry bellowing the Tennessee fight song to an unrecognizable tune.

Mack filled a tankard and took it to Courtney. "Drink plenty of liquids, ma'am. Don't let yourself become dehydrated."

"Don't be silly," said Courtney. She threw the liquid back through the bars, drenching the guard. He jumped up and fled the room, shedding red residue as he wind-milled through an invisible door.

Courtney scoffed, "That's the devil's potion. But I would like a glass of water."

Mack groaned, "Oh, yeah. Lips that touch wine, etcetera."

The guard entered the room in a fresh uniform with sharp creases and drew a big mug of cherry lemonade, sloshing it over Courtney's head with evident relish. Mack wiped a few drops from his sleeve and started to lecture the guard. But it was too late. The guard had slouched back on the floor, fast asleep.

Courtney spluttered. "I've never touched the devil's drink and now a cockamamie alien doused me with it. How humiliating. Ugh. Ugh." She sluiced the stuff off jiggly arms, front, and sides. She couldn't reach further than her hips, the rest absorbing into the mud stain on the hem.

"I need a shower. Could you get me one, Mr. Mack?"

Courtney looked so disheveled and woebegone that Mack was sympathetic. They all needed showers, desperately, while Reg and the others were enjoying a spa experience. Mack tapped the guard's shoulder and received a horny fist in the ribs.

"Oof," said Mack as the guard bounded up. Mack did a pantomime of a shower, which registered nothing on the guard's face. Mack acted out a bathtub with water, stepping high over the edge, then sinking down and relaxing. Same result. Finally, he said, "Enough of this crap. I know you understand English. All I want is a nice shower for this poor lady you've cooped up in your inhuman prison. Is that too much to ask?"

The guard raised bushy eyebrows, inclined his head to the side, and left.

"Join the party, Mr. Mack," yelled Barry. "We're having a terrific time."

Mack shook his head. "I'm a failure. Lucas is on top of the Ermie situation. Reg is doing well with the Ivies. And I can't even get a shower for a condemned prisoner."

"It's not so bad being an udder failure," laughed Ellen, slurring the word as she sidled up to Mack.

41

Mack considered whether that was a double entendre or an alcoholic mumble. Nope. She was still Ellen, tipsy or not, and he was tongue-tied.

"Come on, Mr. Mack. Party down," said Peter. "Sorry, I don't remember
your real name."

"What do you remember? Do you remember your friend Chuck who disappeared into thin air, or at least into coach? He still awaits a Christian burial."

"Silly goose. Chuck wasn't religious. He didn't go around dissing Jews, Muslims, and whoever for the fun of it."

"Low blow. Don't forget that a foremost pillar of the church sits a few feet from us."

"Never," said Ellen. "My pillar beats hers by supporting the right church. Sorry about that, Courtney, but you should try a tipple before it goes away?" She picked up the pitcher and stared into its empty depths. "Too late. The party's over."

At which the guard made a grand reentry, carrying a fresh pitcher of red liquid and a satchel. He scooted the pitcher onto the table as Mack said, "Slow down on the lemonade or you'll all pass out."

The guard opened Courtney's cell and snapped her wrist into a wall clamp. He removed items from the satchel and tossed one that looked like a mesh circle on the floor. He slapped a foot-long tube on the wall and unfurled an opaque curtain on the inside of the bars. The guard unsnapped Courtney's wrist and locked it on the wall tube, flipping the curtain closed on Courtney's screams as water cascaded. Oblivious, he stepped from the cell and slid down the wall, resuming his snooze.

"Help me, help me. I'm drowning."

Mack yelled back, "Try the lever on the tube. You wanted a shower, you got a shower. Take your clothes off. We promise not to look."

"Right." Courtney sang as she stripped: "'I'm singing in the rain, just singing in the rain. Singing in the rain, I'm singing in the rain.'"

Peter stuck his fingers in his ear. "You can cut that out yesterday. That's not singing and you're not in the rain."

42

"Good one." Barry slapped a high five with Peter, the only contact Mack remembered them having. Maybe cherry lemonade was a good idea.

"Toss your clothes out, ma'am. I'll see if our hosts will clean them."

"'Just singing in the rain.'" She paused. "Nah. I'll wash them myself, though it probably isn't good for the shoes." Her ample silhouette moved behind the curtain as she shucked off the brogans and kicked them between the bars. They bounced on the floor, waking up the guard. "Maybe he can polish them. They're a little grotty."

The brogans were streaked muddy gray and crap brown. Mack pointed, pantomiming their cleaning. The guard shrugged as only an antelope can, with great eloquence and grace.

"Doesn't look like he's up to cleaning your shoes. But toss your clothes out when you're ready. We'll wring them out and hang them up. You'll be as good as new in no time."

"Good as new in no time," sang Courtney, dancing behind the curtain like flickering lights in a cave.

"Ahoy there," screeched Mack's mic.

"Yo, Lucas. What's up?

"Lots. We've only got a few hours."

"A few hours before what?"

"Before the show trial. Courtney is scheduled to fry at noon tomorrow."

"I don't know what time it is so I don't know how soon noon tomorrow is."

"Well, tomorrow isn't far off. Right now, it's noon today. Does that give you an idea?"

The shower stopped dead.

4

Mack was sad. "That's unutterably evil. Frying a poor old woman like that. And for no good reason. It was an ordinary statue, though possibly gold-plated."

Courtney sang in the background. "I'm boiling in the oil, just boiling in the oil. Boiling in the oil, yeah, boiling in the oil."

Lucas cut in. "She may be obnoxious but they still shouldn't fry her. And we could be next. Ordinary statue, indeed. The Goldies are touchy about their god. The same as the Ermies and Ivies and lots of humans too. Besides, 'He who hates vice, hates mankind.'"

"That doesn't fit. We're not dealing with mankind. Our problem is antelopes. So, cut out the dumb quotes."

"What's the big difference?"

Reg's drawl came over their mics. "Antelopes are taller and some, as Madison said, are better looking."

Mack groaned. "How was your bath, which I envy to death? And do you have any idea how to solve our immediate problem?"

"Excellent bath but no earthshaking ideas, son. Except to ally the Ermies and Ivies against the Goldies. And stall. That might start a war, a diversion so we can escape. Hide Courtney, though that would be difficult. Alert the US Embassy. Reform religion. That's all I can come up."

"How much of it makes sense, Sir Reg?"

Lucas mused. "A couple might be possible. We can't hide Courtney or get ahold of the US Embassy. Like that'd do any good, remembering the problem we had in Mexico. US Embassy, my ass."

"We can play the Ermies and Ivies off against the Goldies," said Mack.

"The Ermies and Ivies agree that the Goldies should execute infidels who attack their gods," said Reg. "I have it on the best authority."

Lucas cut in. "I don't understand why these essentially identical antelopes have different gods. You've only seen the Goldies, but trust me, the Ermies look just like the Goldies, except for skin color. Does it make any sense that different gods made them?"

Reg chuckled. "Differences in skin color are never minor. We all need someone to look down on. Any little thing will do."

"I got it. 'All animals are equal but some animals are more equal than others.'"

Mack rolled his eyes. "Forget the philosophical bullshit and concentrate on how we're going to save poor old Courtney."

"Neither poor nor old," Courtney said. "Nor old and poor. I'm boiling in the oil, just boiling in the oil." Her voice was edged with hysteria.

"It's an authoritarian way of punishing dissent. Maybe the Ermies or Ivies are civil libertarians," Mack grasping at straws. "Could we appeal to their sense of fairness?"

Lucas cleared his throat. "I have a good one for you. 'Those who begin coercive elimination of dissent soon find themselves exterminating dissenters. Compulsory unification of opinion achieves only a unanimity of the graveyard.'"

"I don't know how you remember all those quotes," snapped Mack. "But lay off while we deal with urgent business."

"I don't know how I remember these quotes either. I've never been good at remembering anything before."

"Mack has a point," said Reg. "The Ivies have a semblance of free speech and allow dissent. But they draw the line at blasphemy."

Mack inserted, "So did the Catholics a few years back."

"Yeah. But it's been a while," said Reg. "We've reformed. Now we even tolerate atheists."

45

"I'll sound out our Goldie buddies and see what we can come up with."

Lucas laughed. "You don't have Goldie buddies. Though I'll try talking to Badsr. And you, Reg?"

"My contact is the principal adviser to the Ivie chief. Mack seemed to have rapport with one of the Goldie Big Guys."

"I got along with number two," Mack wondering if that were really true, "but I haven't seen him for ages."

"Which is two hours by my count. Surely relations haven't soured yet."

"I'll get right on it," Mack thinking how to schmooze the Big Guy.

The rest of Courtney's soggy clothes landed on the table and Mack's left foot. "Thank you, Courtney. We'll dry them soonest."

Mack nudged the sleeping guard and received a pike through his shoe. Luckily between the toes. "Sorry about that."

The guard leapt to his full height, towering over Mack. He stifled a laugh at Mack trying to free his shoe.

"Furble snarf." The guard pulled the pike out of the floor and telescoped it back into his pouch.

Mack pointed at Courtney's sodden clothes. When the guard failed to react, Mack picked up a fully armored bra, about 60DDD. He pantomimed wringing it out but it sprang from his hands and jumped back on the table.

"That'd make a hell of a slingshot." Peter stuffed it with "food" cubes and swung it around his head, mistiming the release. Cubes flew like buckshot and opened doors in a circular sequence. But they closed as fast as they opened, too fast to see outside.

They froze. Maybe they weren't prisoners and never had been. Could they walk out as easy as putting one foot in front of the other?

Mack looked at everyone having the same thought. "Yeah, but where would we go? We don't know where we are or what's out there."

"Who the hell cares." Peter rushed full speed ahead, banging into the wall like a sack of rocks, knocking himself silly and collapsing on the floor. It was the first time they'd seen a

Goldie laugh. First, he choked, air heaving through his chest. Then he did fartles, snapples, and popples as Peter dragged his concussed self off the floor.

They pivoted as one as a door opened. Mack broke into a huge smile, rushing to grasp the hand of who he hoped was Big Guy Number Two. "We were afraid you'd abandoned us. We're hearing from our friends but would like to know what's going on. Straight from the source."

The Big Guy raised an eyebrow, gave a curt bow, and motioned Mack to follow, waving the others away.

"I'll be right back."

Peter snickered. "We trust you so. I'd like a liter of single malt scotch, if you don't mind. And a lid of ganja. See what you can do."

"I will not. Our first job is to save Courtney—"

Peter said, "Why the hell's that? We didn't chop down a sacred statue. We deserve saving too. Think about that."

Ellen slumped on a chair, slightly looped, while Madison muttered what sounded like nonsense limericks. Roy was all smiles, like he was waiting for Mack to insist that he come along. Barry described the action to Courtney.

Courtney waved. "Goodbye, Mr. Mack. I hope you get back before I come to a boil."

"Right, Courtney." Mack hurried after the vanished Big Guy.

A door opened to muted sunshine filtered through vines over a walkway, bordered by boulders the size of VW bugs. A thin layer of glassy green covered the walkway, which wasn't as slippery as it looked. Boulders too high to vault littered the landscape and gaps between them were too small to slip through. It was the walkway or nothing.

Two spiffy Legionnaires snapped to attention and saluted as the Big Guy stopped before an enormous door that glowed like solid gold. Sculpted antelopes adorned the door, locked in a mortal struggle with recognizable animals. Tawny felines, enormous yellow snakes, and blond crocodiles. The guards held Swiss Army knife pouches vertically between their eyes, staring straight ahead. The Big Guy nodded and the guards opened the doors, returning to parade rest. The Big Guy bowed and motioned Mack to enter a large room with shimmering lights.

In a single step Mack suffered sensory overload. The lights looked like 3D stained glass windows and looked suspiciously religious. Ghostly antelopes flitted through river valleys and over the tops of flat-topped mesas. Black antelopes and white ones changed color to shiny Goldies. It was like watching an action-packed movie in 360-degree surround. Missiles and religious symbols appeared from all directions, aimed at the viewer. Mack hid his face in his hands.

"Spiffle, spaffle, wiffle, waffle," said a booming voice dripping with honey. The Big Guy genuflected to a Goldie wearing golden tassels, skullcap, and lace pantaloons. The golden apparition must have been a cardinal or the Pope himself. His golden cape was frozen in the horizontal, like he might achieve lift-off as he flitted around babbling.

Behind his eminence stood an altar of buffed gold with a replica of the statue Courtney trashed. Identical statues lined the walls, suspended in air. Reedy music shrieked from all directions.

The garish priest glided uncomfortably close to Mack, chanting with elbows flying and face conveying emotions unheard of outside a religious experience. But Mack didn't feel like having one right then.

Mack crossed his arms. "Shoo. Go away. Stop it."

The cleric fell back as if shot. He held a gold-laced wrist across his chest, coughing and snorting as if from allergies.

"Gesundheit." Mack whipped a hanky from his suit pocket and waved it in front of his lordship's nose. This produced another bout of coughing. Mack turned to the Big Guy. "We should just leave."

With endearing insistence, the golden cleric ushered them to the closest pew. Mack almost teared at the priest's woebegone face and drooping shoulders. Shudders of anxiety shook the priest's gold-bedecked body as he bustled into the row in front of them, carrying a replica of the Goldie god. He set it reverently on the back of pew, right in front of Mack.

"Yo, Mack. Lucas here. You got a second yet? Things are happening left, right, and center. We need to confer soonest."

Mack ignored Lucas as the priest seized an ax and swiped at the statue. He chopped closer and closer until he lopped off a tiny antler. He froze, watching it spiral to the floor. He continued with delicate cuts, severing the other antler. That was a minor preliminary as he swooped the ax in and out, circling the polled statue like a wily coyote, flicking the tip of the blade until it came to rest on the golden dick. A quick slash and the dick hit the floor.

The priest had worked himself into such a frenzy that he was unable to stop hacking. He lopped off the head, arms, left shoulder and collarbone, and right foot. The calf and femur up to the knee, right buttock, and the toes on the left foot. The left ankle, and the right leg up to the crotch. He chopped at the little bit left and reduced the statue to a pile of golden splinters as Mack and the Big Guy turned tail and escaped out of the fancy front doors of the temple, or whatever it was.

Mack said into his mic, "No crises here. Everything's under control. So, what's going on with you?"

Lucas came back. "A large part of antelope culture, similar to human culture, can be distilled to religion. A mix of stuff you can't make heads or tails of. It almost makes our religions look rational."

"Sounds interesting." The Big Guy pulled Mack into an auditorium loaded with objects in all sizes and shapes, colors and textures. "Excuse me, Lucas, but they're taking me shopping. I'll have to get back to you. I can't keep up with the Goldie Big Guy while listening to your prattle."

"Prattle, my ass. You're the one who wanted the low-down on their cultural differences. I'm only too happy to oblige, when you can fit me in." Lucas spit into the mic like slamming down the phone.

Mack asked the Big Guy, "What are we doing here. And where's the translator I know you have the technology for? Surely you're as advanced as the Ermies and Ivies."

The Big Guy stopped before a stack of catalogs, ignoring the stares of his fellow antelopes, who couldn't take their eyes off Mack, the Big Guy, and his six-Legionnaire escort. The Big Guy snapped horny fingers and a Legionnaire found a catalog with pages of video games from bloody wars and Spiderman to the NFL and NBA. The war games featured different colored antelopes tearing each other apart with gruesome weapons. Every one starred Goldies. There was even a travel planner with photos of mesas along a river valley.

A Legionnaire handed a page to Mack, who tried to find a pattern in the software selection. Mack said, "Well, sir. I don't know if we need video games. We'd prefer pizzas and cheeseburgers. Plus, my group specially requested scotch, beer, and ganga. But I assume that's not what this is about."

The Big Guy pursed his lips in a little cupid bow, fingering the shoot 'em up Star Wars software. Then he flicked the same finger across his forehead.

"You need programmers? Someone to evaluate your software? None of us have a clue about software."

The Big Guy stared at Mack, who spoke into his mic. "Lucas, Reg. Do the Ivies or Ermies have computers, software, and computer games? The Goldies are asking me to do something I can't figure out. Have you had anything similar happen?"

"Reg here. Nothing from the Ivies about software. It's something I know nothing about, but I've been listening in. There are developments we really need to discuss."

"Soon. Lucas. You around?" No answer. "Reg. You know I'm tied up with Big Guy Number Two. So, I'll have to get back to you."

The Big Guy stared at Mack, who said, "If you want me to understand what you want, stop pretending you don't know English."

The crowd of Goldies had grown so large that it felt like they might be crushed. The Big Guy waved a paw at the Legionnaires, who cleared a tunnel out of the noisy store. Curious Goldies watched as they hopped onto the moving sidewalk. The Big Guy herded Mack onto an elevator that whisked them to the muted light of the surface of the tepui and strode off without a backward look. The Legionnaires escorted Mack to a sidewalk that brought him down to the others.

"Whoa." Peter, Ellen, Roy, Madison, and Barry surrounded Mack.

Barry pointed. "They took everything. No table, no chairs, no food, and nothing to drink. We don't know what we did wrong."

Courtney shook her rubber bars. "They took my curtain and left me standing there without a stitch. Ellen threw me my clothes and I had to put them on wet. Brrrr."

"Yeah, which was even more traumatic for us." Roy grimaced. "Courtney without clothes crashed everything downhill."

Mack shook his head. "It's probably my fault. The Big Guy took me on a tour and Courtney's in much bigger trouble than I thought. I figured boiling her in oil was a bluff, but it isn't. And the Big Guy wanted me to do something I couldn't understand."

At their blank looks Mack said, "Yeah, I know. What else is new? The Big Guy showed me a catalog of computer games. When I said we had no expertise in software, the Legionnaires marched me back here double quick and that's all I know. Do any of you have computer smarts, software or programming skills?"

Peter did a sing-song, "I went to DeVry Tech. I went to DeVry. I didn't learn much and I didn't graduate. But I went."

"What did you learn?"

"Nothing, except my fellow students had an insatiable demand for ecstasy, speed, and coke. I don't sell plain old pot."

"Only the big time for you, eh? Can you write or read programing?"

"Depends on the program. I covered C+++ and a few others. Of course, that was years ago. We dabbled in alternative operating systems like Linux, but it was too much work. There are easier ways to make lots of money."

"And heeere's Lucas."

"What do you have to add?"

"Sorry you're in a snit. I have nothing to add except James has rubbed up against programming. Though he's not current either. And the Ermies are livid at how the Goldies are treating you. We're treated like kings and queens over here."

51

"I'm so happy for you. Getting the Ermies to help us would be much appreciated. But make it fast so we don't miss a meal, something serious like that. And Peter's education was ancient stuff, Lucas. A waste of time. They've taken our rations so we have nothing to eat or drink. We appear to be on their bad side, for some reason I can't figure out."

Lucas laughed. "Where's your fighting spirit? We have to be ready when our rescuers arrive. Buck up because I've sworn off worrying. Besides, my own news is good for a change. Badsr's life story is a hoot."

"Why do you care?"

"Hey. I caught your church appearance and heard what sounded like swishing and chopping. What was that all about? You didn't say much."

"Oh, man, I grew up with religious parents and still don't understand it."

"Then here's one for you: 'He is sent to school. Little or much, where he imbibes the rule. Of safety first and comfort; in his youth. He joins the church and ends the quest for truth.'"

"Geez, Lucas. That wasn't very kind."

"Reg here. Don't be defensive, Mack. Nothing wrong with going inside
a church. I go twice a week and am no worse for it."

"Yeah," piped up Courtney. "And look at me."

"I rest my case," said Mack. "You're the reason we're in jail and on the Goldies' blacklist. Nothing to eat or drink and—"

"Don't forget the unseasonably hot weather," Courtney shouted. "And the plane crash. And tipping it off the mesa. Maybe the stock market crashed too."

Mack held up his hands. "Okay, a small exaggeration."

Reg said, "It doesn't do any good to point fingers. We'll figure a way to get food and drink for you hostages."

Ellen was shocked. "Hostages? Are we hostages? I thought we were guests. Anyway, we're not starving. They'll probably bring dinner."

Mack smiled. "No one looks like they're starving. I'm not and Courtney isn't and Roy looks pretty good for his age. Even Barry isn't too frayed around the edges. Ellen's looked better, but who's comparing? Madison is about the same as always, and Peter is the same old Pete. Plus, we threw down platefuls of colorful stuff before it disappeared."

Barry shook his head. "It's not that we're hungry. But when they took the food away, they did it with gusto. Like they hated us."

"That jerk guard isn't a barometer for anyone other than himself. Don't let it bother you. Like Reg says, the only important thing is to escape. Or preserve our sanity until help arrives."

Ellen groaned. "And if help never arrives, then what?"

"Then we sacrifice a virgin to placate the gods. You'd better be running for cover."

Ellen turned her back on Mack.

"One problem solved. Now for food and community relations." Mack took the wobbly table leg and banged on the wall.

The guard marched in like he'd been summoned. It was the same guard, though he'd changed uniforms, from silver and maroon to blue and yellow. And his hat was cockeyed.

"Oh, brother," said Mack.

The guard marched up with his chest touching Mack's chin, looking down on Mack's bald spot. Mack backed up and whipped his cap off the sloping table, jamming it on his head. The guard moved back again, his chest touching Mack's chin.

"Ulph. Is there anything I can do for you?"

The guard twisted a button on his chest. It produced a thin, metallic, and all but unrecognizable noise. "Broother."

"What the heck was that?" said Lucas.

"Our guard got ahold of a translator. But it must be an antique because it doesn't work too well."

The guard tried again. "Oooh, Broother.   Ooooops. Diiidn't meean a thiing."

"That's quite excellent. Did you hear that, Lucas? Our first communication with a Goldie."

"You call that communication? Remember that 'Nowadays to be intelligible is to be found out.' I'd just call it 'oh, brother.' Which reminds me: 'Until you have become really, in actual fact, as brother to everyone, brotherhood will not come to pass.' Pretty cool, eh?"

"Ridiculous. You can't be a brother to an antelope and who'd want to be? You've never unveiled a quote that fit the circumstances. Do you just pick them at random?"

"Well, excuussse me. You'd think an aspiring intellectual like yourself would appreciate learned things. Perhaps one isn't such an intellectual as one thinks, eh?"

"That 'eh' stuff marks you out as a foreigner, don't you know? You'll never make it in the States. Not that they'll let you stay. When's your next hearing?"

"I might miss it, since it's next month. Unless you have a secret plan to get us out of here."

"I'm leaning in favor of Billy K.'s idea. Walk out and see what happens."

"Even if we got out, what would we do when we reach the edge of the mesa? Assuming we're not shot first. The edge is too high and vertical."

"I've been thinking about that. The Goldies are cagey, camouflaging the surface. They know about satellites. All we have to do is make an appearance on top, unprotected by netting. We'll show up on a CIA satellite and they'll pick us up straightaway."

"Would you two shut the heck up!" howled Ellen. "Oops, sorry." She covered her mouth like it needed washed out. "The guard is trying to tell us something and you're not paying attention."

"Yes ma'am. Pray tell, what have we missed?"

"Well, he said something about food. And he tried to say something about Courtney we didn't understand. And Reg hasn't been able to get a word in edgewise."

"Hi, Mack. This is Reg. Tell Ellen to go to confession, or at least do a couple of Hail Mary's."

Lucas laughed. "Wasn't that serious a sin, eh?"

"Stop that," said Mack. "Or you'll muck up your remote possibility of naturalization. Real Americans only make fun of Canadians."

"Balderdash. I might have been born in Canada. Or I might have been born in the States. It's a matter of exactly

54

where the plane was when me mum was embarrassed on Qantas flight 2. You should have sympathy for someone who does most of your work. Where'd you be if I were deported? In dire straits, that's for sure."

"That sounds like the real Lucas."

"Yes, Reg, I know you can't get a word in edgewise. Our strategy? I'll check with Mack because he's on top of it."

"How come only you can hear Reg, or are you putting me on?"

"Lucas's putting you on," said Reg. "I'm always available, though seldom consulted. The Ivies and the Ermies will support you against the Goldies."

"I know that," said Lucas. "'We should support whatever the enemy opposes and oppose whatever the enemy supports,' which sounds like a kindergarten game."

"Quotes are a kindergarten game," said Mack. "So, cut it out! We're having a high-level strategy session here."

Reg said, "If Ellen heard the guard right, then Goldie largess will continue."

Mack turned to Ellen. "Well. Did you hear the guard right?"

Ellen rolled her eyes. "Why don't you ask him yourself? I'm not your lackey, like some people I could mention."

"Subtle she ain't," said Lucas.

Mack sidled up to the guard but the guard wasn't having it, turning his back. Mack finally said, "Are you in cahoots with Ellen?"

The guard twisted the knob on his chest. "Daamn, daamn, daamn."

"Are we back on rations with the lovely lemonade, and what's going to happen to Courtney?"

A metallic voice emanated from the guard's chest. Without the long vowels and chirps it sounded like, "You are not to eat at all times. There is to be a period of time when you do not eat. You are not to drink at all times or become drunken. There is to be a period of time when you sober up. Mademoiselle Courtney's trial begins in one hour. Should she be tried by a jury of her peers?"

Peter shook his head. "I don't like the Goldies. They're petty insensitive beasts."

"Not like your own self, eh?" Mack bonked himself on the forehead with his hand. "That dang Aussie's got me saying it too."

Lucas purred, "And I quote, 'Bigotry has no head and cannot think, no heart and cannot feel. When she moves it is in wrath; when she pauses it is amid ruin. Her prayers are curses, her god is a demon, her communion is death, her vengeance is eternity, her decalogue written in the blood of her victims, and if she stops for a moment in her infernal flight it is upon a kindred rock to whet her vulture fang for a more sanguinary desolation.'"

"Hey, Peter. You just got dissed."

Peter frowned. "What's sanguinary? Was that it? I didn't understand it all but it didn't sound nice."

"It wasn't nice. Hey, Lucas. I liked that one. You can do one quote a day. Cut down so we don't overdose."

"Actually, Mack, that was for you calling me an Aussie, but wow. I get a quote a day. What a gift. Thank you, bountiful sahib. Since you can't see me, you should know that I'm bowing to your eminence."

"Can it, duck breath. Think about what the guard said, that Courtney gets a jury of her peers. We'll let her off and that'll solve everything and we can go home."

"Silly goose. We let her off and they'll boil us instead. Religions want your blood or your soul and we'd better get used to it. No one leaves this place alive."

"Gentlemen, gentlemen," said Reg. "The beliefs of the vast majority of the planet may be a small matter to Lucas. But for many, religion guarantees eternity."

Lucas said, "So why don't they embrace the afterlife now, instead of waiting around? If it's so much better there, why stick around here?"

Mack mused. "Maybe only a few really believe. Disciples of Halley's Comet, red Kool-Aid, fundamentalists."

"Or they stay to support religious leaders in the style to which they're enamored."

"Bad to the bone," said Reg. "That's the opposite of spiritual and is sacrilege to the overwhelming majority. Ye of little faith are not peers of Courtney's and shouldn't be on her jury. But the idea of us on a jury is bizarre."

Mack walked back to the guard. "About this jury for Courtney's trial. Are you saying we're the jury? We should have lunch first, or postpone the trial until tomorrow."

The guard acquired two small creases alongside his nose. A sure giveaway for an antelope frown. "Snarfle, fartem, bittle, macquarie, offenbach." He jiggled the knobs on his chest and tried again. "You are the jury but our jury is different from your jury. Our jury is tried along with the defendant. That way the judge finds out everything about the jurors. Then he can properly interpret the verdict. It's too early for lunch. The trial starts in forty-three of your minutes."

"Wowzie, zowzie," said Madison. "All that from snarfle, fartem, bittle, macquarie, offenbach. That's a tongue to make you rock."

The guard said in a tinny monotone, "Our language is the richest most expressive on earth. Much superior to English, which is verbose and inane."

"Whoa there, partner," came a voice over Mack's mic, obviously Billy K. "Don't you go denigratin' my native tongue. English sounds a whole heck of a lot better than a bunch of snarfle farts." He blew a raspberry.

"Sorry about that," said Lucas. "My mic was commandeered."

"And for a damn good cause," said Roy. "Otherwise—"

"Yeah, we know what's otherwise." Mack shook his head. "So, where's the trial and how is everyone going to be on Courtney's jury? You've been kidnapped to other tepuis."

"Forward, harch," commanded the guard, opening Courtney's cell. He pulled her out and shoved her through an invisible door that barely opened in time. Two Legionnaires fell in step with Courtney while another six waited for Mack and the rest. The guard gestured for them to hurry up.

"We're off to be a jury," sang Mack. "A wonderful jury of us. Maybe we'll be reunited. What do you say, troops?"

57

"Howza, wowza," said Lucas. "And I quote. 'The efficiency of our criminal system is only marred by the difficulty of finding twelve men every day who don't know anything and can't read.' I don't want to return to the Goldies. But with only forty-three minutes left before the trial, we should know soon."

"Reg agrees, and that was one of your better quotes. The Ivies have been superb hosts. My bath was a spa treatment. Sumptuous with marble and onyx, cascading water, and custom pool temperature. Maybe it was just to relax us, get us off guard."

Lucas said, "We haven't seen a guard since we got here."

"So, have they come to get you yet? Where are you?" asked Reg.

"The Ermies put us in a right Taj Mahal. We are attended by...I don't know what they are. But I think of them as Ermie maidens, slim lovelies with silky manes, soft voices, and cute skirts. We get a program on the hour, printed in English, listing available activities. We don't have to take part but they encourage us to meet different parts of the community, to appreciate their culture. Also, I chatted with Badsr and he'd like to discuss this whole situation with you."

"Similar for us," said Reg, "though a little different from Lucas. The Ivies put us in private rooms with balconies and a lovely swimming pool. They just now shooed everyone back inside and it looks like something's about to happen. They're setting up plush seats in front of a mega-sized monitor. And you?"

"They herded us along the emerald road, past the grand cathedral where the head priest, or whoever he was, chopped up the little golden statue. Now we're going into a small auditorium. Yep. It's a courtroom, or an antelopian version of one. There's a high bench for the judge and they're putting us on uncomfortable bleachers. There are a couple of tables up front, maybe for lawyers. But only one is occupied, shared by two Goldies. It's like Perry Mason on Mars. We're the only ones here. Well, except for Legionnaires and court personnel, who are wearing blue and yellow uniforms. Our guard showed up in a blue and yellow robe and hauled himself onto the high bench I assumed was for the judge. I guess we should have treated him better. But I lost track of Courtney. Our star defendant is missing."

"You don't have to tell us," said Lucas. "You're on our monitors, the same as we're probably on yours."

"Right. You do look like you've been pampered. Is that Benny in that incredible outfit?"

"Shore 'nuff, 'tis," said Benny. "Lookin' pretty good, don't you think? I really hit it off with this bunch. They understand horses and speed and grace and good breeding, and I'm into all of that." Benny wore a red cowboy shirt with royal blue pants, looking like a gay caballero with white leather tassels and powder blue boots.

"Hi, Reg, and say hi to Betty Boop. Where'd she find a plaid skirt and petticoats? Am I seeing right?"

"More or less. Have you given any thought to what the jury's strategy should be—?"

He was cut off by staccato shots from the judge's gavel. The judge, their former guard, wore a floppy blue and yellow hat with seven pointy tails. He stood silent as the gallery filled with antelopes and the outside doors slid shut.

The Big Guys walked slowly down the aisle to a fanfare of long trumpets emblazoned with blue and yellow flags. The crowd waited as the Big Guys sat in three high-backed chairs. Two Legionnaires led Courtney, who looked drugged, into the courtroom. Her shackles were blue and yellow in alternate links. The Legionnaires escorted her to the other table and set her firmly down, arranging the colorful chain over the top of her chair, suspending her arms at half-mast.

Mack stood. "Your Honor. The defendant should be treated with more respect. You shouldn't torture her until you sentence her to death."

The judge spouted snarfles for a second until he remembered to twiddle his knob. "This court has not decided the case or heard the evidence. The defendant is not automatically sentenced to death. And you are in contempt of this court."

"I'd like to deny that I'm in contempt of this court, but I wouldn't want to perjure myself. In any event, you should treat the defendant in a civilized manner."

One of the Big Guys gave a signal and a Legionnaire released the cuffs from Courtney's wrists. With a heart-rending sigh, she dropped her hands to her side.

"The old girl's still a consummate actress, I see," said Lucas.

Mack said, "Nailed that."

"You're all a big hearty help," Courtney said to Mack. "No wonder we never elected you leader."

"We're solidly behind you." Mack was relieved she hadn't been drugged. "We'll do our best to get you acquitted, no matter what."

"My faith is restored. Yet somehow, I don't believe a word. Only in God do I trust."

"Makes sense to me," said Mack.

The judge beat a gavel on the podium.

"Sorry, Your Honor. I stand moot."

"That's mute," said Lucas.

"And corrected to boot."

The judge gave the gavel an extra hard smash and it fractured. The mallet ricocheted off the high ceiling and fell in front of Courtney. She seized it as the judge looked at the end of his impotent stick, aghast. Courtney toted the blunt end up to the bench and set it in front of the him.

The judge angrily twisted his knob. "Order in the court. The defendant will take her seat. Under no circumstances will she approach the bench without express permission. The audience will stop talking and the baliff will fetch a new gavel."

Mack smiled. "That's bailiff, Your Honor."

"Up here, we call them baliffs. So, mind your own business." The baliff or bailiff had already delivered a fresh gavel to the judge. The judge emphasized Mack's reprimand with a crisp wham on the podium.

"Yes, Your Honor. We are chagrined."

"Keep your chagrin active. You'll need it on many occasions. The jury will now be sworn and we'll begin opening statements. Raise your left hands. You humans with the Riffiti,

60

who you call antelopes of color and no color. Also raise your hands."

The judge checked the monitors for compliance. "Raise your hands. That's terrible. Can't you follow instructions? Raise all your hands. You with the antelopes of no color—"

"Your Honor, that's Arturo and you'd do better in Spanish."

"I don't have a Spanish program for this thing, though we have Portuguese. Does he understand Portuguese?"

"Not even close. Or at least not close enough for Arturo, especially when he's being difficult."

"We'll have no difficulties in this courtroom. Now Mr. Arturo, raise your hand along with the rest."

Arturo blinked and raised his hand.

"Do you solemnly swear to uphold the laws of the Golden Antelopes, who rival the sun? And to obey the instructions of this court, so help you God. Who we call Famigusta, and whose name cannot be spoken aloud?"

"Not me." Mack lowered his hand. The rest of the humans snapped their hands down too.

Lucas said, "'The laws of God, the laws of man, He may keep that will and can; Not I: let God and man decree, Laws for themselves but not for me.'"

Mack glared at Lucas's image on the monitor as he said to the judge, "We don't know the laws of the Golden Antelopes. Even if we did, we don't know which ones are involved in this trial. In fact, the defendant hasn't been told what she's charged with. It couldn't be more than a little property damage, maybe a small fine to repair the damage. And we don't recognize the Famigusta god. Besides, we thought you called your god Radnicharra."

"Shut it," snapped the judge. "Radnicharra is a false god of the no color antelopes. And you know very well what the defendant is charged with."

"Exactly what are the charges, pray tell? You never told us."

Courtney clapped her hands. "Yeah, Mack. Good job. You're okay in my book. Sometimes, anyway. And Mr. Judge,

I didn't mean to damage your property. Just get rid of a false god."

"Outrageous. Stand, madame defendant. You have confessed to the crime of defacing God. The punishment is death by boiling oil. How do you plead?"

"I plead for you to cut out the farce, Mr. Judge. I carved up a statue of a false god. I never defaced an actual god and you have no notion of the…concept. You're godless and apparently unfamiliar with the one true Baptist God. Holding this trial makes you liable for defaming the one true God, who is Baptist. Well, or Protestant, or at least Christian. See, your god doesn't even qualify." She spat, and the well-formed gob sailed true, though a little low, splattering on the front of the judge's fancy box.

The judge jumped up, peering at the nasty goober as Lucas whispered, "'When the consensus of scholarship says one thing and the Word of God says another, the consensus of scholarship can go plumb to hell for all I care.'"

The judge ordered, "Guards. Replace the handcuffs and gag the defendant."

Mack said, "I am chagrined, as instructed. Surely you have freedom of speech in this remote outpost of civilization?"

The judge snarled. "Freedom of speech is not the same as freedom of spitting. The defendant is not free to spit."

The three Big Guys rose and applauded. Horny-pawed clapping swept the courtroom as a Legionnaire reattached manacles behind Courtney's back. Then they tied a golden muffler around her face.

They could faintly hear her screaming, "I can't breathe. I can't breathe." She slumped in the chair and pitched forward on the floor.

"Please, Your Honor," said Mack. "Antelope gags are too big and bulky for petite humans. Unless you remove it right now, you'll lose both the defendant and your plans for revenge."

The judge said, "Revenge has nothing to do with it, but the gag may be loosened." And it was.

The responsible Legionnaire tipped Courtney's chair upright. Her stare circled the judge's face like a red circle around a wrong answer and would have justified contempt charges, except the judge ignored her. "The jury will either be sworn or incarcerated."

Mack smirked. "Incarcerated it is, Your Honor." That'd be an easy way to save Courtney and bide their time until their rescue.

The number one Big Guy rose and spoke for the first time. "Forego the oath." He sat back on the highest perch of the three-tiered throne.

The judge tried to hide his embarrassment, clearing his throat a couple of times. "You may proceed."

Mack said, "Who may proceed? Does the jury have the right to ask questions? And will you read the charges so we know what's going on?"

"Multiple question. Overruled."

"Then take them one at a time. If you can't remember them, I'll repeat them. Separately, of course."

"The jury will be questioned by the—prosecutor. Whether you can ask questions depends on my mood, which is pretty bad right now."

"Thank you, Your Honor. We appreciate your petty indulgence. We repeat our request to read the charges against the defendant."

"We don't do that sort of thing. You know what the charges are or you wouldn't be here."

"We don't know what the charges are, yet here we are. Or we could remedy that defect by being elsewhere. It's ludicrous for us to be jurors for our good friend Courtney. You see, we're biased." Several jurors tittered.

"We know you're biased. I'll take that into account when imposing her sentence. So, don't worry about it."

"Then why bother with a fake jury in the first place? Just declare her guilty and throw her in boiling oil."

"I object," said Courtney. "Frying is too good for the likes of me. I only wanted to bring the one true God to a godless nation. You should be down on your antelopian knees, thanking me. Wait until the US government gets ahold of you. You'll be the ones frying."

Mack groaned. "Thank you, Courtney. With a defense like that we can pack our bags and leave you to your just deserts. Which is to say, fried fritters. Besides, they don't understand sarcasm. Haven't you noticed? They think you're serious and now you're in real trouble."

Mack addressed the three Big Guys. "Gentlemen, or gentle antelopes. We deserve to know the charges against our compatriot. Otherwise, we can't mount a defense. You know what I mean?"

The top Big Guy stood and adjusted his knob to the highest fidelity. His voice came out deep and smooth. "The court will now read the charges." He sat down while the judge fidgeted.

"Okay." The judge jerked a paw at the baliff. "Read the charges."

"Squawk, shriek, screeck, farple, beep."

"Right. We'll get you one right now." The judge motioned to the sub-baliff, who passed the order down the line of richly arrayed baliffs until the last of the lot scurried stage right.

They sat around looking at each other. Mack stared at the judge while Courtney looked at the Big Guys. She mouthed, "The judge isn't reading the charges. He's palming it off on a sub-sub-sub-sub-baliff," repeating it over and over.

The judge stared at the Big Guys, and the Big Guys frowned at the ceiling. The judge finally ordered the baliff to send another baliff to fetch a translator. After the order was duly passed down the line the last baliff suddenly appeared, relishing his moment in the spotlight. He strode up to the judge's podium, trying to keep his eyes off the festering gob of goo as he adjusted his Pince-nez. He read loud and clear:

"Hear ye, hear ye. The Honorable Judge Grdam presiding. The charges against the alien defendant are as follows and forthwith. First, the despicable act of accompanying a giant machine of destruction as it destroyed the vegetation and ground cover immediately adjacent to and quite near the fabulous sculpture of our Lord and God Almighty Most Powerful in the Known and Unknown Universe, resulting in the wanton tipping and near destruction of the sheltering edifice for our Lord and God Almighty Most Powerful in the Known and Unknown Universe. Second, the despicable act of leaving the aforesaid giant machine…"

This went on for forty-six minutes, covering thirty-seven charges. At the end, the humans were as certain of the charges as before they were read.

The sub-sub-sub-baliff, however, was satisfied with his performance. He bowed twice on his way to the last chair.

Mack had nodded off a couple of times but now stood. "Your Honor, I move that all charges be dismissed. Remand the defendant in my custody. The fighter jets of the US Air Force men in blue will soon land on this miserable tepui and rescue us from the likes of you."

"Any grounds?" The judge was polite, perhaps to protect the record.

"A few. First, the defendant was not responsible for the giant machine that crashed next to your sacred site. Any attempt to hold her responsible would run afoul of the world's most basic ideas of justice. Second, the defendant was not responsible for leaving the giant machine on your tepui. In fact, the Goldie government illegally dispatched it off the edge of this tepui without due process, failing to first check the health of its occupants. Third," and it took Mack forty minutes to complete the preliminary motion. He concluded, "The jury has neither been duly empaneled nor has the court been qualified in the practice of international law necessary to decide this case under the protocols of the United Nations. Have you applied for membership?"

"Mr. Sub-Sub-Sub-Baliff, wipe off that gob of goo. Motion denied. The court will take a five-minute recess."

The lowliest baliff suddenly stopped considering himself a star. He pulled on shiny gloves and wiped off the goo, holding his nose as he dropped the residue in the bin behind the judge's podium. The second Big Guy walked up to Mack and made a show of adjusting his new chest knob.

Mack clapped his hands. "Now that you've got the translator hooked up, I have questions. What did you want when you pulled out the list of software? I have a few other questions, but would be very interested in what that was all about."

"Harrumph, Testing, testing, one, two, three."

"Enough already. It works like a dream. Now what are you up to, if that's not a state secret?"

"Hmmm."

"Hmmm, my ass. Let's cut the crap and level with each other. Start by introducing ourselves. I'm Mack and you are—?" Mack held out his hand and the Big Guy took it firmly, crunching small bones.

"Whoops." Mack snatched it back.

"I am Btsht, which may be difficult to pronounce in your language. You have plenty of words that we can't get our tongues around. Pleased to meet you, Mack. We didn't want to get involved with you if we could possibly help it. We've lived on these mesas for millennia, isolated and safe from the outside world. And that's the way we'd like to stay. We *know* that once you discover us, we're goners. And for all intents and purposes, we've been discovered."

The Big Guy smiled. "The translator's pretty good with the lingo, eh? You'll put us in your zoos or on reservations. Because our civilization is far superior to yours, we'd like to avoid that. But once we're discovered, we don't know how to avoid it. We're outnumbered by millions. Your people will be on us soon, so we're in a quandary. The first thing we did was vote. Voting together was exceptional because we never vote at the same time. The Goldies, Ermies, and Ivies, as you call us, are rather competitive."

Btsht wrinkled his golden forehead. "Actually, we hate each other. Goldies know that our culture, government, and religion are superior. Same goes for our infrastructure, competence, and educational system. All superior to the dregs on other mesas. They're not real antelopes, which we call Riffiti. You saw them and I'm sure you understand. They're trash."

The Big Guy looked at Mack to make sure he was following. "But on this single occasion, the threat to our future and way of life required voting by all three races. We agreed to observe the decision of the masses and the vote was catastrophic. The Ermies and Ivies demanded that you be split up. Refusing would have meant certain war with the Ermies.

The Ivies are harmless. So, we shipped your friends off to the infidels. Now we find that isn't enough. The Ermies want you all, and if we don't agree, war looms. We've fought wars for centuries, and we'll fight for more centuries, even if only in your zoos. We had to find out whether you could help program our war machine. Programs are programs. So, can you help us or not? Or are we left at the mercy of the rotten Ermies?"

Mack's head was whirling. The Ermies and Ivies were reading from different hymnals. Lucas would know whether the Ermies sought custody of all the humans. And there might be a war? It felt like a surrealistic game. Why would the Ermies care whether the Ivies and Goldies provided room and board for uninvited aliens? They'd be rescued in a few hours.

5

Btsht fiddled with his knob, staring at Mack.

Mack said, "I have to think about everything you said. Give me a few minutes. I respect your confidence and will do everything I can to earn it."

The Big Guy relaxed and slapped Mack on the back as the judge climbed on the catbird seat.

"Oof." Mack sidled back to the juror's bleachers, finding himself next to Ellen. "Oops, sorry. Didn't mean to step on your foot."

"I'm used to it by now."

"How's everyone else doing?"

"Nasty," said Peter. "I'm not cut out for jury duty. I'd rather be doing damn near anything else."

"Great." Roy shook his head. "We can't go any further downhill. We're at the bottom of the bottom and the only way we can go is up."

"Cheery thought. And you Madison, Barry?"

Barry frowned. "Couldn't be worser. Tired of this crap. I just want to get back to Sun City and see if I'm still in business."

"What difference does it make? You're a millionaire. Business is no longer necessary."

"I don't care about the money. But I love the business. It's creative, fun, and I meet lots of horny widows."

"Oh, yeah. Sun City Security. And you, Madison?"

"I'm writing an epic poem, about antelopes, to grow 'em. So, Cookie lend me your comb. I'll stop when we get home. I know they're superior, their favor hope to currier."

"Interesting. That's what the Big Guy said, that they're way superior. Maybe you can team up with him."

"Order in the court," shouted the baliff. The judge tugged on his jester's hat and gaveled once. "The prosecution will call its first witness."

Mack did a double take at the two prosecutors, the Mutt and Jeff of the antelope kingdom. Mutt said, "I call the jury for adverse cross-examination."

Mack was startled. "I object. We're the jury. We can't be called for examination, cross or otherwise. We're the ones who decide the case."

"Wrong," said the judge. "I decide the case. You're just the jury."

"Negatory," squawked Courtney. "I'm the defendant being railroaded. You're a clown and the jury is here to protect me."

"How'd she get the gag off? Now, madam, if you can't keep a civil tongue and stop spitting, I'll have you re-gagged."

"Yes, sir. I'll be good. But why should I? I'm about to fry. I should go out with a bang."

"Your choice."

"Then I choose not to fry and instead go home to the United States of America where I can be me and no one cares."

"I second that last part," said Mack. "Thank you, Your Honor, for your indulgence. I know it's a weary road you travel, wearing so many hats and putting up with nincompoops."

"Indeed," said the judge. "You're a prime example of the cross I bear."

"Does your religion feature a cross? I didn't know it was part of antelopian theology."

"It's not. It's just an expression, probably picked up from your atrocious television— Oops. Strike that."

Lucas said, "'Nothing is really real unless it happens on television,'" at the same time as Mack added, "But Your Honor. Why would you care that we know you watch television? I'm sure you don't watch it often. You wouldn't rot your brains with trash on screens, like we do. A superior race wouldn't. Oh, I see."

69

Mack turned to Big Guy Number Two, who sat between the two prosecutors. "Your superiority may be somewhat exaggerated."

"Sit down," said the judge. "We're here for a solemn trial. Not for you to run off at the mouth."

"Thank you, Your Honor. I'll keep that in mind." Mack sat down.

His mic squawked. "Reg here. Don't believe a word the Big Guy, whatsiname Btsht, told you."

"Just a sec. Before you go further. What are the odds that our conversations are transcribed with copies instantly transmitted to certain antelopes of all colors and persuasions?"

"Point conceded. But you should know the Ivies aren't threatening war. And they're not demanding more human hostages. But they are appalled at the trial."

"Maybe the Ivies haven't told you what they're up to. But we are hostages, a bargaining tool. Human shields against our rescuers. Or will they keep us here so their cover's not blown? From the viewpoint of the antelopes I see no rational plan that would get us out of here."

"There are a few other possibilities, which we'll discuss at a more favorable time—"

Bang, bang, went the gavel as if enraged. Mack stopped concentrating on Reg and looked at the mad-as-a-hatter judge, who said, "Take the stand. You've been called as the first juror."

"Jurors, Your Honor, aren't witnesses. They don't take the stand. They decide the case. Therefore, I don't have to take the stand."

"Wrong court. Wrong law. Wrongheaded." The judge banged the gavel to ear-numbing advantage. "Get yourself up here, now."

"Yes sir, Your Honor, sir. I didn't realize we'd landed in Nazi Germany, or Stalin's gulag, or Idi Amin's hotel, or—"

"Quite enough of that. Take the stand or we'll provide a cell instead."

"I appreciate the choice, Your Honor. Here comes the juror. Here comes the juror."

"Thank you," said the judge as Mack stood below the high bench. The judge loomed over Mack like an iceberg over the Titanic. "Raise your left hand." Mack automatically raised his right hand.

"Close enough. Now repeat after me, I solemnly swear."

"I solemnly swear."

"To tell the truth."

"To tell the truth."

"The whole truth and nothing but the truth."

"The whole truth and then some."

"Cut the clowning." The judge swung the tassels on his colorful hat. "And nothing but the truth."

"And nothing like the truth."

"So help me God."

"So help me who?"

"So help me God."

"We have a problem. First, I need to know which God. Are you referring to Courtney's God, or the golden statue that met a mishap? Or the God it represents, one of the gods of ancient Egypt, a Hindu god, or some other God?"

"Cut it out. There's only one God and that's the God the oath refers to. The Riffiti God, the God of the Golden Antelopes. The only God. Don't trifle with God."

"I can't swear an oath to an antelope God."

"Don't you believe in God?"

"Don't get me mixed up with that Aussie twit, Lucas. He's the one who's hostile to all the gods. I have a few questions, like whose God, but we won't get anywhere. So, why don't you give it up?"

"I can't give it up. Being judge is my job."

"But I thought you were a jailer, a special envoy from the Big Guys, charged with keeping us in red beer and colorful cubes."

"Never mind. It's enough to swear to tell the truth."

Mack glanced at the Big Guy, who'd finished signaling.

The judge said, "Please take the stand."

"Where to?" said Mack.

"Mr. Baliff, insert the infidel into the witness box, now."

71

"Okay, judge. I can tell your patience is wearing thin." Mack climbed onto a chair with a back twice as tall as he was. "Ready if you are."

The Mutt prosecutor wiggled big bushy eyebrows, walked up to the witness box, and said, "Gibbledy fart." Without a trace of embarrassment, he twiddled a knob beside his ear. "State your name, please."

"My name is Mack McElheney. And yours?"

"Don't be a wise ass. You'll only end up in jail instead of cushy quarters at taxpayer expense."

"Either one's at taxpayer expense and neither one's cushy, right?"

Mutt ignored him. "Where were you on the morning of Juneteenth the fortieth?"

"If that was this morning, you know where I was. Were you in the horde of antelopes that terrorized us after the trauma of a devastating plane crash?"

"Just tell the court what you saw when the defendant." Mutt pointed at a bedraggled Courtney sitting like a lump behind the adjacent table. "When she attacked the God of the Riffiti, the Golden Antelopes, as you call us."

"My understanding is that gods are impossible to attack because they're incorporeal. They have no physical body. So, you can't attack a god or a ghost, holy or otherwise."

"I'll rephrase the question. Did you see the defendant dismember the golden statue of the Golden Andelphian God?"

"No." Mack shook his head emphatically. "I saw her carve a couple of nothing antlers and an obviously over-representative golden dick from a statue. The statue wasn't a god because it had a body. Dismemberment I didn't see."

"Thank you, but the golden dick was and is authentically Andelphian. Do you have any questions for yourself?"

"Well, yes. I question why I wasn't born an endowed Andelphian. Though I wouldn't touch the subject with a ten-inch pole. Should I both ask and answer in the witness box? Or should I get down, ask the question, and then bound back up to give the answer?"

"Just say what you have to say, if there's anything of substance you can think of."

"Good point. My first question is why am I here? And no, I'm not talking ultimate questions. Only why I'm in this place at this time instead of being allowed to return home. You tell me the Golden Andelphians are a civilized race. But you apparently aren't. Instead of treating trauma victims humanely, you level trumped-up charges of blasphemy. Blasphemy went out with the Middle Ages. Why are you seeking revenge on poor creatures who could never physically threaten you?"

"I object," said Mutt. "Neither the question nor the answer is relevant."

"I'll go you one better," said the judge. "The witness is a jester and you should never have called him to the stand. He's the chief trouble-maker of the aliens—er, humans. Just call the defendant. She'll admit everything and we can wrap up the trial."

"I have a better objection," said Mack. "There are plenty of religions that would carve us up if we dissed their god. These include ISIS and fundamentalist Muslims in Iran, Sudan, and Saudi Arabia. Also, Hindus in India, and a few Christians I've known in the good old US of A. But since I can't object to my own question, I ask the court to waive the testimony of the jury."

The judge thought for a few seconds. "We can't forgo questioning the jury, but we can skip this particular juror."

"Gee thanks, Your Honor. I was afraid I'd say something wrong and get in trouble."

"You are dismissed. Rejoin the jury."

Mack scurried back to the bleachers before the judge could change his mind.

"I call the defendant, Courtney," said Mutt as Jeff nodded vigorously in agreement.

"Your Honor," said Courtney. "I'd rather not. I'm feeling unwell."

Mutt jumped to his feet. "Your Honor. She's the defendant and has to take the stand. Otherwise we'd have to postpone the trial and there's no time— Oops."

Mack smiled, rising lazily. "Before addressing the question of *oops*...I join the prosecution in objecting to Courtney avoiding the stand on the grounds of *illness*. Anyone faced with boiling oil may feel a bit queasy. But if you're going to kill her anyway, it makes no difference that she feels unwell. So, rip her apart, Mutt."

Bang, bang, bang, ricochet. "I've had quite enough of you, Mr. Mack." The judge watched the head of the gavel arc onto the prosecutor's table and clatter to the floor. The sub-sub-bailiff rushed to fetch another.

"Your Honor, I suggest in future gavel requisitions that you disqualify the lowest bidder." At the judge's look Mack added hastily, "It was only a suggestion. Back to the question of *oops*. To resolve the issue, I call the prosecutor Mutt, or whatever his name is. We haven't been formally introduced."

"My name," said the lead prosecutor, "is *Josejiménez*. I object to being called as a witness. I have nothing to say that would be relevant to the charges before the court."

"Bullhonky," said Mack. "The prosecutor said *oops*. He's admitted the trial can't be postponed, which means this is a kangaroo court." Mack illustratively hopped around. "Holding us hostage as a defense against our rescue by the United States Air Force men in blue."

"That doesn't make sense," said the judge. "We'd be in more trouble if we executed Madame Courtney than if we didn't."

"I think you've hit on it, Your Honor. If you impose the death penalty without carrying it out, you have a negotiating advantage with the US government. Whether to return us and whether you are outed. Of course, you'd never dare to actually execute her. Our government is gung-ho when it comes to freedom of religion—"

Lucas whispered in his ear, "Freedom of superstition is more accurate."

Mack continued, "...as enshrined in the First Amendment to our Constitution. The trial is a ploy to keep you from being discovered by humans. You're afraid we'll put you in zoos and you want to insure your privacy on these archaic tepuis forever."

The judge leaned over the bench. "You have no concept of justice or the sanctity of religion. Your judgment is sadly lacking in all known particulars."

"Thank you, Your Honor. If you'll sign that, I'll type it up and frame it."

The judge banged his gavel. "And you're in constant contempt of this court."

"I didn't think you'd notice."

His mic came to life. "Good kangaroo court analysis. We loved the hopping around in living color. Me mum would be proud."

"Stow it, Aussie," whispered Mack. "I'm otherwise occupied."

The judge said, "When the trial is over, I'll consider the appropriate punishment for your disrespect of this court. So far you're guilty of thirty-one counts of contempt."

"Well, *thank you,* your Honor. May I call Mr. Josejiménez to the stand?"

"You may not. The issue of postponing the trial is not before the court. The court has already ruled that the defendant must take the stand. If she needs a few minutes from time to time, I'll consider it." He shook his hoof. "As long as she neither spits nor throws up. Proceed Mr. Prosecutor."

Jose `Mutt' Jiménez gestured for Courtney to take the stand.

"But I don't want to," said Courtney.

"Just do your best," said Mack. "We'll raise any irregularities on appeal."

"What appeal?" said the judge. "This is a court of last resort, as you can probably tell from the audience."

"Then scratch that. We refuse to appeal. We'll stake everything on this," and did his kanga hippity-hop, "court."

"Thirty-two contempt charges now, Mr. Mack. Just keep it up."

"With pleasure, Your Honor." Mack hip-hopped out of the jury box to massage Courtney's wrists and give her a pep talk.

"Big help you are," Courtney snapped. "You're not a lawyer, just a lackey of the Arizona State Lottery. And a lousy one at that. Give me one reason I should let you make objections, handle my questioning, or give me advice?"

"Beats me. Except no one else seems to be available."

"I want Nick or Reg to represent me. At least they're Christians."

"My parents raised me as a Baptist, so I'm one, too, kind of."

"That's worse."

"Your Honor, the defendant wishes a change of counsel from my honorable self to the Rev. Nick Resovich. Could you have him shipped over from the Ermies?"

"The Ermies. Oh, the bitter blacks, the antelopes of color. The answer is no. But he can handle the questioning by remote. As you can see, the dispersed jury is on the monitors."

Mack looked and only saw antelopes from other tepuis.

"Behind you," growled the judge. "With the rest of the jurors."

Mack turned to see thirteen monitors displaying everyone not present. Mack took a long look at Lucas, who winked at him, and at Reg, who raised his eyebrows. Billy K. blew a bubble on camera. He'd gotten hold of rainbow-colored bubble gum that shimmered like oily water.

Mack said, "Howdy Fats and Molly and Betty and Arturo, and Rudd Rat." Rudd looked hurt, his pout reaching the end of his pointy nose.

"That's enough," said the judge. "Mr. Reverend Nick, you may proceed."

"Huh, me," said Nick. "I'm not— Well, I'll give it a try. Please state your name." He'd seen as much Perry Mason as the next guy.

Courtney said, "You know my name."

"Yes, but the court doesn't. Tell them anyway."

"My name is Mrs. Everett Courtney Fern Sitton Sherman. Sitton's my maiden name."

"Thank you. What else do you want me to ask?"

"About all the crazy charges they have against me. Whether I crashed the plane on their blooming mesa. Whether I meant to knock that umbrella over. Stuff like that."

"Okay. Did you crash the plane into their blooming mesa?"

"No. I wasn't even driving."

"This is getting nowhere," said Mack.

"Is that an objection?" asked the judge.

"No objection. Only an observation."

"I'd appreciate your help," said Nick. "I don't know what I'm supposed to ask."

"Who does?" said Mack. "Do your best. Start with the laundry list of charges and whether she had anything to do with them."

"Think back to the laundry list of charges. Did you have anything to do with them?"

"Good question," said Mary, patting Nick on the arm.

"Well, thank you, my dear." Nick gave her a hug as the judge rolled big emerald eyes.

"I didn't have anything to do with crashing the plane or knocking over the umbrella," Courtney said. "We didn't even know it was there until the sun came up. All I did was carve a few pieces off a false idol. Mack has a point when he says a statue can't be a real god. A statue is only a statue."

Mutt jumped up. "Objection. The witness is assuming a fact not in evidence, and her assumption is erroneous. Naturally, pending instructions by the court. But whether she can be charged with defacing a god is a question to be decided by the court. Not one to be determined by the witness."

Mutt took a deep breath and made as if to continue when the judge gaveled the objection away. "Overruled."

"I object too," said Mack. "Not only can't a statue be a god, but it can't be God with a capitol 'G.'"

"Too late," said the judge, "I already overruled the objection. We let everyone say what they want before we impose sentence."

"Whoa. Don't you first decide whether they're guilty? Or do you just impose sentence?"

"You have a rather loose grasp of justice. What I say is justice. No more and no less. The defendant and the jury are presumed guilty."

"Tilt. Unfair. Scabs. Culottes. All the obscene things. The jury isn't on trial, so it can't be presumed guilty. Otherwise, how'd we get through life?"

"Very rapidly." The judge stifled a grin. "You have the burden of proving yourselves innocent. I'm here to see how well you do it. So far, you might as well pack it in. I haven't seen evidence of anyone's innocence."

"Wrongo reindeer," said Mack.

"That will be stricken from the record as not funny," said the judge.

"I didn't mean it literally. The defendant testified that she was innocent of all charges except one. There being no contrary testimony, she has established her innocence. Except for one debatable charge."

"Wrongo human. The court decides whether her testimony is believable, and hers isn't. After all she's a blasphemer, vandal, and heretic rolled up into one rotund body. Whatever she says is automatically discounted."

"Then how can she defend herself? She's doomed before she begins."

"There is that. After all, we saw her do it. The other charges are window dressing. But she did exactly what she's been accused of, and she has to pay."

"Do you take Visa or Mastercard? She could buy you a shiny new statue, with thin gold plate. That should be adequate."

"That is contempt number thirty-three."

"I'm glad someone is keeping track. Thank you, Your Honor."

"The pleasure's mine. Now sit down and zip the trap. We get along better when you shut your mouth."

"I've noticed that myself." Mack rubbed his chin. "What do you think of the Ermie and Ivie gods? They're a little different from your gods. At least their complexion is different. And I understand they have different customs, rituals, and commandments. If an Ermie set foot on this mesa would you charge him with blasphemy because he doesn't believe in your god?"

"Your question is nonsensical. First of all, an Ermie would never set foot on this tepui without a visa and express invitation. Second, we wouldn't hold their stupid religion against them unless they tried to carve up our God."

"But you can't carve up a god. Gods are ephemeral. They have neither form nor being. The whole idea of insulting a god is insulting to the god. Don't you see?"

"I understand your ridiculous argument perfectly, but you don't have a glimmer. Who's going to handle the examination of the jurors for the humans? Is it going to be the Rev. Nick or yourself?"

"We'll have to get back with you on that. I have to poll everyone before we know."

"Not exactly. You'll decide right now or I'll decide for you."

"I'll handle the questioning," said shifty-eyed Ef on his monitor. "I'll be a compromise candidate since you can't decide."

"We've decided," said Mack. "Go ahead, Nick."

"No, you go ahead." Nick's round face looked 3D on the monitor. "I've got more important things to attend to, like Mary."

There was a moment of silence as the humans contemplated Nick's whisperings over the last month. Poor Mary.

"Right. I call as our next witness, Big Guy Number Two. My good friend whose name escapes me right this second."

The Big Guy stepped from his high seat and bowed. "No thanks, Mack. I'd rather not." He sat down.

"But since I've called you as a witness, you must oblige."

"Overruled," said the judge. "The Honorable Big Guy Number Two need not take the stand. Have you finished examining the defendant and do you wish to call another witness?"

"Since you put it that way, I could probably scare up a few more questions for the defendant." Though he didn't know how she'd answer. He remembered a movie where a lawyer said only ask a question when you know the answer. "Ahem, Your Honor. I need a few words with the defendant in private. I'm sure you understand."

"Denied. You will proceed at once."

"Reg here."

Mack jumped like he'd been stung by a bee. "I'm in the middle of a trial."

"We know, since we're on the jury. But you should know what we just saw on CNN. The US government will launch an all-out effort to find our missing aircraft. As soon as the Venezuelan government gives permission to enter its airspace."

"I'll stall."

"Contempt number thirty-four," said the judge. "Either ask the defendant a question, rest your case, or call another witness. Assuming they have relevant testimony. I can't imagine that they do, but you can ask before I deny it."

"Thank you for cutting me so much slack. Courtney, tell the court what you were thinking when you grabbed the ax and went after the gold-plated statue."

"Objection," said Jose Mutt. "The statue of our God is solid gold. Without our God we lose eternal life. If the defendant would acknowledge this fact, we might be more lenient."

"I'll give it a shot. Now Courtney, I want you to think carefully before answering this question. Do you acknowledge the Golden Andelphian God is a deity they believe will grant them eternal life?"

"I'm sure these heathens would believe anything. After all, they're only antelopes. That's what I understand and—"

Courtney was interrupted by gavel banging. Jose Mutt made a long and complicated objection ending with "and she should be executed forthwith."

"Okay already," said Mack. "I withdraw the question and ask that the rudely interrupted answer be stricken."

"Denied," said the judge.

"Whatever, but I have an idea."

"About time. We only have a few more minutes before the trial is over."

"You're crazy. You have no concept of due process."

"Yes, we do. We give process that is due and very little is due to a blasphemer and heretic." The judge had turned a shade of purple.

Mack sighed. "Courtney, put yourself in the shoes of the Golden Andelphians. Walk a mile in their shoes, which might be somewhere in the Bible. Or is it walk a mile for a mild, mild Camel? But now that you've put yourself in their shoes, I want you to tell us what your reaction would be if they were shipwrecked on your shores—"

"I live in Arizona. We don't have shores."

"Pretend you have shores. Pretend their flying saucer crashed outside your garden gate. And inside your garden is a golden statue of Jesus Christ. Are you following me here?"

"Yes, I am and I see exactly where you're going. And it isn't anywhere."

"That may be. But what would your reaction be if a nincompoop from the flying saucer chopped up your Jesus? Would you condemn them to death?"

"I would not. I don't have the power to condemn them to death. But if I were the government and could do anything I wanted, I'd boil them in oil. So, you can rest your case."

"That wasn't exactly how I wanted to rest it. Wouldn't you cut the poor antelopes some slack? Let them off with a good talking to since they're only ignorant aliens? Not having been previously introduced to the one true and only God in the entire universe?"

"Objection," shouted Jose Mutt. "Counsel is leading the witness."

"I object to your objection," said Mack, "since I'm not counsel. I'm not even a lieyer. Make that lawyer."

"Sustained and overruled," said the judge.

"Which one is which?"

"Which one do you think is which? That's the one."

"Thank you, Your Honor. Please answer the question, Courtney."

"Compassion and forgiveness are part of the Baptist religion. So, I'd sit down with them and find out if they really meant to dishonor the one and only true God in the universe. And if they did, then FRY 'EM!"

"Thank you, Courtney. You may now jump into the boiling oil." Mack sat down.

The judge asked Jose Mutt, "Do you have any questions for the defendant?"

"After that, none seem necessary. But I'll ask a few anyway. Madame Courtney, do you have remorse for carving up the God of the Golden Andelphians?"

"I thought you were Golden Antelopes, not Golden Andelphians."

"Same thing. Just answer the question."

"I am remorseful that I failed to carve the false idol into toothpicks. I've regretted that failure ever since. The entire world would be a sane and peaceful place if you'd only give up your false gods, get baptized, and join the Baptist Church."

"Point of clarification," said Mack.

Yes," said the judge.

"Which Baptist Church is that? Are you referring to the Southern, American, Hard-shelled, National, or some other Baptists?"

"The American Baptists, of course. The others are false creeds—"

Lucas interrupted, "I have a good one. 'I do not pretend to prove that there is no God. I equally cannot prove that Satan is a fiction. The Christian God may exist; so may the Gods of Olympus, or of ancient Egypt, or of Babylon. But no one of these hypotheses is more probable than any other; they lie outside the region of even probable knowledge and therefore there is no reason to consider any of them.'"

Mack gritted his teeth. "Are Methodists, Presbyterians, Lutherans, Seventh Day Adventists, Mormons, and other Protestants false religions? Not to mention Catholics, Russian, Greek, and Serbian Orthodox? Muslims, Buddhists, Hindus, and all the others? Are their followers doomed to hell?"

"You got that," said Courtney. "You got that exactly one hundred percent correct. Thank you for the clarification."

"Your Honor, in light of the foregoing, I respectfully request that you refer the defendant to a psychiatrist. She should be examined for her sanity. Upon a finding of *non-compos-mentisness*, she should be found not guilty by reason of insanity."

Lucas said, "'When dealing with the insane, the best method is to pretend to be sane.'"

"Cut it out. You're well over your daily quota of quotes."

The judge shook his head. "You raise an interesting question. However, it's not a question that need trouble this court. The insanity defense, so popular elsewhere, is unknown to Andelphian jurisprudence. Motion denied." Wham. "Now Mr. Josejiménez, do you have further questions? Or has Mr. Mack established your case beyond your wildest expectations?"

"I appreciate Mr. Mack's efforts, no matter how feeble. The defendant has established her guilt beyond a reasonable doubt. I therefore ask that you throw her in the dungeon. I now call the jury as witnesses."

"Whoa," said Mack. "What the heck does that mean?"

"You will now testify as jurors. In order and fast, because we're running out of time."

"I don't understand the order part. What order? I'm ignoring the fact that a juror can't be called as a witness. You're trying to entrap us. Dump everyone into boiling oil."

"We appreciate your indulgence, Mr. Mack," said the judge. "The prosecutor refers to the order of your dispersal. Naturally, as the most important, the Golden humans will be called first. Then the Ermies, and lastly the Ivies. Quaint names you came up with."

"Well thank you, Your Honor. So, who's the first of the first?"

Jose Mutt said, "You, of course."

"But I already testified."

"Oh, yeah. Then I call the guy sitting next to you."

"Which side?"

"That side."

"May I introduce to the honorable court and prosecutor, Mr. Peter Vittorio."

"You may not," said the judge. "Witnesses aren't introduced to the court or the prosecutor. They're sworn, then the prosecutor asks their name. Then we find out who they are."

"Okay by me."

"So glad. Go ahead and take the stand, Pete."

"See, Your Honor. If I hadn't introduced him, you wouldn't have known his name was Pete." Mack bowed for applause, but there wasn't any.

"No one cares, Mr. Mack." As Peter sat in the box the judge said, "Raise your left hand. Do you swear by the almighty Riffiti God that you will tell the truth, the whole truth, and nothing but the truth, so help you great almighty Riffiti God, the only true god of the universe, so help you Riffiti God?"

"Sure. What do I care?"

"You should know that the penalty for perjury is instant death. Not the slow and tedious death by oil gradually brought to a boil."

"Instant death sounds a lot better." Peter crossed his legs with a flourish.

"I'm glad you approve. Your witness, Mr. Prosecutor."

"Please state your name for the record."

"My name is Peter Vittorio." He punctuated his Italian twang with hand gestures as wide as all outdoors.

"What was your reaction when the defendant vandalized the golden statue of our God?"

"Objection," said Mack. "Mr. Vittorio isn't on trial so his reaction is irrelevant. You're trying to entrap the jury so you can wreak vengeance on us, as well as on the poor benighted defendant."

"Overruled." The judge whacked the gavel extra hard. "You can only entrap yourselves. Answer the question."

"I forgot the question."

"You forgot the question," roared the prosecutor. "How could you? It was a great question."

"That may be. But I still forgot it. If you could repeat it, I'd be happy to shoot it down."

The prosecutor was livid. Through clenched teeth he said, "What—was—your—reaction—when—the—

defendant—vandalized—the—golden—statue—of—our—God?"

"Oh, yeah. I remember now. I thought old Courtney made a pretty ballsy move. But it was also incredibly stupid. It was obvious you had the firepower and could be pretty nasty dudes."

Mack and Jose Mutt spoke at the same time. Jose said, "I move that the scurrilous portions of the answer be stricken," as Mack said, "I move that the answer be engraved in bronze."

"You're a couple of jokers," said the judge. "Both motions are denied."

They said, "Thank you, Your Honor," as Peter sat in the witness box, twiddling his thumbs.

Jose cleared his throat, which sounded like gears stripping his translator box. "That's not what I was asking, Mr. Vittorio. How did *you* feel when she desecrated the holy statue?"

"I figured it was just a statue. Didn't know it was holy. Still don't."

"Do you find anything holy?"

"I shore do. The golden flesh of the California surfer girl is holy. That includes any babe who looks halfway decent, which unfortunately these days only means about one out of twenty. For example, Ms. Ellen there is a borderline fox. She'd be a full fox except for her crazy religious ideas. Certain strains of pot are exceedingly holy, and I'd include the last batch of coke my dealer got out of Medellin. There's a little restaurant in Santa Barbara that approaches holiness. I'm a mighty spiritual person when you get right down to it."

There was a moment of silence before Jose said, "You are excused, Mr. Vittorio. Excused from testifying further, that is. Personally, I find you inexcusable."

Mack felt a sudden warm spot for Party Down Pete. But he felt sorry for Ellen, who was sobbing. He reached over Roy and patted her on the shoulder. "That's all right, Ellen. Peter's a bit of a swine. Don't take him serious."

"I don't," she sobbed. "But I don't take you serious either. I'm running out of things to take serious, except my faith. I'm tired of everyone making fun of it."

85

Peter left the witness box grinning, hands above his head as if celebrating a big win.

Jose Mutt said, "I call the gentleman on the other side of you, Mr. Mack."

"This is Roy McKittrick," said Mack. "Sorry Your Honor. I didn't mean to introduce him."

"Number thirty-five," muttered the judge.

Roy stood, his eyes wide and wild, doing a hand motion that signified what it always meant. Jose asked a preliminary question and the humans listened to Roy say his full name, fascinated that he could say anything other than what he always said.

Jose said, "Now Mr. McKittrick. I direct your attention to the early hours of this morning."

"You mean when Courtney chopped up the statue?"

"Right about then. When that event took place, what did you feel personally?"

"I had a splitting headache because everything was going downhill." And he did the hand gesture.

"But Courtney was going uphill, isn't that right?"

"Not the way I saw it. When I say *everything* was going downhill, I mean *everything*. You have met Courtney, haven't you?"

"What's that supposed to mean?"

"Whatever you want it to. But to me, it means what it always means." And he did the hand gesture.

"You don't get off so easily. At the very instant when Courtney chopped up the statue of our holy God, what did you feel?"

"I wasn't really paying attention. The little ginky antelopes, the kids, whatever you call them, were driving us nuts. Sticking their tongues out, making insulting gestures. Not even creative. Just rude. Truly, everything was going downhill."

"That's Newton's Second Law of Thermodynamics, that everything tends to chaos. Your one-track-broken-record is a simple statement of basic physics."

"Is that a question, because if it is, I don't know? I just know that's the way things go. I didn't even notice what Courtney was doing. She's a dope anyway."

"Let me ask it this way, then."

"Ask it however you want. Fine with me."

"When the pieces of the statue that Courtney hacked off were inspected by, what do you call them? The Big Guys?"

"That's what Mack calls them. I don't know what anyone else calls them."

"When the severed pieces were recovered, did you see them?"

"Yeah, I saw 'em."

"What did you think?"

"I thought Courtney missed a lot she could have chopped off. And everyone thought the golden dick was pretty funny."

"Do you still think the golden dick is funny?"

"Well, shore. Isn't it?"

"What if someone cut off your god's golden dick? Would you think that was funny?"

"I never seen a god with a dick before, much less a golden dick. So, I guess it'd have to be funny. Don't you see the humor, or are you that stuffy?"

"Guess I'm that stuffy."

"But you're not that stuffy. I 'bout fell off the chair when you introduced yourself. That was a supreme moment, if I may say so."

"Thank you, Mr. McKittrick. But you're guilty of blasphemy."

Mack jumped up. "Hello, hello. Is anybody home? I specifically asked the court if the jury was being entrapped. Whether you were trying to make us incriminate ourselves. I thought you assured me that you weren't. But now I realize you evaded the question. Dang it, Your Honor, are you entrapping the jury? Will we boil in oil?"

The judge said, "Sure looks like it, don't it?"

"I'm heartbroken, Your Honor. I assumed that a cutting-edge species like yourselves would understand basic principles of justice. But you're no more than, dare I say it, racist religious bigots."

"Whoa. Them's fightin' words, which you dare not say in my courtroom. That earns you another ten contempts, so you're up to what, thirty-nine?"

"No, Your Honor, if you're adding ten more then I'm in the mid-forties by now. But before you add the other ten charges, you should consider whether my statement is true. If it is true then it can't be considered contemptible."

"It's contemptible whether it's true or not. Truth is irrelevant, at least in this courtroom. Not that there's any truth in what you say."

"But truth has to be relevant because if it isn't, then nothing is." Mack thought about what he thought he said and what he actually said and whether they were related. "Anyway, that's pretty close to what I meant."

The judge sadly shook his head. "Truth that insults the court is no less an act of contempt than any other insult. Do you deny your status as an inferior race? Or have you forgotten your racist religions and bigoted human history? I'm sorely disappointed. You're supposed to be a diplomatic person."

"Come on, Judge. I've never been diplomatic. And there's no need to be disappointed in me. You should be disappointed in yourself. You perfectly fit the definition of racist. You judge us other than on individual merit. You treat us based on your attitude toward our species and religion."

"Forget it. We're not here to debate esoteric philosophical nonsense. We're here to determine the defendant's guilt and the jury's complicity in that guilt."

"Aha. So, you are entrapping the jury without accusing us of anything."

"You may have an argument. But I'm simply following the legal requirements of the case."

"You're simply following orders, isn't that right?" Mack pivoted and addressed the Big Guy behind him, "Mein Herr."

"We don't feel too good about it ourselves," said the judge. "But that's the way we are. We voted on it and democracy must prevail. Sort of like Brexit. You'll think twice before you crash another airplane on our tepui. Or maybe you won't."

"Won't. We didn't plan it so you can't hold us responsible."

"You're responsible for bringing Courtney with you. That woman is a hazard to civilization. Mr. Prosecutor, do you have further questions for this witness?"

"None, Your Honor. The witness may be excused."

"The witness may not be excused," said Mack. "The jury has a few questions."

"The key word is 'few,'" said the judge. "Make it snappy."

"Mr. McKittrick, How often do you attend church?"

Lucas inserted, "'He was of the faith chiefly in the sense that the church he currently did not attend was Catholic.'"

"Every minute of every day, when things aren't going downhill."

"So, your answer is seldom?"

"Whatever. But enough for me."

"Do you have a quarrel with how others worship? How they decorate their god or their religious preferences?"

"Not unless it makes me go downhill. Then I get upset."

"No further questions. You may step down."

Roy brightened as he swung out of the box and retook his place on the jury bleachers.

"And your next victim?" said Mack.

"The lady who was crying."

Mack whispered encouragement to Ellen. She rose like a zombie and stumbled into the witness box.

Jose Mutt got right to it. "Now Ms. Ellen, what did you think when Courtney attacked the Golden Andelphian God?"

"Statue. Mack has a point. Perhaps the first one he's ever had." Mack smiled back.

"Then what did you think when Courtney attacked the Golden Andelphian statue? Did you consider it an act of blasphemy?"

"I didn't consider it an act of blasphemy because I'm not a Golden Andelphian. But I thought it was rude. Not a good way to act toward those who hold our lives in the palm of their hands. Palm of their horny paws. I wouldn't have done it under any circumstances."

"Are you trying to avoid burning oil or are you sincere?"

"I'm always sincere. That's one of my main faults."

"Are you religious? What I mean is—"

"Yes. I'm extremely religious. But it's a personal matter. Nothing to do with what anyone else believes."

"Do you know anything about the Golden Andelphian religion, our God, or our beliefs?"

Mack rose. "Objection. Multiple questions."

The judge shrugged. "You may answer if you understand the question, questions."

"No."

"Have you any interest in finding out about these things?"

"No."

"Then you believe with certainty that your beliefs are infallible to the exclusion of all others. You believe everyone else is wrong. Whether you know anything about their beliefs or not?"

"Objection. Dangerous grounds here, Ellen. Watch how you answer."

"Number forty-six," said the judge, "or thereabouts. You will refrain from telling the witness how to answer questions."

"Maybe I will and maybe I won't. There's no reason to allow these kind people to be entrapped by your weird ideas of religion."

"Are you suggesting that your religions are any less weird?" The judge clapped a horny fist over his mouth. After scissoring two horny fingers apart, he said, "Don't answer that. We'll not be getting into that thicket."

"I will answer that. I might hypothetically believe all religions are equal, whether they're human, Andelphian, or moonbeamian. They seem to rest on the same foundation, which might be superstition. Actually, I got that from Lucas."

Ellen burst out crying. "That's terrible. Don't you have any regard for the beliefs of others? Have you no spirituality? What's wrong with you anyway?" Ellen's comments were only

90

a few of the many wafting around the courtroom and over Mack's microphone. Not to mention the judge pounding his gavel.

When the outbreak quietened, the judge said, "We'll reserve a special batch of oil for you, Mr. Mack. One that's been used to clean battery acid. That should do you right."

Mack continued, "Or I may hypothetically believe the opposite. That all religions are equally true. Whether they're human, Andelphian, or moonbeamian. That they're not based on superstition. You haven't entrapped me yet. Actually, I've never thought about it, so I have no idea one way or the other. Or would you prefer that I made something up, perjured myself?"

"You're accruing more contempt citations than frequent flyer miles. Of course, you won't be flying for the foreseeable future."

"Wrong about that. I'll fly soon, escorted by the United States Air Force men in blue. Trust me on this one."

"Have you finished with the witness, Mr. Prosecutor?"

"I would like her to answer my last question, which Mr. Mack's red herrings evaded. Would you like the question read back to you, Ms. Ellen?"

"I would not. I remember your 'when did you stop beating your wife' question. I've stopped beating my wife the same as you. Which is to say I have as much faith in your religion as you have in mine. We're in the same boat."

The judge cowered and Jose Mutt shrank into his chair as the Big Guy stalked to the front of the courtroom. "This is outrageous, allowing aliens to put themselves on par with us. Such behavior must never occur in this courtroom or this regime. Put a stop to it."

The judge gulped noisily, to the short-lived amusement of the humans. "Yes, Your Most Honorable Leader, sir. Thy will be done. We will take a short recess and resume the trial when calm is restored to the courtroom."

Boom went the gavel and everyone hopped up. The judge rose less than regally, escaping through the invisible door behind the high bench. The Big Guy was right behind him, continuing a one-sided conversation. "Fartle, blippon, whistle, ripppppp." Mercifully, the door slammed shut.

6

Mack's microphone erupted as Lucas and Reg started talking at once. "Hold it, you two. We're in serious trouble. My group is headed for burbling oil. I don't know how long we can stall before we become tater tots for the hippity-hops."

Lucas said, "Although it cost you a few contempt citations, I loved that description of the court."

"Jail's better than becoming an antelope fry," said Mack. "I bet they eat us afterwards."

"Yeah, but by then it won't make any difference."

"Update from CNN," said Reg. "They've run into Venezuelan bureaucracy. So, the search won't start for hours, if not days or weeks. The request must be submitted in tenplicate to the notary for the district of Caracas, forwarded to the presidential palace, then their diplomatic corps for approval, then back to the Venezuelan president."

Mack frowned. "Why will that take weeks?"

Reg sighed. "The president is on vacation in Sri Lanka, visiting his Tamil mama."

"His mother is Sri Lankan?"

Reg shuddered. "This appears to be shorthand for a mistress of international repute, which has gotten him into difficulty with his Catholic constituency. They may have to call early elections, which means they might not have a president for months."

"So, stalling the trial may not work."

Lucas said, "'Trying to make things work in government is sometimes like trying to sew a button on a custard pie.' But I may have the answer. I told you about Badsr, this splendid new friend of mine. He's following the trial like everyone else in Ermieland. And for some unfathomable reason, you've impressed the poor guy. He will use his influence with the Ivies and Ermies to head the Goldies off at the pass. Get us off the hook and the trial adjourned. Establish interspecies peace in our time."

Mack frowned. "Assuming every word we say isn't transcribed and distributed to the Big Guys on all three mesas. We don't have the luxury of waiting for interspecies peace. When you need professional help, you need it now, and I'm here to serve. So, bring Badsr on."

"You're a goose, but I appreciate you taking a few seconds out of your busy schedule. Let me set the stage."

"Fine, but hurry up. The Big Guy just came storming out of the judge's chambers and the judge won't be far behind."

Mack bowed, but the Big Guy said, "Can it. You're too late for the diplomatic route."

Mack pleaded, "Never say die. Could we explore a resolution to our dispute? It wouldn't hurt to try. What do you say?"

"Do you have a proposal?" The Big Guy looked as desperate as Mack.

"I surely do." Which is exactly when Lucas began describing what Badsr wanted to talk about.

Mack whispered into the microphone, "I'm talking to the Big Guy and this is top importance. Give me a minute."

"You always say that."

"I know. But this is the last time. Sorry about that, Mr. Big Guy, I mean Your Honorable Top Leadership Person, Btsht. See, I do remember your name. Do you remember mine?"

"Of course, I remember your name, you twit," snarled the Big Guy, pointing a hoof at Mack. "Get to the point. What's your proposal to solve this mess?"

"It's very simple."

"Coming from you, it'd have to be."

"If you get us off this mesa and we retrieve the aircraft's black box, you'll never be discovered."

"We thought of that, except for the black box part. We didn't know about that until an adviser pointed out the

94

problem." The Big Guy paced up and down, tapping the beautifully grained hardwood floor with his tiny shoes. Mack imagined wee reindeer feet on his parents' roof.

"What's the problem with such a brilliant idea?"

"Keeping your friends quiet. And the religious problem, the whole point of the trial. We can't let Courtney go free."

"Courtney didn't hurt anyone. She carved three small pieces off a statue. Didn't harm a hair on anyone's head."

"You know better than that. She caused severe anguish for Golden Andelphians and drove the Riffiti bishop bonkers."

"It's bizarre to suffer because a statue underwent minor damage."

"Don't be silly. You know that anguish is in the mind of the beholder."

"Okay, let's skip Courtney. What about the rest of us? We didn't desecrate your god. Do you really believe all this religious stuff, anyway?"

"Of course, I do. I have to. I'm a politician. Where do you think I'd be if I said what I really think? My political career would go whoof."

"So, what's more important: integrity or success?"

"That's a pretty dumb question to ask a politician."

Lucas whispered, "'Politics is like being a football coach. You have to be smart enough to understand the game and stupid enough to think it's important.'"

Mack ignored Lucas. "I stand corrected. But the court should leave us alone because we're not a real jury. You've made us defendants with our butts on the line, the same as Courtney. But we didn't do anything wrong except crash in the wrong place. Surely you could cut us some slack."

"I might but I'm not the only 'Big Guy,' as you call us. The other two together are more important than I am. I retain some integrity, despite your smart aleck mouth. But the issue isn't integrity. It's power."

"I've got an even better one," said Lucas. "'If you've got 'em by the balls, their hearts and minds will follow.'"

Mack whispered back, "Dammit, stop interrupting me and the Big Guy." He said to Btsht, "Did you know that

95

'number two' has to try harder? Let's come up with something that saves both our hides. Figuratively speaking, of course."

"No offense taken. Pinch this." Btsht pulled up the sleeve of his tunic and stuck out his arm.

Mack gingerly touched the exposed part.

"Don't be such a wuss. Give it a big hefty squeeze."

Btsht seemed serious so Mack gave the golden skin a major twist. It didn't budge.

"Pretty cool, eh? Now that's hide. Yours is more like silly putty."

"You win. You're a lot tougher than we are. Where's the oil so we can jump in?"

"Sarcasm will hasten boiling oil. Don't overdo it."

"You promise to think it over? I'll do my best to come up with something. Plus, I've got friends to help."

The Big Guy stopped pacing as the judge walked into the courtroom, sulking. "I have a previous engagement but yes, I'll see what I can come up with too. Sayonara." The Big Guy left the courtroom amongst deep genuflections from the audience.

"Okay," said Lucas, his voice tinny from Mack's mic. "He's gone so you have time for Badsr's suggestion."

"The judge is back. I assume you see that too. Badsr will have to wait."

"He can't wait. I'll tell you his idea, Badsr will know I tried, and that will count for something. I'll be the hero and you'll be the goat. Sounds perfect to me."

"All rise. Oyez, Oyez, the court of the Honorable Grdam the Devious is in session. Attend all who desire justice," said the sub-sub-baliff on the end of a long line of baliffs. He snapped up and down like a jack-in-the-box.

The judge pounded his gavel and sat as Lucas yapped in Mack's ear. "The great thing about Badsr..."

Mack interrupted, "I can't deal with Badsr right now. The prosecutor has called his next juror witness. Are you paying attention to the trial?"

"Yes I am. When will you pay attention to Badsr?"

"I haven't heard anything to pay attention to. If you'd cut to the chase, we'd save a lot of time."

Jose Mutt said, "State your name for the record."

"Call me Madison Mallow Murphy."

Lucas continued, "The Ermies are all bi, just so you know. Anyway, Badsr was touring this other tepui, starring in a soap opera—"

"Was it the Goldie or Ivie tepui?" asked Mack. "Or are there tepuis we don't know about?"

Jose Mutt asked about the statue-carving episode and Madison replied, "Didn't clearly see it. Couldn't say. Ask me 'bout another day."

"But what did you think when you realized what happened?"

Lucas said, "It was the Goldie tepui, but there may be a dozen antelope tribes and we only know three."

"Get on with Badsr's story."

Jose Mutt stared at Madison, who said, "Courtney needed a poet, so I wrote it."

Jose Mutt rolled his big green eyes. "You're testifying in poetic form? Well, if you can't talk any other way...."

Madison had a big happy face, the first time he'd recited for an entire auditorium. "Ahem." He looked around. "'The Golden Thing,' by Madison Mallow Murphy. I saw a golden thing, on a sunrised hill. The thing shone bright, but won't much still. Our Courtney dear, a fright I'm sure. She stormed the knoll and brought bits here. I went afar—"

"Stop," roared Jose Mutt. "How long is this poem?"

Lucas said, "The plot of Badsr's soap opera is interesting. It started with Dufrt locked out of his apartment."

"Thirty-two quatrains, more refrains."

"Enough. You're excused."

Madison had tears in his eyes as he stood down from the witness box. "There's a lot more and—it gets better. Won't you listen, maybe vet 'er? It's a first draft I declare. When I finish, you'll be there. If you thought, you silly fop. 'Stead of yelling only STOP. The world would 'preciate and you sedate." Madison squared his shoulders and stuck out his jaw. "Don't yell at me you twit. For the fan your shit will hit. Then will you see the trend, though your face will—?"

"Stop!" said Jose Mutt. "You are excused. But don't quit your day job. I call the last of the Goldie humans."

Barry swung into the witness chair and the baliff swore him in. Jose Mutt said, "What was your reaction when your friend Courtney carved up the God of the Golden Andelphians?"

"Wait," said Mack. "I'm objecting to that. No one carved up a god. Gods can't be carved up. It was only a statue of a god no one's ever seen or really knows exists."

"Overruled," gaveled the judge. "I've personally seen the God. Answer the question."

Mack looked stunned. "You've seen the god. Well, I hardly know where to begin. Could you tell us where you saw the god, when, and were there any witnesses?"

"Question overruled. I'm not on the witness stand. My comment was superfluous and I hereby order it stricken from the record. The witness will answer the question."

"Anyway," said Lucas, "Dufrt's apartment is right below Badsr, and it was love at first sight."

Mack asked, "What does it have to do with our problem?"

Barry said, "Courtney is a friend of mine, but she was rude to attack our hosts' hospitality. I told her exactly that. She hasn't gotten over the death of her husband, only a month ago. She's still bereaved. What a sad situation—"

"No more questions," said Jose Mutt. "I call the first of the Ivie or Ermie Andelphian humans. Whichever's handy."

Lucas said, "How do you come up with such dumb questions? This is complicated. It was the first time they saw each other and sparks flew. That's all. Take it for what it's worth. Don't ask questions."

"I stand amended," said Mack. "So, it was love at first sight. What does this have to do with us?"

"I'm not done," said Barry. "You've got to know Courtney before you condemn her. Inside that neurotic exterior beats a heart of gold, or at least iron pyrite. You shouldn't judge her without knowing—"

"You are dismissed. Hop down from there. Oh, I didn't mean it," said Jose Mutt as Barry hippity-hopped toward the bleachers.

The judge said, "Who goes first from the Ermies? Hello. Is anyone there?" The six Ermie monitors showed no one paying attention to the trial. They were all eavesdropping on the conversation between Lucas and Mack.

The judge whammed the gavel. "Order in the Ermie jury. Now!" He raised the gavel for a final wham and the head dropped off, bouncing off Barry's back in mid-hippity-hop. Then it skittered along the floor as Barry exaggerated the impact, collapsing in a heap.

"Got it, Your Honor." Mack picked up the head of the gavel. "May I approach the bench or would you prefer that I toss it back?"

"Contempt number forty-four and rising." The judge had forgotten the head was gone and tried to pound the stick. Tap. The judge's cheeks puffed out as he turned a pale shade of blue. "And you, Mr. Barry, get off the floor and back to the bleachers. No more histrionics."

"Anyway," said Lucas, "Badsr was so taken with this Dufrt guy that he dumped his current friend, female variety. It was funny as hell."

"Back to you in a sec, Lucas. I have a delivery to make." Mack tiptoed up to the judge's high bench and laid the gavel head on the edge, retreating under the judge's sour look. "Hey, Lucas. Why aren't you supplying witnesses? The judge has been yelling about it for ages now."

"Oh, sorry. Hey, you guys. Who wants to be the first witness? Okay, it's between Ef and Benny, with Billy K. third. No one else wants to play."

"Question for you, Lucas. So, the guy dumped his girlfriend. Why was it funny, and what the hell difference does it make?"

Jose Mutt said, "That one will be fine," pointing at Ef's gleaming countenance.

"Good luck," said Mack.

"Oh, I left out the most important thing," said Lucas. "Badsr's affair became a soap opera on Goldie TV. The Goldies

99

are suckers for romance. He thought if you romanced Ellen, as a salute to true love, the Goldies might let us go. Anyway, when Badsr's girlfriend came home, she smelled something on his paws."

"I don't want to know."

"I didn't say what she smelled, so you don't have to know. She was hysterical and accused Badsr of being involved with another woman. Make that another female, I guess. But he was able to swear on a stack of whatever the Ermie sacred text is that he hadn't touched another female. Which made her feel better because she knew Badsr never told a lie and then—"

"That one will do fine," said Jose Mutt. He directed his questions at the monitor. "Please state your name."

"My name is Efriam Malachi Malinski." Ef was beaming as if he'd sold a desert lot for a million bucks.

Mack said, "Makes no sense to me."

"Badsr started drinking too much of the Ermie potomassian, might be alcohol based."

"All Dufrt's fault, of course."

"I'm a land entrepreneur and what that crazy Courtney lady did wasn't a concern of mine."

"You mean you didn't care? You thought her actions were appropriate?" Jose Mutt was turning a light shade of blue.

"Badsr couldn't tell whether they were going for a relationship or just a sex thing."

"They're both guys. Take a wild guess."

"I don't like your tone," said Ef. "Of course, I cared, kind of. It was a stupid thing she did. We have enough problems without that happening."

Jose Mutt asked, "Do you believe in God?"

"That's not fair. All guys aren't whores."

"All Aussie guys are, mate. Don't you think? Or don't you think?"

"Stop right there," said Ef. "I was brought up to believe in the original God. The one whose name you can't say. And now I can't remember what it is. But memory is the second thing to go." Ef laughed, slapping himself on the knee.

"And what is your attitude toward the Golden Andelphian God?"

"Which guys are whores and which aren't has nothing to do with having a hot romance to impress the Goldies. They might let us go in the name of true love. Keep your eye on the ball, as they say in Americer," Lucas reverting to Aussie.

"But I don't have a chance with Ellen. She's married and super religious. And I'm borderline heathen."

"Badsr says if you follow the soap opera playbook, you'll corral Ellen easy. Piece of cake."

"I've never been introduced to the Golden Andelphian god. Have you?" said Ef.

"I'm asking the questions. What is your opinion of the Golden Andelphian God?" At Ef's blank look, Jose Mutt said, "Your Honor, please instruct the witness to answer the question?"

"You have to do your best with Ellen. It's our only chance of escape."

"I don't even have lottery odds with Ellen."

Ellen nodded agreement.

"I don't have an opinion so I can't answer the question, Your Honor."

"If he doesn't have an opinion, he can't answer the question. Your request is overruled." The judge lightly banged the gavel. "Either ask a better question or call your next witnesses."

"If you knew the story line, Ellen would be a piece of cake."

"I'm not going to touch that one. Besides, she's listening!"

"I call the Benny guy," said Jose Mutt.

"I won't do it." Benny was resplendent in candy-apple red and royal blue. "I won't be a party to this farce. No matter what I think of Courtney, I'll not lend my voice to having her boiled in oil. Or me either. Mack got it right about this being a kangaroo court. Do your worst. I'm not playing."

"Your Honor. We have an uncooperative witness who challenges us to do our worst. May we invoke the rule?"

Lucas said to Mack, "Well, you remember the golden dick that Courtney carved off the statue? That's apparently the soft version, so to speak. The Ermies claim to be more closely

101

related to horses than antelopes. They regard the Goldies are relative juveniles."

Mack said, "Is this a cross-cultural stereotype? Anyway, Ellen is impossible without real magic. There's a trial going on and I have to protect our people. Benny needs me right now."

"A recalcitrant witness deserves invocation of the worst rule," said the judge. The camera on Benny zoomed back to frame an enormous Ermie carrying a large silver bowling ball, twice the size of the usual kind. The Ermie split the ball open and clapped it on Benny's head. Before it slammed shut, the monitor caught a close-up of spikes inside.

Benny screamed until the huge Ermie rushed back and opened the iron mask, revealing bloody dots covering Benny's face. The monitor zoomed in as the dots swelled and ran down his face, clashing with the candy apple red shirt. The scream came to a gurgling halt.

"Here's the key. Dufrt had no chance with his new love until he converted to the Goldie religion. That's why the soap opera was so popular with the Goldies. Badsr was a professor at a posh university for studly Ermie antelopes. He gave it all up to embrace the Goldie religion and true love with Dufrt."

"You're putting me on. A college for studly antelopes. And the idea is for me to convert to Catholicism to woo Ellen. Like she'd believe that."

Ellen rolled her eyes.

Benny's face streamed with blood, his chin quivering. "I will say whatever you want. I'll be a traitor to my own kind and die young." Forty-seven-year-old Benny was a bloody pincushion.

Jose Mutt said, "When Courtney attacked the statue of our god, what was your reaction?"

"They have schools for every interest group."

"Studly is an interest group?"

"I missed the first part." Benny wiped his face. "I didn't see what was going on until your soldiers attacked Courtney. I was enthralled, watching your juvenile population. They can do a hundred-yard dash in under four seconds. In fact, I timed them at three point seven. They were annoying the hell out of everyone except me. You should sign up for the Olympics.

102

You'd snatch ten or twelve medals in track and field alone. Then there's swimming and such. You can swim, can't you? I mean I've never seen you swim so I shouldn't assume."

"That's enough. The court takes judicial notice of your inability to think."

"I've never known you to lie," said Lucas. "Maybe you fudge the truth but who doesn't? So, when Dufrt wouldn't take Badsr with him on the lecture tour Badsr said, and this is a quote: 'We were so happy for a little while.' And I thought, what's new, pussycat? Who isn't happy for a little while? Even I've been wildly happy for a little while. As long as a month or two."

"How did we get off on this? Badsr's soap opera won't help us escape these tepuis."

Benny was livid, his spots oozing blood. "Of course, I think. I think as much as you do, Mr. high and mighty prosecutor of defenseless guests on your inhospitable mesa. I wouldn't treat my worst enemy the way you've treated us. Where do you get off being such unmitigated assholes? You're a disgrace to your race, or your species, or whatever it is you are."

"Thank you for your testimony. Your Honor, I move that this witness be remanded to the dungeon. An appropriate sentence must be imposed for impugning a superior species."

"Maybe not, but we should try. Dufrt didn't react when Badsr told Dufrt he couldn't go on the lecture tour. So, Badsr told Dufrt that he didn't love him anymore. Of course, Badsr wouldn't let it alone. He reminded Dufrt about their first big seduction scene. It degenerated into a shouting match with Dufrt storming out. Naturally Badsr got blotto and the next day—"

"This is a daytime soap opera, not a strategic plan. Forget it. I have to get back to the trial."

"Motion granted. Mr. Chemalski is remanded to the dungeon for sentencing." The judge snapped his gavel down with finality. "Next witness."

"Why are you throwing Benny in the dungeon, Your Honor?" asked Mack.

"You should pay attention instead of listening to soap operas. It's strictly forbidden for inferior life forms to get involved in Andelphian affairs. Even affairs of an inferior Ermie."

"What are you talking about?"

"I have the transcripts of your conversation with Mr. Lucas right here." The judge fluttered a stack of plastic leaves to the floor. "Mr. Baliff. Take those to Mr. Mack."

The baliff delivered flimsy sheets covered with splotches and purple scribbles. "I can't read these. This is evidence of nothing."

"You have quaint ideas, Mr. Mack. What makes you think you're entitled to see the evidence against you? Pish posh. You've hung yourself out to dry. If you don't watch it, you'll be remanded to the dungeon with the heretic and the bigot." The judge pounded the gavel with a flourish.

"Speaking of bigotry, you protest too much. As for the dungeon, hell no! I won't go!" Mack blew a raspberry and sat down.

"That's number forty-six, as if it makes a difference. Call your next witness, Mr. Prosecutor."

"I call the next alien, from what they call the Ermies. Whichever one is next."

"That would be Billy K. Oops. Sorry, Your Honor. But at least I didn't give you his last name."

"How arrogant to even have last names. Highfalutin' like you're better than everyone else. I'd remand all of you to re-education, but there's no time for that."

"Shucks, darn," said Mack, at the very idea of Billy K. "We'd like to sign up for a six-week re-education course. Let us know if you have openings."

The judge wearily motioned the prosecutor to continue. But the prosecutor had already sworn Billy K. and started the first question.

"Shore 'nuff. That's me, Billyk, if you prefer first names only. See, I kind of ran it together so it'd make you feel better, or make the judge feel better. I like it when everyone feels good about themselves. Did I tell you about my new grandson? He's a corker, that one. He's already asking questions like you ask."

The prosecutor held up a paw and Billy K. stopped.

Jose Mutt said, "I hereby ask you the same question I asked the other alien humans. Must I repeat it?"

"Shucks no. I been thinking about that question you always ask. What was I thinking when old Courtney charged up the hill at that golden statue? Well, I was thinking about the time me 'n my buddy, Corky Conn, we was headin' out toward the narrows in McElmo Canyon. Long about sundown, and what do you think come buzzin' down at us? Right out of the blue? You'd never guess."

"I'd never guess." Jose Mutt shook his head, reared up to his full height, and roared. "And I don't give a good goddamn."

"Move to dismiss," said Mack. "The prosecutor has not only used the name of your god in vain. But he has joined it with an expletive inadmissible in a court of law. The only possible conclusion is that your god is of no real significance other than a swear word. So, I move that the charges against Courtney be dismissed forthwith."

"I wasn't referring to that God," said Jose Mutt. "I apologize to the court if my inadvertent comment was inappropriate."

"You've been led astray by Mr. Mack," said the judge. "But no need to apologize. I recognize the term has nothing to do with the one true God Riffiti of the universe. Mr. Mack's spurious motion is denied." Wham. "Get on with it."

Jose Mutt lowered himself into a chair. "Skip the big lead up, Mr. Billyk. Just tell us what you thought when Courtney hewed big chunks off the most holy Riffiti, God of the universe, and supreme being of all creation."

"I always wondered about that, ever since the woman's lib thing started back home. Whether gods are all men, or whatever the term is for antelopes. Or whether a couple of gods might be women. That might make them a bit more compassionate than the old thunder and lightning types. Them in the holy books."

"May it please the court," said Jose Mutt. "Move to strike the witness's last comment as unresponsive to the question."

"Move to strike the motion to strike," said Mack. "The witness wasn't given the courtesy of completing his testimony. Then its relevancy would have become abundantly clear. But no, the prosecution constantly interrupts. The trial could take half the time and we could all go home."

"You're both in contempt," snarled the judge. "Mr. Prosecutor. You are hereby disqualified from continuing in this matter. Your assistant will take over and complete the questioning."

"But—"

"I don't want to hear another word from you." The judge pounded the gavel. "Mr. Assistant Prosecutor, please proceed."

The tall skinny assistant prosecutor had a prominent Adam's apple and looked like Ichabod Crantelope. He loped around the other side of Jose Mutt and leafed through plastic papers, pushing up spectacles on his bumpy nose and looking through the lower half. "Ahem. Now Mr. Billyk. Restrict your answer to only what I ask. Nothing more. Forget about your history with Mr. Conn in McElmo Canyon. What did you think when Courtney carved up the golden statue of Riffiti?"

"Like I started to say, I was thinkin' about whether gods could be male or female? Your god might be better off female since the male version seems hostile. I assume you reflect the attitude of your god. Then there's the point that it's just a statue, which Mr. Mack keeps trying to say. But no one listens to him. I understand some of that since he talks as much as I do. I do like to talk." Billy K. pushed back as if he'd put the whole thing in a nutshell.

"You do like to talk. I hope you appreciate this may be your last chance ever." The new prosecutor shrugged. "But of course, you didn't answer my question. What you thought about Courtney's destruction of our God?"

"I was gob-smacked. I thought your god still existed. Courtney carved up a graven image. Not exactly an all-powerful omnipotent god."

Lucas snorted into Mack's mic, "'It is ridiculous to suppose that the great head of things, whatever it be, pays any regard to human affairs.' Or to antelope affairs, for that matter."

"Give me a break."

106

"You seem to be taking your own break. You haven't objected to a single question since the skinny guy took over. You must be ready to listen to Badsr's escape plan."

"Move to strike the answer as unresponsive," said the prosecutor. "And also move that Mr. Mack be instructed to stop whispering into his mic while court is in session."

Mack waved a finger. "On this point I call the Big Guys as witnesses, Your Honor. They gave us mics to communicate among ourselves. Their views would be more useful than that of a rookie prosecutor."

The judge said, "You will stop whispering while court is in session or I'll have you gagged like the defendant was gagged." Wham. "Complete your questioning of this witness. Time's a-fleeting."

"No more questions. I call the next guy in line."

"Yessir," said James smoothly. "That's me. And here I am." He tipped his ten-gallon hat.

The judge said, "Consider yourself sworn and let's get on with it. State your name."

"My name is James Dean." He did his signature, an S-shaped hand gesture, straight out of the movie *Giant*. And smiled a quirky little smile, accenting his dimples.

"Usual question," said the prosecutor.

"Usual answer," said James.

"Usual objection," said Mack,

"Usual ruling," said the judge, barely tinkling his gavel.

"Do you rest the prosecution," said Mack, "so the jury can be excused and this trial brought to a merciful end?"

"I have a few more jurors to examine," said the prosecutor as sirens howled and the six Legionnaires, who guarded the Big Guys, rushed into the courtroom.

7

The head Legionnaire yelled, "Fuchsia alert. Evacuate the building. Everyone into the number one shelter. Now. Stop dithering."

The Legionnaires shoved Goldies and baliffs out the open doors of the courtroom with humans at the end of the line. Mack waved at the monitors as they inched out behind everyone else.

"What's going on?" said Lucas. "Why's everyone leaving?"

"Didn't you hear the big soldier tell us to get out?"

"Well, sure. But he didn't say why. There's nothing going on at our end. We're still in our cushy juror seats. Oops, here comes Badsr and we're off for somewhere too."

"Same here," said Reg. "They're rounding us up. Maybe the Strategic Air Command is on its way."

"Maybe, and maybe not. We're back on the emerald sidewalk going down. You can probably hear Roy." Mack nudged his mic in the direction of Roy's usual soliloquy.

Ellen said, "I'm praying for a miracle to get us out of here."

Lucas quoted back at her, "'Whatever a man prays for, he prays for a miracle—Great God, let not two times two make four.'"

"I'm not a man." Ellen was indignant. "It's a miracle the world has let you two live this long."

Mack said to Lucas, "I liked the quote right before we crashed, though I hate to admit it. Do you remember that one?"

"Not sure, since then they come automatically. I tried to memorize a bunch but never could. The one you're looking for might have been, 'Pray, verb. To ask that the laws of the universe be annulled on behalf of a single petitioner confessedly unworthy.' Does that sound right?"

"I am confessedly unworthy, but you two," Ellen raised her voice, "are unworthier by far. Actual heathens."

"That wasn't it." Mack ignored Ellen. "But who said the last one?"

"I don't know who said any of them. What's happening with you?"

"We're jogging down the emerald pathway. What's with Badsr? And how's Benny doing?"

"Reg here. We've been evacuated to an auditorium with monitors on three levels. There are lots of people inside. Make that Ivies. Weird prosecutor you got."

"The old prosecutor's gone. The new one doesn't seem as bad, though we can't tell yet. Have you heard anything on CNN about our rescue? Maybe that's why they're moving us."

"Now we only see CNN on tape, nothing live. Is Courtney still with you?"

"I don't know where she is. We've inside a big auditorium with the same stack of monitors, and *there's* Courtney. She's down in front, shackled in blue and yellow chains. She's a mess, poor thing. Looks like they beat her."

Mack finessed his way toward the main floor, saying excuse me, pardon, excusez-moi. Brawny antelopes ignored his ineffectual elbows on the way to Courtney, who sat with her face propped in cuffed hands. The heavy iron pulled her swollen wrists into a reddened crunch. Her hair was filthy and matted and her face scratched. She still wore brogans that peeked under the table in the middle of the raised platform, surrounded by Legionnaires and flanked by the judge and two prosecutors.

Mack pulled himself onto the dais, striding over to the judge. He stuck his hand out. "Howdy, Judge Grdam. Please condescend to tell me, Your Honor, why is Courtney in such sad shape?"

The judge ignored Mack's outstretched hand. He snapped a horny finger as if flicking Mack away. "Mr. Mack, so sad to see you. I've checked sentencing protocols for fifty contempts of court. There's no precedent. I'm thinking death. What kind things have you come to say?"

Mack pulled his hand back. "Why are you torturing Courtney and why were we brought here?"

"If you think this is torture, you've got an education coming, young alien human. What insipid request are you making on her behalf?"

"Take a close look, Your Honor. She's wouldn't harm a flea. Let her take a shower and rest. Will the trial recommence, or is the farce finished?"

"Contempt number fifty-one, and we haven even reconvened. You have a talent, Mr. Mack. But no one would mind if the defendant bathed. I certainly wouldn't." He sniffed.

"Is that an order for the Legionnaires?"

The judge raised a bushy eyebrow at the closest Legionnaire and said something unintelligible.

"Hey, Courtney. They're going to take off the cuffs and let you shower. Don't get into trouble this time."

Courtney managed to sit upright. "I'm sick, Mr. Mack. This has been too much for my heart." As a Legionnaire reached for the handcuffs, she said, "Sorry sir. But I am deathly ill."

"Would you like to have someone go with you? Ellen or Barry?"

"Oh, yes. Both are fine. Ellen has a way with her, even if she is a Catholic." She made "Catholic" sound like a dirty word.

"I'll see what I can do." Mack scanned the auditorium for Barry and Ellen. "Courtney's sort of rescued," Mack said to his mic.

Lucas came back. "Mayday alert. Badsr's here and things are popping."

"Does that mean the cavalry is on the way?" Mack looked up at balconies for Ellen and Barry.

"The cavalry is not on its way. The problem is a matter of war. If you'd romance Ellen that'd head off the war and Badsr could concentrate on getting us home in one piece."

"Why war and between whom? Is Venezuela involved?" Mack spotted Ellen and Barry straggling down the stairs. "Hey, Ellen. Barry. We need help with Courtney so she can take a shower."

Lucas said, "The Ermies and Ivies claim the Goldies violated the election results by denying Courtney a fair trial. The iron mask they slapped on Benny was the last straw."

"But it was an Ermie who slapped the mask on Benny, not a Goldie. We all saw that. The Ivies and Ermies are looking for an excuse to start a war. Thanks, Ellen. Appreciate it, Barry. Anyway, I can't imagine another species going to war on our account. We're the ultimate 'Other,' foreigners, aliens, unimportant ones."

"Speak for yourself, mate. I feel very important—"

"Yeah, but only to yourself. Guess how important you are to anyone else, except your mum, and maybe Marylyn."

"Leave Marylyn out of it. The Ermies and Ivies are looking for an excuse for war. The last war was Ermies against Ivies and Goldies. They switch alliances according to phases of the moon. You wouldn't believe antelopian history."

"Foreign history is always a hoot, like your own."

"I was born here. Okay, not here. But in the US of A. So, I'm already a citizen and the pilot of the plane will testify to that."

"You mean he witnessed your birth? Who was flying the plane?"

"That lawyer stuff is going to your head. You got a taste of it and you can't stop. You won't be a normal human being if you keep it up. Not that you're that close now."

"Didn't you want to harass me about your friend, Btfsplk? Or was that the guy in Little Abner with the black cloud following him around? And why do so many antelope names start with 'B'? Of course, it isn't the letter 'B.' It's a squiggle or inkblot."

"The judge and Big Guys won't be happy when they read the transcripts and find out you can't tell them apart."

"I can tell them apart. They're nothing alike, but the names are confusing."

"The names are impossible, but we have issues to cover with my friend Badsr. If you'd take time to listen, Badsr would tell you exactly how to woo Ellen and get us off these mesas from hell."

"Since they read the transcripts, we'll need a plan to throw them off." "Dumb. You've just told them we're going to concoct a plan to throw them off."

"Right. We'll do it so they don't know which is our plan and which is a trick."

"Don't worry. Since we don't know, they won't know. We have the perfect cover: basic incompetence. Of course, that's not for publication."

"I won't tell if you won't."

"Back to Badsr. He starred in the most popular Goldie soap opera ever. About an impossible babe to woo and how he did it. Might even work for a clumsy sort like yourself. The plot had lots of kinks, like an Agatha Christie potboiler."

"I never thought her pots did more than simmer."

"So, you're a snob. Anyway, this babe was a looker."

"Stop right there. Have you seen this babe? I mean, is she really a looker and what does that mean for, to, and in connection with an antelope?"

"She was skinny so she was a looker."

"That isn't the same in all cultures. Lots of people love large ladies. A sailing buddy took me to get a beer at a whorehouse on the Baja. The Mexicans cozied up to the fat chicks and passed on the skinny ones. And it's the same in Samoa, I hear."

"You do get off on tangents. So, this is a babe's babe. And—"

"She's an antelope. Antelope wooing may be like experiments with mice. Might not translate to humans. I don't even understand humans, like what women see in men. Though what some women see in women I understand."

"Yes, you told me, more than once. Back to Badsr."

"Too late, Lucas. The Big Guys cometh big time. What a production. The Legionnaires are wearing gold instead of silver. Accented with candy-grape purple. And the Big Guys match. Spectacular. The auditorium is on its feet, whistling and clapping their butts off. Ten thousand horny hands shaking the building. They're marching down the aisle real slow, like 'Pomp and Circumstance.' The rest of my group is seated at a big horseshoe-shaped table with places in the middle for the Big Guys. Thrones encrusted with jewels—"

"You're wasting time when we should be talking about Badsr's strategy with impossible females. They've herded us to an auditorium with similar pageantry. But I won't waste time describing it when you should be trying to match up with Ellen, inspiring the Goldies to let us go."

"Like that would ever happen. I was worried about Courtney but it looks like Barry and Ellen cleaned her up. She looks refreshed and ready for more mischief. One second. There's a problem—"

"Reg here. All three tepuis are getting ready for war. You may recall the Ivies have a single Big Guy, who's a low-key diplomat. And the guy I'm dealing with is his chief adviser. So, I thought I was getting the straight scoop on what's going on. But no—"

"Cut to the chase, Reg. I'm getting worried."

"Taking a page from me, eh dude!" said Lucas. "I'm more worried."

Mack said, "Gotta go. Taking my place at the head table. Courtney is acting out. Put that down. Courtney. Did you hear me. Now put—that— Wow. They didn't put her cuffs back on after the shower. She smacked the judge right between the eyes, like David and Goliath. He collapsed in his big fancy chair with his mouth wide open. Jeez, these guys have really wicked teeth. And the Big Guys are livid. The Legionnaires bound Courtney so she can't breathe. She's rolling around on the floor like she's dying. Maybe that's our solution. But I can't just sit here, even if it's only Courtney. Damn, let this cup pass from me."

"I didn't know you were religious," said Reg. "Surprise, surprise."

Mack bent over Courtney, trying to loosen the cords around her neck. He gave up and ran to the Big Guys on their thrones, doing a fast genuflect. "Come on, Big Guys. Courtney may be irritating, but you shouldn't kill her for smacking the honorable judge. He deserved it, the way he treated her."

The judge lay sprawled, mouth wide open, eyes closed.

"So, let Courtney breathe until she's boiled in oil. Surely that's a reasonable compromise. Otherwise you won't have your circus and the populace will be disappointed. To say nothing of the Goldie pope—"

Btsht zipped a horny paw across his throat and Mack got the message, slamming his mouth shut. Btsht nodded to a spiffy Legionnaire who loosened Courtney's bonds, with predictable results. Courtney got up gagging, cursing the Big Guys and the judge with dangs and darns.

Judge Grdam pulled himself upright and touched a bump on his forehead. He looked like he'd been whacked with a tree. He said, "I'm a barmy battleship." And fell back in his chair.

Mack escorted Courtney to her place on the raised dais, beckoning for Barry and Ellen. "Watch her closely, you hear? No more shenanigans or we'll all end up in the soup. Assuming we haven't already."

"Right, my sahib." The smallest of smiles crossed Ellen's divinely beautiful face.

"Right, boss." Barry smirked as he hauled himself onto the dais, pulling Ellen up after.

"Give us a hand with Courtney," said Mack.

Courtney squeaked, "I can't talk."

"It's better if you can't talk. Now pay attention. We're going to boost you onto the platform so you can go back to your proper seat. Remember that quietness is next to godliness."

Courtney glared at Mack as Barry grasped her hand. Mack tried to boost her up. "Oh, Mr. Legionnaire. Could you please—? Thanks, and upsy-daisy. Whew. Now Reg, what's going on? Sorry to interrupt but Courtney swooped out of control, again."

"The Ermies put their missiles on high alert and called up the national guard. The Ivies have moved us to an auditorium, which you can see on your monitors. The Ivies are supporting the Ermies against the Goldies. I don't know the timetable and I doubt anyone does."

Lucas came online. "'There's no expedient to which man will not resort to avoid the real labor of thinking.' Reg is right. The Ermies are also on a war footing. Troops are marching around and missiles have been deployed."

"This is not the time for quotes. First, they're not men, they're antelopes. Second, the Goldies are meeting for a discussion, not to declare war, I hope. Third, just because they could be contemplating war doesn't mean they're not thinking and—"

"I wasn't referring to the antelopes." Lucas was sarcastic. "We're the ones who aren't thinking. If they want to have a war, let them at it. It's the best diversion we could hope for."

"I bet you have a Billy K. plan. Sneak off in the heat of battle, figuring they won't miss us. Find a secret passage to Caracas International Airport. Right?"

"If you didn't talk all the time, we could come up with something sensible.
There's an easy way out of our predicament, like you pitched to the second Big Guy, whatsiname?"

"Btsht. Yeah, I did and he pooh-poohed it."

"But he was interested in finding a way out if they could keep from being discovered by the likes of us."

"I don't know how we could keep everyone from blabbing. Maybe most of us wouldn't, in exchange for our freedom. But the bragging factor would have to win. How many people could keep quiet after being held captive by seven-foot aliens? And right here on the same planet? There's no way to solve that problem."

"Reg here. I may have a solution. What was the second Big Guy's name?"

"It's easy. Just think batshit and take out the vowels."

"Oh, right. Anyway, what you said makes sense. We promise not to reveal their presence on these godforsaken tepuis and they let us go. That works because the black box is down on the canyon floor. And no one would believe anyone who would say that aliens captured us. If one of my guys, say Rudd Rat, tried to blow the whistle, who'd believe him? None of the others would renege on a promise. Except maybe Fats, if he were depressed."

"Which sounds inevitable for Fats. But the good old US of A has more kooks per square inch than anywhere on earth. So, millions would believe it. Think about Roswell and Area 51. One of our guys would spill it to the press, which would pooh-pooh it. But they'd give it a lot of ink because we'll all be celebrities after our rescue. So, if someone blew the whistle, they'd corner the rest of us. If I were asked point blank what happened up here, I'd have a tough time denying the truth. What kind of story could we come up with? Face it. We're screwed."

"We're really screwed, thanks to Mack," said Lucas. "A so-called leader who reveals our innermost thoughts in written transcripts. We have to stop telling the antelopes our every move. Haven't you come up with anything?"

"No, but I'm been thinking about it between crises. The show's started and the Goldies' filmmaking is quite advanced. 3D digital with seamless virtual reality. It'd win an Academy Award for special effects."

"Oops. Same thing here. How about you Reg?"

"Same as Mack said, in fluorescent living color. Looks like a replay of WWIII, maybe their last little conflict."

"The newsreel is scary enough to be WWIII." Mack was shocked. "But how'd they make individual nuclear weapons? Those things are nuclear, aren't they? The cute little mushroom clouds like little umbrellas, opening to destroy each enemy soldier."

"We're not seeing the same film. I'll bet if you ask them who won the last war, they'd each say they did. It's like Killing Fields II, antelopes split in two with all the blood running out."

"I never thought all your blood could fall out like that, gone in a split second."

Reg cut in, "Okay, I have something better than a Billy K. plan."

"Reg must be prescient because Badsr told me Billy K. disappeared," said Lucas. "Billy K couldn't have gone far but he's not in the auditorium. Maybe he was right when he said we could just walk out and see what happens."

"How could that be?" demanded Mack. "There are guards everywhere. At least there are over here. Legionnaires

116

spilling around corners, skulking in corridors, Swiss Army knives at the ready. And Billy K. walked out?"

"The Ermies aren't running a police state like the Goldies. There are no visible cops, though Ermies make black bears look like pipsqueaks. I reckon Billy K. just walked out. If Billy K. can, we all can."

"Is it still show time there?" Mack sounded worried." The Goldies' area stop-framing the annihilation Ermies and Ivies. Psyching the populace for war."

"It's popcorn and circuses over here, too, but Badsr just showed up and wants a word with you, Mack. Go ahead Badsr."

An extremely deep voice said, "Thank you, bon sahib. Very pleased to talk to the—"

Mack said, "What's this bon sahib stuff? Is that your new name, Lucas?"

"I'm embarrassed. Cut me some slack. A title greases wheels. Sorry about that, Mr. Honorable Chief Counsellor Badsr. My compatriot at the Goldies is an officious intermeddler, can't stand anyone else with a title. Remember Mack, we have to observe protocol."

"Right. I was way out of line. Let's start fresh. Thank you for your kind inquiry, honorable chief counsellor badsr and—"

"You didn't capitalize that."

"How could you tell? Right. I apologize for everything you've found out about me. I'm extremely pleased to meet you, Honorable Chief Counsellor Badsr. You every wish is my command."

"You must allow your compatriot associate to recap the plot of my hit soap opera. If properly applied that would solve all our problems. Could you do that for me, Mr. Mack?"

"I'm honored to listen to the plot. But there's no hope for a romance with Ellen, especially since keeping Courtney out of burning oil is my full-time job. And now Billy K. is missing."

"Don't worry about that, Mr. Mack. We'll find Mr. Billyk, though we're occupied with inferior Goldies threatening war."

"Threatening you with war? I thought the Ermies were threatening the Goldies. Not you personally, of course, but the regime."

"You got it wrong this time. But I can't blame you for the lies you've been told by our sworn enemies, the inferior Goldies. We're never the aggressor. We told the Goldies to give Courtney a fair shake but when it comes to religion—"

"I'm surprised that an ancient civilization, such as yours, would resort to war under any pretext. Much less a war caused by a single alien like Courtney, though she can be difficult. Am I missing something? Or is this an excuse to cover up the real reason you may declare war against your fellow antelopes?"

Badsr cleared his throat. "Goldies are in no sense the same species as noble Ermies. The Goldies are a horrid color, have no sense of morality, and their religion is primitive. They're uncultured and lazy, and they don't often bathe. You must have noticed their lack of personal hygiene."

"I'm not at liberty to say, since the Goldies will decide whether we live or die."

"Ah, ever the diplomat, sort of. Let's start with the soap opera plot that will make the Goldies let you go."

"Forget the nonsense about Ellen. I'm more worried about the war and finding Billy K. He could fall prey to the dangerous creatures I hear inhabit your tepui. Or do you know where he is, so no worries? Or are you too busy with other things right now, or what?"

"None of the above. An expedition to find Billyk will begin soon. It'd be easy to convince the hopelessly romantic Goldies to let you go. When would be convenient for you to listen, for a change?"

"Too much happening here with the trial, war games, Courtney, and escaping. Plus, Ellen's married and considers me a heathen. Set her up with someone else, who she doesn't consider a nincompoop and a heathen. Assuming you can get past her married status."

"I like your style, Mr. Mack but time is short—"

"How do you have time to talk to me and get ready for war at the same time?"

118

Badsr got huffy. "This happens to be top importance, at least to me. Since I'm in many respects the Ermie state, it's important for everyone. But you're right about getting back to the rally, which I need to do right now. I have a blueprint to woo Ellen and get you off these tepuis. If you'll listen."

"Why didn't you just tell me straight off? Is Mr. Lucas already off looking for Billy K.?"

"Way too complicated…" and Badsr was gone.

Lucas said, "That wasn't up to your usual diplomatic standard but hey, I'm off to look for Billy K. We're taking James and Benny and Ef. Nick and Mary are at the hospital, so I don't know what's going on with them. We're wearing special hats to blend in with the bush and the weird rocks. Plus keep the rain off. We just got out on top and it's a right downpour. Badsr sent a guard, maybe so we don't try to escape. He's like the Goldie Legionnaires but taller, real spiffy dresser, even has spats. I don't know how we'll find Billy K. in this deluge. Or get through the thicket and around the huge boulders. The guard uses an electric machete that cuts through overgrown vegetation like water. Now we're back on a path and—"

"Didn't you hear Badsr tell you to brief me on the plot to a soap opera that will solve all our problems? You'd better get on with it."

"I'm too excited being on the top of this incredible place. Everything dripping, long vines, waterfalls everywhere. Goddamn rocks, jammed a toe on one. Whoa. I think that was a tiger. Hey, Mr. Guard, sir, was that an albino tiger?"

Mack heard a growl that sounded more like an Ermie than a tiger. "Lucas, to refresh your likely dim recollection: Badsr was going on a lecture tour without his new love. He was drinking too much and didn't know whether it was a relationship or just super sex. Obviously, nothing to do with Ellen and me. Or Ellen and anyone."

"It is a tiger. It is. A white one with big white teeth and blue stripes. More navy blue or black. Just sitting there. Thought we were goners or he'd hightail it, but he didn't do either. Sat there looking like we were desert. But the guard took his foldup knife and the tiger skedaddled without a sound.

Whew. That was the highpoint of the trip. Well, so far. Now, where were we?"

"Goddamn it, Lucas. Now I'm super curious about getting out of here by romancing Ellen. Badsr sounds so confident that I'd like to hear it. But you're off gallivanting with tigers. How'd the other guys take it? Ef and Benny and James."

"Ef wanted to put the tiger in a zoo but Benny and James were really cool. Benny purred at the tiger like it was a horse. But to summarize Badsr's strategy with you and Ellen, you need acting ability. Badsr will provide the lighting effects for your heartfelt conversion to Catholicism. This will be when Ellen finds out her husband absconded with the lottery winnings. Then you're in like Flynn."

"Anyone named Flynn is probably already Catholic. I wonder if Billy K. got eaten by a tiger or other fearsome creature."

"The tiger's gone, stop changing the subject. You have to try conversion therapy with Ellen…oh my god. Biggest damn snake I ever seen. Bigger than the King Browns up in the Kimberly. More like our scrub python, which is huge. But it's not as big as this thing. We damn near didn't see it, 'cause of the rain. It swung its big old head over the path and took off after Benny. Maybe attracted by the blue pants. But the guard moved fast and sliced the snake's head off lickety-split. It went flying and smacked poor Ef right on the noggin. Knocked him cold. The head alone must have weighed a couple of kilos. We're taking a break to bring Ef around. So, let me tell you Badsr's story. He can engineer a spectacular column of light when you convert. Right in front of Ellen."

"She's not going to buy that crap. And the Goldie rally's getting bloodier. They're taking out a dozen Ermies and Ivies at a time. They split in two and their blood swooshes out the bottom. It makes me glad I don't have a period. Can you just imagine?"

"Omigod, that'd be worse than war. But you have to trust Badsr. He can pull off the pyrotechnics to convince Ellen that you're the real pope's illegitimate son. That combined with her husband stealing all the money…"

"Totally ridiculous and you can tell Badsr that's what I said. I'd love a few hours, days, or a whole week with Ellen. But stop it or I'll find a guided missile and watch the blood drop out your bottom like a swish of red tide. Or maybe not, since I wouldn't have anyone to supervise and all the joy would evaporate from my life."

"Badsr is not going to take no for an answer. Ef is back among the living, though looking real bad. We have to take him back before we can look for Billy K. Well, son of a gun. It wasn't that hard to send Ef back. I wondered what the manhole covers were for. The guard dropped Ef in a hole and he's gone. 'Course Ef's not that big. Hey. Where's Ef? I mean is he okay or what? Christ on a crutch. The guard says it's a first-aid chute and Ef is perfectly okay. He's having a nice hot chocolate about now. That's exactly what the guy said."

"You're a dolt, Lucas. Let me talk to that guy, right now."

"Right. Okay, he's on. Go ahead."

"Hello, Mr. Guard. This is Mr. Mack and I'd like to know exactly what you did with our dear friend, Efriam Malinski. Dumping him in a hole in the ground doesn't hardly sound proper. Not the sort of place for him in his current physical condition."

Mack could hear a scratchy noise and then, "Gibbledy fart buttem," rapidly amended. "Butt out, Mr. Mack. Your buddy is safe and dry and slurping hot chocolate. Cheerio."

"Ef has never drank hot chocolate in his life. What is your name and serial number, Mr. Guard? Immediately put your supervisor on the phone."

"No."

"Well, then I'll assume Ef is okay. Now what are you going to do about Mr. Billy K.? He may be the victim of dangerous wild animals, his life in imminent danger."

"He tried to escape and he can take the consequences. If we find him, okay, and if not, that's the way it goes. Goodbye, Mr. Mack."

"That's a pretty nasty guard you have there, Lucas. He's as congenial as the guard who became our judge. You have to watch those guys. They turn on you like chameleons."

"Gurgle, gurgle, retch. Harrumph. Sorry about that Mack. My hat collapsed and I about drowned. Oh, right. Thanks a lot, James. I'll keep that in mind. James says the hat works better if you wear it over a Stetson, which of course is what he's doing. We're back on the trail. Maybe we won't have as many tigers and snakes."

"Geez, Lucas. You've only had one of each. Crocodile Dundee you're not."

"I'd like to see you stare down an albino Siberian tiger."

"A Siberian tiger in a rain forest? Oh, the Goldie rally is coming to a head. They've worked up to vaporizing an entire tepui. What did you say?"

"We're headed back inside. You should have seen it out on top. It was ethereal with mist rising off the bushes. The boulders are like those poky Chinese mountains in their silk paintings. And little waterfalls, mostly down my neck in spite of the hat. Pink sand and limpid pools. We're already back in the auditorium. They're winding things up here too. Whoops, we're just passing through. We skirted the top ring of the auditorium and everyone's yelling, antelope with burps and farts and loud screechy stuff. Like the trip we took to Morocco. Where they sing like that."

"Bad form, Lucas. You'll never become a US citizen because you score too low on political correctness. Hey, gotta go. Got a signal from Btsht. Our mission, since we've undertaken it, is to bring the new millionaires back unscathed. I hope we pull it off. Catch you later."

Ellen tugged on Mack's sleeve. "I'm coming along because you need help, or you'd already have us out of here."

Mack was enthralled for half a second. "As Courtney would say, 'negatory.' Where is Courtney, anyway? You and Barry were in charge of her. And where's Barry?"

"That's the problem, getting help for Barry and Courtney. If you'd pay attention you'd know. Or just looked around occasionally. See."

He saw. Barry was trying to stay between Courtney and curious Goldies flocking for a closer look. They stuck big noses in her face, poking her and spitting with lots of whistle farts.

"Why didn't you say something? I'm on my way to see the second Big Guy right now."

"Which is why I'm going along." She stared him down.

"Um, yes." She looked so utterly delectable. "If you're coming, get a move on. We can't keep the Big Guy waiting."

"You've done a pretty good imitation of it."

He motioned her down the steps where Btsht stood with arms crossed.

"This is our last chance," said Btsht. "Have you given further thought to our discussion? Or are you too busy BSing with your friend Lucas, giving advice to the enemy, and generally making a nuisance of yourself?"

"Since you put it that way, no sir. But you really should keep bullying antelopes away from Courtney. No matter what you think about her, there's no reason to treat her like dog food. An order from you would put a stop to that. Then we can get on with more important matters."

"Do you have the slightest idea how much you try everyone's patience?"

Ellen piped up, "I keep telling him that."

"Thanks to both of you." Mack stuck fingers between his teeth and blasted an ear-splitting whistle. Deafening, even by Goldie standards. The Goldies harassing Courtney froze, and Btsht blinked. "Please," said Mack to Btsht.

"Right." Btsht snapped horny fingers. Three Legionnaires scrambled onto the dais and pushed away the Goldies harassing Courtney.

"Many thanks, my friend." Mack bowed. "And yes, our discussion is all I've been thinking about, between crises. But let's forget what I've come up with because I see a twinkle in your big green eyes."

"They're emerald. And I have an idea we've touched on."

"I thought so. Something to do with computer programming and your war effort? Too bad you posted all but one of our expert programmers to the Ermies and Ivies, your sworn enemies. Until alliances shift, of course." Could he actually foist Peter on them? "Though I'm surprised we have talents you lack. What's your proposal?"

"You're not as dense as you seem. I am surprised." Btsht belatedly returned Mack's bow. "Since we're on the same wavelength, I'll lay out our requirements. We need a hacker."

Silence reigned. Mack waited for Btsht to provide details while Ellen waited for Mack to stop waiting. Her gaze flicked between the two like a ping-pong ball. Mack finally said, "We have an expert hacker. An honor graduate from DeVry Institute of Technology. He majored in hacking, cutting, and dealing."

"Dealing? Is that a recent advance in computer technology? I haven't heard about that."

"Indeed, it is. Dealing is the ability to splay sites among themselves. This is a form of hacking that confuses everyone who comes into contact. I can see you are already confused. But I am prepared to field questions."

"I have one question. Is dealing a thing that would confound incoming missiles? Divert them to targets chosen by us? Maybe I have two questions."

"And very good questions they are. Peter," Mack yelled at the top of his lungs.

"This might not be the best idea," said Ellen.

"You see, Honorable Btsht, Ms. Ellen doesn't want to reveal our most important military secrets, just to save our own skins. We have a difference of opinion. After all, you are now our friend."

"Where is this Peter?"

"Peter." Mack whistled as he looked for cartwheels, the
cadging of drinks,
or dealing on the sly.

"Something is not right," said Btsht.

"Boy, you hit that on the schnoz." Mack tried not to look at Btsht's nose.

"I'll go look for him," said Ellen.

Mack frowned. "Are you ill?"

"I have discovered practicality."

"What are you two up to?" asked Btsht.

"Ellen has volunteered to find Peter. I think I see him down there, on the other side of the dais."

"What is dice?"

"Don't do that. Courtney and your ruler buddies are on a dais, the big raised thing in the middle of the auditorium."

"Oh, dais."

They watched Ellen skip down the stairs, full skirt billowing. She threaded through jubilant Goldies as Big Guys One and Three whipped the audience into war readiness. Every "whiffle, whiffle, michnifnchuck" sounded like "hip, hip, hooray."

"I'm worried about this war you're so keen on," said Mack. "Your wars look worse than ours. Maybe because ours are now mostly civil wars. Why are you so happy about a war?"

"I plead guilty. War is inexcusable and we love it. There's fireworks and rallies, camaraderie and loose women. Now when I say women, I mean antelope babes. You should see our porn sites. Boy, would that be a revelation."

Mack thought for half a second. "Please. I don't want to know."

"What do you mean? That's half your internet. We deserve equal time. Especially if you're about to *discover* us. Let me tell you about my favorites."

"I don't want to know." Mack's eyes were big, jaws clenched, mouth locked in grimace rictus.

"Two Goldie babes, faces buried. You know, long legs thrashing the air. The close ups and the resolution. Fly you to the moon."

"I'm going to be sick. Have you no sense of propriety? A bunch of gangly animals like yourselves. You should be ashamed."

"We should be ashamed? Humans are the original sin when it comes to kinky sex. Who do you think you are? Celestial beings? Last I heard you were animals too. Don't give me any discriminatory bullshit."

"But you treat us like inferior beings, unworthy of eating at the same table." Mack stopped in mid-outrage, palms up. He took a deep breath, calming, calming. "That's not what we're here to discuss, which is far more important."

"Speak for yourself, buster. We consider sex of supreme importance. And wholesome pleasure. We're not like puritanical humanoids who turn it into something dirty. Even for adults." Btsht took his turn at calming. "Never mind. We're back on track. Maybe Peter can help us both out."

"Peter is my donation to your cause. But he comes with no guarantees, believe you me."

"On that single point, I do. I now remember crazy erratic Peter. I doubt he can help anyone with anything, much less assist the war effort."

"Well, I hope he fails miserably. You hold yourselves out as a superior civilization but haven't learned to live in peace with your identical cousins. Except for skin color."

"We're not kissing cousins. Our differences go far deeper than skin color. I'm sure you'll figure it out, bright fellow you think you are. There are antelopes and there are antelopes. We're the great Golden Antelopes, kings of the tepuis. Lords of the known universe."

"Upchuck. The only question I have is whether Peter's success on your behalf will guarantee our release?"

"Peter's success on our behalf will secure your immediate release. And guarantee the annihilation of your friends. Regrettably, they've cast their lot with the Ermies and Ivies."

"You make me sick."

"Tough noogies. You're lucky I don't take umbrage at your asinine comments. For some reason I'm compelled to cut you slack appropriate to the intelligence of your species. So, mouth off as much as you like. Good day, sir. I'll take Peter with me," as Peter came strolling up.

"I heard you wanted me, Mr. Mack, so here I am." The words were scarcely out of Peter's mouth before two Legionnaires grabbed his arms and about-faced him. Peter's legs beat a cadence in the air as he yelled over his shoulder, "What the hell's going on? Have you sold me down the river, Mr. Mack? Tell me it isn't so. Though it must be—" His voice faded as the Legionnaires jogged down the stairs into the melee of the war rally.

Btsht smiled. "I salute you, Mr. Mack. You're a gentleman and a quisling. We Goldies may be in your debt, though probably not. But we won't abuse Mr. Peter. If he turns out to be the dud I'm guessing he is, we'll return him promptly.

126

Mostly intact." Btsht hustled down the stairs toward the growing pandemonium. In the center sat Courtney, Barry, Peter, and Big Guys Number One and Three.

Mack yelled, "Hey, your ornery eminence. That wasn't exactly what I had in mind. And we didn't settle anything." But he wasted his breath. Btsht took his place with the ruling trio, whispering to his compatriots.

8

"You screwed that up," said Lucas, his voice whistling out of Mack's mic. "Why did you trust Btsht and how do you propose to fix it?"

"Peter will be all right. He's the least of our worries. There are other matters, such as impending war. Then there's Courtney. And where's Reg? Have you heard from him? What are he and the Ivies up to? Have I missed anything?"

"You surely have. What about Billy K.? Has he disappeared off your list?"

"Of course not. But I have to delegate some authority to you. I assume you have that problem under control."

"Your smart mouth is correct for a change. We found Billy K., and guess where he was?"

"This is hardly the time for guessing games."

"Right. We found him in a church, where he was showing Ermies how to make knives."

"I don't believe it. Was he ever outside? Why would they let him make knives in a religious sanctuary? Or are knives sacred to Ermies? And why would the Ermies care about the 'art' of knife-making? Where would he get the materials to conduct a seminar on knife-making? Why are you letting me go on like this?"

"You're my supervisor, and I don't know how to stop you."

"That never bothered you before. Okay, you found the lost sheep, conveniently in church. Is there a problem?"

"Of course, there's a problem. Otherwise I wouldn't demand an entire second of your precious time. We're all in church. Badsr, Benny, and James, along with Billy K. and a dozen Ermie converts to his new knife culture."

"What's the problem?"

"I was getting to that but you went off on a tangent and—"

"Have you heard anything about Ef?"

"He sold ten lots with no electricity or water to the crew at the first-aid station. What they're using for a down payment I can't imagine. And they want Billy K. to promise he won't try to escape again."

"Why is that a problem since he didn't escape the first time?"

"He says he'll try escaping anytime he feels like it. He can't promise not to."

"I don't blame him. How often do you run across an honest man?"

"They'll throw him in the dungeon if he doesn't promise."

"This is nuts. They found him in a church. You don't escape to church. You always say you escape from church."

"The distinction won't sway Badsr. Hey, Badsr, what do you think of Mack's analysis of the Billy K. escape conundrum?"

"Crumb bum dum-dum," said Badsr. "I'm having second thoughts on whether he's qualified to romance Ellen."

"Don't feel like the loan arranger," said Mack. "I've ignored your crazy idea. What's so ridiculous about pointing out that Billy K. didn't try to escape? If he had, he wouldn't be sitting in a church, for Christ's sake."

"What part of 'escape' don't you understand," roared Badsr. "He wasn't where he was supposed to be. With the others. He was AWOL. Surely you can understand that simple concept."

"You win. I resign as Ellen's romancer. Which means you win twice. Let's get to the Billy K. problem, which I don't understand."

Lucas came back, "The problem is honesty. Billy K. respectfully declines to swear he won't try to escape. He intends to wander off whenever he damn well pleases."

"Surely you have a quote to cover that. Oh, goddamn, please, Lucas. I take that back. I apologize. You have the top performance rating in the agency. I promise. If only you don't utter another quote."

"'It is double pleasure to deceive the deceiver.' I'm sure you follow the gist of that one. If not, I'll be happy to explain it."

"I thought you'd cured yourself, but *no*. Quote after quote after quote."

"You egged me on. I mean, sort of. Plus, I can't help it. When there's one that fits, it comes spurting out. Nothing to do with me."

"You're an innocent man. I should have known. But your quotes seldom fit the situation. Why shouldn't Billy K. tell them whatever they want to hear? It makes no difference one way or the other. He didn't try to escape so he shouldn't be punished. We shouldn't level with jerkoffs who keep jerking us around. Antelopes display the integrity of a fingernail. There's no reason to be honest with vermin like that."

"Good job, Mack. That'll look great in the transcripts. How does burbling oil sound?"

"Worse than it does to Courtney. Reason with Billy K. Get him to fudge this one and avoid the dungeon. Then we can get on with avoiding all-out war and escape from this dratted tepui."

"You've made incredible progress on both problems."

"I'm working on it."

"'The most common lie is that with which one lies to oneself; lying to others is relatively an exception.' There's a quote that fits you like a glove."

"Does not. I can't do any better than I can do."

"You're a yo-yo, up and down. Falling to the end of your string, asking for help like you're all unwound."

"Just do it. If you can't talk sense to Billy K., let me. Put him on the horn. I'll spin my magic."

Lucas yelled, "Hey, Billy K. Take a break from the knife business. Mack wants a word."

Mack could hear Billy K. in the background, talking his own brand of trash. "You gotta get the spindle just right. Sight it up against the statue thing over there. You can see— Yeah, I'm a-coming. Hey, guys. Gotta go. The big kahuna is calling. But I'll be right back. Do a little sighting while I'm gone. Hey, Mack. How're they hanging?"

"Hanging good, Billy K. We're glad to hear you're safe and sound. How did you end up in church, anyhow?"

"I admire your ability to relax, Mr. Mack. You are a constant inspiration. I scouted out the top. Boy you should see it. Like Arizona sopping wet. Green stuff and lots of plants, real thick with big hunky rocks. Wasn't what you'd call comfy. So, I moseyed back inside, found this bunch of nice antelope people. Darndest conglomeration and I like them a whole lot. They've never seen anyone make a knife. 'Course lots of people haven't, so I sat right down. They was bored with the church part of things. I would've been. Good old Margaret. Reckon you met Margaret. She laps it up. More power to her. So, I whipped up the makings and showed them how you go about an operation like that. Been doing it since I was a kid. My pa showed me how. The priest fellow must have left or something, so we got on real good and—"

"This is fascinating, but you don't want them to throw you in the dungeon. Then you can't be rescued by our air force men in blue. Whether you will or not, tell Badsr you won't try to escape. That would be a right fine thing to do."

"I don't hardly see how I can agree to tie myself down in one spot. 'Specially the kind of spots they pick, present company such as Mr. Badsr excluded. Regular folk that likes to make knives, I can understand. But bossy ones are not on my list of goodtime bosom buddies." Billy K. paused half a second. Mack could almost hear him scratching his head. "You're not suggesting I lie? I may not cotton to church stuff but I draw the line at intentional deception."

At which point Lucas broke in. "I got the absolute perfect one. 'A sagacious prince then cannot and should not fulfill his pledges when their observance is contrary to his interest, and when the causes which induced him to pledge his faith no longer exist. If men were all good, then indeed this precept would be bad; but as men are naturally bad, and will not observe their faith toward you, you must, in some way, not observe yours to them; and no prince has ever yet lacked legitimate reasons with which to color his want of good faith.' Now is that perfect or what? And I know who said it."

"Everyone knows who said that," said Mack. "Not bad, but a bit long. What do you think, Billy K.? You'd be a prince if you would stay out of the deep dark pokey. We want you available when the United States Air Force men in blue come roaring out of the sky to scoop us up. Before you start citing integrity, think about poor old Peggy Sue stuck at home without you. What if we have no way of finding you? Much less get you back? Whataya say?"

"Nope. Not going to do it. Besides, I told you her name was Margaret. But I'll talk about it with Mr. Lucas's friend, Badsr. He doesn't seem a bad chap, though Mr. Lucas calls him Baddie. And that's to his face."

Mack sighed. "What about it, Badsr? You know none of us can escape these godforsaken tepuis without a helicopter. Which we ain't got. So, cut Billy K. some slack and don't be such a hard ass. If you want to distinguish yourself from your Goldie cousins, or whatever it is you concede them to be, then brush it off. You know in your heart of hearts that Billy K. is a pretty fine guy. I'm sure he'd agree not to wander off without your permission. So, let it go. Have we got a deal?"

"To quote Billy K., nope. We can't allow anyone out on the surface at any time. Except under cover of darkness, in torrential rain or camo clothing, or under the canopy. Even you can figure out why, though it may not make a difference now. But whether you figure it out or not, that's the law. And the law can't be waived for an Ermie citizen, much less an alien. No matter how much we adore the folksiness of the particular alien. Got it?"

"Got it, Badsr. You can be a mighty patient person, on occasion. Billy K. Here's what we're going to do. We will promise my friend, Badsr, that you will not venture out on the surface in violation of Ermie law. This means you will not go out unless it's dark, raining, you're in camo, or under the canopy. Is that understood?"

"You're not my mom or my wife. But I'll make you a deal," drawled Billy K. "If Mr. Badsr will rustle up some camo gear that fits me, it's a done deal."

In his mind's eye Mack could see Badsr rolling his big green eyes. But Badsr chirped right back. "The one thing that pisses me off, but which I admire above all, is the sheer gall of your species. But you got yourself a deal. This has restored my confidence in Mack's abilities, assuming he ever finds time to romance Ellen. The inconvenience of aliens in captivity is more tedious than could possibly have been foreseen."

"Your romancing-Ellen scenario is silly. Though it is a fantasy highlight of my humdrum life. Get back to me when it's convenient. I'll set aside an afternoon. What time is it anyway?"

"It's past time," said Lucas. "Haven't you noticed the obvious problem? Where's Reg? We haven't heard from him for what? Hours?"

"Hey, Honorable Badsr. Are you still there? What's the score with Reg and the Ivies?"

"Badsr split. Apparently more important things to do. Oh, and here's Billy K."

"Thanks, Mr. Mack. You sprung me for better things. I am in your debt and don't you forget it. Any little favor you need, just whistle. You do know how to whistle?"

"When you add whistling to your knife-making seminar, let me know. I'll sit up front."

"Can't you ever be serious, Mr. Mack? I paid you a sincere compliment. A simple grunt would be enough. I'm not looking for undying gratitude."

"I should hope not. I'm sorry I disappoint you, Billy K. But to more pressing matters, Lucas. Has your rally wound down? Ours has. They're into something like a benediction."

"I don't know. We're just leaving the church. And they're letting Billy K. stay inside. The big Ermie rally is right next door."

"It would be. So."

"We're already back. I'll bet our rally is bigger and better than your rally. You should see their Legionnaires. They have really big lances, I guess you'd call them. The Legionnaires run across the floor lickety-split and collide in the

133

middle. It's like lightning exploding and smells like sulphur. No one seems to get hurt but, peee-yew." Lucas sneezed, crackling Mack's eardrums. "I'm allergic to whatever it is."

"Have you seen Nick and Mary? Or the personal nuclear devices we saw in the movies?"

"Hey, James, Benny. Have you seen Nick or Mary?"

"Just got back," said James. "Mary looks a little peaked."

"Shut up, you twit," said Benny. "You know what's going on. Don't make it harder for them."

"Christ on a crutch, I wasn't. It was a simple comment and you snap my head off."

"Hey, Nick, Mary," said Lucas. "How you all doing? Jeez, Mack. Everyone's under a lot of stress and acting like two-year-olds. Especially Benny, looking like measles in his red and blue outfit with the fringe on top. Yes, the boots are cute. Sorry, didn't mean to interrupt."

Nick was frenetic in his soft foghorn voice. "We had holocaust movies, little Hiroshimas. An Ermie General told me the movies are real. The last war killed hundreds of Goldies and Ivies, but he said no Ermies got hurt. Says they're ready to kick butt. Sorry, Mary. I asked him if there was a safe place we could sit out the war, especially for Mary." Mack heard him give her a smooch. "But the General said there wasn't. Said no one's safe. Their missiles chase you until they get you. Down corridors, wherever. They home in on your butt, one on one. A little mushroom cloud for each enemy. The General wouldn't admit anything could get through Ermie defenses. But he bragged about how many Ivies and Goldies they'd obliterated in the last war. Kind of like an extra personal suppository. Sorry again, Mary my love. I'm afraid the United States Air Force will be too late to save us. And then there's Courtney. Have you gotten her a reprieve, Mr. Mack? Seems like I got so many worries I can't hardly think straight." Another smooch for Mary.

Mack said, "Yeah, well, I understand," Mary's stage four cancer pushing Nick over the edge. "But I got the Big Guy to put Courtney on the dais with Barry and Ellen. I'm sure she's all right."

134

"Well, gosh, Mr. Mack. I don't want to sound like a pushy millionaire, but I have a soft spot for Courtney. I'd like to make sure she's all right, if you could check."

"Right. Good point." Mack scanned the floor where the Goldie Legionnaires were jousting, on elephants. Unbelievable, but not terribly impressive. The elephants moved like molasses compared to how fast the Goldies could move on their own. But the electrical strikes were spectacular, lighting up fine hairs on the elephants clomping across the floor. The stench was equally spectacular. Suspicious mounds grew where the elephants lined up, steam rising as lightning coursed over the dais. No one was on the dais except the Big Guys.

"Er, I'll have to get back to you. And Nick, you were a hundred percent correct. I should have checked on Courtney earlier, along with Ellen and Barry. They've gone missing."

Mack stood entranced as lightning orbs skittered around the auditorium. It was like the ball lightning that scared the bejesus out of him as a kid during summers on his grandpa's ranch in southeastern Arizona.

Mack plunged down the steep stairs, dodging Goldies psyched up for all-out war. The dais was at the far wall where the three Big Guys sat on three-tiered thrones. Mack flashed the shit-eating smile he reserved for extreme diplomacy, genuflecting across the floor. He had to dodge elephants and steaming mounds of poo, like a ballerina on meth.

Mack stumbled to a halt, his left foot dripping green goo, bowing. "May it please your eminences." Royal emerald eyes glared at his receding hairline.

"You're going to get run over," said Btsht as an elephant brushed Mack's backside. He tumbled head first onto the edge of the dais.

Mack got up, rubbing a new lump. "Your eminences. I enquire about the health and whereabouts of Courtney, Mrs. Ellen, and Mr. Barry. Where are they? And where the heck did you get elephants?"

"Pssst," hissed Mack's mic. "Reg here. Finally got my mic fixed. What's happening? Things have hotted up over here."

Mack said, *sotto voce*, "Give me a sec. I'm in the middle of finding out what the Big Guys did with Courtney. So happy to hear from you but will have to get right back. Ahem." Mack cleared his throat. "Sorry about that, but—"

"Butt should be your middle name," snarfled Btsht. "Your friends are in protective custody. For their own good, of course."

"Of course. May I see them, your holy omnipotence? And why are they in 'protective' custody? Are your loyal subjects too dangerous for my honorable compatriots?"

"The crowd found out that one particular religious alien bigot is causing the upcoming war. They got a little raucous."

"Okay, we're the bad guys and you're the good guys. May I visit the other bad guys?" Mack whispered, "Hang in there, Reg, a few more seconds."

"I'll take you myself." Btsht stood, bowed to the others, and hopped down. He pointed Mack to the auditorium wall, which magically opened.

Mack stumbled toward the opening. "Reg. We're super anxious to find out what's going on with you and the Ivies. If you could give me a rundown while I tag along with the Goldie Big Guy, that'd be great."

"Gotcha. We've been watching the show from our accommodation. Super plush quarters I told you about. And there's a few things I suspect the Ermies and Goldies know nothing about—"

"You shouldn't tell me. They transcribe our conversations. Or maybe it'll stop the war."

Btsht slung a long arm around Mack's chest as Reg said, "It's not going to be a pretty sight."

"What's not going to be a pretty sight?"

Btsht said, "The war will be participatory for you. We can't shield you. But you have an old friend to keep you company." He motioned Mack onto a steep escalator that curved out of sight below them, like standing on a black run with the lodge between the tips of your skis.

"How's Peter doing?" said Mack. "If he helped, you said we'd be safe."

Reg whispered, "It's like civil defense drill in grade school. Duck your head and kiss your ass goodbye."

Btsht rose to his full height as the down escalator entered free fall. "Peter's a fraud. He knows a smidge of DOS, but that's more archaic than Windows. He couldn't hack a paper bag."

"No problem. You couldn't keep us safe if you wanted to. It's general knowledge that the Ermies and Ivies can knock off anyone they choose."

Reg was talking so quietly that Mack had to cock his head toward his collar. "—goners. Hot oil might be a relief—but why bother with more trial?"

Wharrumph, kerplunk. The escalator stopped abruptly.

Btsht growled, "It's time Mr. Mack took responsibility for causing this war instead of claiming to be an innocent man."

"Oh, right. Blame your testosterone-driven war on poor inferior aliens."

"Oh, Mr. Mack. Poor benighted human that you are. We gave up war a millennium ago. We don't like the Ermies and Ivies any better than we ever did. But we've refrained from killing each other for eight hundred years."

"That's impossible. You showed movies with individual nuclear weapons. As opposed to our nuclear weapons that kill everything for miles."

"I can't believe it either," whispered Reg.

"What part don't you understand?" said Btsht. "We digitalized our old war videos. They were taken in your years 1207 A.D., or C.E., whichever you prefer. About the time your ancestors were killing Jews on the way to the Crusades in your still current hot spot, the Middle East. Humans are simplistic children."

"If you're so technologically advanced, why didn't you know about our black box? And why did you tip the plane into the river valley?"

"Want to take a look, Mr. Mack? The plane isn't there anymore. But forget that. The only reason for this war is you."

"You can't blame us for your religious intolerance. We didn't plan to crash on this crappy mesa."

"No one's disputing that, Mr. Mack. Our failure to annihilate you the second you landed has created an ethical problem. A problem the Goldies, Ermies, and Ivies can't solve. Consider this simple question. What will happen when our kind are discovered by your kind? Now we have," he cleared his long throat, "ethical compunctions. God rest our souls."

"Okay, I understand you don't want to end up in our zoos. But you wouldn't. The whole idea is ludicrous. You're obviously as intelligent as we are—" Btsht glared fiercely. "Right. You're a whole heck of a lot smarter. But we couldn't put you in zoos even if we wanted to. You'd unleash individual nuclear missiles like you did eight hundred years ago, or whenever. Don't be daft."

"You're a little slow, Mr. Mack. Forget the unimportant problems that take all your time. Instead, think. What is most important to you? I'm sure your mother told you not to scrunch your face up or it might freeze that way." Btsht sighed. "I don't have time for you to figure it out on your own. The answer is privacy. Though you might not put us in zoos, you'd never leave us alone. There's be sociologists and anthropologists and native studiers and connoisseurs of our art, and rotten tourists—"

"You have art?"

"Don't interrupt! Busybodies would poke their noses into our affairs. The UN would investigate poverty and female rights. Norway and Japan would solicit votes for commercial whaling. There's be an uproar on whether we could compete in the Olympics. Whether our dietary staples constitute drugs. And you already object to our porn. This might sound frivolous but we'd never be left alone. Tourism alone would be staggering. 'Ve vant to be left alone.' Can you dig it?"

"I can dig it!" said Mack, high-fiving Btsht, who stood stunned. "We also want to be left alone. But instead you've created a final solution for innocent aliens. Plus, there's about a hundred things I don't understand."

"I know."

"Smart-ass yourself. Okay, assuming you're smarter, why did you grab Pete? As if he could help your war effort?"

"We were grasping at hollow straws. Everyone has a learning curve, even antelopes. You impressed me with your verbal tap dance at the trial, though you rapidly became obnoxious."

"So, Pete's average and I tap dance a speck above average. For our pathetic species, that is. I'm guessing the Goldies voted for our immediate demise while the Ermies and Ivies aren't so hot on the idea? Right?"

Btsht didn't say a word.

"And the good guys barely constitute Ermie and Ivie majorities. You're the sole hold-out among the Goldie Big Guys."

"I'm wavering."

"So, I'm stupid to ask you to protect us during the upcoming war. Because you're deciding whether we should be executed, and the Goldies are in the affirmative on the issue."

"You sum up well, except for the upcoming part. The war is a done deal." Btsht indicated thick doors swinging open before them. "After you."

"Real doors. Wow."

"Thought you'd be impressed. It doesn't take much."

"The novelty will wear off." Mack stepped through the doors, craning his head left, right, and center. They were in a stainless-steel vault that could hold a dozen football stadiums. Barry, Peter, Ellen, and Courtney sat in a circle. The single Goldie looked familiar.

"What's going on?" said Reg and Lucas simultaneously.

"We're back in prison, guarded by the old guard. Which is to say the Honorable Judge Grdam."

Mack waved at Ellen, tempted to smack her when she flashed her usual look of disdain. Then at Barry, who waved back good-naturedly. Peter ignored him, and Courtney looked like she'd been attacked by ripe tomatoes.

Mack grasped Judge Grdam's hand, shaking it as Btsht said, "Mr. Madison and Mr. Roy will be along soon. But I must leave you." He spun and exited.

"So good to see you again," Mack said with a straight face.

"You lie like a rug," said the judge. "But then, what's new?" He sighed. "The things I do for political advancement. It doesn't seem worth it since you humans showed up. Before that I was on a fast track to be one of the Big Guys, but no. Out of all the tepuis in all the world, you had to pick this one to crash on. Now I might make Big Guy on my four hundredth birthday. I should live so long. So, give me a break, try behaving yourselves, and we can sit the war out in peace."

Courtney shook off her stupor, oozing hatred at the judge. "Your aimless rambling is what keeps you from being a big shot. Ever think about that, Herr Judgie?"

"Grack." The judge twisted his chair to face away from Courtney.

"Good job of getting us in even worse trouble," Mack said to Courtney. "But I have a few questions for the honorable judge," walking around in front of him. "Your Honor, and I'm not being facetious. I know you have the power of life and death over us and will act accordingly. Is this chamber bomb proof, or is it just a sophisticated incinerator? I saw your war movies, the same as everyone else. So, don't soften the blow, as if you would."

"Grack," he repeated. "I am so tired of you. But I'll answer this one question. No one is safe from our individual, couple, trio, small group, medium group, or large group nuclear bombs. Especially the hydrogen ones you didn't see movies of. Rejoin your friends and leave me to the little solitude I have left."

"Sorry, but I had to know." Mack tiptoed back to the others.

Ellen bowed her head. "Let us pray."

"That seems appropriate in the circumstances," said Mack.

Lucas said, "'The fact of having been born is bad augury for immortality.' I knew that one was going to come in handy."

Ellen's mouth dropped. "Are you spiritually stunted or does the cheap mic make you sound that way? You're interfering with the free exercise of my religion, which I really need right now. It wouldn't hurt to observe the traditions of civilization. Instead you spit on everything most of us were taught to respect. You should be ashamed of yourself."

Lucas's tinny voice from Mack's lapel mic said, "You're getting me mixed up with someone else. I repeat quotes by eminent philosophers. I don't vouch for their value. That's up to you and I see you've decided. Though I agree with the last one, more or less."

Reg's stentorian tones came whistling over Mack's lapel mic. "Leave each to their own religion without making fun of it. Quotes are only a spur to thought; not gospel truth. Many of us are petrified of the future. Don't make it worse."

Mack said, "There's a lot in what you say, Reg. So glad you're back with us. Lucas's latest quote, and I'm more against them than anyone, reminded me of another one he spouted. Correct me if I've got it wrong, Lucas, but you said, quoting whoever it was, 'Go and try to disprove death. Death will disprove you.' That has dash and verve, which is why it stuck with me."

"You got it right, far as I know. I only know them perfect when they come tumbling out. As for the Ermies, the countdown has begun. Several Ermie officers think humans should be crushed first. They have the ultimate smart bombs. Smart, if they know your name or serial number, which programs the bomb intended for you, and it keeps going until it finds you. Works first time, every time. Pretty cool, huh?"

Dead silence.

Lucas said, "Think about it. They don't have bar codes for us, or even all our names. We may be okay. Plus, the first salvo will target the Big Guys. Maybe the war will end when they do."

"Ahem," said a mighty voice, as Judge Grdam materialized in front of them. "You humans haven't a clue how things work. What you call DNA is easily obtained by a laser reader. That's the best way I can describe it based on your puny state of technology. Your genetic identifiers were taken when we discovered you. The Ermies, Ivies, or Goldies can easily dedicate personal bombs for each of you. In point of reality, consider yourselves dead." The judge smirked as he retook his seat.

"So, we're purt'inear dead meat," said Barry.

Mack said, "Not so fast. The Ermies and Ivies are on our side. They wouldn't program smart bombs to knock us off."

"But the Goldies would, like our jailer judge," said Ellen.

"Better than boiling oil," said Courtney.

Reg said, "It depends on who you believe. I think the Ivies are on our side, or at least unopposed to our continued existence. But they're as freaked out at being discovered as the Goldies are. I'm not so certain about the Ermies. What do you think, Lucas?"

"My opinion is that, 'To mourn for the time when one will be no more is just as absurd as it would be to mourn over the time when as yet one was not,'" Lucas said. "Sorry. I couldn't resist."

"Cute, but it doesn't help us figure out the Ermies," said Reg.

Ellen yelped. "That's fuzzy bullshit. Oh," she covered her mouth, "sorry."

Mack said, "None of our captors seem particularly reliable. We can only prepare for the worst while doing the best we can. Do I hear suggestions?"

"You're right. We have to plan an escape," said Lucas. "Or at least keep occupied."

Ellen twirled a lock of hair. "We can't get organized when everything we say gets back to our captors. If we weren't targets, we wouldn't be under guard and key."

Lucas said, "They may not have the balls to knock us off in cold blood, but it'd be easy to target us with smart bombs."

"You're right. But please lay off the quotes," said Mack.

"The last one sucked big time. Everyone's upset about dying, but no one's upset at being born. Though I'd like to have been born later. Much later, to see what's going to happen in our squirrely future."

"That's not what the quote means," said Reg. "But it isn't important."

"It is important," said Lucas. "It means we shouldn't worry about getting killed. It fits war pretty good."

Reg groaned. "You fellas give me a headache. What else should we know about the Ermies, Lucas?"

"I don't know. The Ermies might be spearheading the war."

"So, stop them," said Mack. "Is it because I never tried Badsr's bizarre scheme to romance the unromancable? If I would have taken the time to listen, would that have helped?"

"Heavens no. Btsht told you how dumb we are and how smart they are. The Ermies also think we're a bunch of dolts. Badsr was baiting you. The idea you could dazzle the Goldies by romancing Ellen is ridiculous. Guess they proved their point."

Mack frowned. "There's something funny about that quote, that it's just as good not to be born."

"Lord, Mack. How did you get that out of the quote?" said Reg.

"Forget it. I didn't say something that crazy. But for ninety-nine-point ninety-nine percent of us, maybe for all of us, it makes no difference we ever lived. We're born, live, die, done. Unless religion means something. Otherwise we just pass on our genes. And I'm not thrilled the way my genes passed on. Maybe sullen thirteen-year-olds will eventually grow up. I don't have my hopes up."

Ellen wailed, "Stop it! You've no conception of proper religion. Your values are nonexistent and your morals hopelessly skewed. You can't concentrate long enough to get us out of here or keep us from getting killed. Can't you do anything right?"

"Got an even better quote," said Lucas. "Might have been forwarded by email. 'If a man speaks in the forest and no women is present, is he still wrong'?"

"My god." Mack gasped. "That's the funniest thing I ever heard. A quote I can relate to."

"You're sick," said Ellen. "And you make me sicker."

"I disagree," said Reg. "Not with you, my dear Ellen, but with Mack's conclusion that it's the same whether we live or not. The majority have wonderful satisfactions, children, and

143

most of all, souls. Without being born, there'd be no chance at spirituality."

"Ah, yes," said Mack. "Immortality, whether based on soulfulness or progeny. As for satisfactions, they may be gone when we cash our tickets for the big lottery in the sky. Nothing else has been reported back on. You've bought into my tangent, Reg, or let's blame Lucas. I usually do."

"That's a weird way of looking at things," said Lucas. "Life by itself is enough, though I never refuse communion. What the heck, free grub."

Ellen said, "I will scream. Blasphemy is sickening."

"Hey, Mr. Dude," piped up Peter. "Why are you ignoring me? Are you too ashamed? Tell the nice folks what you did to me? They'd be interested."

"Stand up, Peter," said Mack.

Peter looked at Mack suspiciously as the rest stared. Even Judge Grdam turned around. Peter rose slowly. "Okay. Now what, Mr. Dude?"

"Turn around." As Peter just stood there, Mack said, "Not so fast that I miss it. Do it slower."

Peter grimaced as he did a clumsy pivot.

"That was a little slower than I'd hoped for. But it served its purpose. Where's the famous cartwheel and fun-loving party animal we've come to love and adore?"

"You betrayed me."

"How so? I watched you full circle and saw no scars. Did you have a miserable time with the Goldie computer programmers? Or did they feed you beer? There may not have been dancing girls but you look good, Pete. Do you feel okay? Besides being pissed off at me for trying to find a way out of here, seeing if you had a talent that might help? Sorry you didn't. But I admire your flair for keeping us entertained and our minds off the morbid. I'm glad you're back, fit and healthy."

Peter bowed his head as if to say, "ah, shucks, Pa," as the monstrous doors swept open. Peter raised his arms for a mighty cartwheel as Btsht and the other Big Guys marched in, followed by Madison, Roy, and a dozen Goldie high priests. The religious potentates wore golden lace around golden necks, golden tassels on wrists and waists, flat golden hats and flaring golden pantaloons. Their golden capes stuck straight out behind like they were flying. They chanted, "Spiffle, spaffle, wiffle, waffle," in perfect lockstep like cherub reindeer. Each wore a miniature replica of the golden antelope statue around his neck, which bounced as they sashayed in. They halted in disarray, falling in a clump as Peter careened into them at the end of a perfect cartwheel.

Peter bowed. "Welcome to my humble hangar des planes," with a French or Spanish accent. Hard to tell which.

Mack ignored the Big Guys, rushing to meet Roy and Madison. "Where have you been? We were worried."

"Boy howdy, man—" started Roy before he was interrupted by Btsht.

"Protocol, Mr. Mack. You may attend your compatriots later. First welcome the Goldie Big Guys on behalf of your species. We rather like the term and are thinking of making 'Big Guys' our official title."

"Well, you are hot dogs. But I must be diplomatic, even to those who call us scum to our faces. Welcome, Big Guys. We appreciate the use of your most secure bomb shelter. And your unflinching determination to keep us from harm. Especially since you'd rather see us boil in oil." Mack curtsied. "Welcome, welcome."

The first Big Guy curtsied back. "Thank you for your reception. We need the full names and social security numbers of your compatriots. Those wrongly sent to the Ermies and Ivies."

"Sorry. No can do."

The first Big Guy extended his long arms toward Mack's neck, but Btsht diverted the Big Guy's paws a split second before they would have crushed Mack's throat.

"He's playing word games," said Btsht. "What's on your mind, Mr. Mack? From experience, I assume it's small and of little consequence."

"I'm not helping program smart bombs against my fellow humans."

"But you're not being consistent. I have the transcript right here." Btsht pointed to his broad forehead. "You just said

145

it made no difference how long humans live or whether they live at all. That ninety-nine-point ninety-nine percent, or perhaps all of you don't amount to a hill of beans. Put your philosophy to work. Give us the full names and social security numbers of your dear dumb fellows."

"We were discussing our status before birth. And the natural shortness of life. Not bloody murder. Besides, philosophy is a word game, nothing to do with betraying my friends. You know their names. The transcripts are in that beady little brain."

"Beady perhaps. Little never. But I was being polite. Asking before turning the screws. We'll pick whichever one of you best fits the quisling profile, then put the question in a slightly threatening manner. It won't be difficult to get the information we need. But in the meantime, everyone upstairs. Big pre-war service."

"We'd love to hear why more than a tiny number of Goldie lives have significance. Lead on, MacDuff."

"We achieve immortality," snapped Btsht. "Sorry you'll miss out on that. These," Btsht indicated the gold-attired Goldies, "are the messengers of God. You met the big religious guy. He's anxious to see you again, and is especially interested in meeting dear Courtney."

"We talked about that and you're an agnostic. I have the transcript right here." Mack tapped his forehead. "You said, 'Where do you think I'd be if I said what I think?' Hmmm, you didn't exactly tie it down—"

"Words are slippery things. We proceed upstairs."

Judge Guard Grdam bellowed, "About face." The entourage, excluding Madison and Roy, pivoted as one. "Harch." They marched out the huge doors with Legionnaires falling in behind.

Lucas chirped, "What's going on?"

"Madison and Roy are back and it looks like we're headed to the cathedral to cheer the troops to war. And you?"

Roy sidled over to Mack. "Madison made a hit with his poetry. All them antelopes crowded around wanting to know what we thought of their tepui and how it compared with where we came from. But then it went steep downhill," the last accompanied by the usual hand gesture. Madison peered over Roy's shoulder, his fat pink face beaming.

At which Lucas completed a sentence in progress, "—biggest dang thing. Now we're seated under the whatchamacallit. Lord, who'd know what to call that? The female Ermies—and yeah, you can tell them apart—are covered up head to toe. They love the black stuff. Filmy and sheer, which makes every movement a mystery in motion. I'm glad I'm not an Ermie male because these babes are devastating. Not that they're attractive to humans any more than a sheep might be to a Kiwi. But these chicks are sensuous like a toboggan swooping through the middle of your head. Reckon you get the idea, mate. Oops. Now they're doing prayers, a unison kind of thing. First the big preacher guy does a bit. You know, the whiffle, piffle, snarf thing, and then the whole big bowl of Ermies do the exact same thing. You can probably hear the part where the whole bunch joins in. Kind of like very loud."

Indeed, Mack could, but he couldn't get a word in.

"Then the big religious guy—"

Mack insisted on a word in. "How is the guy dressed? Anything special like the Goldies?"

"Nah. More like Nehru jackets, though not as ugly. Black, of course, pants cuffed and creased. Reminds me of the pants I had to buy for marching band, which weren't as bad 'cause they had a shiny black stripe down the side."

"Lucas. I'd prefer quotes to this kind of blather."

"I thought the religious aspects of the antelope experience interested you. But thankee for warming to the quotes."

"As for the religious part, you've mixed me up with Ellen or Courtney. The second part confirms why your eyes are brown."

"Reg here, your clownships. Sorry. That slipped out. The Ivies are also having religious services. Do you still doubt that war is imminent, Mack?"

"I'm undecided, but I *know* you know humans always do the same thing before our wars. The president attends church with his Cabinet, ad nauseum. So, what's going on with the Ivies, Reg?"

147

"I knew you were being flip, pretending disinterest in religion," Reg said dryly. "Religion is us. Society. The fabric of everything. I *know* you know that. The Ivies dress up like a social occasion. They pray in a one direction with a prayer book, which they read and bob, recite and bow. We're in a fancy white church with astounding special effects."

Mack said, "Goldies the same. Btsht took me into a Goldie church I swore was designed by Spielberg. Big blocks of crystal floated in the air and they're doing it again. Three dimensional voices and lights, music bouncing off the rafters, if they had rafters."

"Well, hey mate. Talk about blather. The Ivies clicked in a translation for us and it's a kick. Maybe a kick in the teeth. Whoa. These are one belligerent bunch of antelopes. I had no idea."

"Christ on a crutch, Lucas. Quit horsing around and tell us what they're saying. Hey, the Goldies kicked in with a translation and I understand."

"Same thing with the Ivies," said Reg. "Just started here too. Vicious bastards. I thought we had hate going on between races, ethnic groups, religions, however you want to break it down. But these guys take the big enchilada."

Mack shook his head hopelessly. "The war will be a doozy. The Goldies say the Ivies have three gods. You won't believe it. A Mother, Daughter, and Holy Dirigible. Led by the bishop or pope guy who kamikazed the miniature golden statue. Did it right in front of me and the Big Guy. He showed us why Courtney's species is the scum of the earth."

Lucas said, "'It does me no injury for my neighbor to say there are twenty gods, or no God. It neither picks my pocket nor breaks my leg.' Don't tell me this one doesn't fit. Blahhhh." They pictured Lucas blowing a raspberry.

"Doesn't fit." Mack voice dripped with mock disappointment. "You missed the whole point. The Mother, Daughter, and Holy Dirigible aren't three separate gods. They're one god."

Lucas yelled back. "*You* missed the whole point. This isn't the Christian religion. We don't know whether they're three gods or one god, or maybe a god and a half. And funny, if you could see the skit for the Holy Dirigible."

"Some of our millionaires wouldn't think it was funny."

"Sorry, Mack, but it's hilarious. There's a Casper kind of ghost shaped like a dirigible and the special effects are incredible. The Holy Dirigible is flitting around the pulpit and the Ermie Legionnaires are taking pot shots, lined up like a firing squad. Wow. They pulverized it. There are shreds of Holy Dirigible floating around the big cathedral like a fractured pinata. It spewed bonbons when they shot it down. Gobbled up by the nasty little juveniles."

"Are you sure that's a church, what with the gunfire and candy? But then, you should see it over here. I'll bet Reg has the same kind of thing going on."

Reg said, "I'm dizzy, off balance the way things are going. The Ivie and Ermie skits are similar. The Ivies are less violent, more lackadaisical. Same Holy Dirigible but an Ivie in a fancy uniform marched over to a small white log, did some hocus pocus, and the log did the rest. It swiveled and destroyed the Holy Dirigible, a huge mustard-colored balloon. And it happened in slow motion, blowing it out the top of the Ivie Cathedral. The balloon exploded in a cascade of fireworks. If I had special effects like that in my humble parish attendance would—balloon."

"But why a Mother, Daughter, and Holy Dirigible? The Goldie god statue was convincingly male."

"Badsr told me about it," said Lucas. "It's complicated. The golden male statue is Radnicharra, the main Goldie god. He sacrificed his life for the Mother, Daughter, and Holy Dirigible. As a result, the Goldies will live forever. Crazy, eh?"

Mack said, "I'm starting to think all religions look crazy unless you're part of the particular one."

"Wow. You might see the light."

"I really don't know. The Goldies are clobbering weird beings I've never heard of. I assume they're Ermie and Ivie deities."

"What are the Goldies doing?"

"A two-ring circus. I assume the Ivie god in one ring and the Ermie god in the other. The Ivies and Ermies seem to have one official god and lots of prophets. The Ermie god is a superman type, huge, black, spouting fire, smelling of fire and brimstone. Plumes of smoke spiral out of his tiny antelope ears and explode into bonfires. Too bad they've perfected smell-o-vision. And the Goldies are kicking butt."

Mack could hear Ellen sniffling behind him. "Sorry, Ellen, didn't mean to say 'butt.' However, Btsht personally booted the black superman through the ceiling. The Ermie god spiraled out of control, black air gushing. It shrank and disappeared above the Cathedral roof. Which I don't understand since we're underground. The massacre of the Ivie god was mysterious because he's apparently invisible, which required very creative choreography. You can't say the name out loud and images are prohibited. The Goldies had a field day poking fun at that. Then the invisible god melted like the wicked witch of the west. They sliced and diced bearded prophets of both gods. Don't get in arguments with these guys."

"Only one of us argues with antelopes. But here's the perfect quote: 'Religion is the daughter of hope and fear, explaining to ignorance the nature of the unknowable.' Admit it, Mack. It's perfect."

"Isn't even close."

"Didn't you notice the daughter part of the quote?"

"It may be unknowable but— Hey, Courtney has disappeared, again."

"Again? You should keep better track of your people."

"Right. And I assume you know where Billy K. is—"

"Billy K. is in front, watching the fireworks. I can see him from here."

"Yeah?" Mack sounded incredulous. "And where's Ef? Did he get back from first aid?"

"He's been back for ages. And Benny is getting along with James because James rode a horse once. Benny is looking the worse for wear. His fancy outfit took a beating after an incident I'll skip. You'd better find Courtney."

"All my people are present and accounted for," said Reg. "We ended up with a pretty good group. Even Rudd mellowed after I found out he was a fallen-away Catholic. I told him that made no difference and welcomed him back to the mother church, if he ever wants to come."

"You've got a heart as big as all outdoors."

"I like to think so. The Ivie show has taken a twist, reenacting Courtney's attack on the Goldie statue. The Goldies aren't going to like this."

"They didn't the first time around. Hope it doesn't cause a war. I'm off to find Courtney." Mack gulped. "Never mind. She's the star. The Goldies yoked her like an ox, in stocks next to the Goldie Cardinal. You should see his hat."

"Forget the hat. What about Courtney?" said Lucas.

"For the folks in Ermie and Ivie land, Courtney's the beneficiary of the Cardinal's whittling abilities. Same thing he did to me, except it's personal for the Cardinal. He carved golden shavings all over Courtney's poor gray head. The crowd is eating it up. I'll have to jump down and save her, like I always do."

"You're a numskull," said Ellen.

"And I love you too." Mack skipped down the stairs as Peter and Roy waved. Barry said, "Good luck. You'll need it." At which Mack missed a step, flying to the ground floor like a snowball in an avalanche. He landed at Courtney's knees. Her face glowed like the golden slivers decorating her head.

"Howdy do, Mr. Mack. I've gained a golden crown for Jesus."

Mack was bruised and out of breath. Btsht bent over him, swearing as only an antelope can. "Fartle, snapple, bibridofry mescalinaroid." Btsht belatedly twisted his knob. "Ignoramus, moron, interrupting an important religious ceremony. You're a lout, second only to Courtney."

Mack blinked at Btsht's huge nose. "Did you say all that the first time, before you turned on the translator? That's most impressive."

"Get up before I have you thrown in the dungeon."

"You need a new line. Something more creative than an empty threat. Put me on the rack, or a bed of spikes. Or one of those things that pulls off arms and legs, or is that a rack?"

Btsht snarled. "And what do you think the dungeon is all about? A spa with king-size beds? Not only will we entertain

151

you with a rack and spikes but we're terrifically talented with electricity. And we have maggots that crawl up your nose and burrow into pea-sized brains. Get off the stage."

Mack groaned as he stood up. He dusted off his Arizona Lottery uniform while looking for his missing hat. "I came down here for a reason and you can guess what it is." He ambled toward his missing hat at the feet of the Cardinal.

The Cardinal roared at the top of his considerable lungs, "Get this goddamn alien out of our sacred house of worship. We need to get on with the war. How dare you dishonor the house of God?"

"Which god are you referring to? I get them mixed up. I thought you had a Mother, Daughter, and Holy Dirigible. But the only one I ever see is the naked antelope with teeny antlers and dangling dick." Btsht yanked Mack back from the Cardinal's slashing pig sticker.

"Whew." Mack dodged again. "Thanks, Btsht. I owe you."

"Indeed, you do. Now begone."

"Begone, my ass," roared the Cardinal. "This alien is guilty of direst heresy. We must put him on trial, the same as the witch who kneels before me."

Courtney snorted and the stocks quaked. "I am not a witch. I am a saved Baptist woman. Wash your mouth out with lye."

Mack said, "You have to shut up so I can work my magic."

"Ah," said Btsht. "So, you want to spring Courtney. If you take her place, that can be arranged."

"Okay, buster. I'm through with foolish games—"

"It's about time."

"I hereby declare diplomatic immunity for the humans on these godforsaken tepuis."

"You what? Don't you think it's a little late? On what grounds do you claim diplomatic immunity? As if we'd recognize it for an alien species?"

"I am the duly appointed leader of this delegation of humans from the United States of America. A sovereign country that even antelopes recognize."

152

"I'll take that under advisement. What about the others? I suppose they're diplomats too."

"No, but they're all millionaires, which is close enough. Well, except Lucas, who is the leader of the Aussies in our group."

"You don't have other Aussies in your group. He claims to be an American, the same as you."

"Give him a break. We're all entitled to diplomatic immunity. Whether based on leadership or being too rich to kick around."

The Cardinal howled. "That's asinine. Being rich doesn't shield a heretic. We won't hesitate to destroy rich Ermies and Ivies in the upcoming war. And the fight against heretics is the most important war of all. Fry 'em." The Cardinal's golden togs had turned green from copious sweat, from the lime ring around his cardinal hat to the chartreuse tassels.

"I thought you boiled 'em."

"We boil 'em in oil, which is the same as frying. Now get out."

"Do you feel okay.?"

The Cardinal leveled his pig sticker at Mack's navel. "Never felt better."

Mack sidestepped the lunge only because the Cardinal telegraphed it. As the Cardinal went tripping by, Mack said, "You don't look well. You're green around the gills and a lot of green around the tassels."

Btsht yelled, "Time out. The Cardinal is right. The trial must be reconvened. The Cardinal will proceed to benediction. Then we will regroup in the courtroom of good Judge Grdam."

"That's no way to treat an old lady, even one accused of heresy." Mack strode over to Courtney. "How're you doing, doll? We'll have you out of there in no time." That was the last thing Mack remembered before his lights went out.

9

Mack woke in a sitting position with his hat on and his suit brushed to perfection. But he had a throbbing headache and when he tried to raise a hand, his wrists clanked with chains of blue and gold. Peter, Madison, Roy, Ellen, and Barry sat ten feet away, staring at him. Courtney slumped in matching chains at the base of the wooden podium occupied by the Honorable Judge Grdam. Next to them sat the famous prosecutors, Jose Mutt and Jeff. Unruly Goldies packed the courtroom, and gaudily dressed Legionnaires surrounded the Big Guys.

Though he was afraid he knew the answer, Mack asked, "What's going on?"

Lucas's voice from the lapel mic said, "The jury reconvened. Rallies have been suspended and we're back as jurors."

"What about the war?"

"Reg here. Same for the war. Temporarily postponed."

"So, I did good. I mean, getting the war postponed. Pretty pretty good."

"That's one way of looking at it," said Lucas. "Of course, you're on trial for your life, along with Courtney."

"Yeah," said Rudd. "We're real concerned about losing your leadership qualities."

"Now, Rudd. Don't forget about hanging together or singly," said Reg.

"I don't have a smart mouth when it comes to religion," said Rudd. "Some things should remain sacred."

"Upchuck city," said Mack. "You getting me mixed up with Lucas."

Lucas said, "We heard that. The antelopes already have the transcript."

"Right. I did keep telling you that. Thanks for the reminder. Intemperate remarks might complicate my defense, or Courtney's."

"Who? You?" said Rudd.

"Reg. Could you—?"

"No problem. Back in your seat, Rudd. Please. Order is restored. Have you come up with a defense?"

"Defense? I don't know what I said wrong. I have a migraine explosion every couple of seconds."

"You don't understand the gravity of the situation," said Reg.

"Why is everyone so worried? Courtney's had her head on the block for ages and no one's worried about her."

"We're worried about both of you," said Reg. "Don't you recall a negative comment about the Goldie god's intimate parts?"

"I shouldn't have said 'dangling'?"

"You shouldn't have said 'dick' either," said Lucas. "But I have the perfect quote."

"No," groaned Mack.

"Yes. 'Laws are like spiders' webs, and will like them only entangle and hold the poor and weak, while the rich and powerful easily break through them.' Told you it was perfect."

"I feel particularly poor and weak. Not like seventeen rich and powerful millionaires I could name. Go ahead, Reg. I'm listening, to you."

"I don't have a sparkling defense but we heard the clunk on your head like ringing a bell. You're lucky your head wasn't split in two."

"I don't feel so lucky. Guess I'll play it by ear."

"As usual," said Lucas.

Judge Grdam entered the courtroom and peered down at Mack. "Finally, you've found your proper place in this court, as a presumed guilty defendant. May your soul rest in peace."

"Oh, gee thanks, Your Honorable judgeship. Do you really need a kangaroo trial before you pass sentence?"

155

"I am happy that I don't have to decide the appropriate punishment for your many occasions of contempt."

"Takes a load off my mind, too, Your Honor. May I hear the charges, against both myself and Courtney?"

"You've already heard the charges against Courtney. She's only here for sentencing. The charges against you are high heresy tantamount to treason. The prosecutor will detail these, if he has time."

"But Your Honor, Courtney's trial wasn't finished. The rest of the jurors didn't have an opportunity to testify."

"That's not necessary. I am ready to sentence her."

"Let me guess what it is."

"Don't bother." The judge slammed down his gavel. "Guilty as charged. Death by boiling oil. But Goldie compassion allows the defendant to submerge before heating, like a frog."

"I don't see how the defendant can thank you enough—" Mack gaped as the judge tipped a gallon of oil over Courtney's head.

Courtney raised her eyes to the heavens, her face glistening like a wet seal. "Thank you, Lord, for the opportunity to serve you better." She clasped her hands in ecstasy.

Mack whispered to Courtney, "I take it the oil wasn't boiling."

"Oh, back off," she whispered back.

"I'm glad it wasn't boiling. We'll use every means at our disposal to make certain you never boil in oil."

"You have no means at your disposal. Besides, I'm happy to be a martyr for God."

"Order in the court. No more whispering," commanded the judge. "And now for you, Mr. Smarty Pants. You may proceed, Mr. Prosecutor."

"Thank you, Your Honor." Jose Mutt rose.

"So, you're back in the good graces of the court," said Mack. "Grand to see you again. I'm ready to hear the baseless charges."

"It appears that none of the charges are baseless. I have a transcript of your remarks to the Pope."

"Cripes. The Pope has more promotions than a cut-rate carpet shop. If you don't watch it, he'll be God pretty soon."

Mutt Jose swiveled and ordered Jeff, "Another charge of heresy."

"Righto, chief," said Jeff.

"Strike that," said Mack. "I take it back. Unring the bell. Let's forget the last impropriety and give me a rundown on the charges."

"You want to cop a plea?"

"Like what?"

"Plead guilty to one charge and we'll dismiss the others."

"Which charge would I plead guilty to and what's the penalty?"

"Plead guilty to whichever charge you like. The penalty is the same."

"Right. Death by boiling oil. Guess I'll pass. Give me a hint what the charges are. Maybe start with how many."

"Fourteen."

"Only fourteen. What are you, a slacker?" At the dull stare Mack added, "So, give me the jist of the charges."

"Think back. I'm certain you remember the creative language you used to describe the Goldie God."

"I take that back too."

"Too late. You said he had teeny antlers and, though I hesitate to repeat it, a dangling dick."

"You didn't hesitate long. I didn't mean anything by teeny, or dangling either, for that matter."

"Are you uncomfortable with a god that has sex organs?"

"Why does a god need sex organs when he's invisible? Oops. Double sorry. I was thinking about our narrow-minded Western religions. I didn't mean to repeat thoughtless heresy of matriarchal religions."

"You simply don't think, Mr. Mack."

"Is that heresy?"

"It leads to heresy, unavoidably in your case. Then there's the teeny antlers thing."

"I must admit, Mr. Mutt, er Jose, I don't know why that constitutes heresy, not that I understand any of this."

Lucas whispered, "You'll like this. 'If you give me six sentences written by the most innocent of men, I will find something in them with which to hang him.'"

"Shut the fuck up."

Jose Mutt said, "The inference of teeny is undersized. To undersize a god is inherent heresy. Surely you can understand a concept that simple?"

"Again, I wasn't thinking. But minor slips of the tongue shouldn't merit the death penalty, particularly by boiling oil. Don't you guys ever do leniency?"

"You'll never learn, will you, Mr. Mack?"

"I imagine I will, when my skin sluffs off in burbling oil."

"I'm sure that's what it'll take. But you're right. These are relatively unimportant charges of heresy."

"Then let's skip the death penalty for those. Make me sit around with Courtney for a few hours. That should be punishment enough."

"Ah, bottomless empathy for your fellow human beings. I'd hate to see how you'd treat another species."

"Look in the mirror and see how you're doing. I couldn't improve on your technique."

Jose Mutt continued as if not interrupted. "Of course, conviction of heresy, whether weighty or not, carries the death penalty. We are sufficiently civilized to have the same First Commandment that you do."

"What are you talking about?"

"Thou shalt not have other Gods before our God. We don't tolerate that sort of thing either."

"Hey, I wasn't putting any gods in front of your shiny god. Or making out that some are better than others. Heaven forbid. But then, I'm not real religious."

"You certainly aren't. Otherwise you wouldn't have committed the biggest heresy of them all. I hate to repeat it and do so only for the sake of justice. To make certain you understand the seriousness of the charges against you."

"I'm afraid to contemplate the horrendous act I committed. Unknowingly, of course, which should lower the penalty far below that of a capital offense."

"Ignorance of the law is no defense."

Lucas inserted, "I was just about to quote that."

Mack said to Jose Mutt, "The men in blue from the United States Air Force are going to kick your butt."

"See me quake. We've removed every trace of your presence."

"Except our physical bodies. You seem equally bent on eradicating those too."

"Are you ready?"

"I'm not ready to be eradicated."

"You called our gods the Mother, Daughter, and Holy Dirigible. That is heresy per se."

"Which part? I was told that's the names of your gods."

Mutt smirked. "Told by whom?"

Mack thought a second. "I've been entrapped. That's what the Ivies called them. Or maybe the Ermies."

"Right. When they burned effigies of our Gods. Was that when you heard the term?"

"When they shot down the Holy Dirigible."

"The Holy Dirigible is the Ivies' idea of a semantic joke. The words for dirigible and spirit are cognates in the Ivie language. Shooting down the Holy Dirigible to them, means shooting down the Holy Spirit. You defamed the Holy Spirit the same as the nasty inferior Ivies. And you defamed the notion of female gods and implied that our gods might be incestuous. Naturally, you must pay the ultimate price."

"Your actions lie outside the realm of civilized behavior."

"I'll not debate such a broad topic but it's clearly within the realm of normal human behavior."

"We may have a few fundamentalists but they're not mainstream humans."

"You mean entire countries fail to represent the mainstream of their citizens? How about Afghanistan, Indonesia, India, and Pakistan? Buddhists in Myanmar and Sri Lanka slaughtering Muslims? Greeks and Turks, France and

Algerians? The innumerable conflicts that slaughter your kind in the name of religion mixed with nationalism. And you call religion the fountainhead of ethics? Don't make me laugh."

"Hey. Do you see me laughing? No laughter from this kid. In fact, I said the same thing, not too long ago. You should cut me some slack since we're on the same wave length. Maybe the religions are at fault. Far be it for me to blame myself."

Mutt's gaze didn't soften.

"Well, how about I resign from the species and you grant me clemency on that basis?"

"You're grasping at straws."

"You're absolutely right. At this point I'd even accept a quote from Lucas, assuming it'd deliver me from befuddlement."

"Got it. Yep. Lucas to the rescue. Dun tiddledy dun tiddledy dun tiddledy dun," a tune resembling *The William Tell Overture.*

"I take it back."

"Too late. Ahem. Now listen up, Mr. J. Mutt. 'Manners are of more importance than laws. Upon them, in a good measure, the laws depend. The law touches us here and there, and now and then. Manners are what vex or smooth, corrupt or purify, exalt or debase, barbarize or refine us, by a constant, steady, uniform, insensible operation, like that of the air we breathe in. They give us their whole form and color to our lives. According to their quality, they add morals, they support them, or they totally destroy them.' Ta da. What do you think of them apples? Awesome, eh?"

"Not," said Jose Mutt.

"*Au contraire.* The Aussie got it right," said Mack. "Congratulations, Lucas. Charges dismissed."

"Playing games doesn't change the law," said Jose Mutt. "Especially religious law. Religion is unrelated to manners. Don't be silly."

"Wrong. You've displayed abominable manners to poor ignorant aliens unfamiliar with your religion. You treat us like KFC."

"You ain't fried yet, so count your blessings. Otherwise I'm a deaf ear."

Mack looked up at Judge Grdam, prepared to launch an objection. But the judge was asleep. "Deaf ear from the judge too." Mack elevated a single finger in the air and roared, "I object."

The judge started banging the gavel, then stopped. "You object to what?"

"I object to you going to sleep. You're supposed to give me a fair trial before acquittal."

"Don't give it a thought." The judge melted into a more comfortable position.

Mack looked Mutt in the eye. "I remember what you said in an off moment, during an earlier trial."

"I'm surprised you remember anything that far back."

"You said you'd grant clemency to anyone who—let me get this right—who acknowledged the Goldie god as the key to eternal life."

At Mutt's shocked reaction Mack added hastily, "Only for Goldies, of course. I'm sure we couldn't be saved by a god not in our own spitting image."

Lucas piped up so loudly that it ricocheted around the courtroom. "'You will eat bye and bye. In the glorious land above the sky; Work and pray, Live on hay, You'll get pie in the sky, When you die.'"

There was stunned silence.

Lucas continued, "That could be sung to the tune of 'Onward Christian Soldiers.' Oops, I turned up the volume when I shouldn't have."

"Boy, you've got that right," said a voice in the background, which Mack recognized as Nick's. "We're tolerant as a rule but tolerance can be stretched to the breaking point. Poor Mary is upset—"

Mack interrupted. "Oh, Lucas, my boy, no. You've blown the only defense I can come up with."

"Don't give it another thought," said Mutt soothingly. "It wouldn't have worked anyway. Only Goldies can believe that the Goldie God grants eternal life. For humans that would be the height of hypocrisy. Even the noble and Honorable Judge Grdam wouldn't accept that."

Clapping broke out behind them, causing Mack and Mutt to turn as one. The Big Guys were on their feet, pounding the bejesus out of horny palms.

Mack bowed as long as the Big Guys clapped, straightening when they stopped. "Does that mean you're granting clemency?"

Btsht said, "No one would believe you no matter what you said. So, conceding the immortality-granting powers of the Goldie God isn't enough. Good job, Mr. Prosecutor. Sorry, Mack. But you'd have to denounce your own gods. I don't suppose you're ready to do that."

Before the words were out of his mouth, Peter and Roy chimed, "Yessa, yessa, massah. We denounce."

Mack said, "I didn't know human gods scared you so much that you needed them denounced. But we could do that. Denounce, denounce, denounce."

"Sincerity, Mack. We need sincerity." Btsht suppressed a smile.

"Based on the events on this tepui, I'm utterly sincere."

"Well, yes. You do seem to be transitioning to heathen. So, you don't have much to denounce. Again Mack, you've come up empty."

"But I'm not a heathen. You're getting me mixed up with Lucas. I'm not particularly religious but I'm not anti-religious, though recent events have made me think about that."

"Reg here, Mack. Many of us disagree. But no offense Mack, if you've taken the heathen label to heart."

"I'm not the heathen sort. Lucas's the heathen."

"The pie in the sky thing," said Reg. "That was terribly impolite."

"That was Lucas and his uncontrollable quotes."

"I will not allow heresy," said the judge. "Religion cannot be denigrated in public. Those who do so, deserve death."

Courtney rose from her stupor with a vengeance, standing tall though bedraggled, clanging blue and yellow chains. She knocked Mack behind her as she pushed her ample body to the fore. "Pie in the sky my eye. You're talking about God the savior and salvation here. You are the ones," she said

162

pointing, "who should be boiled in oil. You should be burned at the stake, dismembered, and your putrid bones thrown to the crows. Amen. Amen." Her head slumped forward as nervous rustling began in the courtroom.

Ellen rose from her spot on the jury. "I've remained silent in the face of obscene provocation. But I rise to defend the honor of the creator of the universe. The one true God, who you spit upon. No matter the consequences I object to the scurrilous quote Mr. Lucas inflicted on this court. He's impugned the sensibility of religious folk everywhere, whether humans or Goldies. God rest our collective species of souls." She blushed. "Thank you," and sat down.

"Okay," said Lucas "I stand reprimanded. Ahem. 'Men have contempt for religion and fear that it is true.' I hope that fixes things. I apologize for the boo-boo. Sorry."

"Holy darn," said Peter. "You don't have to be sorry. There's such a thing as free speech. We may not believe exactly the same but we don't have to. Besides, religion is a pretty boring stuff. Geez." Peter looked around, "I hope I didn't insult anyone."

Mack said, "We promise to reform. We'll ignore the threat to our physical bodies and the souls some suspect we may not actually have. You've done a good job of confirming Lucas's heathenism. But you can't call religion boring when your butt is on the line."

"I promise to reform before everything really goes downhill," said Roy. His hand thrust dropped like a Bach fugue.

"Your Honor." Mutt bowed, smiling. "I've made neither motion nor objection, confident the humans would hang themselves. Their confessions find them guilty, including those remaining silent, since silence in the face of heresy is an admission of heresy. Courtney, of course, is a dead duck. And Mr. Mack is well on his way. But the silence of Mr. Barry and Mr. Madison, and Ms. Ellen's statement that only her god exists, support a conclusive finding of heresy. *Ergo hoc, ergo sum.*"

Judge Grdam peered over the high podium. "Be that as it may, do you wish to call further witnesses, Mr. Prosecutor?"

"May I address the court, Your Honor?" came a nervous voice from Mack's lapel mic. "Er, Mr. Lucas speaking."

"Huh," said the judge.

"When rendering a verdict at the end of this fiasco the court should consider: 'Be careful; with quotations you can damn anything.' Thank you, Your Honor."

The judge fired back, "You've done your part damning yourself and your fellow humans. But you're a day late and a bolivar short with that pathetic effort at atonement. No more interruptions in this courtroom and that goes for you, too, Mr. Prosecutor. Proceed at once."

"Then, Your Honor, I move to add Mr. Barry, Mr. Madison, and Ms. Ellen as defendants."

The judge said, "Sure. But hurry up."

"I hereby charge Ms. Ellen with heresy in the first degree. Heresy in the second degree for Mr. Madison and Mr. Barry. How do you plead?"

Everyone turned to behold the new defendants, already fitted with blue and yellow chains. Mack stood, gesturing wildly. "I object, Your Honor. This is not due process."

"You receive the process which is due. If you have a beef, take it up with the prosecutor. He preferred the charges, which I consider luscious. To preserve my unbiased appearance, I hereby strike that last bit. You may proceed, Mr. Prosecutor, at once!"

Mack said, "Too late, your judgeship. Besides, I have two more objections. Ms. Ellen is a pure as the driven snow and about as chilly. She doesn't have an ounce of heresy in that rather fabulous body. She may have religious biases, but we all have those. So, you should let her off the hook."

The judge leaned over. "Very interesting, Mr. Mack. I aimed my subatomic lust detector at you, and guess what?"

Mack blushed.

"Yes, you know what I'm about to say. I'd never have thought that you, an imminent leader of humans, would be smitten by a female with whom you have nothing in common. What a moron."

"I protest."

"Too much," said the judge.

Ellen sprang up like a weed, chains clanking and clunking, trying to raise her hand.

"Yes, m'dear," said the judge. "Do you need to use the facilities? Or do you wish to *respond*," he chortled, "to your less than secret admirer?"

"We hate each other." Ellen seethed.

"You've seen Hollywood movies," said the judge. "That's the way they all start. But by the last frame there's a little one on the way." He held up a horny paw as Ellen opened her mouth. "No need, ma'am. I think Mr. Mack has a point. Motion granted. The charges against Ms. Ellen are dismissed. She only said there's one god. It is possible that all gods are one, from the Egyptian gods to the penultimate Goldie God. Thus, when it comes to religion, Ms. Ellen may be the fairest of them all. Rather like Mr. Mack thinks she is in another context. Ha, ha, har," leading one to think the judge had his own stash of porn. "Get the chains off the female and reinstall her in the jury box, now."

"But Your Honor—" began Jose Mutt as a Legionnaire scurried to carry out the order.

"Stow it. As for the other new defendants, what's the rationale? Other than the tenuous one you've timidly tendered? I grant leave to conduct *voir dire*."

"Mighty golden of you, Your Honor. But since I'm preferring the charges, perhaps Mr. Mack would like to conduct the *voir dire*."

The judge nodded curtly and Jose Mutt said, "Go ahead, Mr. Mack."

"I don't even know what vor dire is." Mack clinked and clanked as he stood up. "But I'd be happy to ask a few questions to show you're full of beans. Thank you, Your Honor."

"Get on with it." The judge pointed the gavel at Mack like a Colt .45.

"Right. I begin with Mr. Barry, who I know wouldn't speak heresy against any god. Isn't that right, Mr. Barry?"

Barry looked sorrowful in his new chains, clanking. "I am opposed to boiling in oil. If my silence was misread, it's only because I didn't know what was going on. I don't know when I'm supposed to say something and when I'm supposed to shut up. I've tried to look after Courtney but failed miserably. Why did I go on this terrible junket? I am discomfited."

"I move to dismiss the charges against Mr. Barry. His silence had nothing to do with disrespect of the Goldie god or gods."

"Proceed with *voir dire* of Mr. Madison," the judge getting testier.

"Right. Mr. Madison. I know you're the poetical instead of heretical type. So, your silence implied no indictment against the Goldie god or gods, right?"

"Which is it, Mr. Mack? God or gods?" said the judge.

"I'm not sure. I remember the Mother, Daughter, and Holy Spirit. But the statue was Radnicharra, or maybe Famigusta. I confess confusion."

"Let's proceed by analogy." The judge pretended patience. "Your main religion has a Father, Son, and Holy Spirit. Now is that a god or gods? I'm interested on how you come out on that one."

"Still confused, though I know the tradition is for one god. I can't see how the statue god, whatever his name is, would fit that classification. The only thing I thought I knew for sure was the statue isn't the Daughter in your trilogy. The dangling dick comes to mind."

Zing. Mack staggered backward as a flash of lightning hit him between the eyes. He pried open singed eyelashes, slightly cross-eyed as a Legionnaire holstered a Swiss Army knife.

"That smarted. I take back the dang— Nevermore."

"Good move," said the judge. "You may be on death row but there's no reason to mess up your face."

"Now wait a minute, Your Honor. I'm not on death row yet. I haven't been convicted or sentenced."

"'Yet' is the operative term. Have you finished *voir dire* of Mr. Madison?"

"No. He hasn't answered the question and I forget what it was."

Madison rose smiling and raised a pudgy hand. "The Goldie gods," sweeping the hand grandly down in unconscious imitation of Roy. "These glorious gods of gushing goodness,

166

more welcome yea than food t'us." He did the tiniest of bows, "I may have to work on that, add a chorus, refrains of limpid prose, I'm the one as heaven knows. I'm a member you can see, extemporaneous poets' society. My addition the ranks to swell, poetry that rings a bell. EPS for short, and don't you snort. Try your own before you sell mine short. I've been studious, you'll report. So, render I my every cadence, words that sundry all may dance. Let yon jaws drop come what may, my every word is po-et-ic-a'ly. To your question I now turn. What to say, for that I yearn. My silence surely now you know, that just means I create too slow. The Goldie culture, who can know. May be good but this I go—" Madison stopped and said politely, "Oh my goodness, I admit, that the question I forget."

"Mr. Sub-sub-baliff, read the question back," said Mack. There was no response. Mack looked at the judge, who couldn't be seen from Mack's vantage point. He was obscured by Courtney's gentle rise and fall, accompanied by delicate snores.

Mack looked at Jose Mutt, who threw up long lanky arms. "We don't read questions back for aliens."

"Never mind." Mack turned back to Madison, whose moon-shaped face looked like a bleached pumpkin. "You were silent when the alleged heresy occurred only because you were composing a poem. There was no other reason, correct? Certainly, it was unrelated to heresy in the first, second, or third degree."

"Is that a question, can that I ask? Or am I bound to don a mask? What do you want and then I'll say, I wasn't there upon that day. Perhaps I confused a little part, if that's it, then fiddle fart. Oops." He pasted a hand over his mouth. "I slipped into Goldie, don't you see? Otherwise that's never me. Perhaps I should elaborate, or if you'd like, pontificate."

"Oh, please don't." Mack sat down, exhausted. As he slumped on the bench, his chains clanked like sleigh bells

"When the heresy occurred, then my head was like a bird. Thrilling to escape absurd, make the point and save a third. But then it swooned a merry tune and whoops, flew out just like a loon. Heresy, ne'er I see, instead to fly and do poe-a-try.'"

Madison smacked himself in the middle of the head. "Hot damn. Thank you, ma'am. For some of that I'm on the lam. Take a pic and save the cam. Surely that will make the book, oh but then I hate your look."

His face pled for understanding. "I'm in competition, sure you know, EPS to judge, best of show. Perhaps they'll say that I'm a gent who overcame predicament. Guess that means I'm on a roll, came and said and stole the show. What you say Your Honor dear, poetry you'll never fear. So, if you wish a tongue to grease, get yourself down on your knees. When I'm on a roll like this, all the world my hmmm can kiss."

"We'll serve you on a roll, deep-fried," said the judge. "I tolerate a certain amount of leeway. But not inane poetry that fails in rhythm, rhyme, and rationality. Chain time for you, Mr. Madison."

Mack jumped up clattering. "But Your Honor. He isn't charged with bad poetry. He's charged with heresy. Your Honor must admit that Mr. Madison's inimitable poetical style proves his lack of intent to commit heresy. Thus, I suggest, unchain time, Your Honor."

"You may suggest your butt off, Mr. Mack, until it sluffs off in boiling oil. Only I make suggestions, which you may interpret as orders of the court. Sit down."

Mack said, "Mr. Honorable Prosecutor Jose Mutt, sir. Could you enlighten me on why we haven't heard from our compatriots on the other tepuis? We're concerned."

Mutt rolled his eyes. "Don't let it worry your little head. We have no control over heathen others, who will remain nameless. Your friends will be back in touch when their masters allow it."

The judge said, "This faux trial has taken too much time." The Big Guys nodded vigorously. "We'll wait until the war is over to decide whether defendants Madison and Barry should be prosecuted. The war, of course, will take almost no time before the Goldies destroy the infidels. Because this delay will be insignificant, the prosecutor's motion is held in abeyance. The defendants are released in the interim."

Mack was up dancing around, waving his hands as high as he could, about shoulder height, due to the chains.

168

"Bad move, Mr. Mack. I was coming to you and your co-defendant, Courtney. Courtney, of course, has been sentenced to death. That sentence will also be delayed until the war is over. But you, Mr. Mack, are a special case. I've decided, based on advice from higher-ups, that you will be placed on display in the central Goldie square. That should entertain the populace, especially with Courtney in stocks at the same location." Wham went the gavel.

Mack swiveled to catch the expression of the Big Guys. It was obvious who'd decided what. Btsht gave Mack a thumbs up.

Mack said, "I appreciate not being tossed in boiling oil. But the alternative is like being put in a zoo. You're against that for yourselves, your Big Guy-ship, sir."

Btsht didn't flinch. "Life is better than death, especially for poor mortals like yourselves. I did you a favor and the least you could do is act like it."

Mack bowed. "Yes sir, massah, sir. Since there's an intervening war, who knows? Maybe none of us will survive. I'm not excited about being stuck in the open with smart missiles, ready for a big suppository."

"Release Mr. Mack from his chains. He's coming to the square with us. Preparations have been completed for his display, along with Courtney."

A Legionnaire shucked the chains off Barry and Madison. They followed Mack and the Big Guys out of the courtroom, along with Ellen, Peter, and Roy. The same Legionnaire toted Courtney along in a headlock, her neck twisted like a pretzel.

Mack whispered to Btsht as they walked along. "I've had a couple of excellent ideas we should discuss. The first one is how to avoid this war you seem so bent on."

"What's the other idea?"

"If you don't stop twisting Courtney's head you won't have a bread and circus execution. Take a look. The populace will be sorely disappointed if she doesn't make it to the stocks."

Btsht glanced at the Legionnaire pulling Courtney along like an ox with a broken neck. "Our fine soldiers often try for

169

extra brownie points, doing their duty with gusto. Promotions are tight right now, you know."

"I didn't know."

"Knock it off back there." When the Legionnaire failed to respond, Btsht took a vicious swipe at his knob. "Fartle, gibmetaker bobbarino."

The Legionnaire loosened his grasp on Courtney's neck but she trudged along in the same position with her eyes crossed.

"Oh, the poor dear." Mack hastened to her side, arriving at the same time as Ellen. "Please, my dear. I'll take care of Courtney."

"I'm not your dear and exactly how do you think you can help her?"

"I'll straighten her neck like this." Mack gave Courtney's neck a twist. Crack. "Oh, Courtney. I hope I didn't hurt you."

"Grack." She was more cross-eyed but less twisted.

"Compassion." Ellen placed hands on Courtney's shoulders, gently massaging bunched up muscles, cooing. "Straighten your neck when you can. No rush." She whispered three times before Courtney unbent her neck to look around. "Now try straightening up, my dear."

Mack rushed back to Btsht, who said, "What was the excellent idea you had for aborting the war? The one we've hyped ourselves up for, and deserve?"

"No doubt you deserve it. You're as cocky as a Thanksgiving turkey the day before. But no matter how much you've psyched yourselves up, wars aren't all fun and games. I mean, people can get hurt. Well, antelopes too. Even Goldies."

"Yeah, and lots of Ermies and Ivies, if I may borrow your crude vernacular."

"You may. But why are you so hot on killing the other guys?"

"Because they're scum. They're not Goldies. They're inferior beings." "Surely you don't really believe that stuff."

A familiar voice came out of his mic, "'Patriotism is the willingness to kill and be killed for trivial reasons.' And how you doing, dude? Long time no hear."

"Goddamn long time no hear, yourself. Where have you been, and have you been in touch with Reg?"

"Technical problems."

"I don't believe it."

"Good thing because the technical problem was confiscation of our lapel mics. We've missed the last hour or so of drama."

"As we've missed what's going on with you. Your hosts' names are verboten over here right now." Mack glanced at Btsht, who was in a snit. "Sorry about that, Big Guy. I realize we were about to solve the war problem and that should have priority."

"We don't particularly want the war problem, as you put it, solved. We're happy to kick inferior butt and show them who's boss, making Goldies the kingpins for all time."

"Even you don't believe that. It's not a good reason to fight a war just because you might be invaded by Globus tours. There's an old saying where I come from. *Que sera, sera.*"

"That's profound. Definitely a war stopper."

"I got it from a Fifties song."

"I am underwhelmed."

"You shouldn't be. If you have a war, you'll be found out. Firing missiles and blowing the tops off of tepuis will light up every satellite spy system on the planet. Don't be obtuse, Mr. Big Guy. Checkmate. So there."

"Are you quite finished? Yes, you are, because we've arrived."

"Wow." A huge 3D map with wiggly green lights dwarfed the impressive square. A cage sat at a corner of the stage, next to Courtney's stocks. The cage said "Mr. Mack" on a golden plate with grandiose scribbles. Courtney's name was carved on the stocks. "So, you agree the war is a bad idea?"

"Stop and think for a change. You're hung up on visible technology, visible weapons, visible slaughter. The weapons you saw were last used eight hundred years ago. We've made technical advances since."

"Okay. You're hot stuff. You can kill by lasers so your enemies melt like the Wicked Witch of the West, puddling on the floor."

"Slicker than that. We have the neutron bomb you could never perfect. You remember that one, right?"

"But your neighbors have made similar technological advances, inferior as they may be."

"Their inferiority is boundless."

"They will surprise you. War always does. Plus, the United States Air Force men in blue will be screeching down on this very tepui within the hour."

"I didn't see anything in your transcripts about the imminent arrival of an inferior air force. Gosh, I wonder if you might be bluffing? Feel free to consider the issue in your cage."

A Legionnaire seized Mack and stuffed him in the cage. As he strode off, Btsht said, "Let me know if there's anything you need."

"I surely will," yelled Mack at his departing back.

"Another coup for you," chirped Mack's mic.

"I admit this is a low point. So, what happened while we've been incommunicado? And why is Btsht so overconfident?"

"Reg here. Sorry if I stepped on Lucas, but there's an easy answer. They're all overconfident, though the Ivies don't really seem up for the game. It's war euphoria. Soon replaced by war exhaustion and loathing of body bags. Though this lot won't need body bags."

"Right," said Lucas. "Guard your collar mics so we don't lose communication again."

Mack said, "I'll put it in my pocket. They'll never find it there."

"Not until they read the transcript, which they're likely doing right now."

"So, what should I do? Swallow it?"

"Gadzooks, Mack. You're the leader of this fiasco. Why ask us? Make a command decision and say nothing they can transcribe. Tough, I know."

"Let's don't get off track," said Reg.

Mack said, "You mean, like usual?"

172

Mack could almost feel Reg shrug. "Back to the weapons. We don't have a petunia's chance in hell if this war goes ahead. I was shaken at their display of weaponry. Of course, the Ivies say they'll destroy the Goldies in a millisecond. Shortest war in the history of the planet."

"The Ermies have a weapon that looks like a ghost, which Badsr says is antimatter. Whammo. Target no longer there. No fuss, no muss."

"Reminds me of the old films we saw, but without the mess," said Reg. "It only destroys living tissue, not property. Unless they're bluffing, a war won't last more than a few minutes before everyone is destroyed. Why doesn't your Big Guy understand that? The Ivies realize the danger."

"'The moral is obvious: it is that great armaments lead inevitably to war—The increase of armaments that is intended in each nation to produce a consciousness of strength, and a sense of security, does not produce these effects. On the contrary, it produces a consciousness of the strength of other nations and a sense of fear. Fear begets suspicion and distrust and evil imaginings of all sorts.' Hey, Mack, I'm back."

"With a vengeance. Your quotes are too long, boring, and never on point. The antelopes are a bunch of racist boobs, intent on destroying each other for no discernible reason. Totally stupid."

"Surely Mack, war stupidity isn't limited to antelopes—" said Reg, cut short by Lucas.

"That quote was squarely on point. The Ermies developed their weaponry in response to the Goldies and Ivies."

"Gotta go. Courtney's stocks are way too tight. Ellen and Barry tried to loosen them but a crowd is gathering. I have to get out of my cage."

Lucas and Reg could hear him banging on the bars. "Hey you, get me out of here. I've got work to do, people to protect. Courtney's civil rights are being violated. Where art thou, Big Guy, when you're needed. You said all I had to do was yell if I needed anything. Well, I NEED SOMETHING." Mack put his fingers between his teeth and whistled.

10

The Legionnaires covered their ears and the crowd was instantly silent, cringing against a repeat performance. A Legionnaire approached Mack's cage as Barry and Ellen retook their post at Courtney's stocks with Peter, Roy, and Madison peering around the corner of the cage. The Legionnaire paused for a second and Mack reinserted fingers in his mouth. The Legionnaire immediately did whatever opened the invisible door to the cage.

Mack stepped out grandly, throwing a lackadaisical salute at the Legionnaire. He walked up to Courtney's purple face and patted her shoulder. "Don't fret, Courtney. We'll have you out of there in no time."

Mack beckoned the closest Legionnaire, pointing to Courtney. He motioned to open the stock while placing two fingers on his lips. The Legionnaire moved fast, flipping up the center of the stock, releasing Courtney's head and hands. She collapsed in a heap.

"Upsy daisy." Ellen and Barry assisted Mack. "You three. Give us a hand with Courtney." Peter, Madison, and Roy scrambled to help. Barry and Ellen took her arms while Madison and Roy tried to circle her middle. Ellen and Mack levered her up on the radiant emerald floor. The Goldies grew testy during this extended effort, muttering while juveniles swooped too close for comfort.

"Hey, jerkoffs," yelled Mack at their departing fannies. "Cut that out."

Three juveniles made an especially daring plunge, sticking out footlong tongues, their tips trailing along Mack's forehead, nose, and lips. "Yuck, gag, upchuck."

In a reflex like roping a steer, Mack grabbed a tongue, flipped it around his wrist, and decked the attached juvenile. The antelope kid found himself flat on his back, tongue wrung out and tasting icky. He retched himself silly, amusing the crowd no end. Mack hadn't washed his hands since they'd landed.

"Hey, Courtney, what's happening?" She was beginning to come back to life, her face shading purple to red and then white.

Mack said, "Madison, Roy, and Peter on the other side. I've got people to talk to and wars to avert."

"Thanks, Mack." Courtney was gasping.

"Well, thank *you*, Courtney. That's the nicest thing you've ever said to me."

She gathered her strength. "It wasn't easy, you almost being a heathen and all."

"Which makes me doubly appreciative, ma'am. Now stay out of trouble, hear? Hey, Mr. Legionnaire. Over here, sir."

The Goldie Legionnaire knew he was being talked to but had no glimmer why. He inched over.

"Back in the cage. I don't want to stay out here with the juveniles. But I'd like a couch. A sofa. You know. You don't know. Okay, go find someone with a translator."

The Legionnaire scrunched up his long antelope face, but it didn't help.

Mack began an elaborate pantomime, twisting an imaginary knob on his chest. The Legionnaire did the same, an antelope-see, antelope-do sort of thing.

"You crazy?" chirped Mack's mic. "Why do you want to go back in the cage?"

"Shush. It'll work out fine. Much better than dealing with teenage antelopes. I have an idea. I feel sorry for the rest of the guys sitting outside. There's peace and quiet in the cage."

"Ding-dong."

Mack tried more charades but had drawn a real dumb Legionnaire. In desperation he took a stab with, "Fartle, chirple, manitou." The antelope smacked him square in the face.

Mack got up, rubbing his chin. He bowed. "Sorry about that. Didn't mean whatever I said."

175

The Legionnaire bowed back, on automatic. Mack grabbed his long bony wrist and tugged him toward the invisible door. He placed the bony hand on the bars, pretending to open them. Son of a gun, the big lummox finally got it. Mack watched carefully as the Legionnaire triggered the invisible door. It looked like an electric eye at the base of the cage, perhaps reachable from inside.

"Great." Mack stepped back in. "Now all I need is a comfy sofa and food, in case I get hungry, with enough for my friends and countrymen. But since you don't understand a word I've said, I will simply say, 'Btsht.'"

The Legionnaire did a half frown, half glimmer of comprehension. Mack repeated it and the Legionnaire brightened. Mack could almost hear him saying, "Me go get Big Guy pronto," as he turned tail and disappeared into the gathering crowd.

"Made it back," said Mack into his mic. "And the Goldies aren't all smart. I don't think they clock much over a hundred IQ, not much better than us. Maybe their advanced weaponry is balderdash."

"Are you suggesting we egg them into war and call their bluff?" said Lucas.

"Heavens no, Mr. Sensitivity. We have to pay attention to details, see what they're actually able to do."

"They weren't pretending with their little fold-up weapons, flipping a 747 off the tepui. Or the times they zapped Courtney."

"But that's all we've actually seen. Videos and movies are easy to fake, and the mask they slapped on Benny was very low tech. Where the heck is Benny, anyway? You haven't mentioned him for ages."

"They sent him to the dungeon. Remember."

"He's not still in there, is he? You did try to get him out?"

"You got sidetracked by the transcripts of everything we say. That's the first time we found out and we were flummoxed. At least you were. So, we never got a chance to stop them putting Benny in the dungeon. We dropped the ball, or you dropped the ball. I got him sprung a few hours ago." Mack could feel the smirk. "Poor guy was a wreck."

"You mean the Ermies let him out because war is looming? You didn't have to do anything. Fess up."

"I can't keep up with you, Mack. First you think the war's a sham and then you think it's a done deal and we're all going to croak. Now you think it's a fake because you met a dumb Goldie. One dumb Goldie. Big deal."

"I tricked him into putting me back into the cage. What I mean is—"

"One dumb Goldie canceled out by a dumber human."

"I have my methods. You watch."

"We'll all be watching because we've seen you in action. Whoopty-doo."

Ellen yelled up at Mack, "Cut it out. Here comes the Big Guy."

The muttery-snarly crowd parted as Btsht strode through. "What are you up to, Mr. Mack? Is there a problem?"

"Thanks for coming. I didn't believe you when you said whistle if I needed anything."

"First I heard that you'd called. We're starting demonstrations, which I must attend with the General and, of course, the Pope."

Btsht swept the heavily epauletted General forward. The General's shoulders and collar swooned with crowns, pips, and stars. He was sharp in his Persian blue and Tartar red uniform with scrambled eggs piled six inches high on his hat brim. The resplendent pope accompanied him with a heavily brocaded golden cape billowing stiffly behind, so enormous that it took a dozen apple-cheeked choirboys to hold it erect. The Pope's golden miter hat stretched a meter above his sweaty brow.

"Your citizenry is out of control. They whipped up on poor Courtney and she was almost asphyxiated in your barbaric stocks. I got her out while suffering spitty humiliation by unruly juveniles. You ought to train the young ones better, to respect their elders, and—"

"And to respect every odd alien that drops onto our sacred tepui? I think not. Goldies, and even humans, garner the

177

respect they deserve. If you command respect, you receive respect. And guess what?"

"I got it, Mr. Big Guy. But I need something to sit on and regular food and drink. You may not be a signatory to the Geneva Convention but there are minimal standards of human decency. Perhaps even antelope decency, below which civilized beings ought not to drop. You follow my drift?"

"Like dandruff. But we have no time for trivialities."

Btsht turned and escorted the General and the Pope to the brilliantly lit stage. They ascended a golden platform and Btsht introduced the Pope with flowery phrases. With Btsht's single glance toward the humans, they received a translation in English.

"Where'd that come from?" said Mack.

"We're not speaking to you," said Ellen.

"Come on, guys. That was strategy. I do everything to nurture, feed, and keep you safe. But I have to establish authority with the Goldies. So, give me a break. I simply wondered how they turned on the English. Maybe they're not so dumb after all."

Lucas said, "We can't keep up with your flip-flops."

"We all get the translations," said Peter. "Give the poor schmuck a break. He's doing the best he can."

Lucas laughed. "Yeah, but sometimes he seems at the limit of his capacity just staying awake."

"Hey, Lucas. I almost forgot. It's time for six-month evaluations. I'll have to get them to the director as soon as we get back. When might be convenient for yours, dear boy?"

"You're a petty tyrant and Marylyn will curse you if you screw up my raise. Otherwise state employees are slated for a big one and a half percent, which would cover breakfast out on Tuesday next."

"When is Tuesday next? I've lost track."

"Did you hear that?" At Mack's blank look Ellen said, "I knew it. You weren't paying attention to the Big Guy introducing the religious gentleman. He called him the Pope. Now that's heresy. Courtney was right all along. We shouldn't have to put up with heresy, even in captivity. You must protest immediately."

178

"Lord almighty, Ellen. Settle down. It's just a translation. Since he's the head guy for their religion, they call him the Pope. It's not like he's trying to nudge aside the white-haired…or is it the bald-headed gentleman who knocks about the Vatican? So, it wasn't heresy. Just a bad translation."

"Do you really think so?" Ellen had tears in her lovely eyes.

"How'd you like to share this safe and secure cage with me? You are so cute when confounded over some dumb-assed nothing."

Ellen stamped her foot, ricocheting off Goldies who crowded too close. "Dang you, Mack McElheney. I'm a married woman. I couldn't share the cage with you if I wanted to. And I most assuredly don't. Do not." She shoved a Goldie who'd bounced off her. He, or maybe she, decked Ellen like a house of cards. "Whaaaaa," she cried from the floor.

"Oh my god. Just a second. Get me out of this cage. Where's the electric eye beam? I know I saw it." Mack stuck an arm out of the bars, swinging it around, but Madison had already helped Ellen off the cold green floor. The Goldies were crowding closer.

"Get me out of here," yelled Mack. "I can't find the magic beam and where's Courtney?"

"Snarf." The closest Legionnaire opened the cage. "Fartle," he added, which Mack took to mean that he'd better scoot. He skidded out of the cage.

"Where's Courtney?" Mack asked to blank stares. "You mean none of you saw her disappear? How can someone the size of Courtney simply vanish? Grack," he added as the crush of Goldies became claustrophobic. "Out of here. Give us room to breathe."

The Legionnaire moved the crowd back two inches, pressing, pressing. Then another full inch.

We must proceed to the ceremony, where the Big Guy, the General, and the Pope—"

"Waillllll."

"Stop it, Ellen. I didn't mean the real pope. I apologize to everyone I've pained in the universe, including you. But I don't know what else to call him. I mean, that's what the Big Guy calls him, so cut the tears."

Her sobbing subsided to a dull squawk, trailing into a blackboard-curdling hiccup. "I'm sorry. I'm overwrought. Thank you, Madison. And no, I don't know what happened to Courtney."

"She was right here," said Barry. "Then she wasn't. The bad thing is no one noticed. She's been quiet, not like the old Courtney. I like her the way she used to be, maybe cantankerous, but—"

"Barry, I'm sorry to interrupt but we're no closer to finding Courtney. She probably went to the ceremony, so let's check it out."

"What makes you think she's there?" asked Peter.

Mack gritted his teeth. "Because she's not here and that's the only other place she could be."

Peter shook his head. "That doesn't make sense. She could be anywhere. Why would she go to a ceremony with 'godless antelopes'?"

"It wouldn't be voluntary." Mack ground his teeth. "We'll form a phalanx and bull our way through this nasty crowd. Ready, get set, go." Mack gave a roar and ran full tilt into the unyielding chest of a massive Legionnaire.

"Gibble, machittitti, nostradamussness," he said before Mack reached up and tweaked his knob.

"Could you please repeat that?"

"On orders of the Big Guy, you are prohibited from proceeding to the patriotic ceremony. You must stay behind this imaginary line. If you don't, you're back in the cage."

"It's a remarkable language. Tell you what, Mr. Legionnaire. We don't want to go to the patriotic ceremony. We want to retreat further away, to escape the crush of your fellow antelopes. If you could escort us around the stage in the opposite direction, we would be most thankful." Mack bowed, practically genuflecting. For some reason this impressed the Legionnaire, who scratched his head.

"Nothing says I can't do that. This way then." The Legionnaire swept wide around the crowd. They followed as he approached the opposite corner of the stage.

"Perfect," said Mack. The Big Guy sat between the General and the Pope. Courtney was in front with her head in stocks.

The Big Guy said, "We eternally acknowledge the pre-eminence of the Goldies. Remember that God accompanies us wherever we go. She protects us from mindless attacks by aliens and inferior antelopes."

He nudged Courtney's neck with a tiny shoe. "You have heard our personal emissary from God, the Honorable Pope. And the words of wisdom from the great General of our crack troops. Never forget and remember well that the Goldies are the vanguard of civilization. We're the most advanced on the planet, and we shall prevail—"

A familiar voice said, "The Ermies are doing the same thing. Their god can kick the butt of the Goldie god. Here's the quote you're breathlessly awaiting. 'Remember the [blank] people are the chosen of God. On me the [blank] emperor, the spirit of God has descended. I am his sword, his viceregent.' Sound familiar?"

"Well, no," said Roy, speaking to Mack's mic. "I can't rightly place it. Why the blanks?"

Mack said, "Because Lucas is into charades. We have more important matters than guessing games. Like rescuing Courtney."

"We're always rescuing Courtney," said Peter. "We should guess who did the quote. I vote for Italians. We have the best pasta, opera, gelato, cappuccino, and wine."

Mack said, "You're not always rescuing Courtney. I'm always rescuing Courtney, and I never get any help."

Mack could hear Lucas saying, "Whinge, whinge, whinge."

"Maybe the emperor is Roman," said Barry. "I've never heard of Italian emperors, just Roman emperors. Like Mack says, we have to help Courtney. The Big Guy is kicking her in the neck."

"No Irish emperors have there been," said Madison. "But what the heck I'd vote for them. Ellen should my vote support, and if she will, she's quite the sport. The Irish oh, the

181

Irish—" He trailed off, muttering about what could possibly rhyme with Irish.

"You idiots," came a voice over the mic. "It's obviously German. Who else thinks they run things for god?" It was Ef. When it came to Germans one hesitated to contradict a person with a Jewish name, religious or not. Of course, Ef could be German.

"Get real," said Mack. "It could be anyone. It could be Chinese or Japanese, surely among the most chauvinistic people on earth. Along with every other nation and ethnic group. We should include the French and the Americans, if they had emperors. I've never been anywhere the natives didn't consider their nation and religion supercalifragilisticexpialidocious. Almighty government and the local religion teach this to everyone from babyhood. But don't forget Courtney. She still needs rescuing."

"How the heck we going to do that?" said Peter. "We only got around the crowd with the help of this nice Legionnaire."

"By gum, Peter. You've stumbled on the solution. Mr. Legionnaire, sir.
Could you clear a way up to the podium? We have to speak with the Big Guy. Our friend Courtney is under siege."

"And rightly so," snapped the Legionnaire. "She's a heretic. I'm having second thoughts, bringing you here. Maybe I wasn't supposed to let you come this direction either."

"Perish the thought. If your orders were not to allow us to go the way you didn't let us go then you've followed them to the letter. You should be commended."

"Whatever. But I'm not going to escort you to the podium. The Big Guy would kill me."

"Pretty please."

"No way in hell."

"Okay. Guys, let's huddle, because I have a plan." Mack motioned everyone in tight, throwing his arms around the shoulders of Roy and Peter. Madison, Ellen, and Barry snuggled in too. "These guys are bigger than us."

"No shit, Sherlock," said Peter. "It's amazing the things you notice all by yourself."

"I'm not going to say anything because I might say something not nice. Since we can't bull ourselves to the front by brute force, we'll wiggle our way through the crowd as slyly as possible. A twinkle-toes sort of thing."

Madison asked, "Have you tried poetry, or confined yourself to drollery?"

Mack sighed. "Otherwise we might get squashed. When we get there—"

"You're optimistic," said Peter.

"Someone has to be. When we get to the front, lay low until you hear me say charge. We won't all make it through at the same time. And then we'll head for the Big Guy, throw him off balance so I can talk him into letting Courtney out of the stocks."

"Yeah," said Barry. "And stop kicking her in the head."

"That t—" as Lucas interrupted.

"I always keep close track of my personnel. I don't let them slip away like other people do."

"But you don't have Courtney to contend with. Do you really know where all your people are? Benny and Ef and especially Billy K.? I suppose James is still hanging around with Nick and Mary."

"We're all intact. The Ermies cleaned Benny's clothes, down to the white leather tassels. But after the slimy dungeon, the baby-blue boots will never be the same. Billy K. received honorary citizenship after teaching knife culture to the populace. Mary, I'm sorry to say, was hospitalized. But Nick is by her side and we receive periodic updates. James is entertaining the troops. Did you know he could twirl a lariat like ringing a bell?"

"How about Reg? Are his people all there?"

"Reg here. All present and accounted for. I have a good group, quite peaceable. One couldn't improve on either the Ivies or my retinue."

"Come on, Reg. Don't tell me Rudd the Rat has mellowed out or that Fats is less paranoid?"

"Fats hit it off with the Ivies. Rudd has quieted down. Molly, Betty, and Arturo are model citizens."

"I'm dreading the dash to save Courtney. Her nine lives expired long ago."

"Gosh, boss," said Barry in his Tennessee drawl, "if our leader has no confidence in his plan, what should us poor peons think?"

"On the other hand," said Ellen, "we have to rescue Courtney, so unless someone has a better plan—" There was actual silence. "We'll back Mack, until he messes up again."

"Probably take him another two minutes," said Peter.

"Thanks. Since the Goldies are big beasties, think snake, and go as low as you can go. If we have to crawl, we crawl."

"So," said Roy, "How low can you go? Like really downhill."

"That's one way of looking at it. Does anyone know the Goldie word for 'excuse me'? We may have to use it a lot."

Barry pointed. "He's not taking his foot off Courtney."

"I see that. So, let's do this for the Gipper, which is to say Courtney. Ready?"

"Ready," they chorused.

"Then hit it."

They scurried for the front where the Big Guy stood with a foot on Courtney's neck. Btsht led the vast sea of Goldies in a wave, trying to out shout each other. Shrill fartles and snarples cascaded as the humans burrowed their way through the madding crowd.

His first abortive cartwheel found Peter spread-eagled on the emerald floor beneath half a dozen Goldies. The only way to go was exceedingly low. Ellen wriggled up front, joined by Barry and Roy, where they stood looking at hundreds of Goldies swaying in mass hypnosis. Mack proceeded stealthily, slipping and sliding through masses of Goldies, muttering excusez-moi without pause, less than accidentally ending up by Ellen.

"Where's Madison?" said Mack as they pulled back to avoid being seen by the Big Guy, the General, and the Pope. "We'll have to go it alone."

"But what about Madison," whispered Ellen, her voice so sultry that Mack misjudged the sway of the closest Goldie and took a hoof in the throat.

Mack gulped. "No time to wait or someone'll turn us in."

"Turn us in for what?" said Peter. "We haven't done anything wrong, yet."

A huge Goldie picked Ellen up with one hand and held her above his head. Ellen screamed, adding pandemonium to the riotous assembly.

Mack slapped at the offending Goldie. "Unhand her at once." But it was impossible to hear above the pandemonium and the Big Guy's oration.

The Big Guy spotted Ellen twirling above the crowd and chuckled at Mack slapping the big Goldie. Btsht flicked a finger at the closest Legionnaire, who corralled Mack and rescued Ellen. The twirling Goldie flinched like his pocket had been picked.

The Legionnaire stood Ellen upright. When she swayed, he tipped her up with a single horny finger. Mack strained, trying to reach her. Legionnaires surrounded Mack and hustled the humans to one side of the Big Guy. Btsht continued the pep rally as if nothing had happened.

Mack stuck two fingers in his mouth, whistling his screechiest blast. In the first second of silence he said, "Hey, Btsht. Pick on someone your own size instead of beating up little old ladies who wouldn't hurt a flea. Warrior you're not—" A Legionnaire's iron grip clamped Mack's windpipe shut.

"You are a habitual nuisance," snarled Btsht as Mack's half-conscious body pitched forward and landed at Btsht's tiny feet.

Mack looked up blearily. "And Madison is missing. He wouldn't hurt a flea either."

Btsht spat, narrowly missing Mack's face. "You've interrupted a crucial rally. But if you keep quiet and stay behind me, I'll have Courtney moved to the rear. And I'll make sure Madison is found. You have a split second to decide."

"Okay." Mack slithered behind the Big Guy. Btsht barely paused before introducing the General and taking Mack by the ear, leading him backstage, the door magically slamming shut behind them.

Btsht started speaking as Mack's eyes adjusted to the strange green light. "You never let well enough alone. Before this latest incident there was a chance you'd survive the war. Now it's impossible. You've insulted the populace, interrupted the rally, and made a spectacle of yourselves."

"Okay, we screwed up. Just tell us what's going on instead of acting mysterious and threatening everyone."

"Short of locking you in the dungeon under the supervision of a battalion, you always screw up. Though I like the part where you admitted it." Btsht stroked his long chin. "I have to get back before the General pumps them into a blood frenzy."

"You were doing pretty well yourself."

"Oh, honey child. You ain't seen nothin' yet. The General in action is beautiful to behold. But there is one thing before we return. Put your hand here."

"Where? I can't see anything."

"Right in front of you."

"This sounds like a trick."

"I don't have time to argue. Just do it."

Mack stuck out his hand.

"The other hand."

"What difference does it make?"

"What do you care? Just switch hands." Btsht growled impressively, like a grizzly bear with breath to kill a skunk.

"Right." Mack switched hands. Thunk. Btsht laid a small ax next to the green light as Mack stood a second before howling. He stuck the ends of his whistling fingers in his mouth. "Gerbille," he said.

"Take your hand out of your mouth and follow me."

Mack removed his fingers. "You cut my fingers off."

"Oh, don't be melodramatic. I only cut off the tips. You're not even hurt."

"I'm not even hurt," mumbled Mack as they exited backstage. He shook his hand, splattering red drops on the emerald sidewalk. Btsht marched them onto the stage as the General ranted fire and brimstone, arms churning, epaulettes flying, and mouth frothing.

Courtney had been released from the stocks and stood huddled with the rest behind the General, out of sight of the vast Goldie audience. Mack stood with tingling fingers in his mouth, the General's bluster reminding him of grainy black and white films from WWII, generating similar raw emotion in the audience. The General shouted that wars were wonderful for building character. No one wanted to go to war, but the great Goldie nation could never kowtow to the Ermies and Ivies. The General would give his all to make sure that didn't happen, happy to make the ultimate sacrifice on behalf of the Goldie nation.

Lucas's Aussie drawl snapped Mack back to reality. "Been missing me, boss? We're getting the same treatment and here's what I get out of it. 'War is an evil thing; but to submit to the dictation of other states is worse— Freedom, if we hold fast to it, will ultimately restore our losses, but submission will mean permanent loss of all that we value— To you who call yourselves men of peace, I say: You are not safe unless you have men of action on your side.' Your general sounds just like the Ermie general."

"Not my general. Just another crazy. And that goddamn Btsht cut the tips off my fingers."

"All of them?"

"The two I whistle with."

"Ah, sacrificing fingertips to rescue Courtney. Madison will write a ballad and you'll be a folk hero."

"Rescuing Courtney never lasts long. She's out of the stocks but Madison is still lost. Though that weasel Btsht promised to find him pronto."

"You lost Madison too?"

"He never made it to the front when I made the Big Guy release Courtney."

"Wow. Wish I'd been there. Making the Big Guy release Courtney. It must have been something."

"Well, something like that. Ohmigod. Here comes Madison, crawling across the floor in front of the stage. The magnificent part— I got to tell you about the monumental part."

"Please, boss, tell me about the major important greatest part."

"Well, maybe not monumental and magnificent, but impressive. Tiny little footprints all over his shirt, that teal and orange thing he wears?"

Lucas said, "He wore it to the drawing and says it's lucky. He wears it everywhere."

"Tiny little footprints, and they're pink, clashing with the teal and orange. He's struggling to crawl the last few feet. I've got to help him, so here I go."

"Maybe you should get the others to help."

Mack gave a bloodcurdling cry as he raced around the General's upraised arm, scraped by Btsht, flopped onto the raised platform, and grasped Madison's hand.

"Here's a hand up, Madison." But the General's hysterics, Btsht's reaction, and Madison's lyrics drowned him out.

"My travails fruit have born, so I've come to home. My compadres care, my life I bear, without a snare, the villain's lair, now left bare, because I'm here."

As he finished, the General's roar consumed them like a flamethrower, ordering, "Clamp them in irons." Btsht's eyebrows twitched as the Legionnaires bundled Mack and Madison.

The General resumed his harangue. "My fellow Goldies. We will overcome the aliens in our midst and keep our bloodlines pure. Our tepui will remain sacrosanct and our existence forevermore—"

Mack babbled as they were handcuffed. "Poor Madison. Tiny pink footprints on his shirt."

"Shirt hell, ring a bell. My hide they're branded in, that's why they're pink as gin. Marked with my very own, blood imprinted to the bone. Worse than that, I have to tell, my blood's so thin, I fell and fell. Listen to my tale of woe, I slithered through but didn't go. After hitting shanks of steel, they kicked me out a lousy deal. I'd show you scars so deep and bad, pull off this shirt, that's a lad."

Madison struggled against the cuffs as Peter tried to pull the shirt over Madison's head. "Take the shirt and throw it out. It's unlucky, I've no doubt."

"Get the handcuffs off him," Mack commanded the closest Legionnaire. Mack beamed at Ellen's near reverent stare. "Now," he added as the Legionnaire ignored him. Mack stuck his fingers in his mouth, almost knocking out a tooth with the shackles. He yelped, "Ouch."

Ellen's reverence evaporated.

"You do have tiny footprints, all over your shirt," said Peter. "What happened, anyway? We started out together."

"Just cut the shirt, I think that's best. Heavy guys are such a pest. When they step, they don't look where, gave me damage to incur. Plus, there's a thing I must admit, my directions now are just for shit. Oops, poops." Madison covered his mouth, peering at Ellen.

Mack said, "A poet doesn't need a good sense of direction. Especially a millionaire poet. And are you sure you want to rip the shirt off? Maybe we should keep it intact, save it for posterity, hair-raising tales for the grandkids."

"Don't be cruel to Madison," said Ellen. She slipped hands around Madison's shoulders, unbuttoning the top.

"Yowch," said Madison, "I'm such a grouch. Look at how it's tightly stuck, to my skin that's turned to muck. Tiny footprints imbedded are, that's why they're pink afar."

"Heartbreakingly terrible." Ellen had a catch in her voice. Each tug of the shirt revealed another tiny footprint branded in Madison's pasty white skin. "I hope this doesn't hurt too much."

"Oh, no, I go." Madison swooned into a faint.

"The footprints are turning red," said Mack. "They may get infected. It's outrageous that they'd do this to a poet. I must do something about it."

"Why?" said Peter. "You'll just get us into more trouble. I've kept my exuberant personality under control and you should do the same. Better than running off at the mouth, which I can tell the Big Guy is getting tired of."

"Peter. You're my man. But I must draw a line that no Goldie dares to cross. I'm all that's standing between us and oblivion."

Peter scoffed, "That makes me feel real comfortable. I'll keep that in mind when I get an urge to go cartwheeling, drink myself silly, and play grab ass with the girls. But since there are no girls, nothing to drink, and no place to cartwheel, I'm safe for the foreseeable future."

"I beg your pardon. You dishonor this fine specimen of womanhood—"

Peter was taken aback. "I do not. Ellen's not a girl. She's a full-grown woman, and I'm not about to tangle with that one. I'd never call her a girl."

"I appreciate it," said Ellen. "Help Madison up and stop taking his shirt off."

"Agreed," said Mack. "How are you feeling, Courtney? You're looking peaked."

Courtney managed a klutzy curtsy, crossing one filthy brogan in front of the other, almost toppling on her nose, "Thank you, Mr. Mack. You've ridden to my rescue more than the average Lottery official—"

Mack was staggered, clutching handcuffs to his heart. "An average Lottery official? I'd hoped to have risen above that and achieved a special place in your heart—"

"Oh, for Chrissakes. Cut the crap," said Lucas in a tinny voice.
"I hope your crowd isn't as wild as ours. What's your situation, over?"

"Reg here. I've got strategy cooking, which shall remain absent from an antelope transcript. I may have good news soon."

Mack said, "You mean like the war is a joke and they're about to let us go? News like that?"

"Maybe, maybe not."

Mack shook his head. "Our crowd is bananas. The General's over the edge. The scrambled eggs are quivering on his enormous hat and his shoulder boards are flapping. He's doing an audience response thing that's going well. He says something inane, punches the air, and they say it right back."

"Like what?" said Lucas.

"The General just said, 'Erase the Ermies.' He pokes the air and the audience yells, 'Erase the Ermies.' Then, 'End the Ermies,' same old jab and they repeat it. Then, 'Efface the

Ermies,' big shout back. 'Expunge the Ermies.' 'Excise the Ermies.' 'Exterminate the—'"

"I think we got it," said Lucas. "And guess what the Ermies are saying over here? And your general couldn't have half the scrambled eggs and spastic epaulettes that the Ermie general has. Of course, his are all black, glistening yet somber with hidden meaning. Sorry about getting off track," he said as Mack cleared his throat. "Now he's saying, 'Gut the Goldies,' big swoop reaching up like grabbing stars. At the top of his leap the Ermies come back with, 'Gut the Goldies.' The General is a real leader cheerleader. He just said, 'Gulp the Goldies.'"

"That doesn't have quite the same ring."

"It's not easy to be poetical. Ask Madison."

Mack said, "What about your bunch, Reg? Have you converted them to pacifism?"

"I surely haven't. But they're not as bloodthirsty as the Ermies and Goldies."

"I got the perfect quote," said Lucas. "Right on the tip of my tongue. Give me a second."

"I hope you're not losing your touch," said Mack.

"I like your little quotes," said Reg. "Not to demean them as little. And sometimes they're even apropos."

"Apropos, my ass," said Mack.

"Shut up. I've got it. 'To tell the truth, a continent without war is bored—as soon as the bugles start up, it's a holiday—total vacation. And the bloodlust.' About as apropos as you can get, my man."

"Okay. But it doesn't feel like a vacation and I haven't heard a single bugle."

"Just listen." Lucas cupped his hands and trilled into the microphone, producing a decidedly inferior "Toot, toot."

"Ah, the musical fruit. Like the basic Goldie vocabulary."

Their conversation was drowned out as the stadium erupted into an uproar. The crowd answered the General's final challenge: "KICK ERMIE ASS." Then the crowd swirled up the emerald road and disappeared.

11

Mack, Madison, Courtney, and Ellen were left alone. Mack said, "This is our chance to escape."

Ellen rolled her eyes. "Oh, right. You and Madison in cuffs and Courtney exhausted. Just jump off the tepui."

"But darlin', it's only a man in cuffs. The women are free as birds. You can lead us to freedom since the men have failed so miserably."

"You have failed," snapped Ellen. "But there seems to be no way off these desolate tepuis."

"There must be."

"Why? The Goldies never go anywhere."

"Negative thinking because we don't *know* that." Mack used his most reasonable voice.

"We don't know that," mocked Courtney. "What do we know?"

"We know we shouldn't carve up graven images of other cultures. That we do know."

Courtney was shocked. "You're exasperating, only focusing on the short-term. You have no appreciation for the long-term, for eternity, and the health of your immortal soul."

"I don't know if I suffer from one."

"You must, because you're insufferable."

"Thank God we're here," said Ellen. They rounded the last spiral and staggered onto the top of the tepui. Thousands of Goldies were gathered under camouflage in an area the size of the Rose Bowl.

"The Goldies are way over there. Now's our chance."

Ellen said, "Chance to do what? Leap off the edge?"

"Check out the perimeter, scope out the situation, assess conditions, find a chink in their armor, and a make our way to freedom. Ta-da."

"Mack's right," said Courtney before Ellen could object. "Let's check it out."

"At least get rid of the cuffs. They chafe my wrists."

"Oh, you poor darlin'," mocked Ellen.

Madison cleared his throat. "Thinking the cuffs, easy for bluffs, think small hands, and off they sluffs."

"I don't think that'll work," said Mack.

Madison continued as if not interrupted. "My cuffs they chafe, but my heart runs free. I'll search to rout, my enemy. My arms are bound, but my mind's up front. If you see them coming, lay down a bunt."

"I didn't know you were into baseball. In fact, I didn't know you were a sporting person."

"That was just the first part, first verse, first stanza of a whole bonanza."

"Forget it, Madison. We're going scouting. You can work on your latest sonnet while we find a way to escape, get out of cuffs, avoid the war, and go home heroes."

"Just like that." Ellen snapped her fingers. "Oh, we of little faith."

"Oh, ye of little faith. This way, to the right. Path toward the edge."

"I want nothing to do with the edge."

"How you can switch course so fast? When the plane was whicking and whacking you had no problem with ordering me to rescue those hanging over the edge."

"Only because you wouldn't let me help. I volunteered, but chauvinist you wouldn't let me. I've got no problem with the edge when necessary to rescue fellow human beings." She paused. "Which may include getting us off of here before a war kills us all. You win. Edge it is."

"You are among the most sensible woman I've ever met."

"We've not been properly introduced, so go on ahead. You okay, Courtney?" Ellen said as Courtney yelped.

"It's a snake." Courtney danced like her brogans were ballet slippers, whirling into Mack and Madison, sending them sprawling across the path.

Mack looked up at the bobbing head above them. "It's just a boa constrictor, a baby. Wouldn't even reach around you, Courtney. Now get off. It's hard to get up with these goddamned cuffs."

"I'm not helping you up, young man. You've taken the Lord's name in vain."

"You're a jerk." Ellen grabbed Mack's shirt and ripped him upward.

"A jerk for a jerk. I sincerely apologize. I don't want to insult anyone's religious feelings because someone will get hurt, usually me. Sorry, Courtney. If you have a bar of soap you can wash out my mouth."

"I've always doubted your sincerity," said Courtney. "Though you're almost a heathen you are pragmatic, staying off the toes of the one true religion and—"

"Which one might that be, Courtney?"

"You promised."

"I take it back. But you're no longer bothered by that itty-bitty snake."

"Shriek," said Courtney.

"This one is no bigger than the other one."

"But it's not the squeezy kind. It's the kind that that bites you and you die."

"Then let's tiptoe and don't disturb it. We have work to do, edges to explore."

"Cuffs to clip and watch that dip," said Madison.

"Your poetry is improving. But it's tough, navigating a rainforest in handcuffs, ready to trip on the first nasty thing that comes along."

"Slow down," Courtney whispered. She tiptoed where the path took a hairpin turn. Could be straight off the edge.

"Better let me." Ellen slipped around Courtney, then pivoted back. "Definitely the edge. But there's a big sign that might be useful."

"Maybe it says, 'Watch out for crumbling rock,'" said Mack. "I've never gotten a hang of Goldie writing."

"My point is the sharp corners," said Ellen.

"I love the view. Big river winding around down there," said Mack. "Reg said it was the Orinoco. The edge of the sign could pry off the cuffs." He slapped a cuff on the corner of the sign. "Just the thing for slitting my wrists."

Ellen directed, "More on the hasp, away from your wrists."

"I'll give it a shot." Mack sawed the handcuffs across the edge of the sign, which didn't even scratch the cuffs.

"Wedge it open," said Ellen. "Push the sharp edge into the space there. There. No, over here." She pulled the cuffs so the hinge slipped over the edge of the sign. "Now give it a yank."

"Right," said Mack. The cuff split into two pieces. "Come on, Madison, let's get your cuffs off too."

Courtney said, "There's another tepui over there. Maybe that's where some of the others are."

Mack said, "Covered with camouflage like ours. But we can see under it since we're the same height."

"I don't see any humans or antelopes," said Ellen, squinting.

"Ten miles away is too far to see something that small."

"Then how do you know there's camouflage?"

"You can't see it directly. But lean this way. That's it. A little closer." Ellen shoved Mack and sent him sprawling. He skidded toward the edge, which he might have gone over except for the fat leg of the sign.

Ellen rushed up. "Sorry about that. I didn't mean to knock you halfway over the edge."

"You probably meant to knock me all the way over the edge. But I'm glad you did. Take a look." She glared back and he added, "No, I'm not telling you to get a little closer. But look straight down, like I'm doing."

"Yeah. Well." She edged away.

"You're not going to fall over." Mack shrugged. "Madison and Courtney. Are you afraid of heights too? If not, come over here. I have an idea."

"Your ideas scare me to death so I'll stay back here," said Ellen as Madison and Courtney sauntered over.

"Bow wow," said Madison.

Mack pointed. "See the bushes and trees sticking out, all the way down. It'd be tough to climb up, but easy to climb down."

"Right," said Ellen. "Gravity works wonders. And fast."

Mack groaned. "Come on. We can drop from tree to tree and bush to bush. We could work our way off this tepui in a couple of hours."

"We should live so long," said Courtney. "I'd rather boil in oil."

Mack eyed her girth but said nothing. "What about you, Madison? Do you think you could do it?"

"My heart is joyous at an es-ca-pe, but I'm sure I'd fall, all the way."

"There must be someone besides me who'd give it a try."

Ellen said, "Roy would say it's too far downhill, but Peter might try a cartwheel. I can't believe you'd consider such a screwball idea."

"Even you might prefer rappelling instead of a guided missile up your butt."

Ellen turned to Courtney. "That bar soap you mentioned. Do you have it on you?"

Mack shook his head. "I know your type. Forgetting the seven words you used to couldn't say on television, you're most disturbed by 'butt.' Let me think." He looked at Ellen. "Panties."

Ellen howled like fingernails across a chalkboard.

"You're both children," said Courtney.

The tinny voice on Mack's mic came alive. "I've been following your half-hearted attempts. We're at the Ermie Rose Bowl, watching troops do fancy goose steps. Weapons on parade. How about you, besides a fruitless reconnoiter?"

"We're on our own, scouting out the perimeter, scoping out a way to get off this awesomely steep tepui. And I've found it."

"Yes, indeedy," said Ellen. "The usual Mack stroke of genius. He wants us to swing from tree to tree, vertically, which is to say down real fast."

"Well, I heard some of that," said Lucas. "But I couldn't figure out what you were talking about. I've always been into abseiling and stuff like that."

"Have you scoped out the edge of your tepui, old partner? See if there's a way to escape?"

"No, we haven't. Neither Reg nor I, though Billy K. gets around."

"None of you have fulfilled your duty to protect us," shrilled Ellen. "And swinging down the vertical side of a tepui leaves me cold."

"My dear lady," said Mack, "I suspect that there's little that wouldn't leave you cold. But then you did go to Catholic school."

"That's a low blow. There's nothing wrong with Catholic school."

"Not when patent leather shoes reflect up."

"You're a scoundrel."

"Cut it out you two," said Lucas. "We have serious issues."

Mack sighed. "I agree. The war threat is real."

"I've been talking to Reg, who is able to check CNN. Our stellar foreign office is making progress. They've almost convinced the Venezuelans to allow a humanitarian rescue in their air space."

"We've escaped from the Goldies, Lucas. Maybe this war thing is exaggerated."

"You wouldn't think that was funny if you saw Ermie military hardware."

"I'd rather not."

Lucas said, "They have the Goldie pocket knives that can launch nuclear weapons. BBs that blow up cities, maybe an entire tepui, though they say they won't use them. They don't want to destroy property. That might tank their stock market."

"Come on, how could you possibly know that? They haven't been demonstrating weapons like that or you'd be cinders."

"They're showing movies—"

"You shouldn't believe everything you see. I have no choice but to write you down for that. Your performance is sagging."

"Don't give me that, Mack. You remember the stuff where the missile goes right up the butt? Poof, blood falls out the bottom and the guy disappears?"

"You're too easily duped. You probably think computer-generated Hollywood thrillers are real. Hollywood could easily conjure a super-fast suppository to drain the blood from a victim."

"Or a dozen, a hundred, an entire tepui. It's not a pretty sight."

"Of course, it's not a pretty sight, but is it real? That's the question."

"That's not the question. It looks real enough to take it serious, whether it's computer synthesized or not. Go back to the Goldie rally and see what you think."

"No way. I'm working on escape, rappelling off the tepui."

"It's not going to work. I'd love to try but who else would? Maybe James. Probably Billy K. Maybe Roy, but no one else would have a chance. We'd never get this giddy group of millionaires swinging from tree to tree with the ground a mile below. I'll bet half are deathly afraid of heights. And the rest couldn't run a hundred yards in a week. Forget it, Mack. If I were doing your performance rating, you'd flunk."

"You're not entirely off base with your relatively constructive criticism. But I'd hate to march back to the Goldie stadium and surrender, just because we can't rappel everyone off. That's not us."

"Stop grasping at straws or you'll get us killed sooner than later. Especially those left behind. I've got no hope more than, like you said, *que sera, sera*."

"See? Admit it. Better a screwball plan than none at all."

"The Ermies are marching in front of a hundred-foot movie screen, splattering antelope guts. You have to wonder what the Legionnaires are thinking while they parade back and forth."

198

"They're thinking about glory for whatever god and country, and whatever babe they can roll into the sack on the way. I'm sure you have the perfect quote. Or the less than perfect quote."

"There are hundreds. Me mum's book had a whole section on stuff like that. I wouldn't know where to start."

"That's a relief—"

"But now that you mention it. 'A soldier is a Yahoo hired to kill in cold blood as many of his own species, who have never offended him, as possibly he can.' That's just for starters."

Mack shook his head. "Much too serious. We were talking about raping and pillaging and the spoils of war. Not the reality of war. But wherever you got that quote must be where the mighty internet warrior, Yahoo, got its name."

"Of course. You can bet the bank."

"You know the book?" Mack sounded surprised.

"Everyone knows the book."

"I don't know the book. But it sounds like I should."

"Your performance rating is zilch. You should immediately resign your day job and get an education. Enrollment in the average high school would do the trick, even in a place as boondocky as Australia."

"You're entirely too hard on me," said Mack.

"Your problem is that no one's ever been too hard on you."

"Bulls' cud. You never met my ex-wife."

"You were probably too hard on each other. But I do have a couple more quotes. 'Soldiers were made on purpose to be killed.' Simple and to the point."

"Too simple to be erudite. In fact, it doesn't sound intellectual at all."

"They don't have to be intellectual. They just have to be pithy and memorable. The last one perfectly fit the Ermie film. Body parts flying, blood squirting, bones broken, jagged fragments, guts exploding. Hollywood couldn't do it better."

Mack said, "Soldiers aren't made to be killed. They're made to kill other soldiers and may the surest shot survive."

"Perfect," said Lucas. "I was just coming to that one. 'I want you to remember that no bastard ever won a war by dying for his country. He won it by making the other poor dumb bastard die for his country.'"

"Whoever said that said it better than I did."

"You know it's not what you say. It's how you say it."

"Like you mean, the rub's in the rubric?"

"You did your best. I'm sure of it."

"I don't always do my best."

"That's obvious," said a voice. Mack turned to stare into Ellen's limpid eyes. "Do we have to stand here all day while you whisper sweet nothings to Lucas? Driveling inanities over the airwaves, boring us to tears?"

Mack grinned. "Did you have something else in mind?"

"Ooooh." Ellen was furious.

"It's awfully quiet," said Mack. And then it dawned. "Where's Courtney?"

"Oh, my goodness," as close to an expletive as Ellen had ever gotten. "She was just here."

Mack said, "I wonder where she scooted off to."

"Bet you could make an educated guess," said Lucas.

Mack smacked his forehead. "You don't suppose—"

"She wouldn't," said Ellen.

"What makes you think so?" said Mack.

"She must have learned her lesson."

"A death sentence won't bother Courtney, until it's carried out."

"You're a cynic."

"I'm a realist. But we better check. If she goes after the statue again, they'll toss us all in boiling oil."

Lucas's tinny voice said, "You thought the boiling oil was a bluff, the same as the war."

"I only thought they were bluffing about the war but now I'm not so sure. Where's the crash site?"

"Over there." Ellen pointed, as Madison pointed the opposite
direction.

Madison said, "Over there, over there, I think I know where," pointing toward the stadium.

200

Mack said, "How could it be toward the stadium? We haven't—"

Lucas interrupted. "Madison has a point. The roads inside these tepuis shift to come out wherever you want to go."

"Come on, Lucas. How can a road come out wherever you want it to?"

"The Ermies' roads do. I've seen it happen twice. It's probably happened to you and you didn't even know it. When you left the rally, you took the emerald road, right?"

"Right."

"And it came out by the Goldie stadium. First time you'd seen the stadium, right?"

"I never said that, but yeah."

"The first time we took the emerald road it came out in an underground auditorium. When we entered from the crash site."

Mack spluttered. "So, they're all emerald roads. There's not just one of them. But we still don't know where Courtney is."

"That's what I'm trying to tell you," said Lucas. "Even if she found the crash site and reduced the Goldie god statue to matchsticks, there's no way of knowing where it is or how to get there."

"I refuse to believe that."

"Refuse your ass off for all the good it'll do you."

Mack sighed. "There's one sure way to find it. We're on the edge and the crash site is on the edge. All we have to do is walk around the perimeter."

"And you have that much time? How many miles is it around one of these tepuis? Take a look at the tepui I'm on."

"Your stadium looks like a pimple on the edge, underneath the camouflage. If the stadium is two hundred yards long— If proportions hold true—" Mack held up his thumb and sighted along it. "The stadium is about a hundredth of the circumference of your tepui which would make it twenty thousand yards around. That's about twelve miles."

"I'm pole-axed," said Lucas. "I didn't know you knew diddley about math."

Ellen stamped on Mack's instep. "That's enough. Get off the dime and let's get going."

"Which way, darlin'?" Mack hopped on one foot. "Should we hurry off clockwise or counterclockwise?"

"I don't know. But whichever way we go would get us there faster than listening to your inane conversation with Lucas. You don't understand the gravity of the situation. If Courtney hacks up the rest of the Goldie statue, we're all goners."

"You're right. Should we flip a coin to figure out which way to go?"

Madison laughed nervously, screwing up his face and opening his mouth, but nothing came out.

"Spit it out, man. If you have an idea, tell us."

Another nervous laugh as Madison squeaked, "A morn ago we took a spill, crashed a plane, which hit a hill. The Goldies found us then so dumb, when they marched out of the sun." Madison was dancing a jig. "Ahum, ahum, ahum, ahum," beside himself with joy.

"What's that supposed to mean?" said Mack.

Ellen said, "Don't you see, Mack? We look for a hill where the Goldies came swarming out of the sun. See where the sun is now, almost exactly a day later. Good job, Madison." She kissed him wetly on the forehead as Mack stood stunned.

Lucas said, "I'm out of here, ordered to sit with the dignitaries on stage."

"I figured you were already on stage, hogging the limelight as usual." There was no response. Mack shook his head, realizing Ellen and Madison were staring at him. "Right. Madison has a good point. When the Goldies came roaring down on us, the sun was at about ten o'clock from where I figured north was. And they were square out of the middle. So, the crash site is—" Mack squinted. "The sun is at two o'clock so we need to go counterclockwise. Around the side of the stadium we couldn't see after we crashed."

"We couldn't see anything after we crashed," said Ellen. "It was dark."

"You know what I mean."

"I know what you said."

"So cut the crap and hit the road." Mack cocked a thumb and they ducked under the camouflage, finding a color-coded spider web of tracks.

Mack said, "Blue, red, green, yellow, orange, or chartreuse? Which color did we take before? I didn't notice."

"Neither did I. The colors appeared while you were jawing with Lucas."

"Impossible."

"Reality is. And they're not all emerald." She wet a finger and stroked the air.

"No points for you, my dear. Emerald is the same as green. Well, pretty much," Mack conceded.

"Obviously I'm not *your* dear," Ellen huffed. "Never will be. But let's get on with it, though I have a premonition."

As they careened around a blind corner, Madison said, "Gentlemen, Wimbledon." Madison's warning came too late. They were seized by two Legionnaires.

"Take me to your leader," said Mack. "I have important news. And unhand the lady."

The biggest Legionnaire said, "Btshlp macquarie biddenbatten."

Mack reached over and twisted his knob. "Repeata, por favor."

The Legionnaire said, "You're guilty of trading with the enemy, which is treason."

"Oh, lighten up. We couldn't possibly trade with the enemy. They're on other tepuis."

At the Legionnaire's threatening look, Mack said, "Okay, let's discuss this with a power higher than your own."

"Right now, no power is higher than my own."

"You're a prickly sort. Are you related to someone important?"

"The third Big Guy is my uncle."

"Okay." Mack bowed. "Was that adequate?"

He harrumphed, "Not the sincerest bow I've ever seen."

"Yeah, and how many have you seen? I'm sure Goldies don't bow to you. Only aliens end up on your nasty list."

"You're on everyone's nasty list. No one's ever ran across your level of smart aleck before. "

"Privileged, I'm sure." Mack bowed again. "Are we heading off to see your uncle, or not? You know I'm close personal friends with Big Guy Number Two. He outranks your uncle, so let's get on with it."

"Personal friends you're not. He thinks you're a clown. But hurry up because they're wondering where you got to."

"I'm sure you knew where we were all the time. Why weren't you out looking for us if you were worried?"

"We weren't worried you'd escape. We knew you'd trickle back when you got hungry or wanted something."

"We're looking for Courtney and are afraid she might be up to no good. I'm sure you understand."

The tall Legionnaire wrinkled his brow. "Then we'd better get back quick. Get a move on." He shoved Mack in the ribs and herded Madison and Ellen along.

In minutes they entered a white marble stadium jammed with patriotic Goldies. The guard hurried them down a wide ramp that swooped from the highest rampart to the center of a vast stage where the three Big Guys sat on tiered thrones. Hordes of troops marched around the field, raising miniature dust devils, turning their glowing faces sideways as they passed the Big Guys' reviewing stand. The crowd clapped with each step, rollicking the stadium.

Mack's head pounded as they closed in on the Big Guys, watching Ellen daintily place fingers in her ears. The Legionnaire ordered, "Halt," and Mack careened into the Legionnaire, pushing him into the three-tiered stand. It tipped it on its back with the three Big Guys staring skywards, or perhaps at nothing at all.

Mack hopped up, dusted off his uniform, and rushed to pull the Big Guys out of the wreckage. He grabbed Btsht as the Legionnaire pulled out his uncle. Ellen and Madison helped remove Big Guy Number One .

"Got to you just in time," said Mack. "Glad we could save you."

"You dumb shit," said Btsht, and their little world exploded.

12

Blood and guts flew everywhere, throwing the Big Guys and humans clear of the debris. Two quivering masses of red jelly, each the size of a large bread box, sat where the third Big Guy and his cousin Legionnaire had been standing. Mack, Ellen, Madison, Btsht, and Big Guy Number One sat shivering. Their faces and hands were black from the blast, clothes splattered red and gold. The crowd was hysterical, cowering. Then the red telephone rang, the one they hadn't noticed before, tucked on top of the toppled grandstand.

"Btsht here." He juggled the phone on a singed hoof. "What the hell happened?"

Mack heard a thin smarmy voice as Badsr from the Ermies said stiffly, "I'm calling to apologize for the inadvertent firing of a personalized missile, unfortunately coded for your Big Guy Number Three. The humans were invited on stage for the demonstration of our weaponry. They were warned to stay away from the button, but the human named Ef pushed it anyway. Please accept our heartfelt apologies."

Btsht snarled, "What's the point of an apology? Do you think that will avert a war? Of course, we'll retaliate. A special missile will be programmed for your tight ass, Badsr the terrible. We'll program another one for the dastardly human named Ef. Assuming this isn't an elaborate subterfuge on your part. Apology unacceptable."

Badsr replied woodenly, "I did my best, which was much better than not apologizing. Since you can't accept my personal apology, we will program a missile to whiff out your essence of asshole, immediately, if not sooner." The phone slammed down on the other end, reverberating around the stadium.

Btsht jerked the phone away from his awesomely purple face. He was primed to order the annihilation of the Ermie tepui as Mack threw his body over the phone.

"Stop," shouted Mack. "Let us reason together."

Btsht flung him aside as Ellen and Madison rushed up with Roy and Peter. Btsht started to issue an order for all-out war when they flung themselves around his neck. As they bounced off, Btsht said, "Grrrrrrrk," vigorously rubbing his throat where Roy's bone-hard head had dented his voice box. Btsht tried again but the same mournful croak emerged. Mack picked himself up and dusted off his bedraggled uniform, giving up on Btsht and approaching the first Big Guy, genuflecting all the way.

"Excuse me, Your Excellency." Mack tried to make eye contact with the dazed Big Guy. He tried again and gave up as Big Guy Number One staggered in circles.

Btsht turned from purple to green with the effort of giving the order that would end the world as they knew it.

Mack stuck his hand up. "Excuse me, my old friend the Honorable Maybe First Big Guy Right Now, Btsht. This is a wonderful opportunity to chat before you reduce the world to cinders. Let's sit and let the winds of cool reflection waft over us. Then we can sort out our next move."

"Grack," said Btsht as Mack led him to the stadium seats. Soldiers cowered as officers tried to herd them into the semblance of a fighting force.

Mack shook a finger. "Face it, Honorable Btsht. It's been eight hundred years since you've had a real fight. You've forgotten the reality of body bags, or perhaps jelly bags. You've forgotten the fact of instant death from smart missiles. I am horrified."

Roy rolled over and struggled to his feet, muttering. He was covered with suet, like the rest of them. Mack motioned Peter to help Roy before things really started going downhill. "War can get folks hurt, especially ourselves. And uh, yourselves as well. If they had a missile programmed for the third Big Guy, then there are missiles for yourself and current Big Guy Number One, who's still wandering around in a daze."

Btsht's fury hadn't abated a crumb, illustrated by him trying to do eight things at once. He hopped on one tiny foot and strummed a lanky arm across his throat in a signal to attack the Ermies. But the message was never received by the General, who was dazed and looking in the other direction. Btsht shouted silent expletives and pursed his flabby antelope lips in a failed whistle. He aimed a kick at Roy and tried to slash Ellen across the throat with his right elbow. He smashed at Madison's face with his left arm and tried to knee Mack in the nuts.

Mack jumped back. "Now's a good time to tell you why we came back, Honorable Mute Big Guy Btsht. Courtney has disappeared and there may be an outside possibility that she's up to no good. Any suggestions you have are solicited. Such as sending your crack Legionnaires to look for her."

Btsht looked at Mack with slightly crossed eyes.

Mack peered back. Btsht was shell-shocked. "With your permission, sir, I will convey your orders directly to the Legionnaires. Nod if you agree."

Mack automatically took a rapid step backward, which was a smart move. Btsht's tiny foot grazed his kneecap.

"Well, sir, you're not smiling. But I think your head is nodding a bit. May I take that for assent?"

Btsht uttered an especially malevolent "Grack." But Mack sensed a weakening of the Big Guy's resolve to destroy the known world.

"Respectfully, sir. Avoiding further damage to the statue of your god should rate high on your list of priorities. Though I can sympathize with the sorrow you must feel at this terrible time. With the possible elimination of your closest political rival."

Btsht looked at Mack like he was stunned that Mack could know anything about Goldie politics. But ambition, a politician's best friend, won out. He said, "Grack," with a semblance of civility.

"I thank you, sir. Future generations of god-loving antelopes will thank you for your judgment. Avoiding a disastrous war will preserve your religious heritage for generations. I will approach the Honorable General and issue your order forthwith."

Instead of "Grack," Btsht's said something that sounded like, "Getamovin.'" Mack marched directly to the General with Btsht on his heels.

Mack crisply saluted. "The Honorable Btsht, Big Guy Number Two, may already be Big Guy Number One. Particularly if Number One doesn't get his shit straight pretty damn soon. Anyway, Number Two has been wounded in the enemy attack and should be awarded the Goldie order of heroism, sealing his political fortunes for the foreseeable future."

Btsht's face, for the first time Mack could remember, was wreathed in an almost smile. "The Honorable Btsht believes the statue of your god may suffer an enemy attack. But he has temporarily lost the power of speech and motioned for me to relay his orders to you. You will hit the road with your crackerjack troops and find Mrs. Everett Courtney Fern Sitton Sherman. But under no circumstances will you harm her. Got that straight, Honorable General, sir?"

The General had his back turned, watching Big Guy Number One walk in circles of decreasing circumference, suddenly becoming a whirling dervish. The General's eyes were red with fury, maniacal Betty Davis eyes. He was ready to tear the snot out of an owl and bite off a frog's head. He would avenge the wronged Goldie nation with every weapon at his disposal.

When the General turned around, Mack was still holding the salute. This triggered the General's reflexes and started his lanky forearm on a path to return the salute. But the General recovered in time to backhand Mack a good one. Mack bounced like a yo-yo, back into Btsht's ultra-bony knees and left elbow. They penetrated painful inches into Mack's already bruised and battered body, which sent him bouncing back into the General's fortunately rotund form.

"Oof," said Mack as he fell stunned between them. Mack peered up at a spinning camouflage cover as the General snapped a crisp salute to Btsht. Btsht returned it with a horny middle finger.

"General, sir." Mack gasped, testing an elbow in preparation for scrambling to his feet. "The Honorable Btsht, now apparently new Big Guy Number One, has spoken through me. You have your orders. Get with it."

Btsht was trying unintelligible "g" words related to "grack." Like "getamovin" and "getalife" as Mack regained his feet.

"What I meant was," Mack amended. "The Honorable Btsht suggests that when it's convenient you should apprehend dear Courtney before she causes another religious crisis. But don't hurt her. "

"What the hell's he thinking of?" roared the General. "Our enemies, the Ermies, assassinated Big Guy Number Three and his nephew Legionnaire officer. We must retaliate immediately. I heard the former Big Guy Number Two say that right afterwards. I don't believe for a second that he's relaying orders through you."

Btsht shrugged as Mack said, "Well, yes, Honorable General. Btsht Big Guy Almost Number One did temporarily advert to the possibility. But that was before he considered the threat to the health and well-being of the Goldie nation. Before he considered a more appropriate reprisal against the inferior Ermie empire. So, if you could find it in your power to obey your leader, get with it, sir." Mack snapped a super crisp salute and held it as the General thought and considered.

"I'll send a squadron to find the infidel Courtney. But I can't assure her safety and don't believe the Honorable Almost Big Guy Number One, Btsht, cares about her safety. Methinks you've been putting words in his mouth, you filthy alien swine. But first things first. While my brave soldiers corral the heretical excrement named Courtney, I'll assist the Honorable Btsht. We'll perfect our war strategy against the Ermie shitheads." The General gave shrill orders that ended with "shoot to maim, kill, and puncture the scabby alien heretic."

Mack dropped his unreturned salute. "Peter and Roy. Go with the Legionnaires and protect Courtney."

"I heard that," bellowed the General at two hundred decibels.

"Your hearing is acute. Now, let's conference with the Honorable New Big Guy Number One, Btsht. What do you say, Honorable Bigmouth Noisy General?"

The General was livid. "You blasphemous heretic. I don't ever want to hear you say anything like that again."

"I promise to never let you hear me say anything like that again. Thank you for the warning, General, sir." Mack whispered, "I'll only mumble blasphemy. You are hard of hearing, aren't you?"

The General roared, "That's better. Now get out of here while I plot strategy with the Honorable Big Guy and—"

"As Courtney would say, that's a big negatory, General, sir. I must speak on his behalf since the Big Guy hasn't yet regained his voice. Besides, I'm privy to his innermost strategic thoughts. We go back a long way, you know, more than twenty-four hours."

"You are an impertinent jerk. If you weren't a temporary guest, I'd have you flogged to death. After extracting your fingernails, balls, and pecker. One of these days you'll overstep our bountiful hospitality. Mark my words."

"Send me a copy of the transcript with a number two pencil."

"Eh?" The General cupped his ear at Mack's whisper.

"Never mind. Gotta go." Mack scurried to the other side of Btsht. "Let's retire to more private quarters."

Btsht shook his head, pointing at the fidgety hundred thousand or so Goldies scratching and skittering, stunned by the mayhem. Btsht limped to the large podium sitting on its side. He pulled it upright, along with the array of microphones.

"But, sir. You can't speak, can you?"

Btsht looked so frustrated that Mack almost felt sorry for him. The Big Guy clearly wanted the General to address the crowd but was afraid of what he'd say. He might let Mack say a few words but seemed equally afraid of what Mack might say. His eyes pleaded, darting back and forth between the two, pantomiming calming the crowd with shushing gestures.

Mack nodded wisely, "I can allay their fears while you discuss the matter with the General."

The General roared, "Bomb the fuckers. Stuff the entire missile arsenal up their ass and be done with them."

Btsht rolled his eyes and extended horny fingers half an inch apart, telling Mack to say the smallest amount to calm the crowd. Mack smiled and strutted to the microphones. "I speak on behalf of the Honorable Big Guys. But only the Honorable Btsht is hearty and well. He asks that you stay calm for a few minutes while he consults with the General and other advisers."

Mack glanced at twirling Big Guy Number One. "The recent events were caused by a terrible accident. Thank you for your cooperation." Mack bowed and backed away from the podium.

"Grack," Btsht said gratefully, nodding approval as the General scowled.

"We'd better talk," said Mack, backing away. "Over there," pointing behind the tipped-over grandstand. Btsht led them to an invisible door that opened at his approach, closing in Mack's face as the General disappeared inside.

Mack's tinny mic spouted Lucas's inimitable voice. "Good job, dude. Getting them after Courtney and averting immediate retaliation. You may have saved the day."

"Right. For thirty seconds. We can forget it if I don't get in on their conference. What's going on at your end? Did Ef really push the button? I can't believe it."

"I called with a quote because I knew you've been missing them."

"No. Not now. There are other things—"

"'If any question why we died, Tell them because our fathers lied.' I like this one and was sure you'd appreciate it."

"You are flat-ass wrong. We're not defending our fathers or our country. You'll get your butt blown off with your head up it."

Mack banged on the invisible door as Lucas said, "I hope that doesn't mean a negative evaluation. Marylyn would be so upset."

"I'm holding your evaluation in abeyance until—" The invisible door opened and Mack fell inside.

"Grack," said Btsht.

Mack wearily propped himself on an elbow and gradually worked himself up to hunched-over. "Sorry I'm late, but it's been that kind of day."

The General drooled on his gold-bedecked collar. "I told him to keep you out. This is the highest-level security meeting in Goldie history and we shouldn't share it with a snot-nosed heretic."

"General, I fully understand your sentiments. If I were the president of the United States, I wouldn't want an alien horning in on my security council meeting. But the Honorable Btsht is rightly concerned with the power of the Ermie arsenal. You'll probably annihilate each other faster than quick-draw McGraw. This possibility should be considered before launching a retaliatory strike."

"Shit. Goddamn. Hell, no."

"I heard that, General, and it wasn't very nice."

"Makes no damn difference what you heard. I'll cook your keester faster than a microwaved poodle. We must take the Ermies out right this second. There'll be no one left to retaliate and the Goldies will be the kings of the tepuis for all eternity. I say smite the bastards. Kick their collective butts. Avenge the sneaky death of Honorable Big Guy Number Three. And the inner ear imbalance of Honorable Big Guy Number One. Leave me to deal with Honorable Big Guy Number Two. If we act decisively now, we'll never have a war again. I say, drop the big one."

Lucas's reedy voice came singing over the airwaves. "'Oh Lord our Father, our young patriots, idols of our hearts, go forth to battle—be thou near them!—help us to tear their soldiers to bloody shreds with our shells; help us to cover their smiling fields with the pale forms of their patriot dead: help us to drown the thunder of the guns with the shrieks of their wounded, writhing in pain; help us to lay waste their noble homes with a hurricane of fire; help us to wring the hearts of their unoffending widows with unavailing grief— For our sakes who adore Thee, Lord, blast their hopes, blight their lives, protract their bitter pilgrimage, make heavy their steps, water their ways with their tears, stain the white snow with the blood of their wounded feet! We ask it in the spirit of love, of Him who is the Source of Love, and who is the ever-faithful refuge and friend of all who are sore beset and seek His aid with humble and contrite hearts. Amen.'"

"Well," said the General with enthusiasm. "I didn't catch all that, but it sums up my view. Not that I want anyone writhing in pain more than a couple of seconds. I just want them killed stone-cold dead."

Mack whispered, "Great, Lucas. You'll get us all killed. The General thinks I'm on his side." Mack eyed the General as Btsht shifted his attention back and forth. "Think a minute, General. If the Ermies wanted to deliver a sucker punch, they could have knocked you out with a first strike. But they didn't. You should believe their story."

"They couldn't fight their way out of a wet paper bag," snarled the General. "They're backward primitives, unfit to wear the label of antelope."

"Does that go for the Ivies too?"

"Nah. They're a bunch of harmless wimps."

"You can't call the Ermies backward primitives. Their little accident cost you two-thirds of your leadership. What if they were serious and wanted to do real harm? You'd be seeing nothing right now. So, get real, General. You live in a fantasy world of nationalistic grandeur and religious invincibility. You have no concept of the horrors of war, a General on paper only. You've never fought a war. You've only read books and seen a few movies."

The General's blood pressure spiraled as he clenched horny fists, foggy wisps wafting from his ears. "Put this traitor on the rack and pull off his arms and legs. Toss his parts into boiling oil until fried to a crisp. Then serve him as hors d'oeuvres for our combat ready troops and—"

Btsht scribbled furiously and thrust the note in the General's spittle spewing face. "SHUT THE FUCK UP."

The General's three-foot souffled hat collapsed to a pancake. His face fell, and moisture dotted the corners of his eyes. "But Honorable Number One Big Guy Btsht, sir. We've been planning this war all day long and I haven't ever had a war. I surely hope this alien traitor human toad—"

The General abruptly stopped when the next message was thrust in front of his disbelieving eyes. "CAN IT."

"Yes sir, sir," yelled the General. He clanked heels together and cut a salute so sharp that his hat reinflated. He waited and waited for Btsht to return the salute.

Btsht sighed and nudged a finger of his horny left hand against his left sideburn. The General let his breath out in a swish, nearly asphyxiating them both. Btsht turned to Mack, whipped up a larger placard, and stuffed it between Mack's eyes.

The print on the placard was so small that Mack could barely make it out: "This may come as a shock but I don't like you. I've never liked you. I don't like any of you. If there were any way I could keep your kind off of these sacred tepuis, I would do so, no matter the consequences. But destroying the Ermies and the Ivies fails to achieve that aim, no matter the sentiments of my heart. Therefore, I wouldn't declare war on the Ermies if I could think of an alternative. However, we're an honorable race. We gave our word that there'd be war and I'm honor bound to deliver on that promise. I gave the Ermies your DNA so they can pierce your heinie like it's never been pierced before. If you have further suggestions, I'm willing to hear one. But no more than one. Don't take advantage of this momentary courtesy to bombard me with half-witted suggestions like you've done in the past. Sincerely, Btsht." The great Goldie seal was imprinted on the bottom.

Btsht shoved a placard with much bigger print in Mack's face. It said, "You have two more seconds."

Mack gulped. "I won't say *same-to-you-fellow*, Honorable Number One Big Guy Btsht, sir. Though you hate me and my kind, it's better to be a deceiver than dead. Playing war games is losing valuable time you could use getting us off these tepuis. Put us in Bogota. Or Caracas, if you want to be nasty. No one would believe a cockamamie story about prancing antelopes and mutant tepuis. With our squirrely sense of direction, no one could point out where you live. You're safe for the rest of eternity. So, what do you say? Let's ring up the Ermies and tell them all is forgiven. Of course, after they

214

sacrifice their first born in the central Goldie square. Then we can all go away happy."

Btsht finished scribbling, holding up a barely legible placard. "You had your chance and blew it. As usual."

As if a light hit him, Mack said, "Now wait a minute. Since when can you write English, much less speak it?"

Btsht rolled bulging eyes and held up the massive pen clenched between horny fingers. Mack realized it didn't write the way Btsht moved it but with a motion of its own.

"Hey. Let me try that." Btsht handed it over and Mack wrote, "Your mama wears combat boots." It came out with inkblots and squiggles.

Btsht grabbed the pen back and threw a single-fingered salute at Mack.

"Okay. Your mama doesn't wear combat boots. But if I blew it, then what sort of plan would you have accepted? You said you'd do anything to keep humans off these tepuis, and my plan would accomplish that. If you're so smart, why don't you come up with something?"

Btsht's pen wrote, "Because there doesn't seem to be anything to come up with. We couldn't drop you in Caracas without getting caught."

"How about a blimp at midnight, lowered on silken tether to sullen earth? I'd settle for that no matter the wispiness of the tether or the hardness of target earth. Your turn to give creativity a chance."

Btsht flipped the pen over and wrote an incomprehensible something, shoving it in the General's face. The General grasped Mack's arm and they flew back through the invisible door into a stadium with restive Goldies stomping in unison.

Mack's collar mic reverberated with Lucas's dulcet tones. "You tried your best, Mack. Reg and I and our Big Guys have been following your exchanges with interest. But we missed whatever Btsht said. Does your mic blank out when he talks? Some sort of security thing? Should we expect dismemberment? Does that sum it up?"

"Btsht's fixated on the idea that we'd rat them out if they let us go."

"I could point out that 'to die for an idea is to place a pretty high price on conjectures.' But you'd find it inappropriate."

"It's not only inappropriate but nonsensical. We're not going to die for an idea but for the lack of an idea. If you convince your buddy Badsr to drop us at a decent Venezuelan resort, I promise a really great evaluation. Make Marylyn proud. Care to give it a shot?"

"You're grasping at empty air like a desperate old man. They can't return us to civilization without being discovered, showing up on satellite. Maybe they're not blowing smoke."

"If they'd put us on the valley floor, we could float down the Orinoco to the Caribbean. What's going on with the Ermies? War readiness as usual?"

"It's worse and worser. They're afraid the Goldies will fire their arsenal without warning. So, the Ermies are considering a first strike. Of course, Ef's up to his neck in doo-doo and will likely boil along with Courtney. The Ermies have cleared the stadium and assigned us to shelters that will theoretically protect us and their elite from Goldie missiles."

"Sounds like the dungeon the Goldies put us in. I didn't see anything special about it, but supposedly it's like NORAD under Cheyenne Mountain. A smart missile would probably bust any fortress."

"Reg here. The Ivies are continuing with patriotic exercises, briefing us on safe houses. Parades are starting afresh, right now leaving the Ivie stadium. We're trooping along behind my friend, the principal adviser to the Ivie chief, like following the Pied Piper. We have our own merry parade behind an Ivie band."

Mack shook his head. "Reg, do you see any hope at your end?"

"None. I thought the Ivies would oppose the war and they did at first. But now they feel the Goldies have challenged the superiority of the Ivie master antelopes and it's their God-given obligation to protect Ivie sovereignty."

Mack shook his head. "Weird that they're doing the same war ritual as the Goldies."

"Nothing weird about it," said Reg in his inimitable baritone. "Everyone does it. Humans, I mean. That's how it works when it comes to war."

"Crazy," said Lucas. "We learned our lesson at Gallipoli."

"You did not," said Mack. "You ended up in Vietnam the same as we did. And hey, Gallipoli. Wait until immigration hears about this."

"Oh, I meant in the generic sense, like forebears and that sort of thing."

"Lame. But it is a hell of a parade. Same for you, Reg?"

Reg let out his breath. "You two waste time on trivialities."

"Right," said Mack. "Roy and Peter are back with the squadron that went to find Courtney. And they found her. Hey, guys. Good job."

"Not so good." Peter was subdued. "She's not feeling well. We weren't able to stop them from man-handling her. Antelope-handling her, whatever. Take a look."

Mack edged up, shocked. "My god, Courtney. You look terrible. What happened. Tell me everything and I'll see what can be done."

Courtney was quiet as a rock. She looked terribly sad with her misshapen face. One eye was swollen, bloodshot, and slightly askew. A purple bruise spread across her forehead and she didn't even flinch when Mack said "god."

Mack shook his head. "Heavenly days. Where's Ellen and Barry when we need them?"

"Right behind you and happy to be ignored." Ellen patted Courtney on the back. "Poor dear." She took a handkerchief and motioned for Madison to hand over his box of pen and paper. It was so much a part of him that Mack had stopped noticing it.

"What's that?"

"Oh, Macca I say, scant attention you pay. Look a bit, as I open my kit. Now magic you've seen, Courtney's eye I can clean. Back in the—"

"All right already. I didn't know you had a first-aid kit. So, what happened, Pete? Roy?"

"Courtney was totally lost," said Peter. "She admitted wanting to finish off the statue. Perhaps admitted isn't the right word."

"Right. Knowing Courtney, she bragged about it."

"More than you might imagine. She ranted about godless antelopes and demanded that they take her to the 'sinful idol' so she could destroy it once and for all. That got their attention, not that she didn't already have it. And—"

"And everything really started going downhill," said Roy.

"They beat her up." Ellen angrily daubed cotton balls around Courtney's eye.

"Screech," said Courtney.

"That's better," said Mack. "We were afraid we'd lost you."

Ellen said, "We may have. That was more reflex than anything. Look at her eyes. She may have a concussion. They decked her right in front of us. No love tap stuff."

"The big Legionnaire. This guy." Peter pointed. "Reached behind his left ear and hit her with a haymaker. She went down like a sack of cement dropped off a roof, and she's been goofy ever since. Goofier than usual, which is to say quiet."

"Totally out of character." Mack marched up to the head Legionnaire. "Explain your brutality toward a female much smaller than yourself. Well, a lot shorter. Aggravated assault carries a penalty of years in the dungeon, without parole. Did she take a threatening step toward you? Did she brandish an atomic laser or impugn the lineage of your parents? Did she launch a dangerous missile? What justified beating up a poor old woman who wouldn't harm a flea?"

The Legionnaire placed a finger on Mack's nose and flicked, knocking Mack on his butt. "You're all hot air. This heathen woman has been sentenced to death for heresy, which taught her nothing. She committed an act of heresy in my presence. No one does that unscathed. If you'd like to try your luck, be my guest. As my favorite human philosopher would say, 'Make my day.'" The Legionnaire crooked a finger and beckoned, daring Mack to get up.

Mack scrambled up, his nose dripping blood. He ducked and weaved as he air-boxed, doing fancy footwork. "Bullies and jerks have always been my undoing. The only remedy is to bring their superiors down on such cretins like a truckload of rotten cabbage. Bullies are cowards at heart and shrivel when reported to their superiors. The new number one Big Guy will bust you on the spot, out to pasture without a pension."

The huge Legionnaire put hooves on his hips. "You have no idea how much you bore me. The General, my esteemed boss, hates your guts. The same as His Eminence the Pope. And the new Number One Big Guy," peering at a transcript, "'has never liked you.' He'd rather I mopped the floor with you than look at your ugly mug. These being the undisputable facts, I will make our day for the General, Pope, Big Guy Number One, and myself." He pulled his sinewy arm level with his left ear and let fly.

It happened so fast that "telegraphed" wasn't the word to describe why Mack had already begun moving to the right. Though much too slowly. It saved his life but failed to prevent the scraping of skin, tissue, and gristle from the left side of his head. His limp body followed a graceful arc as he spun through the air above his compadres, landing with a whomp.

Peter, Roy, Barry, Madison, and Ellen rushed to him. Even Courtney stumbled over, like a goose-stepping robot with unfocused eyes. Ellen swabbed cotton balls on the side of Mack's head while Barry said, "Give him air, back off so he can breathe."

"There shouldn't be a problem." Peter laughed. "He landed on his head."

Ellen wiped furiously. "That's not funny. He fortunately didn't land on his head. More like his shoulder. It's crumpled."

"He went up like a rocket and downhill like a rock." Roy blinked at Mack as if that would resuscitate him.

Madison emoted. "His open eyes, swirl like pies—"

"Pies don't swirl," said Peter. "You're going to have to work on that one." "Ah pizza pies, swirl like eyes, alight on thighs, oh me oh mys."

Mack shifted the weight off his shoulder, rolling on his back, moaning. "Ohhlilihh. What did I do now? Where am I?"

"I'm not doing much good." Ellen stood and ripped a strip off her skirt. The piece came off raggedly, leaving a modest slit. "More first-aid kit, Madison. Snap it up."

"You made a right mess of that," said Peter. "Our hosts probably don't like miniskirts any more than they like Mack. But I'm an artist, so it's all right by me."

Ellen groaned. "Oh, stow it, Peter. Do something constructive."

"Here, my dear; take the kit, I give you it."

"Oh, thanks, Madison." Ellen sprinkled antibiotic powder on the cloth strip and laid it over Mack's temple. "What a mess." She grabbed fresh cotton balls. "You back? We were worried."

Mack said, "Where's Lucas?" His eyes were unfocused, one dilated and the other with an enormous pupil.

"He looks worse than Courtney," said Barry.

"You rang?" came Lucas's tinny voice. "It's hard to follow what's going on. But it's always safe to assume that Mack got creamed for wising off. Ellen is doing her best to nurse him back to health, oh happy day. And war games are about to begin. I got one hot off the press. 'Small nations are like indecently dressed women. They tempt the evil-minded.' The best part is Mack isn't in shape to tell me I'm a hundred eighty degrees off base."

"Well, you are," said Ellen. "I'm not an indecently dressed woman. I just have a little tear in my skirt."

"What did you say, Lucas?" mumbled Mack. "I shouldn't have opened my big mouth. Someday I will learn. Yes, I will."

Lucas said, "No, you won't. But how are you feeling? We hoped it was just a short in your mic when you hit the ground. Do you read me, Mack?"

"What did you say, Lucas? I'm not hearing too good, and I can't see too good either, and my face feels burned. Where's my hat? The worst part would be losing my hat." Mack moved an inch as if to go look for it. "Oh my god, my shoulder. I don't think I can walk."

Peter groaned. "You don't need a shoulder to walk. You'll be okay, especially when you realize Ellen is busting her cute little butt for you."

"God, I hate you," said Ellen. "Come on Mack. Get up. You, too, Courtney. Pry yourselves off the ground and let's get going. And Peter, go get his hat. It's right over there. Otherwise, they'll leave us here."

Mack's head lolled back and forth as he tried to zoom in on Ellen's voice. "What's that? Who will leave us here?"

"Reg here. Unless you stick with your hosts you won't have shelter from the storm. Your only chance of survival is underground."

"Maybe our only chance of survival is— I'm woozy." Mack laid the uninjured side of his face on Ellen's shoulder, apparently without ulterior intent.

Reg said, "I'm worried about you, my boy. You took a shot heard around these little worlds. But you were saying?"

"Really dizzy. Our only chance of survival is getting off these tepuis before the fireworks begin. I'm going to be sick." Upchucking sounds filled the airways as Mack's compatriots left the immediate vicinity.

"Gag. Okay, I'm done. For now. Come on back."

"It'd be better if you came over here," said Peter, "or if we moved you out of the mess. You're a sight. Come get your hat," Peter twirled it on a finger.

Mack tried to roll over. "You must admit this has been an adventure. Plane crashed and up to our knees in mud. Dust-deviled by whirling dervishes. Big Guy Number Three and his cousin blown up all over us. And no one's had a shower except Courtney, and it did her no good. Damn the lottery and my big mouth. I am going to reform."

"And when will you begin this reformation?" said Ellen as Peter shrugged, setting the hat aside. He helped Roy lift Mack by the elbows and carry him away from the stench. Ellen lifted the bloody strip off his head and folded it over, reapplying it. "It's almost stopped bleeding but he'll have a scar."

Peter said, "Mack looks like bloody hell."

"Thanks, Pete. I needed that. Anyway, thanks for finding my hat." Mack gingerly propped it on his head, titled

221

away from the bad side. "See, I'm my old self. We'll follow the dust cloud inside. See what's going on."

Peter stuck out a small box. "Would you like a breath mint?"

"Thanks, Pete." Mack popped one in his mouth. "Hope I didn't wilt you," he said to Ellen as she lifted the refolded strip off and stared at the deep scrape.

"No problem. Try getting up."

Courtney stood hunched like a buzzard, eyes twitching and jerking. Mack tried standing, grimacing all the way. He finally made it, the left side of his head glistening like raw steak. "Looks pretty good, eh?"

Peter said, "You look like I picture death. You hit your head harder than you think."

"The hat hides the bats in the belfry I see," said Madison. "Your head is ill, you took a spill, perhaps a pill will fill the bill."

"Oh, please." Mack held his head with both hands. "Onwards. I'll shamble along."

"Why?" Courtney stared at Barry as he took her elbow. Ellen helped on the other side. "Why?"

Lucas's faraway voice said, "I've got a great quote to go with that but I can't remember it. Can anybody help me out?"

Mack groaned. "I hope you forget all those damn quotes."

"I like his quotes. His quotes are jolts. Only dolts would wish to bolt."

Mack almost smiled. "Thank you, Madison. I'll try cutting him some slack."

Roy struck a pose and swung his huge paw. "Mack is going downhill."

Ellen shook her lovely head. "We were worried when you bit the dust like you were shot from a cannon. But you've done nothing to endear us since, except claim you've learned your lesson and can control 'the mouth.' But you can't do it, can you? You haven't a hope."

Mack sighed. "You're right. I'm always out of line, and my war wound is acting up." He put a hand on the wrong side of his head and blanched like an almond. "Ooohhheeeeeee."

222

"Our sympathy is rapidly diminishing."

"Why?" demanded Courtney.

"My dear." Mack swung an arm halfway around Courtney's waist. "You're in worse shape than I am and it's my fault. Let's get something to eat and a little bonus we deserve."

"Yeah, and what's that?" said Peter. "Your surprises are never good."

"Why?" said Courtney.

"Barry and Ellen, give me a hand." Mack motioned. "She'll be all right when we get going. I'll not say another word."

"That'll be the day," said Peter. He took Courtney's hand and helped her onto the emerald road. They headed down into the heart of the tepui, as fast as they could stumble.

"We're a sight." Ellen smiled. "Like Dorothy and entourage, approaching Emerald City for an audience with the Wizard."

"And of course, you're Dorothy, so we're your entourage," said Peter. "Persnickety, I'd say."

"You're so literal." Ellen stamped her foot.

"That was a bit like Dorothy," said Mack as they stood staring at a high portal that looked like a Chinese gate. Barry and Peter searched the blank wall for a mechanism to spring the invisible door.

Ellen said, "I don't get it. The Goldies walk up and doors open. We do a body cavity search and nothing happens."

Mack leaned against the side of the fancy gate, clasping a hand to his head. "Mustn't talk like that. I'm a poor weak male and you knock me into a cocked hat."

"Which takes no effort at all."

Courtney snapped out of her reverie and marched up to Mack double-quick, shaking a finger in his face, "You should have your mouth washed out with soap. Spouting obscenities like that in front of this fine upstanding young lady…" trailing off like she remembered Ellen wasn't a Baptist.

"You're feeling better." Mack's attempted smile was defeated by the left half's failure to perform. "I didn't mean to offend. I got carried away by the reservoir of testosterone that's accumulated in the last year or so. Pardon, madam. Pardone," accompanied by a bow that grazed the portal and the door slid open. Roy and Peter fell on their noses as Madison and Barry ran through the door with Mack, Courtney, and Ellen.

"Where the hell are the lights?" asked Peter. "We can't see where we're going."

"Doesn't matter." Mack pointed. "The emerald road glows like aisle lights in a theater. It'll be easy. Maybe Ellen would like to link arms and skip."

"Oh, you." Ellen rolled her eyes.

Madison gushed. "I love this thing, a ring a ding, I'll take a fling, my chimes to ring. Ain't it grand?"

Mack shook his head. "That last part didn't rhyme. You're out of character."

"I was interrupted, corrupted; another second's time and I would've dubbed it. So, slam shut your mouth, as you've promised, and we'll rejoice, you doubting Thomas."

Madison took an extra big breath, promising an epic poem, as Mack said, "You win, Maddy my man. Now go down, 'til Roy's found. Sorry, couldn't resist."

"That was terrible," said Peter as Roy intoned his usual. They sped through the near darkness along the glow of the downward spiraling road.

Mack pointed. "That looks like a sliver of the stage, like looking through a slit. Everyone quiet." They could hear marching and a loud voice droning as Mack motioned them toward a fork in the road.

"Which way, Sherlock?" said Peter.

"I always take the high road," said Mack.

"Right," said Ellen. "I agree because there's no room on the down fork," which was jammed with Goldies. They tiptoed behind Mack. In seconds the upper fork turned into a bridge swaying under their collective weight.

Ellen whispered hysterically. "It's going to collapse."

"It was built for those larger than ourselves." Mack gestured at Courtney. "Go on. No worries, mate, as Lucas would say."

"You rang, dude?" came Lucas's thin voice.

"No, but we found an underground stadium that must hold a hundred thousand plus." They stood at the top of a stadium with the stage far below. A vaguely familiar figure stood in the center of the stage as lines of Legionnaires marched around it. The stands were filled with Goldies rhythmically clapping and shouting at regular intervals. It sounded like "Oy Vey."

"The voice sounds familiar," said Mack.

"Well, yes. It's me," said Lucas.

Mack said, "I mean the main haranguer below. It's our old friend Judge Grdam, jailer sans humor. In our tradition of brass ballsiness, we'll demand food, grog, and seven showers." Mack punched his fist in the air, attracting the attention of the closest Goldie, who shot him a look of unadulterated hatred.

"I think we ate it this time," said Peter.

"Get going." Mack plunged down the stairs with Judge Grdam's voice rollicking over Mack's translator, "—times that try antelope souls—"

The crowd clapped and swayed, rocking the stadium, drowning out the judge's harangue. "—must strike a decisive blow for peace—that will preserve the antelope way of life for—"

Lucas's voice came filtering through. "You'll appreciate this one, Mack, so listen up. 'The purpose of all war is peace.' Told you you'd like it. Told you so."

Mack stopped, and said wearily, "I'll concede you that one but only on the condition that you cut it out permanently. Is that a deal?"

"That's the worst deal I've ever heard of," said Lucas. "What do I care whether you concede me one? Respond on the merits, man. The quote was squarely on point."

"No more quotes would be more on point."

"It's on point. Admit it."

Ellen said, "It's squarely on point. Give him one, Mack."

"I'd be giving him one if I admitted that."

"Then how's it not?" demanded Lucas.

"Well." Mack stopped short. "Of course, the purpose of all war isn't peace. The purpose of all war is war."

"Yeah, but both sides figure they're going to kick butt big time, which will achieve instant peace. So, the purpose of all war is peace. You can't deny it."

"I deny it."

"But without reason. Out of sheer stubbornness and cantankerousness."

"Oh, yeah," said Mack. "Troops, charge," and Mack ran smack into a leering Goldie. The big Goldie picked Mack up by the nape of the neck, brushing the injured left side of his head.

Mack screeched. "Unhand me, you ruffian, and take me to your leader."

"I'll leader you, you little nitwit," said the huge Legionnaire. Mack belatedly recognized him as the one who'd almost knocked him to kingdom come. The big Legionnaire was prepared to do it again, flinty fist cocked beside a crooked smile.

"Whoops." Mack ducked so fast he slipped the Legionnaire's grasp and rocketed down the stairs, bouncing off huge Goldies that shivered only slightly. He plunged through the marching ranks of goose-stepping Legionnaires onto the stage.

Judge Grdam stopped in mid-rant. "Not you again. I thought you'd gotten lost, or eaten by wild animals. Guards! Guards!"

"Now, just a wee second. We're your guests and you're not treating us like a civilized species would treat their guests. Look at my face."

"No worse than ever. Guards. Seize him."

Guards grabbed Mack's arms. "We demand food and showers. Well, how about a cold cup of water in his name, or whatever name? What are you planning, a public execution?"

"Great idea. But no time for that."

"I demand to see Big Guy Number One, my good buddy, the Honorable Btsht."

"Horrible to see you again." Btsht appeared behind the judge. "Whatever made you think I was your good buddy? You sure know how to push the envelope. Handcuff him."

The huge Legionnaire materialized beside Mack. Btsht nodded. "Keep him in sight at all times. You got that?"

"Yes, sir." The huge Legionnaire saluted.

"Wow, sir, Honorable Btsht. You got your voice back. I was worried but am so happy to hear you talking again. I respectfully request food, water, and showers for my friends—"

"And they shall have them in spite of how unworried you actually were. You will stay in sight and out of trouble." He snapped horny fingers. A Legionnaire snapped ceiling-fan-sized titanium cuffs around Mack's sagging wrists. A cluster of Legionnaires corralled everyone else, taking them to a table behind the stage. One of Mack's handcuffs was taken off and snapped around a corner stanchion. Mack watched them eat as the Goldies continued speechifying.

"Psssst. Throw me something to eat. I'm weak from hunger."

"Sure," said Peter. "Catch," tossing orange cubes. The huge Legionnaire diverted them with a lanky paw, knocking them high in the air and catching them in his upturned mouth.

"Wow," said Mack. "That was great. Did you start out with popcorn and work up to Chinese food. Or was that a reflex proving superior Goldie ability?"

"My highest ambition would be to drop you in boiling oil. I would so enjoy that."

"I know you're sincere. But surely your advanced civilization feeds prisoners between bouts of starvation and torture."

"Nope. Shut up and listen to the honorable judge. You might learn something, though I doubt it."

Mack shut his mouth, thinking how much better life would have been if he'd kept it shut for the last thirty hours or so.

The judge wound up the crowd, tighter and tighter toward inevitable explosion. He said, "—protector and defender of the faith—Golden Macaroon Award of Religious Fitness—filthy swine before the protractor—the Good, the Great, the Only—the Fabulously Pious, His Eminence the Most Grandeur and Grandiose——the late Bishop, Cardinal, now Pope and successor to God."

His final comments were drowned out by tumultuous applause as the stadium exploded in columns of purple, lavender, and chartreuse smoke. His holiness swooped from the ceiling in a chariot of gold drawn by six albino tigers. The Pope swung a golden bullwhip, snapping it in lock-step with the crowd's over-the-top clapping.

"I think I'm having a religious experience." Mack placed manacled hands on his heaving chest.

"Well, who the hell isn't?" said Peter with his mouth full, transfixed at the spectacle.

The chariot skidded onto the stage, bounced, and slid to a stop. Two albino tigers snarled, scant inches from Mack's nose.

13

"Nice kitties," said Mack as the Pope stepped from the chariot and colorful rockets ripped the air. Solid blocks of plasma displayed golden antelopes bounding over mountains and up raging waterfalls as tigers sniffed Mack's crotch.

"Snarl," said the closest tiger, holding up a paw the size of a catcher's mitt. A playful swipe sent Mack reeling backward and hanging by a gigantic handcuff off the corner of the stage, spiraling above his feasting compatriots.

"Arrmrg." Mack grabbed his newly sprained wrist as it turned purple and green.

"Here." Peter ran under Mack's spinning feet and gave him a boost onto the edge of the stage. The tigers surged to take a closer look at the weird human.

"Bad kitties." Mack slapped at the tigers. Sniffing nostrils flared as they sprang, fortunately still attached to the Pope's chariot, which brought them up short and unhappy at Mack's continued existence.

The Pope's cape flowed horizontal behind him as he flung himself onto the elevated center of the stage. He snubbed the judge but embraced Btsht, kissing him on both cheeks. Btsht, not to be upstaged, smooched back with a distasteful expression.

The monitors changed from a dozen heroic scenes into a single gigantic production. The history of the Goldie religion was illustrated in the space of forty-seven jam-packed seconds. Even the tigers sat quietly during this astonishing exhibition. First came the MOTHER, wafting ethereally over the crowd. Her goldenness eclipsed the most brilliant sunset in colors from key lime to burnt sienna. The MOTHER birthed the

229

DAUGHTER in a supremely tasteful fashion. More golden sunsets pulsed around the huge arena. She in turn birthed the GOLDEN SON, or Radnicharra, or Famigusta. Mack couldn't make out the Goldie script. Then the GOLDEN SON hit the big screen with gusto. He wielded a super big Swiss Army knife that shot lasers every which way, destroying buckets of Ermies and Ivies.

Mack shook his head as Lucas's muttering bit into his consciousness. "Hey, Mack. Our show is better than your show."

"No way. The Goldies can outdo everyone in tackiness and noodle-headed popery. Snarling albino tigers nearly did me in. They've put on the greatest opening ceremony since the Olympics."

"BFD. The Ermies featured giant elephants thundering out of the heavens. They pulled a super-tank with sixteen madly swiveling turrets. It shot movies over the top of the Ermie stadium like a mad sky-writer. None of the wussy Goldie stuff for us. We're patrons of Ef."

"How is the poor soul? I hope he isn't a scapegoat like me."

"You'd better sit down, because this is going to be hard for you. You sitting?"

"Cut the crap. What's with Ef?"

"Efriam Malachi Steinmetz is an Ermie hero with a title. The Illustrious, Revered, and Honorable. He did what the Ermies had been afraid to do. Fire the first shot and knock off a Goldie Big Guy. That must have shredded the Goldie morale to tatters, giving the Ermies the psychological upper hand. They might have been antsy about war for the last few hundred years but they've embraced Ef with vigor and verve. They put a big HERO badge on his chest, mostly obscuring him. You should see him with his little black cap and silky tunic. He's wearing sleek pantaloons and platform shoes in patent leather with twelve-inch heels, like a midget on stilts. Billy K. made a black switchblade to go along with Ef's spiffy new outfit, and Ef sold out the Ussery Pass development. It'll be interesting to see how folks in Phoenix deal with their new Ermie neighbors. I'd like to be there when the first Ermie shows up. You know how open-minded that Fountain Hills-Paradise Valley bunch is."

"I'm shell-shocked. I thought the Goldies were nuts but the Ermies sound worse. The Pope did a swoop around the stadium with a golden-rocket backpack. He's wearing full dress regalia with golden lace and tassels that twirl like a bar hussy. Little golden statues of whoever it was Courtney dismembered, flit around behind him. It's like Follow the Leader in virtual reality. The audience is part of the action, a truly religious experience. Now he's calling for all good Goldies to come to the aid of their country. Smite the nasty Ermies and Ivies and dunk their nasty false gods. Eradicate the indecency of their inferior cultures."

"I have the perfect quote."

"Please don't."

"Ahem. 'The clergy repay this friendly recognition of their place in society by an almost unfailing devotion to the constituted authorities. When they take part in rebellions, it is almost always against subversive usurpers, not legitimate rulers. At all times and always they have been the bulwark of orthodoxy in politics— Their prayers always go up for kings, not for rebels and reformers.' I know you can't see it, good buddy, but visualize me taking a bow. Thank you. Thank you. Oh, please. That's enough applause."

"If you only had a brain. There's no rebellion. This is a war among city-states, like in ancient Greece. Not a civil war. The day you come up with an appropriate quote is the day we're rescued. I wonder if we'll be celebrated for discovering an intelligent alien species."

"You can't really call these guys intelligent. Going to war over little or nothing."

"Well, they're no dummies. Their reason for going to war is not exactly nothing. Though after my whack on the head I can't remember what the reason is. Except we *might* out them."

"They're going to war to prove that their god is better than the other antelopes' god. My god can kick your god's butt and I'll show you by kicking yours. I came for Carnival in Rio. I had no intention of getting involved in alien rivalries."

"And I didn't want to have my fingertips chopped off. Or having to save Courtney from becoming the fattest French fry on the planet. Or losing the left side of my face and wrenching my wrist out of its socket. Or having my best dress uniform spattered with antelope gore, or missing lunch today. I did so want a shower."

"I'm sure everyone's with you on the last part."

"Our pope floated onto the stage with his great cape, godliest hang glider you've ever seen."

"Bullhonky. Our pope-type guy is even better."

"You may have a pope-type guy, but this one actually is the Pope. At least that's the translation."

"Don't be dense. We get the same translation for the top religious guy over here. What else would they call them? Ayatollahs?"

"You need to brush up on political correctness. Our pope is exhorting the Goldies to dismember, destroy, demolish, devastate, disfigure, decimate, despoil, deface, disable, defile, debilitate, debase, debauch, degrade, disgrace, dishonor, desecrate, defame, demean, discredit, and…the one I like best because Courtney might have inspired it. De-dick the Ermies, and the Ivies too. In the name of Mother, Daughter, and Radnicharra, or maybe Famigusta, amen. I missed a few words but that was a near quote. The Pope illustrated each d-word, greatest acting ever."

"You have a fanatic on your hands. Which reminds me. 'Onward Christian Soldiers, rip and tear and smite! Let the gentle Jesus, bless your dynamite.' Admit it, dude. Apropos."

"Hmmm. Go away, nasty kitty cats." Hiss. "Okay, I can't admit you've come up with a winner but if you won't tell anyone, that wasn't too bad. It reminds me of the one about pie in the sky."

"They're not intentional. They are magically sprung by a stimulus that straightaway brings the quote to mind."

"Say what?"

"To recall a quote from me mum's big book I have to somehow be reminded of it from something that happens. Or what someone says. I can't just come up with a quote on request. Do you understand what I mean from what it was I think I said?"

Mack groaned. "Have you heard what's going on with the Ivies and Reg's crew? We haven't heard anything for ages. Meanwhile, I'm in handcuffs. The Pope is conjuring up illusions while my buddies gorge their faces. And the nice kitties fantasize about eating yours truly. They hiss and spit and breathe all over me. They must have had anchovies for lunch."

"Reg here. Sorry about your struggles, Mack. I wish the variously colored antelopes would stop defaming the real pope." He sighed. "But Lucas probably doesn't consider it defamation; only politically marginal. You haven't heard from me because we're having no problems. The Ivies are the greatest, though I am worried about these rallies and the frenzy they've worked themselves into. And yes, we're having our own, similar to yours. The Ivie rallies may not be as impressive, but they are veering out of control. We're still treated as treasured guests with box seats high over the arena. The Ivies are following the same script as the Goldies and Ermies, though our 'pope' is low key. He was chauffeured in a long white, dare I say it, popemobile."

Lucas laughed. "That's what we call backpacker's buses back home, ah, what they have back in Australia." Silence. "That's because they're so full. No population control, you know."

"Hardy, har," said Mack. "Go ahead, Reg. I apologize for Lucas's interruption."

"Well." Reg forced a chuckle. "The Ivie pope began a low-key address that escalated. Molly and Betty escaped to the surface but were bored until they saw an albino tiger. It was the size of a bobcat. Your story will make them feel a lot better, Mack. Oops, we have company. Talk to you later."

"Thanks, Reg. Though I can't picture the Ivies working themselves into a frenzy."

Lucas said, "Though theoretical allies, the Ermies consider the Ivies inept. They'll be worthless in the upcoming war."

"Oh my god—"

"Kitty got your tongue?"

Mack said nothing.

"Hey, Mack. What's up?"

Mack's voice shook. "We're having a funeral."

"Yeah. So? It's not one of you, is it?"

"I figured it already happened, when I wasn't around."

"You're not making sense."

"A funeral for the third Big Guy and his nephew. The Goldies that Ef blew to smithereens. The Pope conjured see-through coffins out of thin air. Two tall athletic antelopes are blobs of red jelly, right over my head. The size of bread boxes, big bread boxes. Good thing I didn't eat. The Pope is flitting back and forth like a roadrunner in front of new Number One Big Guy Btsht. Back and forth in spurts, off the edge of the stage suspended in mid-air. He's super good with the rockets on the back of his cape. You wait for him to dash his brains thirty feet below but he never does. The audience is going nuts. The Pope is demanding revenge, reprisals, recriminations, repayments, retributions—I won't list them all. The patriotic Goldies are eating it up. Here's a toast to the next war. May no one survive. Which is to say no Ermies, Ivies, or humans.

"His demise wasn't so unfortunate. Big Guy Number Three gave me a lot of grief before Ef's missile sprayed us with gore."

"I'm surprised at you, Mack. Justifying the demise of an intelligent being just because he gave you a hard time. If that were the rule, they'd be few of us left."

"You're a comedian, ha, ha. Besides, I'm not so hard to get along with."

"Not as long as everyone does what you want them to do when you want them to do it. Then you're okay. Otherwise, kerflooey."

"So, you'd rather that those who give you a hard time are granted eternal life to do it in perpetuity."

"No. But I wouldn't rejoice at having them blown away."

"You're just a better person than I am."

"I've been telling you that for practically forever. But, damn. You made me forget it."

"Forget what?"

234

"The apropos quote. 'We are always making God our accomplice, that we may legalize our own inequities. Every successful massacre is consecrated by a Te Deum, and the clergy have never been wanting benedictions for any victorious enormity.' Stand and marvel. Pretty good, eh?"

"Sucks. Our respective popes aren't consecrating a massacre but seeking revenge. They're consecrating a massacre before it happens."

Lucas sniffed. "I know that. I was quoting from the Ermie viewpoint. What our pope's doing. Celebrating a victorious enormity."

"Of rather short duration, I'd guess. Those damn cats. Go away, nasty anchovy-breaths. My wrist is killing me and I'm famished and I'm sick to death of the Goldie pope. I have to get out of here, Lucas. So, sayonara for now. And here goes."

Mack bent like a pretzel around the handcuff. He inserted the fingertips of his undamaged hand in his mouth and blew a mighty blast that shocked the great stadium into silence. This aborted the clapping as the Pope poised in midstep on the edge of the high podium, plummeting to the floor as Btsht, the new Number One Big Guy, stared daggers. Mack yelled. "Get me out of these things and away from the bad kitty cats. I am ready to dine." He added as an aside to the Big Guy, "Ambidexterity can be a gas, eh?"

A snarl crossed the Big Guy's face as he summoned the huge Legionnaire. Mack placed his fingers back in his mouth. "Stand back or I'll deafen you. I'm only asking for common courtesy, a bite to eat, and a warm shower. The minimum required of a civilized species, such as you purport to be."

In a single stride the Big Guy stood with his face in Mack's. "I still have an ax and this time it won't be just your fingertips. You've pushed me too far."

"I haven't pushed you nearly far enough."

The Big Guy reached for Mack's throat at the exact second the two closest albino tigers pounced. This made the Big Guy say with feeling, "Sheeeee-it. Get these goddam cats off me. Trainer, big Legionnaire. Heads will roll."

"Maybe your head will roll first." Mack stood back as the Big Guy wrestled an albino tiger with each hoof. His tunic

235

shredded and blood spurted, threatening to drench Mack and his compatriots.

Peter yelled, "I didn't know you could still whistle. I thought the Big Guy cut off your fingertips."

"I'm too busy to discuss it." Mack blew a whistle that would go down in the annals of Goldie lore, holding the blast for fourteen seconds. The albino cats flew off the Big Guy and covered their ears with their paws; the entire auditorium was incapacitated, unable to think or walk straight, while Mack's whistle rent the air. The Big Guy staggered free and received sloppy first aid.

"Enough already," said the Big Guy weakly. "Uncuff him and put him with his friends for a bite to eat and a shower. He really needs a shower."

"Why don't I just throttle him instead?" asked the huge Legionnaire.

"Right." Mack deafened the entire Goldie population, with gusto. "Shriek, caterwaul." The huge Legionnaire numbly loosened the cuffs, letting Mack free.

"Thank you kindly. Send your first-aid guys because I need stitching up. Well, after you finish with Honorable Big Guy Number One, Btsht. I count him among my esteemed acquaintances."

Peter yelled, "Mack, duck."

"What's that?" The tiny shoes of the Goldie pope landed in the middle of Mack's back.

"Take that." The Pope's booster rockets wafted him gently onto the platform next to Mack's doubled-up body.

"Give me a second and I'll give you a super-duper genuflect, or have I already done that?" Mack rolled onto his side, then the other side, checking out the easiest way to get up.

"You are a despicable heathen and fit only for the—"

Mack interrupted with a whistle. The Pope draped golden doilies over his ears, his eyes rotating in opposite directions. "The Big Guy has spoken and we've got a deal. Give me a hand down, my good antelope," he said to the huge Legionnaire.

"My pleasure." The Legionnaire flipped Mack over the side with a kick to the midsection.

"Catch him," yelled Peter as Mack fell into Courtney's outstretched arms.

"Got him." Courtney beamed all over her huge face. "Hope you're doing better." She bounced him up and down.

"You've saved my life, Courtney, what little I have left. I see you're doing better—not an entirely good thing because the Goldies might not boil an invalid. But, could you put me down, please?"

"Sure." Courtney lowered him to the floor. "Sorry about that. I was really glad I caught you."

"And I was even gladder. Is there anything left to eat?"

"One of these days—" Ellen handed him a plate of multicolored cubes and a foaming mug of red grog.

"Yeah. One of these days what?"

Madison said, "One of these days, you'll come back dead. And why will that be, maybe something you said? We'll stutter along, without a clue, and think back on you, boohoo."

"Oh, that is so sweet, Madison. And to think you made it up on the spot. You'll go far with the extemporaneous poets of America. In the meantime, does anyone have any idea how to stop the war? Because I haven't an inkling."

The festivities reconvened as Mack scooped up colorful cubes and tossed them in his mouth. The Pope dashed about the high platform as if uninterrupted and new Number One Big Guy Btsht looked smug, though tattered. The transparent coffins of jiggling red jelly continued their slow descent toward the frenetic pope.

"It wouldn't hurt to say a prayer," said Courtney.

Ellen nodded. "She has a point."

"Maybe a few more tankards and a hot shower will help us think better," said Peter.

"All I can say," started Roy before Mack interrupted him.

"We know," said Mack to Roy and then to Madison, as he opened his mouth, "and Madison. I don't want you to overtax yourself."

"But, hey, hey; I have something to say." Madison waved his arms.

"Okay." Mack was reluctant. "Shoot."

237

"I've thought and thought and thought and thought and then I thought some more. And my considered opinion is, we should bolt the door."

"What do you mean?" asked Peter. "Why would we bolt the door? We don't even have a door and if we did how would we lock it?"

"When I say bolt, I mean we run for it, 'cause rappelling's better than vaporizing."

"That's truly the worse rhyme I've ever heard." At Madison's wounded expression Mack grimaced. "Well, the sentiment was fine. And I've reached the same conclusion. After all, the Goldies don't seem to care if we disappear. Maybe they'd rather we did. Scouting out the tepui would keep us out of trouble, or at least me out of trouble. That'd let Courtney escape boiling oil and me, too, while getting us out of this madhouse. The Goldie war jamboree is depressing."

"Terribly depressing." Ellen looked sad. "It gives me the heebie-jeebies. The Goldies are warmongers intent on their own destruction. Along with everyone else, especially us."

Peter held up his hands. "We shouldn't go rushing off until we've finished eating. And we'd better take enough food to last awhile. I'm tired of feast or famine. This is only the second brewski we've had since we've been here."

"We've only been here thirty hours." Barry shook his head. "How many beers do you need in thirty hours?"

"I wouldn't need any if I had a little reefer."

Mack patted Pete on the back. "Good point on provisions. See if the guard will rustle up a batch of cubed stuff to go."

"It'll be growing your gut." Barry rubbed his tummy. "That stuff's pure butter. No wonder it melts in your mouth, all over your hands, and down your face." He handed Courtney a towel and she delicately patted her mouth.

"TA, TA. TWEEDLEDUM." The call was answered by, "TA, TA, TWEEDLEDEE," as trumpets sprouted from the sides of the huge auditorium. The opposite trumpets gave answering calls, blaring in a round robin, sweeping the auditorium and erupting in a military cadence that sounded like the Triumphal March from *Aida*.

238

Mack laughed. "Hey, Lucas. The Goldies have elephants too."

"We're way past elephants over here," said Lucas's tinny voice. "Our pope is prancing around on lasers like they were stilts. What a showman. And I think I heard trumpets. You know what they say."

"What who says? What are you talking about, Lucas old sod?"

"Gotcha. 'It is forbidden to kill; therefore, all murderers are punished unless they kill in large numbers and to the sound of trumpets.' Heh, heh, heh."

"Pretty cute, aren't you, suckering me? Still, you should see the Goldie trumpets. They're six feet long and look like pure gold. Did you hear we're making a getaway? I want you to cover for us, let us know what's going on. Create a subterfuge if necessary. Can you do that?"

"That won't be a problem since the transcript of this conversation is already winging its way to the desks of the Goldie, Ermie, and Ivie movers and shakers. Assuming it isn't there already. You're fortunate you're doing my performance evaluation instead of vice versa."

"No one seems to care whether we escape."

"Yeah, I heard that. But don't press your luck."

"We should start talking in code, maybe pig Latin, eh? Okay, here goes. Eway tendinay ootay amscray. That should fix their translation machines. We get in trouble from literal translations because English isn't literal. Every word has a half-dozen meanings depending on nuance, inflection, and context. I don't know how anyone understands anyone."

Ellen groaned. "You're the most literal of the lot, and your wrist is looking scary. You probably shouldn't have purple and green lines running up your arm."

"Hmmm." Mack took a look and winced. "Is that a facade of concern concealing the inherent romantic inclination of your heart? Or is there another explanation? I'll think about it."

"You open your mouth without thinking. And your thoughts are obscene, lascivious, and self-centered." Ellen huffed off to help Peter fill a bag with colorful cubes.

"Romance isn't obscene," Mack said to her back. "You may be married but I've never heard you say a kind word, or any word at all, about your old man. Your darling husband. Am I missing something here?"

A helpful Legionnaire provided a contraption like a big bowling bag to carry the food. And an aluminum cylinder that looked like a miniature a beer keg. As they scooped up the food, he said, "Bon Voyage," and flapped a horny hand in a friendly wave.

"Do you think they're onto us?" said Mack. "Nah. Couldn't be."

Lucas agreed. "Impossible."

"Hey, nice Mr. Legionnaire fellow, could you give us directions to a picnic table topside? Next to a waterfall and a hiking trail with a view of the river below?"

The nice Legionnaire pretended to wrinkle his brow. "Gee whillikers, that sounds like fun. I sure wish I could join you instead of being stuck inside this smoky auditorium, listening to patriotic and religious bullshit."

"Somehow, I think you're putting me on. But I'm sure you don't have a clue about the history of religions and nationalism. So, you don't appreciate the madness."

"And you'd be right in spades. But I do follow orders. Which door would you like to leave from?"

"I'm always suspicious when things are easy. Could there be an ulterior motive to let us wander the surface of your noble tepui? Or am I missing something?"

Ellen shook her curls. "You're always missing something here, there, and everywhere. I'm sorry I have to put up with you until our eventual rescue—"

"You are an optimist if you think we'll be rescued."

"My hopes are buoyed by your constant reference to our air force men in blue. What is your fixation with fly guys? Did you have a seminal experience in your youth?" She tee-heed.

"Oh, that's pretty funny, all right. I'm shocked you'd lower yourself to engage in shady word play. How unfundamentalist Catholic."

"Catholics aren't fundamentalists. Fundamentalism is reserved to Protestants and—" She interrupted herself at

Courtney's sidelong look, "Don't worry Courtney. I'm not including Baptists in there."

Mack was puzzled. "Why ever not? Some folks say Baptists are to the right of Genghis Khan." Courtney shot him a piercing look.

Ellen pursed her cupid lips. "I was talking about Muslims. The nasty ones in Afghanistan and Iran, Saudi Arabia, places like that."

"Watch it or you'll have an Intifada. The thing they put on Salman Rushdie," said Peter.

"That was a Fatwah," said Mack.

"Then why'd you say Protestants?" Courtney stared at Ellen.

"I meant televangelicals. That might not include Baptists."

"Well, it might include Southern Baptists and Holy Rollers but not American Baptists. We're the soul of reasonableness and light."

"Right." Mack sighed. "From now on I'm completely ecumenical. Open-minded, nonjudgmental, and tolerant of all intolerance."

Ellen was sarcastic. "You are such a good person. For your information, the relationship between my husband and myself is not up for discussion with the likes of you."

"You mean there's still a relationship? Never mind." Ellen's glare was scathing.

"Sometimes you're terribly over the top, old man," said Barry. "But the grub's packed and the keg's in webbing, easy to carry. And the nice Legionnaire says to follow him when convenient."

"One moment. Did you get that last bit?" Mack pointed at the Pope, the General, and Btsht. They stood with lanky arms draped around each other's shoulders as the Pope droned the benediction.

"—thank thee for thy guidance and blessing as we proceed to smite our dangerous and deadly enemies. Your grace and beneficence will light our path for the launch of heat-seeking missiles—"

241

Mack shook his head hopelessly. "I can't take it anymore. I can't believe any self-respecting god would let a pope get away with stuff like that. Where's lightning when you need it?"

"I heard that," said Lucas, "and I know you're awaiting the wisdom of the ages in response. Ahem. 'One must make a distinction between what God Himself has said and what the clergy has said in his name.' Hey, hey. Whataya say?"

"This is going to blow you away, but I like it even though it assumes the existence of one or more gods. And you're no Madison, ho, ho, ho."

"I am flummoxed, but you're just saying that so I'll stop serving up pithy quotes. But no reverse psychology for this kid. No siree. I'm unswerving in my search for truth. A three-dimensional philosophy to serve the common man. Wisdom for the ages as a guide for everyday life. Except for that and with special thanks to me mum, I accept your bounteous gift at face value. Thankee, thankee. I am encouraged no end."

"I'll go along with the 'no end' part. You jump around like a catatonic kanga. The Kanga Kid. That's you to a T. And henceforth you'll ever be. Hey, Madison. What do you think of that?"

"My lord, my god, my everlasting bippy. You think Lucas's bad, Mack's twice as lippy."

Madison took a bow to applause from everyone except Mack, who groaned. "We'd better be going. Don't forget, Lucas. Keep us apprised of important events. Kanga Kid, that is."

"I like the Kanga Kid label. Sounds like an outlaw anti-hero. So, good luck from the Kanga Kid, and as the nice Legionnaire said, 'Bon Voyage.'"

The Legionnaire led them to the back wall where a door opened, everyone filing through except Mack. He took a last look around the huge auditorium.

"Done with that bunch, I hope." Mack stepped through the door, which slid shut with finality. "Maybe more done than I thought." He ran to catch the group winding its way up a bright orange spiral, amazed that for a change, it wasn't raining. He came up on Ellen as she helped Courtney along.

"You two okay?"

"We were," said Ellen.

"Well, excuse me. Though I know I'm inexcusable. But I have a question. Nothing personal. Don't get all het up."

"Yeah?" Ellen was seized with disbelief.

"I've never thought anything about religion or politics or war. Nothing about what we're smack dab in the middle of. But you—both of you—are religious experts. At least you know a lot about two particular religions. Given that, do you see how strange a religion looks to someone who doesn't know anything about it? Like the Goldie religion? I know you'll say their religion is weird, made up by screwballs. But don't you find it peculiar that every religion is perfect right down to the last decimal? And every other religion is crackers. It's almost as if religions were just made up. What do you think?"

They looked blank.

Mack squinched up his eyes. "Do you both *know* your religion is infallible and that all others are false? Baptist and Catholic are both Christian, but they're very different. And neither recognizes the validity of the other, does it? Now don't take offense, ladies. I'm just asking."

Courtney cleared her throat. "You probably know what I think. Of course, American Baptists have it right and the others are flat wrong. No offense, Ms. Ellen."

"How can I not take offense?" Ellen acted as if she were dodging an adder while aching to stomp it to smithereens.

"Bulletin, bulletin," said Lucas. "I have an update."

"Yeah, so what is it?"

"'Religion is the opium of the people.'" At the absolute silence Lucas said, "I was just trying to help."

Ellen blinked. "That's not fair. Besides, some communist said that."

Peter smiled. "I'd like a toke of that opium stuff, or whatever's available." The keg swung dangerously to and fro between him and Barry.

Madison said, "It's a commie, Mommy; let me say. Did the opium bloke, make your day?"

243

Courtney was resolute. "Better dead than red. The commie bastards wouldn't dare trifle with me. I'm a true-blue American, through and through."

"Watch it, buster." Barry was off balance. "We'll be sliding down this nasty orange ramp like a toboggan if you don't stop swinging the keg."

Roy struggled along with the bag of food on his shoulder, watching the wildly lurching keg. "We'll all be going downhill, posthaste."

Mack spoke into his mic. "See the trouble with quotes, Kanga Kid? A few more like that and we'll have a revolution."

"I expected a pithier comment from a philosophical genius like yourself."

"I've turned over a new leaf. I'm not going to piss off any more religious persons because they really take it serious. The Goldies aren't alone."

They'd reached the end of the road where sun dribbled through camouflage onto a color-coded road sign.

Mack grinned. "I like the signpost."

Ellen grimaced. "We're abandoned, they're starting a war, and there's no way off this nasty tepui. You have an acute sense of the nonsensical."

Madison brightened. "The sun's shining, yet Ellen's whining. From Roy's bag, we'll be dining. It's home for which I'm 'pining. Every cloud has a silver—"

"And we have a keg of the finest Goldie brew," said Peter. "Lead on, fair leader. We'll follow you to the death. Or at least to the edge of the tepui. Maybe there's a super slide to get us down."

Barry dumped his end of the keg on the ground. "It's not exactly light beer."

"What'll it be?" Mack surveyed the colorful signpost. "Blue, red, green, yellow, orange, or chartreuse? A color-coded road system would be great if we had a map."

Ellen rolled her eyes. "But we don't have a map. We haven't started and we're already lost."

"We can vote if that'll make it easier." Courtney was sarcastic. "The typical know-nothing electorate."

Mack was surprised. "What's this, Courtney? I've never heard you intimate an interest in politics."

"What you don't know, buster. I was the chairperson of the Democratic Party of Pinal County. I was a kingmaker."

"I am impressed, especially with 'chairperson.' Okay, command decision it is. We'll take the red road. I've always been partial to red."

"Like a bull," said Ellen.

"I'd have picked chartreuse," said Barry. "Because it's not a run-of-the-mill color. It might take us somewhere interesting."

"I like blue," said Peter. "It matches my eyes." He fluttered long eyelashes as Ellen made retching noises.

"Green would be my pick," said Courtney. "My birth stone is emerald."

Mack shook his head. "No one can lead a bunch of renegade millionaires. It makes no difference which way we go, as long as we find the edge."

"Yellow and orange, that we've spurned. Hope it don't, get us burned."

"Enough of that," said Mack. "We're off, so hoist the keg. Do you need a hand with the bag, Roy? Madison, give him a hand. It's humongous."

"Humongous donges, carry longest. I'm your boy to tote with Roy."

"Thanks, Madison." Mack stifled a laugh, which came out a burp.
"I picked the red road because it leads to the edge and there may be a perimeter path."

Ellen shook her lovely curls. "That doesn't compute. We were on the edge earlier and there wasn't a path."

"We didn't walk around the whole thing. Which reminds me. Stay close, Courtney. Don't go wandering off on an independent mission."

"Whatever do you mean by that?" said Courtney. "Okay. I'm a poor weak soul when it comes to serving God."

Mack rolled his eyes. "Head' em up and move 'em out." And miracle of miracles everyone started at once.

Courtney's eyes lit up. "Hey, Mr. Mack." Her brogans beat a tattoo on the red road. "I just realized that's beer. We can't have the devil's juice with us. That's expressly forbidden. Haven't you read about not looking on the grape when it has turned?"

"This isn't grape. Just a little hops and sugar, a bit of barley or rice. Besides, we need something to drink to keep from drying out. So, don't push it, Courtney. Now, Courtney, I'm warning you," as she attacked the keg with her fists. She sent it swaying to and fro, pushing Peter and Barry down the road like drunken sailors.

"Whoopsie daisy," said Peter as he tripped, barely saved by a cartwheel. The keg sailed through the air, landing next to Barry, who was stunned. Peter shook his head. "What did I trip over?"

"It's okay." Mack walked toward the keg. "You didn't hurt anything and Barry is only shaken up. Oh, dear me, the keg is leaking. Get away from there, Courtney."

"I tripped over an antelope." Peter pointed toward the bushes. "It was a little fellow, sticking out in the road. Didn't you see him?" Peter ran back up the road. "He must have gone into the bushes. Let's take a look."

"Why?" Mack was puzzled. "Did you hurt him? Lay off that, Courtney."

Peter raced back. "He was hurt. Something's weird."

"Find something to drain the keg into before we lose it all. And get Courtney away from it. That's all we have to drink until we get off the tepui. Come on guys. Get going."

"Here." Ellen swiveled the keg. "Gravity works as well up here as back home. Now it won't leak."

"Let me at it!" Courtney teeth were clenched.

"Find handcuffs and tranquilizers darts," said Mack as Courtney grappled with the keg like a sumo wrestler. Mack made a dive for her the same time as Barry, and they hustled her away.

"Here's the little guy." Peter dragged a Goldie juvenile into their midst. "He didn't get far, maybe distracted by Courtney. She's good for something, see?"

246

"Right." Mack scrunched up his brow. "Of course, Courtney's good for something and I'll think about what that is when I get time. Down Courtney. Stay over there. Survival comes before silly religious rules."

"Not silly." Courtney pouted. "Families are ruined by demon drink."

"And many expeditions have died of thirst. Do something Christian and go minister to the poor little Goldie. He looks like a house fell on him."

Peter smiled. "I always wanted to corral one of the little buggers. They're nasty, stirring up dust devils and playing hell with my allergies. But this little guy looks so forlorn."

"He looks like a DeGrazia painting," cooed Ellen.

"Not really." Mack raised an eyebrow. "He has big blue eyes. DeGrazia did brown."

"Well, he looks like a DeGrazia painting with blue eyes."

"There's no such thing. Maybe his blue eyes brown you off."

"Actually, his blue eyes make me blue. He looks so scrawny and woeful. I've never seen an antelope like that. They always look well fed."

Courtney sidled up. "He does look terrible. We should do something."

"Yeah," said Mack. "Maybe give him something to drink."

"You wouldn't dare." Courtney was incensed. "That'd be contributing to the delinquency of a juvenile."

Mack took the little Goldie paw. "My good little antelope, is there anything we can do for you? Peter didn't mean to trip on you. What are you doing out here instead of inside with the rest of your clan?"

The little Goldie looked like he'd been living in a garbage dump, tawny skin sprinkled with scabs. He sat bedraggled on the glowing red road as tears formed in his big blue eyes, sliding down his face.

"This kid's either a consummate actor or he's in sadder shape than I thought," said Mack.

"You're an old softy." Ellen nudged Mack in the ribs.

247

"Oh, thanks a lot. He doesn't have a translation machine so I don't know how we'll communicate."

Madison jumped up and down. "My lord, my liege, with thee I plead. Let's give our all and have a ball. What I suggest the kid to aid, is give him clear a nice charade." Madison continued jumping up and down as he did charades. "Bigger than a bread box," spreading his hands. "He's lost his socks," pointing at the kid's tiny naked feet, pretending to pull socks on.

"We don't have time to look after the little fellow. We have to get off this misshapen mesa before it explodes into World War Ill."

"Oh, sure." Ellen shook her head. "Leave him to the likes of the Big Guy and the General. Or the Pope and Judge Grdam, the compassionate ones. If we don't take care of him no one will."

"Maybe he has a mother—" Mack tried weakly.

Courtney groaned. "Maybe he had a mother, ye of itty-bitty heart."

"You could take care of him while we find a way back to civilization. Not that Venezuela would be much of an improvement. What are you going to do, anyway? We have no medicine and we don't know what they eat."

"We sure do." Ellen pointed. "We have a whole bag of food. Hey, Roy. Bring the bag over here. Yeah, Madison. Give him a hand."

Roy brought the bag over and Madison laid it on its side, sliding it open. They stared at a congealing mass that seemed to pulsate like a telltale heart.

Mack laughed. "So that's what you get when you mix yellow, orange, green, brown, and gold. Looks like rotten spinach with mold."

"That's all we have to eat," said Ellen. "And with your smart mouth, who's going to be able to?"

"Guess I shouldn't have jiggled the bag." Roy looked forlorn. "Now our food's gone way downhill." But this didn't stop him from swiping a finger along the edge and tasting. "Hmmm."

Ellen wrinkled her forehead. "What does that mean?"

"The kid will like it. Sweet with an oniony back taste, layered with the hearty flavor of chalk. Too far downhill to salvage."

"Oh, ridiculous." Mack slathered a bit into his mouth. "Hmmm, let the kid try it." Mack beckoned the kid over, taking his paw and dipping it in the goo.

"Look at him go," said Courtney. "He was hungry."

"He'd have to be." Mack watched the kid dig in. "Enough charity. Let's get the show on the road, the bright red road."

Barry frowned. "I don't know if we should let him dig his filthy little paws in there. It's all we have to eat and who knows where his horny hands have been."

Peter laughed. "No one is going to eat it now."

"What else is there?" said Barry. "On the other hand, the ladies have made a friend for life, or at least until his next meal." The little Goldie had slurped his paws clean. Now he was nuzzling his golden antelope nose around embarrassing parts of Ellen and Courtney.

"If we get hungry enough," said Madison, "we'll have to eat the stuff."

Mack looked hopeless. "So, now we have a mascot. What's he up to?"

The Goldie kid scurried into the bush and everyone followed, except Mack, who stood with hands on his hips. "Come back, guys. We have places to go and things to do."

"Don't be so hard-headed," said Ellen. "There's an entire camp set up back here. A dozen little antelopes, street children."

"There go the rations. It won't take two shakes for little Goldies to polish off the entire bag."

"Lucas here. War games on schedule. So, what's going on with you? It sounds like you've run into a pocket of poverty. Maybe Ermie propaganda is right on target. Which reminds me. You ready?" Lucas yodeled.

"We aren't ready," Mack yodeled back.

"Tough noogies. 'The greatest of evils, and the worst of crimes, is poverty. Our first duty—is not to be poor.' Squarely on point since we're escorting millionaires."

"Good of us, isn't it? Helping Peter and Courtney and sweet little Ellen fulfill their duty not to be poor. Not to mention your bunch. Kind of makes you proud."

"You're just jealous," said Ellen. "You could work for the lottery a hundred years and you'd never be a millionaire. Of course, I'm giving half of mine to the Church."

Mack raised both eyebrows. "I'll bet that makes hubby happy. No wonder you're here by yourself. You'll probably have court papers waiting when you get home, so hubby can get his half before you give it away. Assuming you get back. Maybe you don't have to worry after all."

"The only thing that bothers me is your smart mouth. How could the lottery let someone like you deal with its big winners? Or any member of the public? I'll set them straight when we get back."

"You are an optimist. Or maybe you'll be the first off the edge of the tepui."

"Hey, hey, hey. Ho, ho, ho," came Lucas's squeaky voice. "'The value of money is that with it you can tell anyone to go to the devil.' And you just got the ultimate performance rating."

Mack held his hands up. "I hereby dedicate my life to mollifying our millionaires, especially the millionairesses. I am a servant of rich people. If they prefer to take care of a scabby antelope instead of escaping to civilization, far be it for me to quibble. I await your every order, ma'am. Bowing and scraping now."

"They're starving," said Courtney. Everyone stared at the skin-and-bones antelopes sniffing at the bag held by Roy and Madison.

Mack shook his head. "Up to you guys whether we give them the bag of food or hoard the nasty contents for ourselves. Fats would suggest the former and remind us that karma returns threefold. Besides, who wants to eat a mishmash that looks like baby poop after it's stirred by filthy paws?"

"Your philanthropy is mind-boggling," said Ellen. "Crack it open, Roy. Give him a hand, Madison."

They moved the bag onto a rock and flipped it open. The Goldie juveniles were delighted. They dug in, horny fingers flying from bag to mouths in a mishmash of color.

Madison beamed. "Helter skelter, watch 'em belt 'er. Suck the fodder, sans the bother."

"Yeah, that was a gem," said Mack. "Why is the Big Guy letting these poor little fellows go homeless? They should be part of the happy Goldie family. Something is amiss in Goldie society."

"You are so sensitive," said Ellen. "An uninformed observer might think you had a heart."

"Fooled them. I'm as heartless as they come. Especially when it comes to the Big Guy and the Pope not taking care of their own. What did these little fellows do wrong?"

Peter nosed around the ramshackle camp. "Hey guys. Check out this TV."

"Interesting," said Mack. "Reg and Lucas have access but this is the first TV we've seen, and in the possession of homeless teenagers. I'll go along with incredible, Peter old sod." The humans left the little Goldies slurping the contents of the bag as they gathered around the odd TV set.

Mack fingered the set. "I've never seen one thin as paper."

"The best part is it's got CNN." Peter pointed. "I'd turn up the volume if I could figure out how it works."

"No knobs." Mack fiddled with the set. "Pretty spiffy." It flickered pictures of the usual crisis in Gaza. Mack must have found the volume because the sound came on at the same time a Goldie juvenile knocked him on his butt, turning the sound off as fast as it began.

Mack sat up. "What the hell was that about?"

The little Goldie stood wiping his face, licking horny paws. He ignored Mack, who jumped into his face. "I asked you a question, you little snot. What do you have against sound? It'd be good to hear proper English for a change."

"I'll give you proper English," said the little Goldie.

"What did you say?" stammered Mack.

251

"You heard me, Mr. Dude. You want proper English, you got it. What does it take to please you? Oh, yeah. Thanks for the grub."

"A ticket home would bring great satisfaction. But ignoring that, where's your translator? What's going on here?"

"Translator, smanslator. The elders have been having you on. Not that it was difficult. They don't need translators. Almost everyone understands or speaks English."

"My name's Mack McElheney, representing the US of A. Pleased to make your acquaintance." Mack stuck out his hand.

"You're quite welcome." The kid stood slouching, paws in the bulging pockets of his filthy tunic.

Mack dropped his hand. "One normally volunteers one's own name when someone proffer's their own." At the kid's blank look Mack said, "So what's your name?"

"Name's Mkcht. Let's hear you say it."

"Mikchit."

"Not even close."

"So, Mkcht, why are you hungry, out here in the middle of nowhere, instead of with the other Goldies? And why can't we turn up the sound?"

"Your food would be disgusting if we weren't desperate. I hope that's not what they gave you for your trip."

"No, it's not what they gave us. We managed to mess it up on our own. And how'd you know we were on a trip?"

"Classified."

"Which means you have close contact with folks back home."

"This is our home."

"Not the nicest I've ever seen. What did you do to deserve this?" "Nothing."

"There must be more to it than that. Where did you pick up American English?"

The little Goldie bowed at the television. "Thanks to your almighty tube de boob."

"So, why can't we listen? Right now we have a great deal of interest in CNN."

"Yeah, we know."

"How do you know if you're estranged from society? What do you know about us anyway?"

"Everyone knows about you. You're the alien agents bent on destroying life as we know it. That much has filtered down."

"You didn't seem surprised to see us. I feel like I'm swimming in molasses. Is this kid evasive or am I insensitive?"

"It could be a combination of factors," said Ellen.

"Look what the kid has around his neck," yelled Courtney.

"Settle down, Courtney. It's just a little golden statue. Not a false god. For these kids it's probably more of a fashion statement."

"No," said the kid. "It's more of a religious thing." At Courtney's menacing look he said, "Maybe I take that back. I remember the story about this alien person." But he didn't look frightened.

"Lay off him, Courtney. Now why can't we turn the TV up?"

"It's for your own good. Besides, we have our orders. We're not allowed to let you listen."

"Why would anyone expect that we'd *stumble* over you? And why do you follow orders? And what orders didn't you follow that got you kicked out of the sweet little setup inside?"

"I don't know what makes you think it was so sweet. Of course, alien parents may be more understanding than Goldie parents."

"Doubtful," said Mack. "And who could understand you twerps? Come on. Give me a hint why we can't see what's going on with CNN."

"You can see all you want. You just can't hear. Maybe you can read lips. I've heard even non-deaf people can pick up a bit."

"They think I'm a smart-ass! I've met my match."

"Bet your bippy. Got that from old *Laugh In* reruns."

"You have reruns? I figured Goldies were so advanced that you only had original programming."

"Huh. That's your idea of a joke? Sorry I forgot to laugh. Anyway, thanks for the grub and we'll see you around." The kid turned his back and snapped the food bag shut. "You'll find it lighter."

"Okay, you little ingrate." Mack seized him by the frayed collar. "We'll have answers now."

"You're a big bully." The kid feebly tried to pull away. "I'm in no shape to deal with a couch-potato American. If it were a few months ago, when I wasn't a mere shadow of myself, I'd mop the road with you. Scrape red tarmac into your open wounds. Unhand me, you jerk."

Ellen tugged at Mack's sleeve. "What are you doing? He's a poor little kid. Why are you picking on him? Just because he won't turn up the sound? You're not a nice person!"

"Oh, Ellen, Ellen. He's our ticket off this tepui and you want to let him go? I'll bet the kid knows an easy way off this thing. Ain't that right, kid?" with a terrible Bogart imitation.

Ellen said, "Oh. I thought you just wanted to watch TV."

"I should turn you over my lap and paddle your little—"

"You'd like it too much, and I'd punch you out if you tried. So, get your mind out of the gutter. And let the kid go, you're choking him."

Mack pulled the kid around and the kid's head drooped onto his chest like he'd passed out. Mack dropped him and he sprang to life. "Great little actor too. Now kid. Let's get down to brass tacks," the Bogart imitation sneaking back in. Mack cleared his throat. "I want to know why we can't have sound on CNN and why you're ostracized. But most important, how can we get off this dreaded tepui?"

"I'm not going to tell you." He thought Mack's raised hand meant something so he ducked. "Oh, shit."

Courtney stuck her face in the kid's face. "I wouldn't have my hand where you've had your mouth. Who's got the soap? Come on. We have some, don't we?" She looked at Barry and Roy, who shrugged.

"Anyway," said the kid, outnumbered. "They kicked us out because we finished school and didn't want to go to work. We wanted to do other things."

Mack frowned. "What do you mean?"

"Whataya mean, what do I mean? *Other things* means *other things*. Don't you speaka the English?" The kid clunked an ear against a horny paw. "Or don't you hear well?"

"I'm gonna kill 'em," bogarted Mack. "Let me at 'em."

The kid laughed. "That's the worst gangster imitation I've ever heard. Don't quit your day job, man."

"I am truly going to kill him." Mack grabbed his collar. "What's this not wanting to work stuff? You don't seem old enough to work."

Lucas's tinny twang cut in. "Don't you know, Mack? Surely you recognize this: 'And though you presume that authority here is but a shadow and that I dare not touch the lives of any, but my own must answer it, yet he that offendeth, let him surely expect his due punishment. You must obey this, now, for a law—He that will not work shall not eat.' You do recognize it, don't you?"

"Don't you have something to do on your own tepui? Maybe keep Billy K. from wandering off or Ef out of major diplomatic incidents leading to war? And no, I don't have the vaguest where that's from, though it sounds biblical."

"That's not biblical," said Courtney. "That's communist. I can smell it. I'll bet that was the Commie Manifesto."

"Doesn't sound biblical to me," said Ellen. "'Course there was the 'offendeth' thing. So, it might be from before communism."

"I don't see why you shouldn't have to work to eat," said Mack, "unless you're too young or unable."

The kid broke in. "Don't you have vacations after working long hours, when you're not working and you still eat? Why shouldn't we have a gap year when we finish school? Besides, you're right. We're too young to work. It might stunt our growth."

"Okay. I don't care about this stuff anyway. I was just curious. What I really care about is getting off this crappy mesa and why we can't listen to CNN. So, shoot."

The kid pointed horny fingers. "Bang, bang. You're dead."

"I'm gonna kill this kid." Mack tightened his grip, tearing the kid's shirt to the waist.

"That *is* a false god he's got on the chain," said Courtney. She made a wild grab for it and slipped, landing at his feet.

The kid stared down at her. "You're a bunch of crazies. I'd rather go to work than put up with stuff like this, man." He said the last word with extra sarcasm.

"You're right." Mack helped Courtney up while keeping between her and the kid. "Give us a hint how to get off this tepui and we'll leave you alone, so help me whatever god you prefer. Could you do that one little favor for me?" At the kid's look Mack said, "For us?"

"I have orders about that too. Do you think I just happened to be sticking out in the road? Stop and think, if that wouldn't be too taxing. Why do you think the elders let you go without a whimper? You single-handedly started the first war among the Island Sky nations in over eight hundred years. Does letting you walk scot free strike you as unlikely, or perverse? Or perhaps overshadowed by an ulterior motive? Whataya think?" At the blank looks the kid said, "You do think, don't you?"

Ellen said, "We're burdened with a leader who reacts instead of thinking."

"Well, la de da. Is that your excuse or do you blindly follow whoever happens to be in front of you? Do you have a mind of your own or is Mr. Dude the best you can do?"

Mack said, "I take personal umbrage at such a scurrilous attack on my leadership capabilities. Or I would, if I had any."

"I've seen the transcripts, so umbrage your ass off. I'm my own antelope, beholden to no other. Particularly not to my political maniac of a father—" The kid stopped short.

"And who might that be?"

The kid said nothing.

Mack looked the kid up and down. "You don't look like the Pope, even if the Pope slimmed down and gave up celibacy. And you don't look like the General, though it's hard to tell what he looks like under all the gold brocade. Don't tell me you're somehow related to a Big Guy?"

The kid didn't flinch.

"Maybe not a current Big Guy. And you're not related to the third Big Guy or you'd be at the funeral. So, are you related to the original first Big Guy who's still spinning like a dervish?"

The kid gave Mack a look. "I didn't think so. But I see a family resemblance with an acquaintance. You're Judge Grdam's son."

"I'm not related to the 'honorable' judge and I'm not a male." The kid was embarrassed.

"Oh, right." Mack did a double-take at the torn shirt. The kid wrestled to pull it together, covering six miniature nipples. "Sorry, my dear."

"As Ellen would say—again from the transcript—I'm not your deer."

"That was a pun? Then you're Judge Grdam's daughter, female child, doe, whatever?"

"Not exactly, but then, it doesn't matter. A close relative was high up in the government but is now on the outs. Because of you aliens and incidentally, Judge Grdam. And you're headed for a fall."

"That was *real* subtle. But we appreciate the warning. I take it we're supposed to find our way off the edge of the tepui precipitously, and good riddance."

"To bad rubbish."

Mack rolled his eyes. "So, there's an extremely dangerous way off the tepui which they want us to take. Tell us where that might be so we can stay away from it. But more importantly, is there an easy way off this damned mesa? And what difference does it make how we disappear, dead or escaped?"

"Big difference. They want an easy way to get rid of you—"

At Mack's faked shock, the kid said, "You're not just trouble-makers, you're heretics. But we'd prefer you had an accident instead of doing it ourselves. Clean hands and all that."

"We know there's no love lost—"

"You're a master of understatement. But no, we can't help you. We don't want to get in more trouble or they'll stop

257

food deliveries. They'd execute us for treason if we let you escape. Not that there's a safe way off the sky islands."

"I see. Your gratitude is heart-warming."

"Gratitude for mashed-up slop? We can give it back if you feel shortchanged."

"Ah, no, we're happy to feed you on behalf of your esteemed elders. We expect nothing in return. Not even civility. Your father is right, kid. Get a job."

"You're a master psychologist, Mr. Dude. The Goldie society owes us a living for a year or two. We've been working our tails off. See." The kid swiveled around.

"Right, Goldies don't have tails."

"Ahem, young lady," came Lucas's voice. "'The state, it cannot be too often repeated, does nothing and can give nothing which it does not take from somebody.' Get a job, kid. Unless you're too young, too weak, or stupid."

"Who's that idiot?" The kid looked at Mack like he was a ventriloquist.

"Another master psychologist. Can it, Lucas. I'm in the middle of delicate negotiations."

"Yeah, I can tell. It's obvious why you're on the outs with the Goldies while we're the revered guests of the Ermies and Ivies."

"Oh, please. We have special circumstances. Fortuitous events resulting
in religious wars."

"Right. And who's responsible for that?"

"Courtney."

"And Mack. Take personal responsibility. Don't forget Mack."

"We could never forget Mack," said Courtney and Ellen in unison. "Besides," said Courtney. "God always comes first."

"Depends on which god," said the kid.

"I'm turning over a new leaf," said Mack. "From now on I'm the epitome of diplomacy. Henceforth I'll ruffle no feathers, or fur."

"Right," said everyone in unison, including the kid.

"Well, I intend to try harder. Thank you for the valuable information. Without your help we might have fallen to our deaths."

"You almost sounded sincere," said the kid.

"I almost was," said Mack.

Peter said, "What are we going to do for grub, kid?"

"My name—"

"Your name," said Roy, hamming it up, "is Mkcht Josejiménez. And I love it kid. I just love it." Roy flipped a high five, which the kid automatically returned.

"Roy's kind of cool," said the kid.

"Hey, kid," Roy whispered in her ear. "Where could I score some weed? I'm almost out and you're the first decent Goldie I've run across. Try the stuff I have left." Roy rolled a joint one-handed, inserting the end in the kid's mouth.

"Roy, cut that out," said Mack. "The lottery told you to leave illicit substances at home. I can't believe you crossed national borders with illegal drugs. You're contributing to the delinquency of a minor and the kid's father is a prosecutor. We could get thrown in the dungeon."

"Stow it, old man," said the kid. "Goldie jails are country clubs, unless you commit a political no-no or violate a religious taboo." She slapped another high five with Roy, who laid a flame on the joint. They retired to the rear of the encampment.

Roy said as he disappeared from sight, "I got a medical Mary Jane license, ha, ha."

"I'm sorely disappointed in Roy," said Mack. "A millionaire with the Arizona Lottery should be setting an example for alien youngsters. And I'm disappointed in Goldie youth for stooping to drug abuse."

"Oh, come on, Mack," said Peter. "You lived the aftermath of the sixties. Don't be a stuffed shirt. Besides, you can't abuse an inanimate object. You can only abuse yourself." Peter gave Mack a big wink.

Courtney said, "Mack is perfectly correct and we should back him to the hilt. When we get back, I'll ask the Arizona Lottery to forfeit Roy's winnings. He's practically a felon, just not convicted."

"I wouldn't go that far, since he has a medical marijuana card," said Ellen. "But Peter and Roy are unsuitable emissaries for meeting an alien culture. This is a historic occasion and we shouldn't blow it." Her eyes glazed over at Mack's look. "No throwing stones at Roy."

"This is an opportunity," said Mack. "If Roy gets the kids ripped, they might give us the information we need. We could be off this tepui in minutes." He inched toward Roy's smoke-in, the others following.

"What are you old fogeys up to?" The kid sat in a circle with Roy and the others. The kid's eyes already looked a little foggy.

Mack said, "We thought we'd keep you company. See what's going on. Shoot the breeze. Compare cultures. See what you're into."

"And mostly try to find a way off the tepui." The kid bounded up. "You demean our homeland. How'd you feel if someone said the US of A was a wasteland? How'd you like that, huh?"

"No offense, kid. I thought you were supposed to mellow out on that stuff, experiencing the brotherhood of the entire human race. Make that the antelope race and the human race."

"Racist pig. You can't compare yourselves to us. We're the most advanced civilization on the planet and you're in the stone age."

"Better than the *stoned* age."

"I knew you were an undercover pig. Go away. We prefer Roy's company."

"Hey." Peter pushed into the circle. "I could use a hit of that."

"Yeah," said Roy. "Have a sit down. The rest of you are welcome too." At their disapproving looks he added, "You don't have to inhale to be welcome. So, sit."

Mack beckoned them forward as Barry said, "You wouldn't happen to have regular tobacco? I left my cigarettes on the plane."

Madison said, "I feel happy, oh so happy, it's so sappy, how happy, I feel."

"That's a contact high," said Roy. "Flop over here, Madison. Madison is our resident poet, artist, free spirit. Hey, Maddie, have a hit?"

The kid said, "Sure. We got some old fogey drug. Hey, guys, something for the gentleman with the funny accent?"

"I don't have a funny accent," drawled Barry in his Tennessee twang. "That's the way Southern Gentlemen and real people talk."

"I'd rather you didn't smoke," said Ellen to Barry.

"Well, my lovely friend, I'm sorry, but I need a smoke in the worst way." Barry held out his hands. "They're shaking."

"Smoke's smoke, isn't it?" said Mack. "I can't believe you're okay with pot and not with a mere cigarette."

Mack's mic came alive as Lucas said, "Come now, boss. Here's one on tobacco from 1600 A.D. I don't know who said it, but the date stuck in my head. 'A custom loathsome to the eye, hateful to the nose, harmful to the brain, dangerous to the lungs, and in the black stinking fume thereof, nearest resembling the horrible Stygian smoke of the pit that is bottomless.' And if that isn't enough for you, here's a slightly later vintage, a real kicker: 'Tobacco dryeth the brain, dimmeth the sight, vitiateth the smell, hurteth the stomach, destroyeth the concoction, disturbeth the humors and spirits, corrupteth the breath, induceth a trembling of the limbs, exsiccateth the windpipe, lungs and liver, annoyeth the milt, scorcheth the heart, and causeth the blood to be adjusted.' So, tobacco has been known to suck since the 1600s. It's beyond me how a plaintiff could win a tobacco suit, four hundred years later."

Madison said, "Why let suits by cancer coots, when hundreds of years it's killed the brutes?"

"Couldn't have said it better myself," said Mack, "though the meter's suspect. But pot's no better than tobacco."

"Au contraire." Roy was flying. "You can't smoke twenty or forty joints every day like you can cigarettes. One's enough, almost." He offered the tube. "Have a hit."

"You are quite the philosophical species," said the kid. "The only difference is one's legal and the other's not."

"Not quite," said Peter. "We have legal medical marijuana in Arizona and we know tobacco's more dangerous."

"Doesn't sound like it," said Mack. "Smoke is smoke and the more you suck, the faster it kicks your butt."

"Try a hit of this stuff," said the kid. "It'll kick your butt." She blearily held the joint toward Mack.

"Cripes, kid. I'm not looking for something to kick my butt. Since you're in a mellow mood, how about giving your new good buddies, Roy and Peter, a tip? Like how to avoid falling off your lovely tepui."

"You are really smooth, and since you are, I'll tell you how." They leaned forward as the kid whispered, "Stay away from the edge." She broke up, slapping scrawny thighs with horny paws.

"You've got your father's sense of humor." Roy slapped the kid on the back. That made her swallow a massive inhale and break into serious coughing. "Sorry about that." Roy cackled.

"Hey, not a problem. Let's retire to the next bush. I have a stash that you might be interested in." They trailed off with Peter close behind.

"You're doing just great," said Ellen to Mack. "Really cozying up to them. We should be home in no time."

Madison smiled goofily. "What about we tag along, go and see, where they've gone? Maybe I should try a bit, it's been a while since I had a hit. Then again, perhaps I'll stay, see what—"

"Sorry to interrupt," said Mack, "but you weren't heading to stardom with that one. The other little Goldies might be more helpful." Mack sidled up and they melted away faster than Mack could say a word.

"Any backup plans?" said Ellen, as Mack did an about-face and strolled back as if nothing had happened.

"We'll liberate Roy and Peter and scout out the perimeter. Of course, we'll have to be ultracareful. Madison, are you up to walking around? I'll help you up."

"Hey, I'm fine to toe the line. Let's hit the road and do our time." Madison struggled to his feet with Courtney helping.

Courtney said, "I'm fed up with this den of iniquity." She rushed the bush that the kid, Roy, and Peter had ducked behind, crashing through and taking it out by the roots. "Aha," she yelled as the others ran after her. "Committing felonies, dabbling in sin, and destroying your brain cells. What few you have left." With a roundhouse slap, she knocked the joint out of the kid's mouth. Then she ripped off the necklace with the golden icon.

Mack snatched the necklace out of her grasp and handed it back to the kid. As he hustled Courtney backward, Roy stood frozen with his hand in a large burlap bag.

Courtney shouted, "Let me at 'em. They're offending against God and common decency." At Mack's look she said, "Come on, Mack. You weren't stopping this and someone has to." She did a fast shuffle with her brogans and tried an end run, cut off by Mack with help from Barry and Madison.

"Give us a hand, Ellen." At her crossed arms Mack said, "You're all sass and no substance. Watch Courtney so we can get out of here. You do recall our common cause, don't you?"

Ellen reluctantly stepped up to Courtney. "My dear, we'll get back to principles later. But first we need to pull together so we can escape."

"Thank you, Ellen. Thank you, Courtney." Mack nodded. "Our first priority is keeping Courtney out of boiling oil. Not to mention myself. Assuming the war doesn't find us with a missile up our butts."

"You are gross and despicable," said Courtney. "It'd take all the soap in China to put your mouth in sanitary working order."

"I remind you, Courtney, that reality requires pulling yourself together. Roy, Peter, are you ready?"

Roy had finished stuffing every pocket and Peter was in the process as Roy embraced the kid. "Love you kid. Anytime you're in Phoenix you have an open invitation, stop by and crash. We'll have a good old time, stop the world in its full blast assault downhill." They smashed high fives and hugged each other, Peter joining the fraternal farewells. Mack, Ellen, Barry, and Madison looked on, while Courtney turned her back.

"Good luck, guys," said the kid tearfully as they waved goodbye. As they turned to leave the kid yelled, "And hey." They did an about-face, looking at the kid. She said, "Stay away from the edge."

14

The sun's position made it barely after noon, searing through the camouflage. The road glowed red; thorny bushes and razor grass grew along the side, bordered with boulders the size of trucks. Peter and Roy caught up with the main group after a quarter of a mile. skipping along like kids under the influence of excessive hopscotch.

"Hey, guys," said Peter, doing a shambling cartwheel as he passed them on the right. "That was fun. Thanks for making our day. Have you noticed?" He was out of breath, tottering as he tiptoed in front of them. "Roy hasn't gone downhill for almost an hour? We're making progress. I know I am."

Peter looked back. Roy was bent over in the middle of the bright red road, stuffing a leafy substance into already full pockets. "Oh, pshaw," said Peter. "I lost something. I'll be right back." He skipped back, shooing Roy aside to scrape at the aromatic leaves littering the road.

As a gust swept by Roy said, "It's all going back down the hill, poor Peter. But worry not because I don't do cartwheels. My pockets are full." They skipped off to join the main group marching down the radiant red road. All except Courtney, who charged at Roy and Peter like a bull.

"Caramba," said Peter, dodging Courtney as she careened by, smacking into Roy. After two out-of-control backward leaps, Roy tripped. He barely dodged Courtney's brogans as she stumbled and fell on her ample backside. Roy jumped up like bread from a toaster, rushing to where she sat.

"Here, Courtney, my poor downhill darlin', let me help you up." Roy tugged at her left arm, which dangled funny.

"That really hurts." Courtney smacked Roy with her other arm. "I have a problem."

The others gathered around, Ellen ministering to Courtney's arm, gently flexing it.

"Another catastrophe." Mack shook his head. "Can she walk?"

"She only hurt her arm. Not her legs," said Ellen. "She'll be all right. Nothing broken. See."

"It feels broken," wailed Courtney.

"What's going on?" said Lucas's thin voice. "Did someone get hurt. Did you go too close to the edge?"

"It's dear Courtney," said Mack. "In spite of our counsel, she got ticked off at Peter and Roy. They copped some pot, maybe you heard."

"No lie. That's amazing."

"Yeah. Well, they did. Courtney disagreed with their decision and almost decapitated her arm in the process."

"You can't decapitate an arm," said Ellen.

"Tell her this," said Lucas. "It might make her feel better. 'Tobacco, coffee, alcohol, hashish, prussic acid, strychnine [and perhaps I should add pot], are weak dilutions; the surest poison is time.' Let me know what she says."

"That is sheer balderdash," shouted Courtney at the top of her lungs. "It doesn't excuse felonious sin. Tell Lucas I said that."

"You want me to repeat it?" Mack said to Lucas.

"That won't be necessary. Have you reached the edge? Are you going to rappel off?"

"We'll know in a minute. We're almost there."

"What do you mean, we're almost there? You don't know where we are," said Ellen.

"See. Right over there." At their quizzical looks Mack said, "No. That way, where the bushes end. There's nothing beyond that."

"Isn't this where we're supposed to be extra careful?"

"You do a scouting report. We'll stay here where it's safe. A chance for you to illustrate the superiority of female leadership. I'm obviously hopeless in the leadership category."

"You certainly are." Ellen did a swallowing exercise. "I'm ready. I'll do it."

"Take a second to get over the shakes. Peter or Roy might have something to calm you down."

"I'm perfectly fine."

"Perfectly fine." Mack drew it out.

"I'll go and scout the edger out, save the damsel from a shout," said Madison.

"Oh, you dear thing." Ellen planted a soppy kiss on his forehead.

"Right," Mack exhibiting ill-disguised envy. "Never mind. Barry, Madison. Come along. Let's have a look see." They followed without a word, moving cautiously through the bush, away from the abrupt end of the red road. Mack pushed aside the last bush to see the long winding river below, and the silence shattered.

"Surprise, surprise," said a virile voice. Btsht strolled up as Legionnaires surrounded them, pulling them back from certain death.

Mack said, "I thought you were otherwise occupied, building the crowd up to a blood frenzy, celebrating your religion while mustering your army and air force. Along with underestimating your enemy and generally making a fool of yourself."

Btsht smiled. "I sometimes think that there are parts of you I'd miss but I always reach the opposite conclusion. You're lucky I'm in a mellow mood. There's so much you don't know and have no means of comprehending."

"I'm not the loan arranger."

"You're clever with empty words. I'm the new Number One Big Guy—and your frolic is over. Your luck has played out. I take it you catch my drift."

Mack's complexion was pasty. "You mean—"

"That's right. Consider the last two hours as a cigarette before facing a firing squad. A last supper of carefree hours wandering the tepui before your number is up and your chimes rung. Your life spinning before your tiny minds' eye with your pipsqueak contribution to the universe folded, bent, spindled, creased, and canceled. The court will enter final sentence in your case as only a superior civilization can. With equanimity and speed."

Mack shuddered. "I don't like the sound of that. But I'm relieved you weren't conspiring to send us catapulting over the edge to our death."

"Under no circumstances. Our juvenile outcast dope addicts have quaint ideas. We reserve the pleasure of witnessing your public execution."

"Ahem," said a voice from the vicinity of Mack's collar. "The Ermies are officially aggrieved at this terrible news. They remind the Honorable Btsht that 'the State calls its own violence law, but that of the individual crime.' Take that, you big lummox."

"Thanks a lot," said Mack. "That was one of your timelier quotations but you're not helping the situation. Ermie irritation at our demise carries no weight."

"I swear on my performance evaluation that I am entirely sincere. The same as the Ermies, Ivies, and your fellow humans."

"I am so relieved."

"I object," said Ellen, staring Btsht in the eye. "You haven't convicted most of us of anything. The majority are blameless."

Mack sighed. "You forgot to add that those who have been convicted are innocent. And we're bone-weary of the Goldies' dreadful hospitality. What about Courtney?"

"Her too." Ellen never took her eyes off Btsht. "She doesn't deserve a death sentence, especially in boiling oil."

"Ah, my esteemed colt-like alien." Btsht grinned. "You are correct, temporarily. You have not been convicted of a capital offense. You've been acquitted of one. That's if my sterling memory serves, and of course it must. However, your future is uncertain because we're not finished with you. What sentence do you recommend for Courtney? Assuming you had the authority, what sentence would you impose on someone who almost destroyed your god?"

Ellen stared back. "My God can't be destroyed. And I wouldn't do anything to someone who defaced or even destroyed a statue of my God. No. I take that back. I'd make them write on a blackboard a hundred times, 'I will not make fun of other gods.'"

"Wouldn't that constitute an admission that there are other gods?"

"Okay, I'd make them write, 'I'll not make fun of icons depicting those who others believe in as a god.' We're not barbarians who'd execute someone for expressing an opinion. We believe in free speech."

"Some speech is freer than others. We'll explore the parameters at a formal get-together."

"Spoken like a true bureaucrat," said Mack. "We're shaking in our boots. When is our formal get-together and is war still penciled into the schedule?"

"Funny you should ask. The war has been suspended. The Ermies and Ivies have agreed on a momentary moratorium."

"Do they realize that you're only doing that so you can launch a surprise first strike?"

Boom, was the sound of Btsht's horny hand as it connected with Mack's jaw, knocking him two feet to the left. "How do you like that for a surprise first strike?"

Mack clutched his face as he regained his balance. "Typical sucker punch by the sucker leader of an uncivilized sucker culture. And I didn't like it one bit. The Ermies and Ivies will take this as a lesson of your first-strike capabilities." Mack fingered his jaw. "Yowzah, that smarts."

"Good," snarled Btsht. "Get them out of here."

The Legionnaire captain herded the humans down the red road as the early afternoon sun filtered through the canopy.

Ellen said, "You told them off good, Mack. Though you said you'd turn over a new leaf and would never again ruffle feathers or fur. Or was that so long ago it slipped your mind? It must have been a whole half hour ago."

"I'm not perfect. I continue to suffer for my sins."

"That I don't mind. But I do mind that *we* continue to suffer for your sins. Leave us out of your future sin-suffering."

"Oh, for Chrissakes. Lay off the poor guy," said Peter. "He does the best he can. It may not be much but he's sincere. Well, usually sincere and he sometimes tries."

"Gee thanks for the support," said Mack. "Actually, I thank you for those almost kind words. They're better than nothing and far better than Ellen's." He stuck his tongue out at Ellen, thumbs in ears, waving his fingers.

"Juvenile." Ellen turned her lovely head with a swish of auburn curls.

Madison said, "I think what we must do, is put the past behind our shoe. Trudge on down this road of life, yet do our best to end this strife."

"That's the old es-spir-it-tu," said Roy, weaving all over the road. "I say, my friends. This road may not be downhill but it sure does snake all over the place."

"I vote with Madison," said Courtney. "Conciliation is our motto today."

"Too bad it wasn't yesterday's motto," said Mack. "But I've been out of line. I won't swear to be perfect since we know I can't. My actions will speak louder than words."

Ellen groaned. "Oh, please. Okay, new leaf, new page, new start, new deal." To Mack's utter disbelief, Ellen marched up and took his hand, shaking it heartily.

"Wow. A new start. I'm impressed." Mack covered Ellen's hand and held it.

She jerked away. "We'll see how long this lasts."

"Whoa," said Roy, shakily. "Everything's going uphill. I never thought of it before. But there's not much difference between things going uphill and things going downhill." He illustrated his perplexity with a complicated series of hand swooshes. "But I feel real happy, folks."

Peter giggled and nodded assent as he scooted down the ruby-red road with Roy. Legionnaires flanked them in front and back, with Btsht nowhere to be seen. At that moment they passed the bush where the kid had tripped them up, recognizing it because the kid stood there with her scruffy compatriots, waving gaily as they bounced by.

Roy high fived the kid while Peter pounded her on the back. The kids still waved as Legionnaires shoved Roy and Peter back in the procession. In minutes a familiar looking portal opened to the interior of the tepui and they spiraled down between white walls, entering a large auditorium.

"We done stopped going downhill," said Roy. "Where the heck we at?"

"The bottom of a pit," said Peter. "Weird place. Look at the funny corners with high pulpits at the ends and little pulpits in front."

Mack said, "We're back in court. The Goldies in the little pulpits look amazingly like our old friends, the sub-baliffs."

"But there's no jurors' bench," said Ellen. "Or prosecutor's table. Or defense table for that matter. Where are we supposed to sit?"

The Legionnaires disappeared, leaving seven humans with twenty-five Goldie baliffs glowering down on them.

"I'm dizzy," said Courtney. She shifted uneasily, scuffing her brogans, pressing her head with her hands.

"No wonder you're dizzy." Mack pointed. "The room is revolving. But the corners aren't moving."

"We're on a turntable, Mabel, couldn't get off, e'en if we're able," said Madison. "Watch us spin, what a state we're in. Like rollin' a joint, or passin' the gin."

"No need for either," said Barry. "This is a natural high. We're on a big Lazy Susan. Madison got it right."

"It's not going fast enough to make us dizzy," said Mack. "But I'm glad we didn't eat that mish-mashed up food. Oh, boy. Here come the judges."

The twenty-five Goldie baliffs stood as twenty-foot-high doors opened under blinding spotlights. Robed figures took their seats in the high pulpits as a sub-baliff shouted, "Be seated."

"Yeah, and where do we sit?" Mack looked around.

"Down," they were instructed. A baliff from each corner shoved them on their butts.

"Be careful there," someone said, accompanied by an especially loud plop. Courtney hit the deck, cursing with sugar, heck, and golly darns.

"We are deeply honored." Mack struggled to his feet and was knocked down by the closest baliff. "Actually," he said, not bothering to struggle up, "we are deeply bruised."

The Goldie in the high pulpit practically spat as he said, "You will stand when you address the court."

"We tried that, Your Honor. But to paraphrase Courtney, your dad-blamed baliffs keep upending us. If you would call off the dogs, we'd be happy to stand with reverence when addressing this honorable court. And, if you could turn the spotlights down a bit, we could see who we're so reverent of."

One spotlight blinked off and Mack brightened. "Well I'll be darned. Where the heck you been, Your Honor? It is so very good to see you again. I should have realized that this trial required the appearance of the foremost trial judge in Goldie history. Your Honor, the great and glorious Judge Grdam, we salute you. Would there be the possibility of a chair? Or seven chairs? We would appreciate that."

The judge roared, "You would appreciate it like you appreciate everything else. But the baliffs will no longer knock the humans over when they address the court."

"Well thank you, Your Honor, for that generous dispensation. We will, of course, be eternally grateful. Would it be appropriate to ask the honorable court what the heck is going on?"

"You didn't stand."

"Does that mean you couldn't hear me."

"That means you're already in deep doo-doo."

"So, what's new?" Mack unfolded into rigid attention, setting an example for his fellow Americans.

"Actually, I'm Big Guy Number Two now. Remember how you used to think that Big Guy Number Two was your particular friend."

"I take it I should disabuse myself of that idea right about now."

"That is entirely correct. And the reason you are in this courtroom is easy. Big Guy Number One, Btsht, your supposed former buddy and friend, has convened the court as a favor. You requested it on behalf of your doomed companion, Courtney. Maybe he's more of a friend than we thought. You asked that we spare Courtney, and in his beneficence, Btsht has granted your request. On the condition that one of you replace her. After all, we must have revenge, because heresy cannot go unpunished. If you would like to volunteer as a replacement for Courtney, she will be spared. At least we won't knock her off just yet."

"How do you propose we find a replacement for Courtney?" Mack was dumbfounded. "No one's going to volunteer. I'm preferring charges against your short-tempered president and former friend of mine. He struck me in the face without warning or provocation. Well, without much provocation, if he had any regard for free speech."

"There you have it. We're against speech that insults us or our sacred gods. After all, Number One Big Guy is the president."

Mack mused on an answer as his collar mic erupted in static that resolved into Lucas's nasally voice. "I'm again to the rescue. You, or someone, should be reminded. 'When a president does it then it is not illegal.' You must admit it. Big Guy Number One, the Honorable Btsht, is the same as the Goldie president."

"I wonder who said that?" Mack frowned as Judge Grdam clanged a shiny stainless-steel gavel.

"Who said that is not germane to this trial but the sentiment is apropos. It reflects reality."

"It must have been a guy from one of those South American countries," said Barry in his Southern drawl.

The judge banged his gavel like a piston on fire. "The topic of who said what is out of order. Kindly proceed."

Courtney lumbered to her feet, irate. "I don't want anyone substituted for me. I want to go down in history as the first martyr at the hands of the uncivilized Golden Antelopes. The intolerant, antiquated, backward race discovered in the last backwater of the planet. I'd rather boil in oil than have someone take my place, thank you very much."

"You're out of order. Gag her and put her in chains." The judge gave the bright new gavel an extra clang. The order was rapidly carried out with Courtney draped in blue and yellow chains and a golden Pamper around her face.

"Are you okay, Courtney?" Mack listened.

"Mumble." Courtney vigorously shook her head, no.

"Just so they didn't make the gag too tight. The chains are a big improvement, colored aluminum—" Mack fingered them. "Light though ultra-strong. You are doing better by our dear friend, Courtney. What did you say was next, Your Honor?"

The judge leaned over the bench. "Calling volunteers. Who will take Courtney's place?"

Roy sat in a lotus position with a stupid grin on his face. Peter looked in every other direction. Barry put his hands in his pockets, whistling tunelessly, staring at his shoelaces.

"How about you, Ellen?" said Mack. "I'm sure you'll volunteer to replace Courtney."

There was no answer, though Ellen looked at Mack without blinking.

Mack laughed. "Saving yourself for the wee children back home with hubby, the love of your life? After the wee children, of course. You wouldn't want to leave them as orphans, sad and bereft without their loving mother. A mother who's off gallivanting on a junket with never-you-mind."

"No matter how difficult it might be for you to understand, I have responsibilities. How about you, Mr. Mack McElhenny? We know you haven't an earthly care or responsibility and are therefore the best substitute for 'our dear Courtney.' You make me sick with that one. You have no responsibilities that anyone knows about. No one cares whether you live or die."

"I'm not hiding behind an ex-wife and daughter who I haven't seen for months. But I won't sacrifice myself for a woman condemned to death for intolerance of other religions."

"Why is that, Mr. Mack? You've become most intolerant toward all religions. Well, second to Mr. Lucas. Not that you admit it, but you reek of it."

Mack bowed. "You'd have been wrong if you'd said that yesterday. But recent events have made me less charitable toward all these infallible yet completely different religions. Perhaps I'm poorer for it and my intolerance is no better than Courtney's. But I don't translate contempt to action. I neither carved up a golden gewgaw nor would I ever."

"You wouldn't physically carve it up, but you'd denigrate it to death with your insidious mouth. You match Courtney tit for tat."

"Ahem," said the judge, who amazingly wasn't Judge Grdam. They gawked as the judge continued, oblivious of their stares. "This is amusing but we're making no progress toward finding a substitute for Courtney. Is it your considered position that no substitute is necessary? That we simply dump her in boiling oil?" The honorable judge whoever-it-was bent his lanky form over the pulpit, granny glasses perched on his humongous nose.

"What the heck's going on?" said Mack. "What happened to our old friend, Judge Grdam? Have you done a David Copperfield on us? And who are you?"

"And who are you, Your Honor?" instructed the new judge. "I am disappointed you don't recognize me. Perhaps it's the robes when you're used to seeing me in a business suit."

"You mean you're Josejiménez, our favorite prosecutor? You don't look like Josejiménez."

The judge jumped up like a rocket, though not very high. "This is outrageous. Why do we put up with these impudent heathens? Dump them all in boiling oil and we'll get on with more important things."

"Sorry, Mutt Judge, Your Honor, sir. It did take me a second. You were at the next counsel table but we weren't formally introduced. I had more contact with your partner, so I apologize. But what did you do with the Honorable Judge Grdam, and what's going on, anyhow?"

"You're wasting the time of this court. If you'd pay attention, you'd notice there are five judges. You're being judged seriatim. Flunking badly, I might add. Think back to when you first walked onto the turntable. You're on your second judge, and as your compatriot Mr. Roy would say, it's all going downhill. In fact, Messrs. Roy and Peter form the basis for further charges. Grand theft of a quantity of vegetable matter from the orphan child of a former prosecutor."

Roy shambled to his feet, swaying. "Well, hell, Your Honorableness. We didn't steal it. The kid gave it to us. He told us to help ourselves and we did. And why is he an orphan?

Being an orphan is really going downhill." Roy waved a hand about. "The poor kid's out in the boondocks living on nothing, penniless and hungry. Hanging out with a bunch of other orphans. We fed him, though all we had was that slop you gave us. What sort of society treats its future leaders like they should fall off a cliff?" Roy did an especially low swoop and ended up on his back, staring at ceiling lights. He added, "We didn't steal nothin'."

Lucas's voice screamed from Mack's collar mic. "Got the quote of the century. This one fits good. Listen up. 'For de little stealin' dey gits you in jail soon or late. For the big stealin' dey makes you emperor and puts you in de Hall o' Fame when you croaks.' That fits Btsht, the big kahuna of the Goldie nation. Us'ns over at the Ermies and Goldies are on Mack's side and will help in any way we can."

"The quotes have been a dandy help," said Mack. "They've greased the wheels of our relationship with the Goldies. Their number one Big Guy Btsht will be especially sympathetic to us now."

"But you've always said that truth is an absolute defense. You'd excel with a performance evaluation based on backtracking."

"When it comes to diplomacy, truth is irrelevant, superfluous, and obscene. I've learned that much in the last two days."

Judge Mutt said, "When nearing the end of life, knowledge often snowballs. Based on the last exchange, I charge you with defamation of Btsht."

"No one defamed Big Guy Number One," said Mack. "Unless you count Lucas, who's in the custody of the Ermies, beyond your reach."

"I heard no denials when Mr. Big-mouth Lucas maligned the Honorable Number One Big Guy. None of you even blinked, much less denied the slander when he was accused of 'the big stealin.' Silence is assent."

Mack shook his head. "That's warped Goldie logic. We're not putting up with it, no siree. You haven't a clue whether Btsht has done big, small, or medium stealin', or no stealin' at all. The most you can say is you don't know. Those rising to the highest political office are almost always less than innocent babes in the woods. Cutthroat competition is what politics is all about."

"You're wasting what little time you have left. But there remains one question before the court. Who is willing to substitute for Courtney?"

"Get real. No one will volunteer to boil in Courtney's stead. She's not our favorite human on the tepui."

"Blub, blub," said Courtney.

"Take off the gag." Mack stared at the judge. "She hasn't insulted you, Your Honor, and she has a right to defend herself."

"We know how she defends herself," said Judge Mutt. "She attacks other belief systems without knowing anything about them."

"We all have our faults. But you must be curious about what she's trying to say. She's probably refusing to accept a substitute. Which would cut the charade short and adjourn this hippity-hoppity court."

Bang went the gavel and Mack was tightly bound. When Courtney's gag was off, she said, "I will accept no substitute. I and only I will boil as a martyr for my God. So, lay off the others. They have little or no moral sense, except Ellen, though she's a Catholic. But a relatively nice Catholic."

The judge banged his gavel but Courtney continued, "Morals is what religion is all about. For the glory of American Baptists worldwide I look forward to, nay fervently hope for, my day of glory." She sat heavily, grinding the mechanism of the lazy Susan to a halt.

From behind the blinding lights Btsht said, "That will be quite enough. I ordered a substitute and thus someone will be substituted. Ignore the heretic and decide who should boil in her stead."

"Right," said Judge Mutt. "You will each stand and describe why you should not be boiled in oil as a substitute for Courtney. Though it makes no difference since several of you will likely swim in oil soon, however briefly. Do the right thing and let a foolish old heretic off the hook."

Mack said, "Shove it."

"Get this thing revolving," ordered the judge. "I don't want to be stuck in this job any longer than necessary."

"And why might that be?" said Btsht in the burning brilliance behind the judge. "Are you afraid to dispense justice? Is your temperament unsuited to judicial office? Should you be replaced?"

Judge Mutt blanched. "Merely a slip of the tongue. We will proceed with dispatch, zeal, and vigor henceforth." He spat at the nearest sub-baliff. "Get the stage moving at once." He resumed in a grand magisterial voice. "Mr. Mack will state why he should not be substituted for Courtney."

Mack said, "What part of 'shove it' don't you understand? As long as I'm cuffed and chained, I'm not one to play your game."

"Wowee, zowee," said Madison. "Mack is poet material, hopefully blooming before his burial."

"Take his chains off, Mr. sub-baliff," said the judge, adding sotto voce, "and how is the floor repair coming?"

"Yes, sir," said the sub-baliff, adding in a whisper, "not too good."

The judge motioned the fifth sub-baliff to remove Mack's chains and the fourth sub-baliff to assist the floor repairmen.

Mack stood on a slant as his chains clattered to the tilty floor. "Thank you, Your Honor. Even aluminum chain's a pain."

Madison's eyes rolled in ecstasy.

"I regretfully decline to substitute for Courtney. But I'm interested in hearing from my fellow Americans, since you insist."

Judge Mutt said, "Next."

Roy staggered up at the urging of the sixth sub-baliff. "Unhand me, you varlet. For my next trick, watch carefully so it doesn't go downhill, boom." Roy stuck a meaty hand in his bulging pocket and with the other, peeled a filmy paper from his jacket pocket.

His other hand appeared with a quantity of vegetable matter, which he sprinkled into the vee of paper. Quick as a flash he rolled it one-handedly into a taper of perfect symmetry, whipping it into his mouth and bowing as Peter flicked his Bic. Fragrant smoke curled lazily toward the judge.

"That's quite a trick," said the judge. "But smoking pot is expressly forbidden to non-Goldies. That's a sacrilege against our religion. Buds are reserved for use during the worship of our God, or Gods, depending on how you look at it. And ignorance of the law is, of course, no defense. This demonstration means you volunteer to take Courtney's place, Mr. Whatever-your-name-is. It escapes me this exact second."

Mack's lapel mic came alive, rattling and reverberating. "Many moons ago someone said this. 'The soul is only the thinking part of the body, and with the body it passes away. When death comes, the farce is over, therefore let us take our pleasure while we can.' This should be Roy's motto. Oh, yeah, Judge Mutt. His name is Roy."

"Name's Roy." Roy whipped the glowing joint from his mouth, tiny smoke rings around the words. "Excuse me for about a minute." He held his breath for thirty-two seconds.

"You haven't answered the question, Mr. Roy," said Judge Mutt. "Will you end the farce of your shallow life, exchanging your worthless body for that of the convicted heretic, Courtney, so help you God?" Roy was concentrating on a second humongous inhalation and failed to promptly respond. The judge said, "I asked you a question, Mr. Roy. Answer under pain of perjury."

Feeling slightly woozy, if not actually flying, Roy expelled the small amount of remaining smoke. "If the pain of perjury is less than the pain of boiling oil, then I'll go for perjury, though I'm dead set against going downhill faster than I already am. Thank you for your kind consideration." Roy bowed and plopped on the floor, passing the joint to Peter.

The judge said to Peter, "One tiny hit of that and you're convicted of heresy. And you know the penalty for that, Mr. Blond-whatever-your-name-is."

"My hair is golden." Peter viewed the joint cross-eyed, torn between the fragrance and the judge's threat. After a split second he added, "Which should make me a Goldie. What the hell," and took a drag.

Mack was torn between flicking the joint out of Peter's mouth and yelling at the judge about the stupidity of such a law. He opted to do both at the same time, sending the joint curling in an airy trajectory as the stage began revolving. That launched the flaming joint into an orbit that ended on the judge's head, igniting what little hair Judge Mutt had left.

Mack said, "That's the dumbest law I ever heard of— My god, you're on fire." Mack rushed at the judge, joined by a phalanx of Legionnaires batting at the judge's head. The joint flew back toward the hapless humans, directly into Madison's open hand.

Madison slapped the joint into his mouth and gulped it down. "The evidence is gone, the joint be done. I took it on the bone, the credit's mine alone. Next time you flip a cone, please think and hold the phone."

"Doesn't work," said Mack. "They're spelled the same but they don't rhyme."

"That's all right okay. On paper they'll look to pay."

"Forget it. Your Honor, I hope you've recovered, and Madison, sit down."

"I saw that," said the judge, pushing away the Legionnaires. "You did that on purpose. Not only are you guilty of heresy. I don't mean you personally, Mr. Mack. But the blond guy and Mr. Whatsiname Roy. And you, Mr. Mack, are guilty of trying to burn down a judge, which is a mighty serious charge."

"Oh, come off it, Your Honor. There's no evidence to support a heresy charge against Roy or Peter. And I didn't mean to do anything other than terminate a budding act of heresy, so to speak. So, let's get on with this charade because you've suffered no real damage." Mack did a double take at a smoldering patch on the side of the judge's head "Well, no serious damage, yet"

"Makes no difference that the poet guy ate the joint. No difference except he's also subject to a charge of heresy. I saw them smoke it, or eat it in the poet's case. I smelled it and you threw it at me. Then it burned me and I'm upset." The judge brushed smoldering hair away from his watering eyes. "I'm sure you can tell."

"Yes, bandying about heresy allegations when they can only be brought by a prosecutor. And you're no prosecutor, Your Honor. Not anymore. So, don't let the fond memories of your previous profession cloud the unbiased judgment required of a judge. Besides, smelling the so-called evidence, which no longer exists, means you must recuse yourself. You'll be a witness and must turn these proceeding over to another judge. Anyway, there's a new judge lurking in the wings, so give it up. That's what you want, isn't it?"

The judge leaned over, whispering, "Well, I do and I don't. It's best not to cross the Big Guy and I look at it from his viewpoint. I'm in line to become Big Guy myself, someday, if I live so long. And I wouldn't want to be sassed in front of the entire Goldie nation. Anyway." He banged the gavel, "Objections overruled. Formal charges of heresy are entered against all the aliens. Well, except the Ellen fanatic, who should be charged with something equally dire, but I don't know what it is. You're in it together so let the trials begin." Bang.

Judge Mutt was gone, replaced by a new judge whose appearance shriveled the humans in their shoes. There was no mistaking a judge decked out in gold lace and tassels with a golden hat higher than a wedding cake and a golden cape flying behind in perfect erection. They cringed at the Judge Pope and their likely high executioner, swirling a bowl of steaming oil in his horny palm.

"Ah, my dearies. The time has come for you to be judged for heresy, every filthy last one of you. I can't tell you how happy I am to be in this place at this time with you in front of me awaiting judgment. I am delirious with happiness."

"You truly are delirious," said Mack, "and we are equally delighted to have you sit in judgment of us. But a judge must be unbiased. You can't come to court having already decided the case."

"Justice is blind…" The Pope was interrupted by a blast of static from Mack's mic.

"Hear ye, hear ye," yelped Lucas, "The opportunity is golden. 'In dark ages people are best guided by religion, as in a pitch-black night a blind man is the best guide; he knows the roads and paths better than a man who can see.

When daylight comes, however, it is foolish to use blind, old men as guides.'" Lucas blew an impressive raspberry. "Take that, you doddering old fool."

The Pope was apoplectic, his face glowing red. Long hairs spurted from his ears, like blow-out party favors unwinding. The steaming bowl flew from his clenched paws and spewed across the pulpit, oil cascading down the aisle in rivulets, sweeping toward the humans quaking on the jerky lazy Susan. The Pope's towering hat fell over his eyes and the long rigid cape lost its starch, collapsing in a sodden mass of golden jelly around the back of the Pope's gigantic chair. He stood with difficulty and the cape stretched to a golden film. He clenched a fist and unleashed a torrent of language that made the audience tremble, shake, and shudder. "You [thirteen unprintable expletives deleted] cock-sucking alien swine," spraying spit over the audience. "Who had the brazen gall to utter such heresy in the presence of God's emissary on earth?"

The alien humans, save one, were less than shell-shocked. Courtney loved it, while neither Peter nor Roy gave a rat's ass. Barry paid polite attention, and Madison composed an impromptu soliloquy, fortunately undelivered. Only Ellen was upset.

Mack said, "It was an Aussie. I'll tell you what I'll do to repair the damage, your lordship. His performance evaluation is due. I'll give him a zero on reverence. Would that be adequate, or are you truly pissed?"

"I am truly pissed." The Pope sprayed slobber over the hapless baliffs. "I am not a blind man. I am the seer for my people, the most holy and spiritual of the Goldie nation. The earth will cease turning if I have anything to say about it."

"Spoken like a true pope," which got Mack an elbow in the ribs.

"You're going too far," said Ellen. "He may not be the real pope but making fun of him is like making fun of the real pope, and I don't like that."

"You there," roared the Judge Pope. "You will approach the bench. I have another bowl somewhere." He reached inside the pulpit, where small cauldrons skittered on orange-shimmering hotplates.

Ellen stood and took a step before Mack grabbed her arm, hauling her back. "Don't go there. Just because he tells you to do something doesn't mean you have to do it. After all, he isn't the real pope." Ellen looked at him quizzically as he said, "Look at his hat. It's melted. You don't have to do what he says."

"You are in ultimate contempt," screamed the Judge Pope. "You will be summarily boiled in oil until your skin sluffs off and then—"

"And then, we've been speculating. Are you really going to eat us?"

"Disgusting. You're unclean. No civilized being would eat such as you. You deserve to be cremated. We'll scatter your ashes off the Golden antelope tepui so you can join your compatriots. May God rest their souls."

Mack said, "Lucas says there's no evidence that a soul exists."

"Aha," said the Pope. "There's no evidence that the human soul exists. But we have conclusively proved the existence of the Golden Antelope soul. That is an established fact. And don't you forget it."

"I wouldn't forget it if there were the slightest evidence of its truth. But it belongs in the realm of the assertions made by folks who claim to have been kidnapped by aliens. But if you say it, the dumb Goldies believe it. Isn't that how it works?"

The Pope's face turned from red to overripe eggplant, his jaws quivering. "You are the anti-Famigusta. Yea, I say, Mr. Mack is the anti-Famigusta. He'll be dealt with appropriately."

Mack rubbed his chin, wondering if he needed a shave. "Is the anti-Famigusta like the anti-Christ? Or the same as the anti-Radnicharra? Is that what you're accusing me of?" The bristles were rough on his partially severed fingertips. He definitely needed a shave.

"Compared to the anti-Famigusta, the anti-Christ is an also-ran. The anti-Famigusta foretells the destruction of civilization as we know it, the downfall of our sacred religion, the degradation of our young maidenhood, the—"

"I've been wondering about that. Whether there are female antelopes and, if so, where are they? Do you have them

282

cooped up in the inner courtyards of your living quarters? You are a pretty peculiar species."

The Pope suffered a sudden migraine, lowering his forehead on the horny palm of his paw. The tatters of his golden hat fell over the edge of the pulpit, landing with a plop, snapping the Judge Pope to attention. "The impudence of the human species is a loathsome thing to behold. I've done my part. Let this cup pass from me." The Pope yelled at the closest baliff, "Get that hat back up here, pronto. And as for you, Mr. Mack. It's difficult to know where to begin. Females are us since we're bisexual. Overt females have been the downfall of honorable Goldies through the ages and are thus relegated to courtyards, as you put it. Actually, we put them on a pedestal, but pedestals are forbidden in religious ceremonies. You are so observant."

"Congrats on settling down the popish twit," said Lucas. "Here's another one for the old chauvinist pig."

"You should talk, being an Aussie," said Mack.

"'It is indeed a burning shame that there should be one law for men and another law for women. I think there should be no law for anybody.' Aussies can be feminists too."

Mack scoffed. "Your erudite quote has nothing to do with men and women. It has to do with laws. Have you wondered why there's so many laws when you and I don't seem to need any at all? Have you never asked yourself *why* we have all these lurking laws, or do you like laws?"

The Judge Pope was banging his gavel, reducing the pulpit to kindling. "You will zip your trap," he ruled.

Mack said, "Won't. There's nothing left you can do after you've sentenced me to boil in oil. Have you asked yourself what laws are needed to keep your personal self on the straight and narrow? As opposed to the laws required to keep the other fellow on the straight and narrow? There are many more of the latter. Which reminds me of our first meeting."

The Judge Pope thought back, scowling.

"If your memory needs refreshing, you committed the ultimate heresy. A heresy far worse than that allegedly committed by poor Courtney. She only lopped off a couple of antlers and a golden dick while you reduced the identical image to shreds. I assume that means you too should be fried, dyed, and liquified."

"Legionnaires," roared the Judge Pope, "Gag him!"

In a twinkling Mack was gagged and bound. He rolled across the floor like a tenpin and fell into the depression at the edge of the stage, stuck where the turning floor met the stationary part reserved for judges and baliffs. There he slowly clumped and clacked. The snarling edges frayed his bonds as silence otherwise reigned. It dawned on the Judge Pope that they were getting nowhere. He bowed his head. "We must protect the record. Legionnaires, do your thing backward."

Lucas's voice erupted from the tiny piece of Mack's uncovered collar. "It's hard to believe how well the Judge Pope has illustrated our great thinkers. The thoughts our admittedly inferior species has passed down for generations. Catch this one. 'Religion is excellent stuff for keeping common people quiet.' Now admit it. That is perfect. We're the common people and the Pope is the embodiment of religion. And boy has he kept you quiet. We're on the edge of our seats over here. You're on live TV. You're stars!"

When Mack's mouth was freed of cotton quilting, he said, "Fat lot of help you are, Lucas my boy. Ellen, among others, will reject your sentiment. She doesn't think this pope has a connection with legitimate religion, however defined. Much less embodies it. But point taken. I'm giving you an excellent rating on the entirety of your performance evaluation. Marylyn will be so proud. Naturally, I'm only saying this for the TV cameras." Mack looked around. "But I don't see any TV cameras. I can't imagine how this is televised. And I don't know why the Goldies would allow it."

Lucas laughed. "It's the ratings. You also can't imagine how the other antelopes are eating it up. It's adventure TV, sort of like *Survivor*. Which isn't a bad comparison."

"So, someone's making buku bucks from us. But any advantage in going viral is meaningless if the Ermies are still preparing for war. Not that you'd like to give that away to the Goldies, so give me a veiled hint. And have you heard from Reg and the Ivies?"

The Judge Pope bellowed, "I didn't loosen your bonds so you could gossip with your jerk friends. We have serious business going on here. Now that you have your freedom, I expect exemplary behavior. Or the chains will be reattached forthwith. Have I made myself clear?"

The humans started talking at once. Madison danced a jig as he said, "Clear my dear, I'll have a beer. My throat is dry and that's no lie. So, give a break to us you hate. And we'll behave or kiss me Kate."

"Yakkety yak, don't talk back," said Roy. "I'd try to rhyme but I don't even know how to spell it. I'm so happy to be free and no longer rolling downhill." He bowed to the judge, who tried to get a word in edgewise.

"Your Honor," said Ellen. "I don't agree with your politics or religion, but that's your problem. Of course, it's becoming my problem, but I'll be tolerant until I croak."

Peter said, "I'm for the beer Madison mentioned. Us humans are delicate beings and need lots of liquid to survive. We're ninety-nine percent water so we must constantly replenish. Otherwise we dehydrate. That's something you should look into, your popishness."

Courtney started giving the Pope the silent treatment but reconsidered. "Hallelujah, I am free at last. Do your worst, you old tyrant."

Whatever Barry said was drowned out by the Pope's snappy retort. "I didn't make myself clear. Legionn—" He was cut off as the stage shifted and a new judge appeared. This one brandished a tomahawk and was dressed fancy like the Judge Pope, yet completely differently.

This judge's hat was flatter than the Pope's, though just as golden in a punctured sort of way. Gold crammed the bill, stacked on top of itself in swirls and curlicues. Thick golden lines bisected intersections that made it look vaguely French. Instead of a cape this judge flaunted epaulettes. They realized this was the General when he yelled, "Atten-hut. Line up. Move it forward, mister. You there. Back. What's the dumpy lady doing? Baliffs, get these people into a semblance of order. Now!"

The baliffs swarmed all over them. They punched Peter and Roy back in line and tried to make Courtney stand up straight as Ellen snarled and kicked one of the mousy little baliffs where it hurt. He rolled up in a bundle so tight the other baliffs couldn't pry him out of it, finally rolling him off stage. They primly returned to their baliff desks less one, while the judge conducted an inspection.

"Not bad for a bunch of alien trash. You have three seconds to begin your individual recitals. Why you should or shouldn't be substituted for Courtney."

The humans looked at each other to see who would go first. When nothing happened the Judge General thundered, "Sound off." After a split second's pause, he ordered, "Right now."

At the continuing silence Mack put his hand up. "None have military training so they haven't the vaguest what you're telling them to do. If you'd like, I can help."

"Carry on," snapped the General.

"What he means is, state your names in order. Starting at the far end with Barry."

"Barry here."

"First and last names." Mack caught the Judge General's look predicting violence.

"Right. Barry McCafferty, sir."

They carried on from Barry through Courtney, Roy, and Peter. Madison said, "Madison Murphy of the County Cork Murphys." Ellen gave a weenie of a salute. Mack crisped a salute so sharp the General's eyes bulged.

The General gravely returned the salute, which looked a little sloppy after Mack's herculean effort. The General ordered, "Barry McCafferty. You will immediately state why you should or shouldn't be substituted to boil in place of Mrs.... Gulp." He plunged on, doing fairly well. "Mrs. Evernet Courtney Far One Sit on Sharm On. Proceed forthwith."

"Well, Your Honor, sir." Barry gave a late salute. "As a Southerner and chivalrous to the root of my being, I'd be tempted to substitute myself for Courtney. Excuse me if I use the diminutive of her noble name. But a substitution would be contra-chivalrous because she'd rather be a martyr. Who am I to deny her the simple pleasures of her heartfelt religion?"

Mack was on his feet. "I object. There's no need to proceed with this farce, sir," shouting the last word. "Until you prove the efficacy of your god beyond the shadow of a doubt. How about a little lightning display? That might convince us to substitute for Courtney. If your god actually exists, then we're in deep doo-doo. Otherwise not so much. The proof is in the pudding. We require actual steaming pudding before being obliged to step into boiling oil, sir." Mack crackled a final salute and stood at attention.

The General didn't bother to return the salute, immersed in thought so deep he was lucky to pull himself out of it. His glazed eyes revolved to meet Mack's stare. "The Goldie God is Good and Golden. The Pope said so. You don't need more proof than that."

"But we do need proof. Let me give it a go. And please remember this is only hypothetical and I mean nothing by it. I'm only giving the Goldie god the opportunity to display his or her awesome powers, since I get mixed up whether it's a him or a her. I invite you to display those powers on a puny creature like myself. I'd be particularly obliged if you'd make sure the Pope isn't eavesdropping. This is only a demonstration-to-make-a-point."

The General seemed to nod and Mack said, "Hey you punk Goldie god. Our god can whip your butt. You've a fake farty god without the slightest juice. If you have any omnipotence whatsoever, let it go now. Skewer me with lightning. Stunt my growth. Singe my hemorrhoids. Tamp my tater. Do your stuff or forever hold your peace." Mack cocked an ear, listening for thunder and lightning.

"Don't be an ass," ordered the General. "Gods don't condescend to challenges by inferior beings such as yourselves. He wouldn't give you the time of day because you're so far beneath him as to be an ant. Your empty name-calling doesn't prove a thing."

"It proves the Pope is napping, eh, Herr General. But you're right. So, let's ascend a level or two. Where has this Goldie God appeared to you and what witnesses do you have?

287

I need street addresses, first, last, and middle names, dates, and circumstances. So, give."

"Folderol. Gods don't appear to mere mortals like myself, much less to the likes of you. Gods appear only to priests and popes, and sometimes on tortillas. And these miracles don't happen every day. It's not the kind of stuff for a court of law."

"Since this isn't a court of law, I don't see what that proves. Hey, Lucas. Are you still there? Do you have a relevant quote?"

"Squeal, spit," said Mack's collar mic a second before Lucas's dulcet Aussie drawl oozed. "Mack, me man. I'm proud that you recognize the finer philosophical things such as live in me mum's book. And yes, I have a sterling example. 'One single well-established fact, clearly irreconcilable with a doctrine, is sufficient to prove that it is false.' Fits like an artificial limb. What say?"

"Not." Mack reconsidered. "Well, in a backward sort of way. Since Herr General can't come up with a single solitary instance of his god's actual existence, then maybe Senor Famigusta del Tortilla doesn't exist. Those who assert a proposition bear the burden of coming up with at least a single fact to support it. A negative can't be proved. Such as whether a particular god or unicorn or UFO or other figment of someone's imagination doesn't exist. Or am I getting confused here?"

"Poor Mack," cooed Ellen. "You've been confused your whole life. You can't expect enlightenment at your advanced age."

"You're not helping our case." Mack glared at Ellen.

"Nor are you." Ellen glared back harder.

"I got it." The Judge General snapped his horny hooves and sent his golden epaulettes shimmering. "I can prove the existence of the Goldie God. Look around you. He made these terrific tepuis. And us. The Golden Antelopes."

"Well, yeah," said Mack. "And he made us too, the scurrilous human race, and the Ermies and Ivies. I guess we owe a lot to your Big Guy god."

The General was taken aback. "No. That's not possible. He wouldn't have made you. You're a nuisance, the bane of our existence. You want to put us in zoos."

"We'd settle that red herring right now, but I don't want to get off track. The only question is how you know we, or even you for that matter, weren't concocted by a big joker? Or another god? Or Jasper the unfriendly ghost? Or the diabolical tenets of mother nature? Or a UFO? Or a red horny apparition wielding the jaw of an ass while stirring the fickle sands of time? The planet has been screwed up big time with more gods than Carter has little pills. Surely you have witnesses to prove who's responsible for this sorry mess."

The Judge General sounded like he was sobbing, great gobs of anguish escaping his throat. "Ain't my bailiwick." He gasped. "I need to call the Pope for consultation. I'm here to provide order and inspiration. To kick a little Ermie butt when called upon. To extinguish the Ivies on command. This 'who created what' stuff is way above my chain of command. So, stow it and I'll do my thing. The thing for which I'm especially commended and which got me promoted all the way up to general in the first place. Stand up straight or I'll have you all on KP. You there, soldier. Get down and give me a hundred."

"Who me?" said Mack.

"He's no soldier, more a draft dodger. Budge an inch and he's a grinch," Madison danced around like a retarded fireman. "He's a cadger, and a badger. Give a damn, or he'll be at yer."

Lightning struck the edge of the floor, canting it as the Judge General disappeared in a poof of nothingness. Big Guy Number One, His Omnipotency, the Right Honorable Btsht, materialized on his throne, flanked by Legionnaires. One Legionnaire calmly holstered a spiffy little lightning-spitting tool into his scabbard as smoke wafted from a jaggedly charred streak that intersected an imaginary line that ran from Mack's groin to the space between his feet.

15

"Whooey," said Mack as the smoke cleared. Btsht banged a super-terrific king-size gavel, as big as his honorable self. It took both hands to wield it and made the auditorium ring like a bell the size of LA.

"Enough of this tomfoolery," said Btsht. "Now we get down to cases. You will each state why you shouldn't be substituted for Courtney. Then I'll rule. Bear in mind that your substitution will speed up your demise by mere seconds. So why are you resisting and making such a big fuss, anyhow?"

Mack said, "So, why bother? Don't you have better things to do? Like planning a nuclear holocaust? Wiping out life on the planet? Exterminating other branches of your species and generally behaving like a jackass?"

The Right Honorable Btsht sat frozen. He willed away the tremors that threatened to cripple his bodily functions. "You vill never learn. I mean you will never learn. What will it take for you to acknowledge your betters and grasp the rudiments of diplomacy? You need discipline that only government can provide, a lesson in humility. Guards. Draw and quarter him."

The head Legionnaire looked puzzled. He hesitantly, half step, pause, half step, lunge, led his troops into battle. Mack said, "Over here fellows. This is my best side and you can set the easel up over there. Try a charcoal likeness. Then you can shower me with quarters and we'll call it even."

The head Legionnaire looked quizzically at the Right Honorable Btsht, whose blood pressure had rendered the omnipotent head of the Goldie nation a brilliant scarlet. His head seemed to swell and then deflate. Btsht's howl rocked the courtroom and sprayed the multitude. "Drawing is not artwork.

Drawing is seizing his extremities and stretching them like plastic-man. The quartering follows like topsy. Grrr, grrr, grrr."

Mack grimaced. "Let's not be hasty. If you need an apology, I'm happy to oblige. I'll attend diplomat's school if need be. After all, I'm new at the game. Certainly, nowhere near the pro that you are, Your Omnipotency, the Right Honorable Btsht. Let bygones crumble behind us and begin with a fresh slate. I know that will be difficult because, as usual, I'm at fault. But face it, Your Honorableness. Not all of us can be as perfect as you naturally are." Mack did a triple genuflect, looked up furtively, and did three more double-quick.

"The problem with you," Btsht had calmed down considerably, "is you lack governance. Of all the humans and antelopes in all the species on all the planets in all the solar systems in all the galaxies in all the universes, you are most in need of governing. You know what I mean?"

"I love this place," came Lucas's metallic voice from Mack's collar mic. "It presents opportunities a philosopher can only dream of. Ah, yes. 'To be governed is to have every opinion, every transaction, every movement noted, registered, counted, rated, stamped, measured, numbered, assessed, licensed, refused, authorized, endorsed, admonished, prevented, reformed, redressed, corrected.'"

Btsht was stuttering before Lucas finished the quote, resolving the stutter in a shout. "That's exactly what I mean. If there's anyone on the planet who more deserves folding, spindling, and mutilating, I don't know who it'd be. Mr. Mack severely needs governance and I'm here to make certain he gets it. Guards—"

"I must say," said Mack, "that I disagree. No one should have to put up with government unless someone is bugging someone else. The whole point of government is to keep those poor unfortunate souls, who distress us to death, from distressing us to death."

"You distress the holy heck out of me," said Btsht. "I can't find one redeeming attribute in your scrawny countenance. You have a smart mouth and a not-so-smart brain. Such a combination uneasy lies before authority."

"Come now, Your Honorableness. I've never lied to you. In fact, I think that's what most distresses you most, that I refuse to lie. This governance thing is another cob in my cud. Why should anyone have to be registered, counted, stamped, or put up with being governed in the first place? The main reason for government is to give jobs to politicians and Big Guys, to keep you in the style you love best. As long as I don't distress you, you should leave me alone. Of course, it'd distress you no end if I didn't pay taxes or contribute to your upkeep and support. You might expire of malnutrition. That'd be a *real* bummer."

"There you go again." Btsht's face twisted in a snarl. "You'll never learn. We should drop you off the side of the tepui in a gunny sack, concrete overshoes, something like that. I sure wouldn't miss you. Gack," he added at the absurdity of missing Mack.

"Well, Your Honorableness. I'd miss you and yours like the dickens." At Btsht's skeptical look Mack said, "I'm not kidding. This has been the highlight of my life. It's not every day that you come across an alien race, speaking from our perspective, of course. And one as intelligent as yourselves. We may have our differences, but don't you think it's rather a miracle? It must be tied up in this religious stuff we keep running into. Head on ninety miles an hour into a sheer brick wall. Doesn't it strike you that way? I know it does, because we had interesting conversations before your elevation to the highest office on the tepui. But finding another intelligent species. I know you won't admit that we fit that category. But we're a near intelligent species. After all, you watch our television. How smart can you be? Yeah, I know you think I'm beating around the bush. But this whole episode puts the value of our respective religions in question. How can we have gods who made us in their own image when our images are so cock-eyed different? Or plain cock-eyed? Whoa. I see you gather my meaning."

The clashing gears in Btsht's mind were plain. A tic devoured his bushy right eyebrow, encircled his bulbous head, and dropped south. His entire body convulsed into a giant jerk, kerboom, Btsht fidgety on his throne. "We've been through this before, more or less. You should know enough to keep your trap shut, but no. I'll ignore your last series of idiotic comments, for now. And we'll get on with following the law in these kinds of cases—"

"Stop right there. How many cases like this have there been? Have other inferior humans ventured onto these tepuis and met their demise, unbeknownst to our lowland species? And what law could you be speaking of? If others of our ilk haven't blundered into your affairs before, how could you have laws to deal with it?"

Btsht's expression made the answer remarkably clear as Mack said, "Right. You are the law, the Big Guy. Actually, the Really Big Guy of Omnipotency Stature. And what you say is the law. Does that cover it?"

"Pretty much," drawled Btsht. "So, we don't keep covering the same ground, I'll make it extra clear. The law requires you to decide who should be substituted for Mrs. Courtney."

"Do you mean 'should' in the sense of 'deserves to be'? Or in some other sense, such as 'volunteers to be'? Language can be slippery."

"Can be my ass. All languages are slippery, some more than others. And yes, we're looking for personal responsibility. Who 'should' be substituted for Courtney? And since we're at it, I may grant a reprieve for everyone else. All this unnecessary bloodshed." He shrugged massive shoulders as if the weight was beyond his capacity to bear.

"But we haven't had bloodshed— Yes, it would be better not to have further bloodshed. I didn't mean to belittle the death of former Big Guy Number Three or his nephew. Sorry about that."

"Concerning your soliloquy about our respective religions. Oh, no," said Btsht as Mack opened his mouth, "I didn't mean you had a close connection to religion. But what you said about our religion was heretical. And I'm having a super-tough time ignoring that. In fact, I may be unsuccessful."

"Just do your very best," said Mack, soothingly. "Declaring the validity of any religion is heretical to at least three fourths of the world's population. Or in the case of antelopes, sixty-six point six percent of the antelope population. Heresy is in the eyes of the beholder and I prefer to avert my gaze."

"I've given you a king's X for past deeds. But the law, which is myself, requires you to decide who 'should' be substituted for Courtney. In the sense of 'deserves to be.'"

"You mean…" began Mack. But he couldn't go on.

"You mean," said Ellen, "who is most deserving of death by boiling oil. So, we have to decide who's the worst of the us? Is that what you mean?"

"What part of 'should' don't you understand?" said Btsht. "That's exactly what I mean. We will explore your psyches, plumb your depths, delineate your kinks and crooks." He rubbed horny hands with relish.

"Wait a cotton-pickin' momento," said Mack. "What's that I spy in the corner? Behind the klieg lights you hid yourself behind. Is that a red eye and is this an episode of reality TV? Fess up. You're in it for the ratings, aren't you, Your Honorable Big Guyness?"

"You are quick as a whip on trivialities. But it's none of your business. If there's one thing I know, it's that Big Guys don't last forever. One must make one's packet while one can. So, proceed." With both hands he lifted the gigantic gavel and dropped it on the metal grid. As goong, goooong, gooooooong, reverberated through their heads, he shouted, "That's an order."

Lucas's hearty-as-a-kangaroo accent cut through the five-cornered courtroom like a dull stiletto. "Avast there me hearties. The Ermies love your show and the Ivies are also glued to their sets. So, don't let us down. Shout your innermost secrets because it's the law and I quote, 'Every law is an infraction of liberty.' The less liberty, the more law, and the higher the ratings. Those of us out of danger applaud you." They could hear tumultuous clapping over the reedy microphone.

"Why, oh Lucas, have you abandoned us?" Mack's hands were clasped and sweat dripped down his face, glistening in the brilliant light. "But then, enough of this claptrap." Mack stood on his tiptoes and looked Btsht in the eye. "We're not playing. We'll not be quislings to rat on the foibles of our fellow human beings. Especially not to entertain a bunch of antelopes. So, forget that action, Jackson."

"But you will." Btsht had a less than enigmatic smile. "We have a guest judge to help you along." Btsht rose and swept an arm behind him.

A door slid open and in walked a refurbished Judge Pope, resplendent in gold from head to toe. His new cape stuck straight out behind as, with a gut-wrenching smirk, he swept onto a pulpit alongside Btsht.

"So, get along with you," said Btsht, "Mack, old buddy, old pal. Why don't you go first?"

"Because I don't want to." Mack turned his back and sat down.

"That wasn't a question," roared Btsht. "Turn your smiling face around and get on with it or I'll sic a battalion of Legionnaires on you. They'll be happy to turn your various body parts around, separately, one at a time."

"Says you. I call your bluff." Mack stood with hands on hips, facing away from Btsht, who nodded his head. The Legionnaire commander arrived at Mack's side in less than a second, spinning Mack around to face Btsht. Mack stood with his head awhirl but managed to squawk, "I will not rat on myself."

"But you will." Btsht again gave a small nod.

The Legionnaire was resplendent with parallel bars on his broad shoulders. He unholstered his tool and flipped open a single blade. "Your hand, please," he said kindly.

"Nah," said Mack.

The Legionnaire took Mack's hand, inspected it, and dropped it. He took the other hand instead, and lowered the serrated blade on Mack's raw fingertips.

The Legionnaire moved to excise the raw ends, but before he made contact, Mack said, "Right. Now what exactly was it you wanted, Your Excellency? Both Your Excellencies, that is."

The Legionnaire's reflexes weren't what they'd been in his youth. He failed to stop before all four fingers lost another millimeter, transforming them into bloody stumps. Mack screamed, "Hay Sus Chris Tay, Momma Mia Cahones supremo.

295

That hurt like holy heck." He closed his mouth at the Judge Pope's expression.

Mack gasped, gingerly sucking his fingers, his face scrunched at the metallic taste of blood. Btsht said sweetly, "Your laundered autobiography, please. We'll rely upon your compatriots to fill in the dirt."

"Glub," said Mack.

"Don't talk with your mouth full. If you can't remove your foot, at least remove your hand."

Mack smiled a shaky grin, swallowing his gorge. "My name is McElheney Melchior McCafferty, Mack for short. I have other ambitions but apparently am a career employee of the Arizona State Lottery, charged with escorting these lucky new millionaires to the dream destination of their choice. Carnival in Rio. I hope we make it. I am unmarried and live in Tempe, Arizona. What more do you want?"

"We want dirt," said Btsht, as the Judge Pope cast an evil eye on the proceedings. "We need all the facts to decide whether you should be substituted for Courtney in the golden oil."

"Hey, Mack," erupted his mic. "Your graphics are super. The Goldies have a black cauldron sitting on little black legs. When they fade to commercial, they pan the bubbly oil. Nasty looking stuff. Kinda makes you shiver."

"Thanks, Lucas. Getting back to show biz—no matter how disappointing, there is no dirt. My parents lived in Milwaukee until they moved to Green Valley, which is in Arizona, and I visit them when I can. I have a daughter, Alicia Amber, who lives in Phoenix, right next to Tempe, but her mother won't let me see her. Next month we're in court about visitation. I can't imagine what else you'd want to know."

"What we're interested in is what you haven't told us," said Btsht. "Don't let us down here. You're supposed to pay child support, correct?"

"Of course."

"How far behind are you?" said the Judge Pope.

"I'm pretty close to paid up."

"Not even close, are you?" said Btsht. "I'll bet your erstwhile friends have contrary information. Any volunteers?" He motioned the head Legionnaire to do his stuff.

Based on the reaction as he prowled behind the humans, the Legionnaire's tool doubled as a cattle prod.

"You, there," said Btsht, pointing at Peter. "What do you have to say about Mr. Mack's sanitized version of his pristine life?"

Peter grimaced. "Mack's okay. He's not any further behind on his child support than the average bear. He said there was something weird about the decree. No one knows how long he's supposed to pay. And I don't know nothing else." Peter blew a raspberry and received an extra jolt with the cattle prod. A camera close-up caught his agony.

"Enough of this crap," said the Judge Pope. "Mr. Mack is a porn freak. He spends his free time surfing the net, checking out the nastiest sites. But only if they're free. He's partial to two babes getting it on."

Btsht inserted his two cents. "I offered him porn with two Goldie babes and he almost barfed his cookies. Thus, to porn freak we add racial bias and discrimination."

Mack howled. "Where did you come up with this scurrilous crap?" He risked a glance at Ellen. "Goldie porn sounds disgusting."

"Heidi ho," said Btsht. "You should be sentenced to watching videos of hot tamale antelopes. Guess how bad yours's sounds to us."

The Judge Pope ignored them. "Cookies. The cookie net service has amazing information on all of you. Tread lightly in your denials or we'll nail you to a cross."

"I'd willingly be nailed to a cross, or boiled in oil," said Courtney. "Stop the nonsense. There's no reason to torture these people."

"What's this?" demanded the Judge Pope. "Mrs. Goodie Two-Shoes defending a pornographer. So much for the morality of your religion."

Courtney yelped, "I'm not defending a pornographer. I'm defending a human being." Mack bowed gravely. "The charges against him are unproven. Just because you say something doesn't make it so."

"Admirable chauvinism on behalf of your species. But we only speak the truth. We're not half-cocked Christians who'll defend anything, no matter how inane."

"That's not very nice," said Mack.

"You're one to talk." The Judge Pope's vertical cape bumped against the back wall as he bobbed and weaved. "Let's look at another of your pristine group. Who's that guy, sitting over there?"

Roy shuffled to his feet. "Name's Roy Cartwright McKittrick. And this whole thing is rapidly going downhill. The only bad thing about me, and I'm not denying it, is I hawk a little pot on the side. I keep the natives happy and finance my own stash so I can smoke as much as I want. Along those lines, I have an offering for you and yours, Your Poperyship." During the first sentence, Roy rolled a tight joint, one-handedly. He followed with five more during the rest of his speech, flipping a couple to the Judge Pope. Roy lit another joint.

"That tears it," said the Judge Pope. "This is heresy. The hemp flower is sacred. You can only smoke it on solemn occasions of the Goldie religion, during the Festival of Radnicharra and the fortnight immediately following."

Mack said, "Roy's just supplying market demand. No matter how much I disapprove of the particular market, it doesn't hurt anyone very much."

"Hurts me to the core," said the Judge Pope.

"Yeah, but you're an artificial audience. Which is to say religious. I've recently found that rationality and religion rarely hold hands. You're too gnarly to hold hands with anyone."

"I'm the epitome of religion but I'll ignore the personal affront. How's that for turning the other cheek?" The Judge Pope turned his head sideways.

"I didn't know that was part of your religion. But then I know almost nothing about it. I know you have a mother, daughter, and holy ghost. Which I innocently mistook for a dirigible, thanks to the sneaky propaganda of your sworn enemies, the Ermies."

"Thanks, Mack," said Lucas.

"And you're into tassels. Skullcaps that fit around pygmy antlers. I've seen you pray with little blocks of wood around your scrawny wrists, fastened by leather thongs. You genuflect and pray five times a day toward another tepui. Your holy books are both old and new, whatever that means. You revere the family and natural marriages. Which I suspect means male and female only. You have five duties that will lever you into the kingdom of your particular heaven, including giving alms and digging wells. Have I missed anything?"

"I stand amazed. Where did you find this out?"

"Lucas told me about it from a pamphlet he saw, and I never realized until this very second that it had to be in English. Fancy that."

"You missed quite a bit, but it makes no difference for infidels. We're not out to convert you. After all, you're lowly humans."

"It's coming back to me. Your sacraments consist of fasting for the birth of a prophet whose name escapes me. Maybe it was Radnicharra, but I get it mixed up with Famigusta. You have five commandments that I know nothing about except the alms and digging wells. You apparently exclude hospitality for alien others and require various pilgrimages. You separate males and females in church and out of church. That exhausts my knowledge."

"Superficial at best," smirked the Judge Pope. "You've entirely missed our spirituality and essential goodness. And the fact that our religion is the only valid religion in the history of the universe."

"I did sort of know that. It must have been intuitive."

The Judge Pope cleared his mighty throat. "But we're not here to test your knowledge of the noble Goldie religion. What kind of ratings would that garner? We're here to check out your foibles and failings. Next." He crooked a horny little finger at Ellen. "You there. Go right ahead."

"I'm Catholic," said Ellen. "I have no failings."

"Oh, come now. I recall nasty stuff about you from the transcripts. You left your children to come on this boondoggle of a trip. What else lurks in the shadows of your murky life?

We're here to find out and find out we will. Are there volunteers to reveal the deep dark secrets of Mrs. Ellen?"

"None," said Mack. "We're not traitors to our own kind. We'd rather choke on bile, fry in boiling oil, or suffer frostbite before turning on our fellows."

"We can arrange that if you'd rather be boiling, biling, or biting before blabbing. It's not because she's your own kind. It's because she's a, how do you call it, babe, that inhibits your tongue. Lust guides your brash refusal. Your fantasies about Ellen are common knowledge."

"You are wrong." Ellen shook her head vigorously. "My husband insisted I go on this trip and leave our children with their grandparents in Sun City."

"Did you know there's a little hanky-panky going on while you're gone?" The Judge Pope chortled. "What's a husband to do while his wife's away for two long weeks?" He snarfled, saliva running down his chin.

"You are a dirty old man, more like the anti-Christ than any pope I ever heard of. You couldn't hold a candle to the real one." Ellen sniffled.

"You are faithless to your children and allow your husband to philander. This is only the surface of a deeply flawed being. Your deep dark secret is that you're hornier than a toad, randier than a rake, and more spreadable than pure fruit jam. Disgusting. You rut like a rabid rabbit."

Ellen turned the color of an overripe persimmon, spluttering, "That's entirely untrue." It was apparent that she was lying like a rug. "My husband is running the family nursery and is busy with his four-wheel-drive club." Ellen gasped for breath.

"Ah, you mean he's watering the garden and pruning the trees? Spreading the tiny trunks of the bonsai saplings and planting his seed while remaining faithful to you during your crash and abandonment on this remote tepui. Paraphrasing your less than secret admirer." The Judge Pope bounced up and down like a little kid, his equine face split into a lascivious grin.

"That's completely unfair," said Mack, eyeing Ellen with fresh appreciation. "You're giving her a load of grief for no reason. There are no way cookies on her computer would show her husband cheating. And it's exceedingly remote that they'd prove that she's a lascivious nymphomaniac." Though Mack was clearly hoping, his face scrunched in anticipation at whatever the Judge Pope might cite as an unimpeachable source.

"I have the list right here." The Judge Pope waved a long piece of plastic. "Though we can't quite figure out what popesicle.com is all about. Her favorites include nymphomaniacs.com, chippendales.com, and the winner, sexwithpriests.com. The last one comes up several times a day."

"I see. Perhaps the nymphomaniac site is a favorite of Ellen's husband. Who knows, maybe he's bi." Obviously hoping Ellen was, for all the good that'd do Mack.

"That's outrageous," howled Ellen. "Totally outrageous." She stared into space.

"They probably don't know anything at all," Mack said soothingly. "They're blowing smoke, making it all up. The facts are probably the exact opposite." He surely hoped not.

"Ratings are up," said Lucas, his reedy voice swirling from Mack's mic. "You're knocking 'em dead. Or the Judge Pope is setting you up to be knocked dead. Which reminds me of the reason I rang. 'We should always be disposed to believe that that which appears to us to be white is really black, if the hierarchy of the Church so decides.' And hey, the Judge Pope is as hierarchical as they come, say what."

"Conceded, conceited. Enjoy yourself while we're grilled to see who fries first. I thought you'd have more compassion for us, but instead you're glued to the great wasteland."

"Order in the court," roared the Judge Pope. He took the humongous gavel from Btsht's grasp and slammed it on the reverberation plate, with what should have been foreseen consequences. As the sound barrier broke over them in waves of pulsing energy, the pulpit throne imploded. This ejected the Judge Pope and Honorable Btsht like bowling balls, who rolled through the baliffs into the humans.

"Well howdy, partner," said Peter. He barely had time to pass the joint to Roy before he caught Btsht flailing by. Peter grabbed him by a horny paw and hung on for dear life, like dancing a highland reel.

"Mighty fine." Roy finished off a dandy-deep drag, stuck in a happy hempy time warp, before noting the Big Guy's mighty fine run downhill.

Mack and Ellen bore the brunt of the avalanche, knocked over like nine pins. They fell head over heels backward with the breath knocked out of them, next to the Judge Pope laying in a heap of gold damask, his chest rising rhythmically. Barry, Madison, and Courtney surveyed the damage.

Madison was the first to speak, starting slowly but gaining momentum. "Baffling bits of blackened batshit, what's that hanging off us all? Might it be the roly-poly's, done in badly by the fall? Trust a preacher if you reach 'er, now he's gone and done us all. You might think the preach is studly, but I think his gender's mudly. Then who else would wear gold laceys? Bet with priests he's oft off baseys."

Those still conscious tried damage control, picking bits of black baliff costume off the Judge Pope's crumpled finery, but it was too imbedded to remove. Roy and Peter tried to prop the Big Guy up on his tiny feet, but found he was an extra ultra-Big Guy. They braced him up for a few seconds, thinking he was balanced, but he always came tumbling down. Between attempts they discussed strategy over a freshly rolled joint, which Roy rolled faster than Btsht could fall over. Legionnaires scrambled to assist the clean-up and resuscitation but it took eight minutes before the show was back on the air and the Judge Pope in a fresh costume. The Judge Pope was finally propped on a new pulpit throne next to a still-dazed Btsht, who looked like Bill the Cat. Mack recovered as the Judge Pope gingerly touched the humongous gavel on a new and much smaller reverberation plate.

"This court will come back to order. We must make up for lost time and ratings."

"Right," said Mack. "We hereby cease and desist. Where were we, anyway? I can't remember a thing."

"We finished with Mrs. Ellen." The Judge Pope was pale and peaked. "Next is the person on her other side. I don't believe we've been introduced."

"Nor will you be. I was reprimanded the last time I introduced a witness to the court."

The Judge Pope peered. "Oh, I know that one. Another heretic. Mr. Peter the Wop."

There was a collective gasp from the humans.

"Oh, now what?" The Judge Pope was exasperated. "Think ratings instead of interruptions."

"We can't tell you," said Mack.

"You will tell me," ordered the Judge Pope, raising the gigantic gavel.

Mack shook his dizzy head. "I forget what the question was. Have you ever considered, Your Omnipotency, going out for the all-world rugby team? You'd be a shoo-in. I got bumps on top of severe injuries and am not fit to think."

"So, what else is new? But we're getting off track, again. Mr. Peter, Peter, pecker eater, stand and deliver."

"Sho' nuff, Your Orneriness." Peter twice failed to stand before swaying unsteadily to his feet. "I got a little business propositional thing for you, Monsignor Golden Antelope, sir. You think you can make a fortune with a boring TV show featuring clumsy humanoids, yeah maybe. But it's nothing compared to what it is that you and I and the Big Guy could do, exporting this cannabis sativa you got growing up here on this tepid tepui, torrid, whatever it is. We're talking big bucks. Big big bolivars. Enough to buy the whole tepui. Have you ever thought of relocating? Perhaps to a warmer place, a little less rocky? Maybe a sweet little Caribbean island where you'd never have to worry about fog and cold drafts. Or those horrible rocks you got all over the top of this place. Where you could sit under a palm tree, sipping banana daiquiris while perusing the sunset. We could put the Jamaicans out of business. Off those Rastas, yeah. The crap they pass off as decent ganga, compared to the stuff you got growing up here—"

The Judge Pope said, "Heresy. Pure unadulterated heresy. Yet interesting. But we'll have to wait until our next commercial break. Not that I want you to lose your train of thought, which I see is tenuous."

"Not tenuous. I mean business and I'll not lose this thread of thought. Not, not, not." To illustrate his seriousness

303

Peter attempted a cartwheel, landing resoundingly on his northern Italian ass.

"I can see you're trying to concentrate, but your heretical proposal must wait until the break. Now we'll get on with why you're slated for burbling oil. Not that we couldn't arrange a full pardon in proper financial circumstances."

"I can't think of a single reason why I should boil in oil. Plus, I've gotten attached to Courtney, though I don't know why. Business first."

"Not on your life. I have the lowdown on you, Mr. Peter, and it's about as low as you can go."

"I doubt you have the vaguest idea how low I can go."

"You'd make a limbo champ look rigid. The cookies on your personal PC are quite revealing. Mr. Mack hinted that Ms. Ellen might be bi, and perhaps her husband too. But there may be a little more fire than smoke around your little red rosy, Mr. Peter Peter, etcetera."

"I'm a part-time cop. City of Scottsdale. I love babes. You're espousing heresy. Don't allow your future wealth to go slip, slip, slipping away."

"You should be more discreet, Mr. Peter Peter. Certainly, more discreet than you've been in the past. You're a part time cop who runs a florist shop on the side. Here's a list of your favorites, internet-wise. Now listen up, everybody. Number ten is chickswithdicks.com, nine is buttmen.com, eight is—"

"Now wait a minute there, Your Honorship," said Peter. "The buttmen.com site is all babes. Babes have butts, too, you know."

"So, I've heard," said the Judge Pope, distastefully. "I take it you admit the charge of bi-manship? So, there's no need to read the rest of the list?"

"Hey, sweetheart." Peter was cheerful. "I subscribe to the proposition of doubling your chances of a date on Saturday night. And if Lucas's listening in, that's by good old Woody Allen. Let's hear it for Woody." Peter clapped rambunctiously. "Great movies." Peter was joined, first uncertainly, and then with genuine enthusiasm by the studio audience.

"Was there e'er a heart to dare, a father ne'r to himself hath sa'r. My daughter looks so good I dare, lock me up right now foursquare. I'll work on that, see where it's at," said Madison.

"They weren't clapping for the kink, if that's what it was," said Mack. "But Woody Allen made some decent movies. Keep that in mind."

"Oh, yes. We know you're as white as the driven snow," said the Judge Pope. "You may take your former place, Mr. Peter Peter, pecker eater. The guy on your right. Come on up here, sir. And state your name for the record."

"Don't see no record, but my name is Barry, Barry, quite contrary. May you go to Tucumcari. I'm fixin' to make a move on Madison's monopolization of rhythm and blues."

"Your real name, if you please."

"What difference does it make what my name is? You're going to do us in so we might as well go out with pizzazz. No reason to wait and be crushed under tiny antelope hooves."

"You're not listening." The Judge Pope leaned over the podium, whispering. "You could be pardoned. It depends on the ratings, so try and loosen up. Appeal to the masses and reveal your innermost secrets. Pander baby pander."

"I can do that," said Barry. "When it comes to life or death, I know which side I'm buttered on. Fire away, you all."

"We didn't find anything very incriminating on your cookies. You're a stalwart member of the Sun City community. Owner of the biggest security firm in the area. But we did dig up a little dirt."

"Make sure it stays little."

"I wasn't finished. You used to be a Tennessee state trooper, a big cop with a big gun. One rainy Tennessee night you chanced on a couple in lover's lane. Right?"

"Might have several times."

"You found a lithesome young couple engaged in the throes of coitus, is that correct?"

"It happened more than once, right."

"And when you found this young couple so occupied you did the unthinkable. When they began to scurry back into

305

their clothes at your untimely arrival, you stopped them and ordered them to finish. Isn't that also correct?"

"I might have come too early or someone might not have come early enough." Barry flashed a soft grin. "You do bring back memories, Your Honorship. Thank you for that one. It's been a long dry spell. Whether you know it or not, memory is the second thing to go. Those were the days my friend, we thought they'd never end. But they did, dang it."

"I am aghast. Such behavior is squarely against the tenets of the Goldie religion. Contrary to the precepts of Radnicharra." Not only his horny finger but his entire body trembled.

"You mean, your lordship—" Barry staggered backward, smacking his forehead. "You mean such behavior was at one time endemic in the Goldie population? That things got so bad that your god had to step in and put a stop to it? Do you have a commandment against Goldies ordering other Goldies to 'keep on going'? Or does it have to do with watching? Of course, you didn't accuse me of watching. Only of ordering completion. But you seemed to imply that I was watching. Should I keep my speculation to myself?"

"I am livid—"

"Yes, you are. In fact, you're purt'inear purple, Your Honorship. We may be due for a commercial break. I know Peter Peter is looking forward to one."

"Is the human species devoid of shame? That's the question this court must answer." The Judge Pope gathered his dignity, lifting golden quilts and adjusting his golden cape.

Peter shook his head. "If you think that'll reap ratings, you'd better take remedial television production. I can't muster enough shame to do you any good, and I'm sure Barry can't either."

"Which says it all. Ye of little shame will never enter the kingdom of heaven. Your shortcomings make you the prime candidate to replace Courtney in the burbling boil. Next."

"I object." Mack jumped to his feet. "It's unfair to judge us according to the tenets of your religion, which we know nothing about. And yes, I know ignorance of the law, religious or otherwise, is no excuse. It may not be an excuse but it should

306

be enough to avoid the death penalty. You act like you're the center of the universe."

"Well, yeah." The Judge Pope was puzzled. "We know the earth tilts, creating the seasons you poor mortals suffer in the north and south. The superior Goldies are in the middle, where the weather is stable. The center of the planet, the solar system, galaxy, and universe. We thought humans might be sufficiently advanced to know that. But apparently you aren't. How peculiar."

Mack said, "Not peculiar in the slightest. You're completely wrong, the same as if you thought the earth was flat. Boy are you screwed up."

The Judge Pope foamed as he tried to form words. "That's," splutter, splutter, "that's heresy. We are so the center of the universe."

"Are not. But don't take my word for it. Look it up on copernicus.com or flatearthsociety.com."

"That's only your viewpoint. For that you are hereby sentenced to death by boiling oil. Immediately if not sooner. Guards, guards."

Mack paled. "Ahem. I didn't mean to overstate it. Human religions made the same mistake for hundreds of years. You are neither behind nor different from your fellow religious nuts. Perhaps an older pope made a decree and it never got updated. Don't take it personally, and we'll forget it ever came up."

There was loud applause from the vicinity of Mack's mic. "Way to back off, dude, plus you present the perfect opening for me mum's luverly book. 'Every great scientific truth goes through three states: First, people say it conflicts with the Bible; next, they say it has been discovered before; lastly, the say they always believed it.' For Bible you can substitute the Book of Radnicharra or Famigusta, the Koran, the Bhagavad Gita Hindu thing, whatever it is. I don't think I got the name right. The Book of Mormon or a hundred others. Name your poison."

"The Judge Pope has already named our poison and it's a toasty one. French fries are us," said Mack.

"Oh, for Christ's sake," said a rejuvenated Btsht. "The Judge Pope spoke in haste. Ignoring the ratings, we're engaged in a single task. To find a proper substitute for Courtney since you're so all-fired incensed about the possibility of losing her."

"But you never asked whether we were so all-fired up about losing her that we'd volunteer to take her place."

"Again, you miss the point. It's not who'll volunteer to take her place, but who deserves to take her place. Which of you is the most reprehensible? That is the question."

Mack laughed. "If the equation included you, Your Number One Big Guy Honorableness, and the Judge Pope, you would really get the ratings and a different result, moral reprehensibility-wise. I bet there's a gazillion Goldies, and Ermies and Ivies for that matter, who'd be glued to their sets. Maybe toss in the General too. I'd watch it."

"Funny, har, har," said the Judge Pope. "We will proceed with the proceedings. Didn't I already call someone to the extermination box? Examination box, that is."

"Yeah, well, you called Roy a while back. But you never followed up. So, Roy's next, and good luck." Mack bowed as Roy ambled up with a stupid grin across his big shiny face.

"Heidy ho, you all. I got that from Barry. I have run across a conundrum. I would normally be up here..." Roy paused for a discreet puff, holding his breath for a few seconds before expelling. "...telling you how everything is going downhill. But it doesn't seem any better if things go uphill, which means I've reached a philosophical crossroads. The uphill-downhill question is what you gentlemen should consider. That would really grab the ratings. This 'who's going to boil in the oil' bit is getting long in the tooth. Let us instead attack the important philosophical questions in life, then everything else will fall into place. So whataya say, guys? You with me on this one?" Roy peered at their poker-faced countenances. "Apparently not. Your souls are dull and you've left your adventurous ways behind in your dotage. You've done gone downhill."

"Don't sass the court, you hippy-dippy dope," said the Judge Pope. "This is a serious affair—"

"Yeah, rating-wise. We know."

"You interrupt me one more time and your ass is grass. So wise up."

"Yes, sir." Roy saluted sloppily.

"You will now recite the most distressing occurrence in your entire life. Dwell particularly on whichever one was most macabre. Can you do that?"

"With ease, your Judge Popeship. The worst thing I ever done was drag a whole paper sack of weed up on the deck of my former sailing vessel, trying to roll a joint in a gale. Whoosh. Whole goddamn sack gone. I must have been ripped." Roy paused sorrowfully. "I cried."

"It's not improper for an inferior human, such as yourself, to lose a batch of the holy herb because you had no business with it in the first place. The only improper action was intending to smoke it."

"Hain't you never heard, waste not, want not? I am a Franklinian at heart. Besides, it wasn't on this dratted tepui that the dreadful incident occurred. It was far out at sea, off Catalina Island, right about where Natalie Wood inhaled seawater, which is outside your jurisdiction."

"I'll ignore that, for now. But think hard," urged the Judge Pope. "Was there another incident when you were under the influence of the sacred drug, like you appear to be this very instant? Your behavior is hardly the stuff a host expects of a guest."

"Same to you fella, in a vice versa sort of way. The problem is I imbibe more that I should, about daily. So, I don't remember much."

"If you can't remember, why do it in the first place?"

"Because it always seems like a good idea at the time. Like right now. Tell you what, Your Judge Poperyship. I'm having a lot better time than my compatriots, with the possible exception of Peter Peter, who seems to be having a worse time than ever. You didn't treat him too good."

"And I'm losing patience with you. We know there's something horrific in your past, but we haven't had time to find it. So, what is it?"

"Oh, that." Roy sighed. "I must admit it wasn't a shining moment. In fact, I'm still a bit sensitive about it. Which is why I can't talk about it. Sorry about that."

"Let's see if we can help you along. For starters, where's your wife? You are married, aren't you?"

"Well, yeah. If I wasn't married, I'd have crashed downhill years ago. You see it's my lovely peppy spouse who keeps me going."

"Then, where is she?"

"Danged if I know. She didn't make the plane in Miami. We grabbed a cab to visit a friend in Coconut Grove. Good buddy named Dave. Did you know Peter Peter used to live on a sailboat in Coconut Grove, the marina that is? Now isn't that the biggest coincidence you ever heard of? Anywho, we were down at Dave's house. He'd hired Haitians to build a fence around the property and we showed up when the fence was halfway up. Dave told the Haitians he wanted peepholes in the fence. You know, so he could look out on the street without being seen, which is a good idea, depending on your occupation. So, the Haitians scrambled together in a big huddle, scratching the hard clay with sharp sticks, yelling back and forth at each other until finally the Big Guy Haitian— Now hey, isn't that funny? They have Big Guys too. The Big Guy came over. We were sitting right there when it happened. And the Big Guy said, 'That's going to cost more money if'n you want peoples in the fence.' I can tell you, Your Honorable Popeness, I 'bout split a gut and so did Dave. And when the smoke cleared, we had a couple of more joints—"

"I don't follow what this has to do with your wife, her absence, or the worst thing you ever did."

"Well, Your Honorship. You have to stop interruptin' and pay attention. As I was about to say, when the smoke cleared my wife wasn't there anymore. We spent an hour looking for her, all the way up until I was about to miss the plane. We even made the Haitians tear down part of the fence, in case they might have stuck her inside, gotten the wrong idea like they did with the peepholes. And to this day, though I guess it was only yesterday, I don't know what the heck happened to good old Cole. I know she's ticking along somewhere, and I'm

310

pretty happy for her about now, since she missed this weird trip. Weirdest trip I ever been on, and tell you what, I've been on some weird trips."

"We're getting nowhere fast," growled the Judge Pope.

"Oh, yeah, ratings. I forgot." Roy turned humble. "Hope that don't mean everything is going downhill for Your Honorship. Or even uphill for that matter."

"You are easily distracted. Take a deep breath."

Roy took a really deep breath. Actually, a deep toke.

"You can let it out now," the Judge Pope, conscious of the dead air. "I said you can let it out now. Let it out, now, damn it. Pay attention. Can't you hear?"

Roy gazed at nothing, continuing a full fifty-seven seconds. Then he let his breath out slowly, piping it between his crossed eyes, searching for the slightest bit of smoke. "Cool," he said. "Not a trace."

"I hate to ask, but what was that about?"

"Waste not, want not, but don't ask. Now let's see where we were. Something about the most embarrassing incident in my long and varied career. Was that it?"

"Not simply embarrassing, you dunce. We want dirt. Immorality. Nasty bad stuff. The worst thing you ever did. Now what was it?"

"It was a sin of omission. It's what I failed to do that I should have done. I let a buddy down. I let him down the worst way you can let someone down. I let him expire. I will never forget it the same as I can never forgive myself. Once again you were right, Oh Omnipotent One, Judge Pope of your people, seer and sage. I was ripped." Roy raised his hands, shooing away possible gasps of disbelief. "Yes, I was. And while so occupied I failed to notice that my friend—" A sob caught in Roy's throat, and he turned his head. "I can't go on," he gasped.

The Judge Pope stood, clapping. "That was good, boy. You might get an Emmy for that. I might even pardon you." He stopped short, glancing at the Big Guy, who was scowling. "I'd ask the Honorable Number One Guy Btsht to pardon you, but that doesn't seem to be in the cards. But we need the gory details. What did your friend expire of and why didn't you notice his distress, which must have been obvious? Don't stand there like a big dumb dog. Give."

"Well, yes," stumbled Roy. "I screwed up. My friend turned a bad shade of green. Not that faces have too many good shades of green. He plunked down on the table, his head, that is. And then. I can't say it."

"And then what?" asked the Judge Pope with exasperation.

"I skedaddled. I split. I left the premises forthwith, if not sooner. Actually, I didn't leave quite that soon. I did pick him up by his hair and look into his eyes, and they were vacant. Then I left really fast. You see, I was worried. You had to know the circumstances."

"You split?" said the Judge Pope with evident glee. "You actually ran, leaving your poor friend to expire, alone and friendless? Is that what you did, you lowest of scoundrels?

"Actually, yes. But there's more."

"I can't believe it gets worse. So, what happened next?"

"'Couple of days later I was down by the harbor— This all happened in Mazatlán, you know."

"I didn't," said the Judge Pope sarcastically.

"Well, it did. And while I was walking by El Capitan de la Noche, the really big thing happened. Yessiree. I was flabbergasted. There was good old Damian. So, I told him I owed him a drink for leaving him stranded, just because I thought he was dead, collapsing on the table like that. And we had ourselves a rip-roaring laugh before we went out on the town."

16

"Legionnaires," shrilled the Judge Pope. "Draw and quarter that one. We'll have ratings, yes, we will. Prepare for a close up on camera three."

Roy yodeled, "Now let's tarry here a small minute. Renewable ratings are better than one big bang. I've got a thousand and one tales, only getting warmed up. Don't do something I especially might regret forever. Which seems might occur in the next few seconds. Help!" Legionnaires swarmed Roy, gleefully folding his arms behind his back.

"Remember this," said a staticky voice from Mack's voice mic. "And mark it closely. 'Hold always the sign of blood in horror. Take care not to shed or stain thyself with it, for the mark is never washed away.' And I'll betcha you can't guess who said that one."

"Out of order, out of order." The Judge Pope pounded the gargantuan gavel lightly. "That stupid quotation has to do with humans not offing other humans. It has nothing to do with a superior race of antelopes eradicating inferior vermin. So, got you."

Mack raised an admonitory finger. "Roy has a good point about the ratings. Better to string it out and build suspense."

"I was a bit pissed," said the Judge Pope. "Discretion may be the better part of whatever."

The Judge Pope nodded to the Legionnaires and they unhanded Roy. He cautiously moved his stricken limbs. Then his fingers twirled a smokable remedy for the tension that had built up inside him like a kettle about to whistle.

"Next," said the Judge Pope before Roy could open his mouth.

"You asked for it," said Mack, shoving Madison to the fore.

"Great to be here, pass the beer. Thought you'd never, let me near. Ask away, what you want. I'll defer, and never taunt. Not a thing, I have to hide. Fire away, I think I've died." Madison was in ecstasy at being center stage.

"Keep your eye on the ball, young fella," said the Judge Pope. "We're here to turn your insides out. The only question is what you did that you're most ashamed of. And don't get too stupid with the kindergarten rhymes."

"You've hit on it exact, the worse I've done is miss the fact, of membership in the grandest claque. Practice, practice is my mojo, though that's a long tough road to hoe-hoe."

"Tougher for us than you. Besides, not being chosen for membership in a dingy poets society is hardly a venal sin."

"Then blameless stand I here, maybe now I'll take that beer."

"You are a dolt," yelled the Judge Pope. "You're no better than the rest of them. We have the goods on you. Don't try to deny it. You're an alcoholic and compulsive gambler. Not exactly the least blameworthy of your species."

"You're on the rope, good Judge Pope. My vices hurt, no one nope. 'Cept myself, and that's just soap. Try and pin a sin on me, that should be your destiny. What I do, hurts no one else, but makes poor you, sort of jeal'us. Unless my act, scars another, then it's not, your business brother. Morality's basic is stay away and let me be. Otherwise you're all at sea. Unless you have one princ-i-ple, you have none, it's so simple. So, answer that you black-robed quack, tell us all where else it's at."

"I'm not on trial."

"Nor are we, I think you said, something else, to bow your head. Yet you say, yourself to be, a top-notch pope, so fiddle-dee. Drop words of wisdom please, make us fall onto our knees. A simple guide is all we ask, sure to in your genius bask. There must be one thing at least, you can prove so good is greased. Let us in on your big key, the lynchpin of morality. For

314

if you have no thing to tell, then might as well slide down to hell."

"Hmmm. So, you're a philosopher poet who insists on putting his hosts on the spot. There are many absolute rules you must follow for morality. First you must worship the Mother, Daughter, and Holy Spirit—"

"So bad was I incorrigible, to prefer a holy dirigible."

"Well, yes. And you must pray five times a day with leather straps and wooden blocks. You bow with your head toward the holy site on a nameless neighboring tepui, where the holy Radnicharra ascended to heaven." The Judge Pope started getting into it, his cape expanding to fully erect. "Every day you must read the new and old book of our holy scripture. And tithe to the church, which is the most important rule of all. Never sit on the same side of the church as those of the opposite sex. And pay close attention to everything I say. Those are the big important rules and there are lots of others."

"Others always are there, and I hate to bother. But methinks you missed the biggest part, got the horse before the cart. Where is there morality, the right and wrong that we can see?"

"Wrong is not doing those things I tell you to do and right is doing them as fast as you can. Pretty simple, don't you think?" The Judge Pope looked pleased.

"What about the wholesale slaughter, that perhaps begins a morrow? How you hide behind a rit-ual, and pretend it makes you spirit-ual."

"This is claptrap. You've lulled me into forgetting about ratings, which is what we're here for. You are guilty of the vile sins of alcoholism and gambling, which inevitably lead to poverty. Defend yourself, man. Pretend you're a noble creature aspiring to the pinnacle of antelopehood. That may be too lofty to comprehend, but try. You've sunk so low, that dread vices seize your soul." The judge smiled.

"Really easy let me say, won a buck the other day. A million bucks that is, struck oil like Jed and his. Gamblin's done real good by me, single malted whiskery. Never say these vices suck, they have brought me extra luck. How you like it now,

JP? Bet it makes you limp with glee." Madison clasped hands in front of his face, tittering.

"Time is running out and we weren't able to come up with more dirt on you. So, get back with your fellows. I'll sum up so you can vote."

"What's this voting stuff?" said Mack as Madison scurried to the bleachers with a smile across his broad red face.

"You never pay attention," said the Judge Pope. "We told you after the dirt was dug up, you had to vote on who is most shameful and should be substituted for Courtney. Then we can get on with the boiling oil and the war to end all wars."

"Are you sure you aren't descended from Genghis Khan and the Mongol hordes? You seem somewhat to the right of Adolph Schicklgruber. "

"Heresy per se. The mere idea that we're descended from the human race makes me want to puke."

"Well, you're certainly not ascended. Your idea of fair play makes us look tame. And making Americans look tame is almost impossible. It's like having real gladiators on reality TV. Survivor to the nth degree, public executions, blood and gore for the masses."

"At least we're honest about it," said the Judge Pope. "You simulate everything from sex to violence. You're a bunch of wimpy losers unable to compete in survival of the fittest. We're happy to be the number one civilization and number one we'll stay, because you don't have the gumption to compete with us. But again, we're sadly off track. That's what you'll be voting on, who's the worst of your lot. You have stiff competition going."

The Judge Pope summed up with relish. "First, we have Mack, the leader of the pack. The philistine father who fails to pay his child support because it slips his mind. Understandable considering his pea brain. And if that weren't enough, he's partial to kinky porn. And the porn he's partial to is so kinky it makes him upchuck to contemplate the equivalent by a superior race. The applause meter is ready to hear from the studio audience. So, without further ado, let's hear it for Mack."

The applause was riotous. Waves swept over the studio that had magically expanded into a great auditorium filled with antelopes. The top was so high the uppermost occupants were obscured by clouds.

The Judge Pope became impatient at the length of the applause, gaveling before quieting the audience. "Thank you, thank you. You are a marvelous audience." Boy was he pissed. "Mr. Mack has reached ninety-nine point four-four on the applause meter. Since that's a scale of one hundred, it's difficult to see how he can be beaten. We may already have a winner in the who-will-replace-Courtney-in-the-boiling-oil sweepstakes. But to be fair to Mr. Mack, we'll give the others an opportunity to score higher."

Mack said, "That wasn't a fair vote. Though I wouldn't like to vote for or against my compatriots. So, maybe it's better this way. Forget I said anything."

"Oh heavens, no. You are perfectly correct. This isn't the official vote. The official vote, which is your vote, comes later. Right now, we're registering sentimental choices, which allows the studio audience to participate, helps bolster ratings, and serves to break later ties."

"This is a preposterous nightmare from which I hope we'll soon awake."

"Whatever," said the Judge Pope. "Next is Mr. Peter Peter pecker eater. Mr. Bi-bi baby, hello. Mr. Peter is guilty of the sin that dares not say its name, at least among the inferior races. Goldies are far more enlightened, encouraging priests to be priests. Now, audience, consider a human doing something like that with another human. Let's hear it on the applause meter." And whammo, the meter zoomed toward the ceiling, up, up, near the top.

"Whoa," shouted the Judge Pope. "You didn't quite overtake Mr. Mack, Peter Peter. But you scored a solid ninety-seven point five-three. A credible tally, but you may slip into the background, Mr. Peter Peter."

Mack raved. "I don't like the looks of this. And furthermore, I don't understand it. Since when is a little forgetfulness in paying child support—I'm not that far behind. Only a few months. Or viewing wholesome two babe porn— But then, you voted—"

His mic erupted in static as Lucas volunteered, "I have the answer, dude. Though you seem to have lost much of your dudeness. 'The end justifies the means. To reach a certain goal, one must vanquish everything that stands in the way.' That fits like a shower curtain."

"What are you chattering about? I don't get it."

"You're too numb to get anything right now. The goal is ratings and you're the most visible of the Goldie hostages."

"Things are getting desperate over here. When are the Ermies or Ivies going to launch a rescue attempt? We're waiting."

"They never said they would but we are hugely sympathetic. Doing something about it, would be a whole 'nuther thing."

"Order in the studio," said the Judge Pope, pounding the massive gavel. "Of course, the ends justify any means. Next after Peter Peter is—"

"You may be right," said Mack. "But you're spinning your wheels and wasting time. Courtney doesn't want a substitute. She prefers the martyr route. You wouldn't—"

"Which is exactly why we're running a substitution derby. Why let the heretical old biddy get her rocks off by dying for a false god? We can make a packet and boost ratings. It'll be a grand old time, boiling you in front of the entire Goldie nation."

"Have you no shame?" Mack's tone designed to smite a Neanderthal.

"Not that I can think of. Next is your personal favorite and I admit a certain partiality myself. The lovely Ms. Ellen, though she doesn't count for much in antelope terms. But she's a spunky, coltish thing, and I can see you might admire her spirit, if nothing else. There is the fact she's a closet nymphomaniac, so she'd probably wear you out. But it's impossible to get her in bed in the first place, unless you happen to be a priest. I mention that yours truly is not just a priest, I'm the Judge Pope. So, you can imagine the spectacle if I chose to engage in a little animalphelia, condescending to engage with the equivalent of a sheep, baa, baa, babykins."

Mack said, "Urp," fighting down a gorge, as Ellen loosened a wail to shake the shingles from the roof.

The Judge Pope laughed uproariously. "Poor woebegone humans can't take it on the firing line. Ms. Ellen presents a credible substitute for Courtney. I've always been partial to priest groupies who sustained me on my rise through the ranks. We all need something to cling to."

"Is that the same as from each according to ability and to each according to need?" said Mack.

"I heard that." Courtney was irate. "Nothing can save godless communists and I'm looking forward to martyrdom. Nay, I'm anxious. So, quit the cock and bull games and light the fire under the oil."

"We've already lit the fire, and we'd love to oblige," said the Judge Pope. "If it weren't so satisfying for you. If we pulled out your toenails and fingernails, you might reconsider your enthusiasm."

"That's a firm negatory. I've suffered pain my entire life. I bore children. I saw them grow up mediocre. I saw love go wrong. I saw cotton fields dry up and blow away. I buried a husband and two infant children. But through it all, God was my rock. More pain, no matter the intensity, is no big deal. Now don't get me wrong. I probably won't lift my countenance to the heavens and glow with the glory of my redeemer while frying. I'll likely blanch and cry. But one thing I'll never do is recant. Martyrdom is me."

"I understand your position completely." The Judge Pope took the hefty end of the gavel and bopped Courtney on the top of her wooly head. She went down without a sigh.

The Judge Pope said, "Before Courtney rudely interrupted these proceedings, I was about to present Ms. Ellen to the multitudes for judging. Poise your horny hands and all antelopes vote, NOW."

The applause meter swelled upward, inching ever higher, cascades of clippity-clops reverberating off the walls of the gigantic auditorium.

"Congratulations, Ms. Ellen. You have beaten Peter Peter by a nympho nympho. And you've come within a chinny-chin hair of Mr. Mack. Your score is ninety-eight point ninety-eight. The Goldies love you but your martyrdom has been dashed on the rocks. You may take a seat, sweetums."

Mack took Ellen's unfeeling arm and guided her to the rear where Peter and Courtney lay in a heap. "You're okay in my book," said Mack. "Don't let these cockamamie Goldies get to you. Our air force men in blue will soon come swooping out of the sky and scoop us up, taking us home to our loved ones. If you have any disappointment upon arrival, give me a call." Mack handed her a card embossed with the Arizona Lottery logo.

"Thanks, Mack," she said listlessly.

"That's my phone number at the bottom, with my email address." He poked a shaky finger at the card

"Right." She stared at the card without comprehension.

The Judge Pope's voice boomed out. "Though they've inadvertently entertained us, the remaining humans are minor miscreants. This includes Mr. Roy, the downhill guy who may or may not have seen the demise of a comrade. Mr. Barry, who commanded the copulation of innumerable frequenters of lover's lane, getting so close he probably singed his nose hair. And Mr. Madison, poet supreme, whose inane verse fails to hide the sad fact of his gambling and alcohol addictions. The humans will vote, deciding who will be substituted for Courtney, their favorite religious fanatic. Guards, revive her. We don't want her to miss the debate."

Seven Legionnaires were instantly on Courtney, lifting and slapping her silly, to no avail. They tried smelling salts so awful that Madison gagged on the threshold of a new verse and Roy plunged a hand into his pocket and pulled out a joint the size of a cigar. The aroma of its ignition brought Courtney around, as Mack jumped to his feet.

"None of us should be substituted for Courtney because it would be against her religion. If you want Courtney to respect your religion, you must respect hers. Out of deference to Courtney and her heartfelt religious feelings, neither I nor Ellen, Roy, Barry, Madison, or Peter, will substitute for Courtney. No matter how much we'd love to. We hereby withdraw from competition for the honor."

Btsht rose and bowed slightly in the Judge Pope's direction. "You're taking this too lightly, Mr. Mack. You seem to think that nothing is going to happen to anyone. That this is a game soon to be interrupted by men swooping from the sky. Little blue men are a myth. This is reality. We're creative with boiling oil, which is suffused with sulphuric acid. And we don't just dunk you, which would be terrible showmanship. Males are suspended above the boiling cauldron, suspended upside down for the first dip. Your scalp burns off in a split second, making you appreciate the immediacy of your demise. After your scalp dissolves, you're suspended spread eagle in a horizontal position. Then we slowly lower you so that whatever hangs lowest burns off first. Who can tell me exactly which appendage will be first to burn off in the second dunking?" Btsht smiled as he looked them up and down.

"I see we have no volunteers," said Btsht. "Funny how Mr. Mack is silent. Though it doesn't matter after the first two dips, we burn the remaining appendages separately. Mr. Mack will tell us why the evil that lurks in his heart fails to justify his substitution for Courtney. Come on, Mr. Mack, I can't hear you."

Btsht stood with a horny hand cupping a tiny ear. "Where is your bravado now?" Btsht paused to gloat. "Now we unveil—voila!"

A gnarly black cauldron shot onto the stage, skittering from side to side on four tiny rollers, frothing as it slid to a halt at center stage. Oil slopped over the side and hissed as it ate through the floor.

"Gulp," said Mack.

"Don't make me repeat the question," said Btsht. A human-shaped harness spiraled from the heavens, jerking to a halt thirteen inches above the steaming cauldron, swaying.

"Hmmmm." Mack cleared his throat and squared his shoulders. "Am I man or moose, mousse or mouse? Is the supposed evil that lurks in my heart sufficient to justify my substitution for dear Courtney? Compare the three acts on the same moral plane, one by Courtney and two by myself. Which one did the most violence to society, tearing the social fabric asunder? That depends on which social fabric we're talking about and who's doing the judging. My favorite porn hurts no one else. Being behind in child support hurts my kid, though I wish it would only hurt my ex, who I loathe. Courtney's actions had a major impact on the Goldies. Thus, my sins are nowhere near as weighty as poor Courtney's, god rest her soul." Mack bowed his head to a smattering of applause from his compatriots. The applause grew as it dawned on them that if Mack won, they'd all win.

"Snarkle, static," went Mack's microphone as Lucas said, "We'll mount a rescue party because we must. But if we're late, Mack, console yourself that your sins are as common as roadkill. And I quote, 'If only there were evil people somewhere insidiously committing evil deeds and it were necessary only to separate them from the rest of us and destroy them. But the line dividing good and evil cuts through the heart of every human being. And who is willing to destroy a piece of his own heart?' That may also apply to antelopes, though limited to Goldies. I wouldn't want to get on the bad side of the Ermies and Ivies by lumping them in too."

"Gosh no, and we wouldn't want you to," said Mack. "We could do with a bit of rescuing this very second. The Honorable Btsht, Big Guy Number One, is about to render judgment."

"Forget the rush to judgment," said Btsht. "As long as the ratings are up, we'll listen to your blather. But I'm sick of the silly quotes. Why would a mother give such a subversive book to her gullible offspring? Mr. Lucas's dear old mom must not like him much."

Btsht held up a horny paw. "That's a rhetorical question. The last silly quote illustrates my point. So, no one's perfect and there's a streak of good and bad in everyone. Whoopteydoo. What a revelation. But from where I sit there's a bright line between good and bad, between Goldies and humans. We're the good guys and you're uncivilized schmucks. You may have the opposite opinion, but what do you know? Not much."

Mack said, "Since you're governed by the god of ratings, there may be a better way to liven up the show. Which reminds me. You haven't had a commercial break for a long time. And there's a proposal pending, submitted by the

Honorable Peter Peter. Filthy lucre may overshadow your ratings race. Plus, I wouldn't mind some refreshment. Even a cup of cold water in the name of the Judge Pope wouldn't be amiss. A few hors d'oeuvres to keep body and soul together until you can rip 'em apart."

"A commercial break may be in order, but not right now. What interesting idea do you have to boost ratings? It'd be difficult to improve on the Judge Pope and my honorable self displaying terrific erudition on the big screen. Everyone loves watching us put exasperating aliens in their place. And we promise the goriest finale ever seen on TV. But we're always open to ideas. Fire away, Mr. Mack."

"Thank you, Big Guy Number One, but first I have to lay a foundation. This plan is so unique and earthshaking that you may not immediately see it's overwhelming merit." Mack drew a line in the air. "Imagine the most important people in the kingdom on your show." Mack shushed Btsht with, "Yeah, I know. You're already on the show. But remember the quote about the big stealin' and the little stealin'. How the latter illogically carries the greater penalty. Think about it and visualize. Becoming emperor requires huge risks and successful crimes. Think back on your own career. Of course, you don't have to tell us out loud, but you might come to the same conclusion."

The Big Guy started to nod but squelched it with a shrug as Mack continued. "You don't have to reveal all the dodgy things you did to outfox everyone on the way to the tippy top of power. Obviously, the accidental removal of a former Big Guy was dumb luck. However—what if—? The great wasteland would reap unparalleled ratings with a leader like you in prime time. Why Btsht, you pale. Does that mean you agree that such a program would be a resounding success? Though, of course, practically over your dead body?"

Whang, whang, kerplump, splinter, went the gavel that Btsht had wrestled from the Judge Pope and slammed on the pulpit podium, burying it to its tiny hilt, leaving three inches of handle above a forest of slivers.

"That was a remote hypothetical," said Mack. "I didn't mean for you to take it personally. Perhaps—"

Lucas broke in, "Oh the hell you didn't. Personal is exactly how you meant it and I know why. Because, as usual, you wanted to make a point. And the point was, and I quote for the benefit of your favorite Goldie Big Guy, 'What is hateful to thyself do not do to another. This is the whole law, the rest is Commentary.'"

Madison jumped to his feet. "No tit for tat, how about that? If that'd work, you'd bell the cat, scrape us off the welcome mat. Do the rule, you witless fool, perhaps for Goldies, not so cool, but they're stubborn, like a mule. Maybe now, they'll fight a duel, Mack and Btsht, out of school."

"Oh, shut up," said Btsht, "and sit down. We'll take that commercial break and you imbeciles can fight it out over a keg of lemon beer with chunkies on the side. A well-fed cast gets the ratings and even humans deserve a last supper. Peter Peter will come with me while the Judge Pope supervises preparations for a final vote. Fifty-two minutes from…" A triangle appeared and Btsht hit it with a chrome rod, ding, "Right now."

Btsht rose as Legionnaires escorted Peter through the alcove behind the pulpit.

"Hey," said Mack. "We can't vote if one of us is missing."

"Don't worry. You'll get him back soon enough. He won't be gone more than a few minutes."

Btsht made a regal exit. On the way out, he tapped the steel thread holding the harness above the roiling cauldron, sending it swaying, drawing every eye in the auditorium.

Peter yelled as they escorted him from the room. "I give my proxy to Mack. No make that Ellen. Or maybe Courtney, ha, ha, ha—" His voice disappeared as the sliding door closed behind him.

"So, who gets your proxy?" yelled Mack at Peter's disappeared back. "A fine kettle this is."

"A fine cauldron, you mean," said the Judge Pope. He levered the gigantic gavel out of the splintered pulpit, poised for action. Ding, he banged the gavel at the edge of the previous catastrophe. "We will take a straw vote. See where everyone stands—"

324

"That would be divisive," said Mack. "You're thinking of ratings but we're not going to fight among ourselves. No one believes you'll do anything before we're rescued. Brinkmanship is our favorite game."

"You beg for it, don't you?" The Judge Pope stood on tippy toes, leaning over the pulpit and shaking a nasty looking paw at Mack, making the gold lace around his wrist danced like a tambourine. "Well I'm going to give it to you. Legionnaires."

Three Legionnaires paused in midstride. The leader held a huge keg of lemon beer above his head. He set it on a fancy stand while other two balanced trays pyramided with multicolored cubes. The head Legionnaire said, "Yes, your holiness."

The Judge Pope laughed nastily. "Take Ms. Ellen and bundle her into the harness. Let's see how long Mr. Mack and company avoid divisiveness. Though I'm not normally a betting pope, I bet they'll be at each other's throats in the heartbeat of a hummingbird."

"Don't do that," yelled Mack as Legionnaires jammed Ellen into the harness. The head guy swung her in a long figure eight above the burbling cauldron, her ragged skirt flapping against her knees, but she was silent as a lamb.

"We'll do a head-down swoop first, burn off the long chestnut hair Mr. Mack finds so lovely. He probably fantasizes about using it like the tissues which are no doubt situated next to his stack of two babe porn."

Mack held up his hands. "You win. We lose. We promise to tear each other asunder. Let her down."

"I don't know." The Judge Pope slowly swooped a horny hand lower and lower. Ellen turned upside down and the grungy denim skirt billowed in waves as she vainly tried to keep her thighs covered. Her downwards progress mimicked the Judge Pope's gestures, swoop by swoop as the harness dropped inch by slow inch.

Mack howled, "We agree to whatever you want us to agree to and we agree to it now. We'll do whatever the ratings require. Stop it, damn it."

"Well, gosh, since you put it that way." The Judge Pope pointed a horny finger in Ellen's direction. This stopped her descent as she finally whipped her skirt into submission. The ends of her long hair fizzed and sparked on the surface of the bubbling cauldron.

The Judge Pope turned his finger over and Ellen flipped upright, paler than driven snow. "No harm done, dearie. Besides, you only lost split ends."

Mack groveled. "Thank you, your heroic holiness."

The Legionnaires helped Ellen out of the harness but were forced to duck and weave because Ellen came out clawing. "Forget that crap, Mack. The creep judge is blasphemy on the name of the true pope." She slashed her fingernails across Mack's face, leaving four lines oozing red. "I thank you for stopping my humiliation but you had no right to interfere. The jerk pope must pay."

"Ahem, my dearie." The Judge Pope raised a snooty nose. "You're risking a real dunking. If you continue to misbehave, I'll burn your witchy face off before lover boy can save you."

"Don't threaten me, your fraudulency." Ellen was on fire, shimmering. "I have no regard for the heathen you call Mr. Mack, and you are even more contemptible, preying on the weakness of a devout Catholic. You'll dance in hell before your silly pronouncements affect my conduct."

The Judge Pope stuttered, "Oh boy, oh boy, oh boy, oh boy—" rubbing horny hands so fast together that sparks flew.

"Stow the histrionics." Ellen was gasping. "I have no fear of you. My only concern, like Courtney, is doing right by my God. Kowtowing to the likes of you betrays my God. I'd rather fry than put up with your crap. So, if you have the balls, and I don't think you do, go ahead and do the dirty deed." Ellen stood stock still, staring straight into the Judge Pope's bulbous eyes.

The Judge Pope covered his inability to meet her gaze with rapid fire yapping. "You'll now decide who is to perish in Courtney's stead. After we debate the ultimate question: is there a god and if so, is it the Catholic god, the Baptist god, or the Goldie God? No other candidates seem relevant."

"Don't be obtuse," said Ellen. "No one can answer a question like that. The Goldies will agree that the only real god is Goldie. The Catholics and Baptists will choose their own gods, which some would say are the same."

"I've always been partial to the Egyptian gods," squeaked Lucas over Mack's mic. Everyone ignored him.

"First, the straw vote to see who replaces Courtney," said the Judge Pope.

Mack tried again. "No one should replace Courtney. She doesn't want replaced and we don't want to replace her."

"I'll replace Courtney," said Ellen.

The Judge Pope was aghast. "You're doing this so the Catholic god can win? What will happen to your orphan children? Will your erstwhile husband or aging parents be suitable surrogates in your absence? I think not. You're selfish to even suggest such a course. Courtney should nominate a substitute. What do you say, Courtney?"

Courtney lumbered to her feet, rubbing her eyes. "I nominate myself to be substituted for myself. You seem dense for a Goldie, a judge, or a pope. Why would you ask such a stupid question?"

"Stupid questions make you think, and if you think about the question, it's not so stupid. Considering the relative intelligence of our species, my questions are brilliant. And your responses are dim-witted."

"Doubtful," said Mack. "Debating the existence of three gods out of thousands has nothing to do with who should fry in place of Courtney. There's no reason for Courtney to bite the dust. She may be obnoxious at times, but who isn't? You shouldn't execute Courtney for knocking a few knickknacks off a statue of a never-seen god. And there's no logical reason why anyone should be substituted for her. She doesn't want a substitute. And no one wants to substitute for her. With the momentary exception of Ellen—"

"I'm not being momentary. I'm serious."

"Cut out the horsing around," came Lucas's inimitable voice. "You're beating around a low shrub. Whether you should believe in God, whichever god, was given eons ago. Well, I assume it was eons ago. Get this. 'You must wager. What will you choose? Let us weigh the gain and the loss in calling 'heads' that God is. Let us weigh the two cases: if you win, you win all; if you lose, you lose nothing. Wager then unhesitatingly that He is.' It's the 'unhesitatingly' bit that makes me suspect it was a while back. But it makes perfect sense. You can't fault the logic."

"It's absurd," said Mack. "That's a sellout, an abdication of integrity. A belief in superstition suspends reason, and here, Lucas, I'm parroting you. Anyone who would believe without evidence deserves a god. With thousands to choose, from how can anyone figure out which god to wager unhesitatingly on? It's a mug's game."

Ellen was miffed. "And you're a mug. Unless you believe in God, there's nothing left."

"To the contrary. Anyone who'd believe in a god would believe anything. Apparently."

"I like it lots," said the Judge Pope, rubbing horny hands with relish. "Claw her throat out. Go for the jugular. Crap on her principles. Deny her beliefs. Yea, I beseech thee, accept the existence of the omnipotent omnipresent Goldie God Radnicharra, and the unnamable known as Famigusta. Made flesh through the Mother, Daughter, and Holy Spirit."

Mack rolled his eyes. "I'll always think Dirigible. But I could never go for her jugular except with butterfly kisses."

Ellen looked like she was going to be sick.

"On the other hand, I recognize the unbridgeable divide between us—"

Ellen was livid. "There's more than one divide, buster. Not only have you become a heathen in front of my eyes, questioning the existence of the being who created you, but you're tacky, and I'm a married woman. Have you no shame?"

Mack smiled. "I'm like the Goldies in that regard. But unlike the Goldies, I seldom feel shame because I try to never do anything to be ashamed of. I may be an irremediable smart-ass, but I bear malice toward none. Or at least very few."

"That's not good enough. You should respect the beliefs of others, instead of running them down at every opportunity."

"You respect my beliefs far less than I respect yours. Why are you upset at someone who is slowly coming to the conclusion that the idea of gods is nonsense? I'm not threatened

328

by your belief in a god. Why are you threatened by what you consider my silly disbelief in one god out of thousands?"

Ellen said, "Calling my most personal and sacred belief nonsensical shows a complete lack of regard for me as a person."

"Oh, lady, no. We may consider each other's beliefs similarly, but I have a fantastic regard for your person. However, the clotted gray mass in your head drives me crazy, but only about religion and your undying hostility toward my own sweet self. Two tiny defects out of a million possibilities ain't bad."

Courtney harrumphed, "You're bad to the bone, Mack. You prey on married women of outstanding character, harassing them to death."

"She looks pretty healthy, thanks to me."

"You *are* an irremediable smart-ass," said Courtney. "Plus, you have no respect for the institution on which our country was founded, the Christian religion."

"A very recent phenomenon for me. Do you also believe I have no respect for Baptists in particular?"

"Roger Williams of Rhode Island, an outstanding Baptist, was a founding father."

Mack said, "Wasn't he the one who above all else preached religious tolerance? If that had been observed on this particular tepui, we'd all be in a lot better shape. Especially you. Of course, that was a rhetorical question."

"I still have an answer."

"The Judge Pope might enjoy an explanation. And we as your potential substitutes are also interested. So, shoot."

Courtney stood up straight, looking less of a dumpling, though the grimy dress remained a disaster, fringed with moss and green cubes. "I was in shock from the crash. When I saw that thing glittering on the hill, it made me mad. It was an antelope. I can understand a statue of a human god, including those of other religions, but the antelope was obscene and I couldn't take it. I've tried to put up with Catholics, present company being okay, and other religions, but I've never seen one that worshiped anatomically correct animals. I came unglued. In retrospect, I might have acted hastily. Not that I want to back out of martyrdom."

"I take it you've never seen the Hindu gods," said Mack. "They have a popular elephant god named Ganesh. If we'd crashed in India we'd be in big trouble because you would've chopped off its trunk, or something worse."

"I've never seen an elephant god. Why do they worship an elephant, anyway?"

"Don't ask me stuff like that. I can't keep up with the hundreds of denominations of Protestants, Catholics, Muslims, and Jews. Much less Hindus Buddhists, Sikhs, and a thousand others. Besides, it's not really an elephant. It's a human with an elephant head."

"That might make a difference," mused Courtney.

"You mean you might not go berserk in India. That's a relief, or would be if we could teleport there."

"Hello," said the Judge Pope. "I hope you haven't forgotten me." They vigorously shook their heads no. "How nice. Mr. Mack is beginning to question the existence of any god, including the Christian ones, Catholic and Baptist. And the Goldie God too. I don't much care about the Catholic and Baptist gods but the Goldie God holds a special spot in my heart—"

Mack smirked. "Like it provides your livelihood, without which you wouldn't live high on the hog."

"Your political instincts are terminally lacking. The Christian gods don't seem workable either, this father, son, and godly ghost. What kind of ghost is that anyway? But denying the Goldie god is a bad move. I believe we've found a substitute for Courtney and need look no further."

The Judge Pope cupped an ear for a response from anyone but Mack.

After a few seconds, Roy stuttered to life. "Well, we'll miss you Mack. It won't be fun watching you go downhill." Roy turned to the Judge Pope. "Oh, don't do that to poor old Mack."

"Does that mean you're volunteering in Mr. Mack's place?" The Judge Pope had a nasty grin on his wide antelope face.

"Golly no, he won't go. Leave him low, you dinky schmoe," said Madison. "What's a schmoe?" said Ellen.

Mack said, "One of those fat ghosts from the Little Abner comic strip, years ago, before your time. I research important stuff like that." His look turned quizzical. "Except it was a shmoo. Not a schmoe."

"But schmoe I thought it had to be, 'cause shmoo don't rhyme quite right for me."

"Right. Poetic license. But I refuse to substitute for Courtney. I've learned to just say no."

"You don't have to substitute for Courtney," said the Judge Pope soothingly. "All you have to do is acknowledge the existence of the Goldie God."

Mack sighed. "I'd surely like to. It's not as if I have moral qualms about saying I believe in a particular god out of thousands. But I've reached the point that I doubt gods exist, much less an alien god on a godforsaken tepui that's the spitting image of antelopes who harass us night and day. I didn't feel like this when we crashed. In fact, I've always figured there was a god, though I never really thought about it. But this mess forced me to a different opinion. You've hardly provided a fitting example for believing in your god. It'd be easier to believe in a Goldie devil."

"Hark," came Lucas's honied drawl. "Mack is a contrarian who denies what anyone else says. But suggesting the existence of a devil, even a Goldie devil? Here's the appropriate quote from me mum's book. 'That there is a Devil is a thing doubted by none but such as are under the influence of the Devil. For any to deny the being of a Devil must be from ignorance or profaneness worse than diabolical.' This absolves Mack of all guilt."

Mack frowned. "That's a switch."

"It is. Because Mack denies the existence of the Goldie god he must be under the influence of the Goldie god. Based on this quote."

"Obviously a logical conclusion."

Lucas groaned. "Shut uppa your mouth. I'm trying to help and hope I don't have to lead you through this twice. Even a big dumb Goldie is going to suspect the logic if you keep opening your trap."

"I stand mute."

"Well, that's a first, so you must be under the influence of a god," said Lucas.

Bang, crunch went the gavel as the Judge Pope applied slightly too much force to the second bang. The gavel was again buried up to its tiny neck, next to the hole Btsht had created moments before. The Judge Pope tried to twist the gavel out of the wreckage. "We will poll the jury on the existence of the Goldie God. And the two Christian ones as well."

"What two Christian gods?" said Ellen.

"Shut up," said the Judge Pope. "We're talking about the Baptist and Catholic gods. You first, there. Yes, you. Now pay attention."

"Who, me?" said Barry as Peter came bursting into the huge auditorium, the result of a mighty shove.

"Well, I'm back." Peter skidded to a stop in front of the Judge Pope.

"Then you can go first," said the Judge Pope. "Since you've not heard the question, it's whether you believe in the Catholic, Baptist, or Goldie God."

"Be forewarned," said Mack. "It's a loaded question."

Peter sighed. "Isn't it always. But before we get into a religious thicket, the possibility of a deal is a bit remoter than before. So, let the Judge Pope do his worst. We could still come up roses, maybe."

"That's reassuring."

"I did my best, which often ranks up with your best, Mack. Things turned bad when I lit a joint for the Big Guy. He doesn't smoke, even religiously. I don't understand where he's coming from since that's what we wanted to talk about in the first place. Now what's this god question? Why is the Goldie bunch hung up on gods and graven idols when they have the best ganga on the planet? The very best. I can't remember any better, anywhere, anyhow."

Mack shuddered. "Even if it was better somewhere else you wouldn't remember. Short-term memory loss and all that."

"What was the question?" Peter looked up at the Judge Pope.

Peter's question about the question gave the Judge Pope time to extract the buried gavel, rather too suddenly. The gavel catapulted end over end in a slow arc, the handle flying gracefully into Peter's outstretched hand. "Whoa." Peter fell as the massive gavel pulled him to the floor. He put both arms around the big end and, with Mack's help, they got it off the floor. But try as they might they couldn't lift it onto the pulpit in front of the glowering Judge Pope.

Peter peered at the Judge Pope, who looked glassy-eyed. "Don't tell me you've forgotten the question too?"

"Baliff," croaked the Judge Pope. A baliff instantly appeared, handing the bulky gavel back to the judge. "You may approach the bench," he said to Peter.

Peter stared at him.

"What that means is you will get your sad sack ass up here right now." The Judge Pope held the gavel high in the air.

"Well, I would, but you might have a gavel accident and I'd rather not be in the neighborhood."

"Guards," yelled the Judge Pope. In a single shake of an antelope's tail Peter had his arms pinned behind his back. Squarely under the dread gavel.

"Yessa, yessa. I am here. Please be careful."

"You do remember the question, don't you?"

"I think I do," said Peter. "And the answer is no, no, and no. If you have no other questions I'll go back where I was. Right now, if that's okay."

The Judge Pope pasted on a wet antelope smile and laid the gavel on the uncrumpled corner of the pulpit, leering down at Peter. "You might want to rethink your answer, sonny. There's such a thing as heresy and you've just committed it. I'm sure the penalty for heresy hasn't escaped your memory."

"It comes rushing back this very second. Whew. I need to amend part of my answer."

"I'm so pleased your memory has returned, so I'll allow an amendment. But you only get one try, so don't screw it up."

"Oh, no. I'll be *real* careful. May I explain my vote."

"Get it over with."

"Right. Well, I was raised by a devout Italian mama. That explains my no vote on the Catholic part. And I've never had much truck for Baptists, who are too straitlaced and never seem to loosen up. Sort of like Catholics. Which leaves me with the Goldie God. All of a sudden, I have a definite belief in that dude's existence, sir." Peter bowed.

"Ass-kissing is no substitute for sincerity, but it helps. On the other hoof, it's not enough. No one would suspect that you believed in a god, much less the omnipotent, omnipresent, grand, and glorious Goldie God. One of the signs of lying is the fact you called the Goldie God a dude, but she's female, mostly, and so not a dude. You hereby join Mack in the category of probable substitutes for Courtney. Return to your compadres, you sorry sack of scat."

"I don't how to thank you enough, so I won't try. Your shabby treatment is so predictable. I'd be an idiot to lick your almighty golden booties." Peter nudged Roy and took the immediately proffered tube, lighting it with gusto and sending an obese smoke ring shimmering toward the Judge Pope. The ring settled reverently over the Judge Pope's head, onto his shoulders.

The Judge Pope held his breath as the approaching blimpoid descended, but when it broke across his broad nose, he inhaled with predictable religious results. "Ooommm." He forgot himself to the extent that he held the sharply inhaled breath.

After thirty-seven seconds he exhaled, releasing zero smoke. Roy and Peter applauded, pounding their hands with enthusiasm. "Bravo, bravo," as the rest looked on with apprehension.

"Oh my gosh, I am afear'd. The mouse has failed, the cat to beard. But if and when, he says a word. I'll be first, my loins to gird. Hark and now he drops his jaw, bet it's sure to lay the law. If that's the course, it takes with us, we should try, and catch a bus."

The Judge Pope rose as if levitating, airily waving a horny hand like a fairy wand. "I am experiencing a vision. Yes I am." He fell silent, distracted by the golden lace shimmering around his wrist.

"That's enough of that," said Btsht, sitting next to the Judge Pope with a thunderous kerplop. "The question is belief in the Goldie God. The Catholic and Baptist ones were an afterthought. Roll call time. Mr. Mack and Peter Peter are down for summary execution. There remains the possibility of a deal to spare Peter Peter's obnoxious life. That would be at most momentary because I do not approve of ganga for any purpose, religious or otherwise."

"Spoken like a true despot, though on this single issue I tend to agree," said Mack. "Which means I should also be spared."

"Doubtful. There are more pressing issues. We're about to annihilate the Ermies and Ivies, which will render your compadres dearly departed, so sorry. But first we'll finish this part of the program. With that in mind, I continue the rudely interrupted roll call. Ms. Ellen, I can guess your response. A big yes to the Catholic Big Guy, a quiet no to the Baptist one, and a resounding rejection of the true Goldie God. What say you for real?"

Ellen arched an eyebrow, freshly bowling Mack over. She said softly, "You got that mostly correct, Your Excellency. But in spite of what I've heard my entire life, I suspect the Baptist god is a cousin to the Catholic one. But I couldn't begin to judge the proper position of the Goldie god in this triangle. It may be after Vatican II that the Goldie god is as good as any other, though the opposite may gain official acceptance. My position is that I don't know. I won't know until the real pope issues an encyclical."

"You mean you don't have a clue what to believe until you're told what to believe? Is that it?" Btsht sneered.

Ellen smiled dazzlingly. "Now that you point it out, I guess that's the way religion works. Isn't it the same for the Goldies? Until the Judge Pope or the Goldie Bible, whatever you call it, tells you what to think, you don't know. Your mind's a vacuum until you're told what to put in it about religion, right? Come on, 'fess up. What you said is exactly the way it is for any religion unless you invent your own. Gee, I hear no denials, no snappy repartee. Did the kitty get your tongue?"

Btsht twirled the gigantic gavel like a baton, the Judge Pope watching transfixed. "Doesn't matter," Btsht snapped. "As usual you've gotten yourself off the hook. But there's no reason to let you wait for a ruling by your inferior pope, especially since we don't intend that he find out about the Goldie religion. You will have to take a position right now." Btsht lowered the gavel onto the tiny unsplintered part of the pulpit.

Ellen frowned. "I'd have to study the matter. Look at doctrine, your history of miracles, and what has been achieved by your saints. I'd have to find out everything about the Goldie religion and god before I could make an educated decision. You wouldn't want me to venture an opinion without knowing what I was talking about, would you? It's not the kind of thing you'd do, is it? State an opinion without knowing all the facts?" She smiled like an angel.

Btsht said stiffly, "Not hardly. You may take your seat."

As Mack stood, a familiar voice resonated from his tinny collar mic. "You've said the magic word and now the blackbird of paradise swoops down and gives you a hundred dollars. 'There is no creed so false but faith can make it true.' Obviously, the magic word is faith. As soon as we're reunited, I'll lay that hundred dollars on you, Honorable Big Guy Btsht."

Mack groaned. "As if you had a hundred dollars to your name and he has use for US currency."

"It might help him bribe his way out of trouble, which should be any minute when the US Marines land to rescue us."

"It's not the Marines, silly. It's the US Air Force men in blue." Mack stopped short. "Has CNN said when the men in blue will be landing? We're getting a little uneasy over here. You flit from garden party to reception plying the diplomatic circuit while our existence is far less pleasant. Most of us have been sentenced to death and we're tired of it. What's the news?"

"The news," said Btsht, "is if that Ermie schmuck friend of yours keeps interrupting, your microphone will be melted down to pins and needles, on which you'll be impaled. Tell him that."

"You just did. Which reminds me. Why didn't you take it away before?"

336

"So we can track everything you're up to, but you keep avoiding the subject. Let's face it squarely so we can get to more important things, such as dealing with the Ermies and Ivies. Let's see how the rest of you vote on the religious options so we can decide who will be substituted for Courtney."

Mack shook his head "Let's cut the charades and relax, get off this silly religious kick. Spend the time settling the utterly stupid dispute you have with the Ermies and Ivies."

Btsht spluttered, "Stupid!? It goes to the question of our existence, which is hardly stupid. You don't realize the consequences of our discovery by a savage backward species. We've tried to avoid contact with humans for centuries and until these last two days of infamy, we were entirely successful."

"You seem hardly less savage and backward than ourselves. You enjoy religious prosecution and intraspecies hatred, which are arguably the two greatest defects of supposedly inferior humans. How are you any better?"

"Big difference," said the Judge Pope. "We have the one true religion and won't tolerate false religions devaluing our own."

"Of course, unless you consider the opinion of Ms. Ellen and Courtney. But speaking for myself, I'm sick of this religious bullshit. Can't we get to something more interesting like, um, almost anything? Maybe your astounding advances in technology, or Peter's business proposition. Anything besides religion."

"Amen," said Peter.

Btsht raised his finger. "Guards." He pointed at Mack. "I've had my fill of your perpetual impertinence."

As Legionnaires grabbed him, Mack said, "I've been filled with impertinence forever. But I understand your concern and will try to do better." They tied his arms behind his back.

"Much too late. Take him over there and keep him quiet." The Legionnaires did their duty, two guarding him on either side while the third stood behind Mack with a horny hoof on his shoulder and the other over Mack's mouth.

Btsht said, "Who's next?"

"I already went," said Peter. "But I agree with Mack because religion isn't my bag."

"I can understand that," said Btsht as Barry, Madison, and Roy shook their heads in agreement. "But you're not setting the agenda. You will answer all questions when asked. Or you'll automatically be substituted for Courtney. Do I make myself clear?"

They continued nodding their heads with equal vigor, glazed grins spread from ear to ear.

Btsht was pissed. "What is the closest you've come to believing in anything related to religion? With particular emphasis on the Goldie religion?"

"Er, Big Guy Number One, sir," said the Judge Pope. "Maybe I should cover the religious questions. Take the strain off while you prepare for strategic moves against the Ermies and Ivies."

"Request granted on the condition that you stay away from the holy weed during questioning."

"That was an accident."

"Right. You may proceed, temporarily."

The Judge Pope said, "Mr. Barry. Do you pledge allegiance to the Goldie religion and accept all its tenets? Each and every one?"

Barry jumped up, blinking a couple of times. "Well, Your Honor, I don't know what the Goldie religion exactly believes, though I'm sure it's honorable and moral. I was raised a Methodist, though I'm not one right now. Kind of back slid. So, I guess I just don't know."

"That's not good enough."

Courtney struggled to her feet. "Sit down, Barry. The Judge Pope is out of line like he's been ever since we laid eyes on him. And what was that about no creed being so false that faith makes it true?"

"Don't blame that on me," said the Judge Pope. "That was Mr. Lucas from Ermieland. We're not responsible for that bunch."

"I'm tireder than Mr. Mack of this whole rigmarole, but for a whole different reason. You're the one, Judge Pope, who makes blasphemy in your mouth. You make fun my humble faith."

"I didn't make fun of you, Courtney."

"Well, your god is pornographic. I wouldn't show its picture to a child, yet you bandy it all over. It's disgusting."

"Now wait a minute, Courtney. You're the blasphemer. You're the one who chopped off the holy horns and the holy—"

"Don't you say that." Courtney raced up to the pulpit, shaking a finger halfway up the Judge Pope's left nostril. Little hairs tickled her forefinger, causing her to crook it.

The Judge Pope grabbed the gavel with both hands and lifted it above his head. As it started its descent toward Courtney's poor grey head, a shrill blast rent the air, shattering the heavy metal gavel a millisecond before it split Courtney's skull.

17

Everyone threw hands and horny paws over their ears, staring at Mack. He dropped the limp appendage of the Legionnaire, whose hoof had covered Mack's mouth. Mack stepped through, around, and over three unconscious bodies, smiling at the Judge Pope.

"Hey, Judge Pope. I saved you from destroying your career and being shamed forever. You shouldn't hit a defenseless old lady, even a heretic."

"Say what?" The Judge Pope cupped an ear in a horny hand. Gavel slivers dotted his face from the blow-back of Mack's horrendous whistle, and Btsht was sprawled next to him, knocked half stupid. The metal heart of the gavel had hit him between the eyes.

Mack was all smiles. "I know you're half deaf. But I congratulate you on the shape of an antelope's horny paws, for whistling that is. If I had paws like that, I could deafen an empire in one fell swoop."

"You dang near did," said Peter. "My ears are ringing and it isn't entirely from holy weed."

Madison puffed himself up. "He blew a blow for charity, such a thing's a rarity. Selfless is he, I must say, saved our Courtney, one more day."

Courtney's reaction was overwhelming as she smothered Mack with kisses.

Mack fended her off. "Thanks, Courtney. That's enough. Please. Hey, I thought you wanted to be a martyr for your faith. I did you a disfavor. Blub, blub, blub," as she kissed him on the mouth.

"Thank you, Mack. It wouldn't have been proper martyrdom to be whacked with a gavel. You've saved me to witness for my Lord in boiling oil. I prayed and my prayers were answered. In a funny way, Mack, you're a holy spiritual person."

Mack thought, 'Yeah, me and Donald Trump,' wiping his mouth on the back of his sleeve. "Death holds no terror for you, eh Courtney. You're like that Harry Belafonte song, living forever because of Christmas Day."

"That's the central tenet of being a Baptist. You rise from the grave, whether hit with a gavel or boiling in oil. When I boil in oil, they'll write a hymn about it." She sang to the tune of 'Bringing in the Sheaves,' "Boiling in the oil. Boiling in the oil. That has a ring to it, so lyrical. I'll live forever hereafter." Courtney's face shone as tears coursed down her face, splashing her dress.

"I know what you're thinking, Mack," came Lucas's singsong voice. "I have your exact sentiments at me fingertips, or actually on the tip of me tongue. 'It is certain because it is impossible.' Fess up. That's exactly what you're thinking."

"That is not helping." Mack gritted his teeth.

"Oh, Mack. Get off the pontifical kick. If I'd said the opposite, you'd argue about that too."

"I didn't say you were wrong. I said it wasn't helping. And yeah, I can always take the other side. It's probably true that almost nothing is impossible, though an overstatement."

Ellen was snooty. "You can't make the other argument, can you, Mack? You're too enmeshed in your new atheistic world to tolerate human goodness and ethics."

"Please, Ellen. Don't do this."

"If he did take the other side, your side, it would be to schmooze you up," said Lucas.

Mack motioned at the Judge Pope. "You can have my collar mic." But the Judge Pope was busy picking splinters from his great wide nose.

"No substantive response, eh Mack," said Ellen. "You're foxed by ethics and goodness."

"I can make the argument." Mack's tone was robotic. "Without discriminating against any particular religion, they

341

seem unrelated to ethics and goodness. But almost anything is possible, even unsubstantiated promises of religion, no matter which one. I've thought about it for hours on end."

Ellen sniffed. "You paint with a mighty broad brush, Mack. Discriminating against all religions."

"It's a lot fairer than siding with one against all the others, which you and Courtney do every day."

"Boring," said Roy.

"Yeah. Get off it already," said Lucas. "Sorry I got you started. It can be summed up fairly for the religious and unreligious alike. 'Religionists and anti-religionists each made their irrefutable points.' Or, 'The light of faith makes us see what we believe,' and 'Nor do I seek to understand that I may believe, but I believe that I may understand. For this too I believe, that unless I first believe, I shall not understand.' How's that for religion in a nutshell?"

"You're the nut and your foolish quotes are the shell," said Mack. "Whatever you said makes about as much sense as—"

"As you do," said Ellen. "Actually, that was pretty good, Lucas. You finally got the religious side of it. We do believe to understand. We're not know-it-alls like Mack. We seek and pray to find the way."

"Wow," said Madison. "Bow wow, holy cow."

"I'm sure she's not aspiring to membership in the extemporaneous poet's society," said Mack. "Sorry no pithy rhyme sprung forth."

Madison raised his eyebrows and launched. "Hey, hey, whataya say? When Ellen speaks, we all give way. A brand-new poet, comes this way, but Mack of course, will have his say. From epic sway, let us pray, no Ellen nay, and Mack makes hay—"

"Attention," said a grandly coiffed and robed figure, who rolled shell-shocked Btsht to the left and the Judge Pope to the right, pulling a tall chair in between. "I've been selected to take over for the temporarily and slightly incapacitated Judge Pope and Honorable Big Guy Number One. We're going for big ratings, which I know can be achieved."

342

"It can't be," said Mack. "Where have you been? Not that I'm glad to see you, but welcome back anyway, Judge Grdam."

"I'm surprised you remember my name."

"I could never forget it. You look pretty spiffy in your new get up."

"I am the judge. Permanent appointment now, you know."

"I didn't." To all appearances Mack bowed respectfully.

"So, let's get on with it. We begin with the quotes contributed by your turncoat, Mr. Lucas of the traitorous Ermies, who will suffer extreme prejudice. You must believe to save your carcasses from deep frying. All will believe except for the unlucky one who fries. Make that plural. For if you believe you will understand, and if you understand you will believe."

Mack sighed. "We all said we believed, except Courtney, who you're bizarrely bent on rescuing from her fate. And Ellen, who always gets off the hook."

"No one would believe you," said Judge Grdam.

"But you have to believe we believe to understand we believe."

"Good argument. Unfortunately, I don't believe that you believe. You're a scoundrel who'd say anything to save his own skin. That goes for your druggie friends too."

"At least up here it's a holy drug. But ye of little faith. We hereby raise our right hands in unison." Mack turned to Barry, Roy, Peter, and Madison. "Hold them high, boys."

Roy and Peter had difficulty deciding which were their right hands, putting up one and then the other before settling on the wrong ones.

"Close enough. Now repeat after me."

"Now repeat after me," said Roy and Peter.

"I'll ignore that." Mack shushed them before they could repeat that too. "We hereby acknowledge—" They repeated it. "That we believe in the Goldie God and whatever tenets his religion consists of."

"Stop it right there," said Judge Grdam. "You know full well the Goldie God is female."

343

"Give them another chance," said Lucas's whispery voice from the tiny microphone. "I've got the perfect quote. 'Belief in, and dependence on God, is absolutely essential. It will be an integral part of our public life as long as I am governor.' Just change the last part to 'as long as I am on this tepui' and everything will work out all right."

"That's ridiculous," said Judge Grdam. "When it comes to religion there's nothing you could say that anyone would believe."

"Then why are you dicking around with this charade?" said Mack. "If you reject Courtney's sincere and heartfelt pleas to fry on her own, pick one of us and get it over with. Stop boring the pants off the entire Goldie nation, which is no longer glued to their sets."

Mack snapped his fingers. "I stand corrected. You haven't denied Courtney's heartfelt pleas to 'boil in the oil.' Hey, Courtney. Do you want to renew you petition with the new judge in town?"

"Well, I surely do, good old Judge Grdam. I remember you from back when I got my shower. I haven't had one since and I could sure use one." Everyone nodded in vigorous agreement.

"And that was back when you were only a guard. Look how far you've come in two short days, which I attribute to your association with me. Based upon that connection, I respectfully ask you to boil me in oil. Quit harassing these heathens. It wouldn't do them any good to burn in oil. I earned it, I deserve it, and I demand it. Thank you for your kind consideration." Courtney made a sort of a curtsey, crossing her brogans.

"Sorry. I have my orders—"

"Zo," said Mack, stretching to full height. "You haf your orders. You were born a half century too soon. You should have been German."

"That's unfair," said Ellen. "That's racist."

"I'm sorry. I hesitate to say some of my best friends are German, though I occasionally enjoy the company of at least two, including my mother on rare occasions. I don't like to be bossed around. Wives, mothers, at least mine, Germans, and

344

governments, not to mention religions, love to tell me what to do. So, I stay away from them."

"You're smug as a bug in a hug," said Madison.

"You're an oaf," said Ellen, signaling to Madison she wasn't talking about him.

"Thanks, guys," said Mack. "And I take it back, Your Honorable judgeship, about being German. I got carried away."

"Thanks a lot," said the judge. "Though I can't possibly believe you, do you all sincerely believe in the Goldie religion?"

"We discussed it before you showed up. How can we tell you one way or the other when we don't know much about it? We've heard of the Mother, Daughter, and Holy Diri— Ghost. And someone said the statue Courtney chopped up is Radnicharra or Famigusta. We remember the golden tassels and skull cap. The wooden blocks and leather thongs fringed in gold. The Judge Pope is a constant reminder, though I'm not sure what it all means. I remember you pray toward the other tepui, but don't know if it's the Ermie or Ivie one. You have an old and new book and five duties, though I don't know what all they are. Except alms for the poor and drilling water wells. That exhausts the hearsay I've run across. I can't see too much wrong with it, but I don't exactly relate to it either."

"I'm here to help. We go to church every Thursday and imbibe the cup. We pray while facing a tepui that will remain nameless, and do whatever the Judge Pope tells us to. I don't know any more except the rituals. But we're the chosen people of God and will live forever if we do the things we're supposed to do. That covers what the Judge Pope would say if he were able." The Judge Pope was still preoccupied picking wooden splinters out of his face.

"Got it," came Lucas's scratchy voice through Mack's mic. "There couldn't be a more preposterous religion and I quote: 'Altogether, both the glory and the tragedy of Israel may be traced to the singular idea cherished by its people—the exalted, conceited, preposterous idea that they alone were God's chosen people.' I'm sure Mack has something to say."

"You got that. Lest poor Lucas be thought anti-Semitic, he's quoting stuff his short-circuited brain hands him on a platter. Without deliberation. The second thing is, that applies to all religions. Not just Judaism. Every religion is the chosen of its particular god, which is better than all the others. The Jews are not alone on this one."

Judge Grdam reached for something and realized it wasn't available. "Baliffs. I need a gavel." In seconds he had a reasonable facsimile of a normal sized gavel and started banging away like there was no tomorrow.

"Order. Order. We're way off subject again. You're out of order, Lucas and Mack. I'd love to let Mack fry, but public interest requires that we go through the motions of finding a substitute."

"It certainly does," said Mack.

Judge Grdam said, "You likely can't do any better describing your religions than I did ours. I order Ms. Ellen and Courtney to describe theirs forthwith."

"That is not a problem," said Courtney, "depending on which way the test goes. What do I have to do to flunk it?"

"That's easy. You only have to know nothing about your religion."

"But I can't tell a lie. It'd be against my religion. Unless the lie is worthwhile, such as getting me into boiling oil. But I don't know how I could tell a lie at this stage in my life. So, what's the wages of lying? Telling you I don't know a thing about the tenets of the noble American Baptist religion? Would that make me a potential French fry again?"

"I'll skip you. Ms. Ellen. State the principle tenets of your religion, Roman Catholicism."

"Heavenly days. Everyone knows what Catholics believe, whether they're Catholics or not."

"That's not good enough. Someone might think you were covering up a lack of knowledge."

"Not hardly," said Mack. At their looks he said, "Sorry to interrupt."

"I think we make a great interruption team," said Lucas. "Cut out having Courtney and Ellen describe their religions because I have a definition of Christianity at my tongue tip. It should adequately cover Catholics and Baptists alike. 'Christianity: A religious system attributed to Jesus Christ, but really invented by Plato, improved by St. Paul, and finally revised and corrected by the Fathers, the councils and other interpreters of the church. Since the foundation of this sublime creed, mankind has become better, wiser and happier than before. From that blessed epoch the world was forever freed from all strife, dissensions, troubles, vices and evils of every kind; an invincible proof that Christianity is divine, and that it is to be possessed of the very devil himself to dare to commit such a creed or doubt its origin.'" They could visualize Lucas bowing.

Mack groaned. "It's a good thing you're an Ermie hostage, out of Goldie reach. That definition must be satirical, and might even be unfair."

Ellen pounded her chest and Mack hoped she didn't injure anything important. "You surprise me, Mack, and sometimes for the better. I didn't know you could say anything good about religion. Are you feeling well?"

"You didn't let me finish," said Mack. "It's not the fault of Christianity that the world continues to slit each other's throats. It's partly the fault of all religions. Us versus them, and that will never change. But I see Judge Grdam is upset at the digression."

"Pissed is more like it." The honorable judge held the gavel in a threatening manner. "Get on with it, Ms. Ellen."

"That's Mrs., and of course, I'm intimately familiar—" she backtracked at Mack's leer, "extremely knowledgeable about Catholicism, having been baptized as a baby and brought up in the—"

"Exactly the problem with it," interrupted Courtney. "You're baptized, sprinkled that is, when you're too young to know any better."

"Ahummm," said Ellen in her I'll-let-that-one-go manner. "We baptize babies to save them from hell, in case they die in infancy."

"They're not sinners in infancy so you don't need to baptize them. I should know. I'm a Baptist."

"Now is hardly the time to get into the finer points of Original Sin."

"Which doesn't exist," growled Courtney.

"In any event, we believe in the Bible like all Christians—"

"But you're not allowed to read it," said Courtney. "Your Bible is filtered through priests."

"Used to be." Ellen smiled sweetly. "But that's of no importance now. We pray the same as other Christians."

"Yeah, using beads. We pray direct, and when I say we, I mean American Baptists."

"Courtney, you're getting on my nerves. Could you take a break while I'm talking to Judge Grdam?"

"Hardly," said Courtney. "Your prayers go through the pope, who's practically your god. You do whatever the pope tells you and popes have been a din of iniquity since time immemorial."

"Time immemorial was a long time ago." Ellen was fluttery, trying to preserve the peace. "Not anymore."

"Only in reality, not in doctrine." Courtney gestured rudely. "It took Protestants and the Reformation to rescue the Catholic Church from infamy."

"Enough of that." Ellen grabbed for Courtney's hands, unfortunately missing, a fingernail scratching Courtney across the cheek.

"The Catholic witch wounded me." Courtney brushed at the thin red line. "Let me at her." She lunged and tripped.

Lucas's voice shredded the pregnant silence. "They did a great job with camera angles on the Ellen/Courtney spat. And now a replay. Which requires an on-point quote. 'There is no wild beast as ferocious as Christians who differ concerning their faith.' You'll be proud of me, guys. The Ermies are letting me do the closed captioning live. No five second delay."

Mack said, "Quit using quotes to incite Ellen and Courtney to riot. We have enough problems."

"Sounds like Northern Ireland, another example of Catholic-Protestant cooperation." Lucas laughed. "Cut the crap, Mack. You have no more sympathy for religious squabbles than whoever it was I quoted."

"Maybe, but I'm more circumspect. I know the difference between a game and when it's serious, and Northern Ireland was serious. I thought you were an agnostic or something, uninterested in religious wars. If you'd cast Momma's big book of quotes out of your pea brain, we'd be better for it. At least I would be and I think the Honorable Judge Grdam would agree, and perhaps also—"

"The Honorable Judge Pope agrees in spades." The gold-bedecked figure was starting to pay attention, rubbing a face that looked like a plucked porcupine.

"You may now recuse yourself, Judge Grdam," said the Judge Pope.

"My honorable self and Most Exalted Big Guy Btsht will resume our positions of authority."

Judge Grdam slunk off as Btsht rolled a high-backed chair next to the Judge Pope, who muttered, "What the hell happened? One second I was wreaking vengeance on the heretic Courtney and then my gavel exploded."

"It was a good thing you had your nose in the air," said Mack, "or you might have lost an eye."

"I thought you were in protective custody. Where are your guards?"

"I gave them the day off. They've been putting in too much overtime and I was afraid you'd get in trouble with the wage and labor people." At the judge Pope's severe look Mack added, "I meant well."

"I'm sure you had something to do with the exploding gavel. Where were you at the time?"

"I was in protective custody, minding my own business."

"You're whistlin' Dixie. I'm mighty suspicious that you somehow made my gavel explode. It wasn't that old."

"It probably suffered internal stress when Btsht crunched it through the top of the bench pulpit."

"Very well. We'll appoint a Big Guy commission to look into it. Meanwhile, what were we discussing? No, no. I don't want you to tell me. I want to pick up the thread on my own. We were looking for a substitute for Courtney in the boiling oil."

"That's correct," said Btsht a little too heartily. His eyes were glassy and he still sat clutching the diamond-hard kernel from the exploded gavel.

"Ah," said the Judge Pope, turning from contemplation of Btsht's condition. "Yes, but what was the question?"

"I remember it exactly," said Mack.

"Oh, yeah." The Judge Pope was suspicious.

"Yeah, you made Ellen and Courtney outline their religious beliefs to see if they were the same."

"I don't remember that. But it makes sense. Maybe we all have the same god. Courtney will have to apologize when she realizes that, and we can all go home happy."

"Medics," called Mack. At the Judge Pope's quizzical look Mack said, "You've suffered a severe blow, sir. You may need medical care."

"Oh, Mack," said Ellen, which focused his immediate and undivided attention. "Follow the judge's cue and get us off the hook. The bogus pope may be right. We may have the same god with different names."

Mack shook his head hopelessly. "Your pope probably wouldn't recognize a female god. But point taken. I hereby withdraw in the interests of sanity. My own."

"Withdrawal heartily granted," said the Judge Pope. "Now Ms. Ellen, you were saying about your god—Please describe your god with exactitude, if you would be so kind."

"Well, certainly. He's—"

The Judge Pope interrupted. "Our god is female so they can't be the same."

"That's probably a myth. Gods aren't sexed."

"One can hardly envision them having sex," snickered Mack.

"This is a serious discussion, Mack McElheney," said Ellen, and Mack almost swooned. It had to be serious. She'd said his entire name. He was smitten as Ellen continued. "Our God is all powerful, omnipotent, omnipresent, and all good. I can't add much to that. I assume your god is the same."

"Well, sure," said the Judge Pope. "But all gods are super-antelopes, everywhere at once, and good guys. That's not what distinguishes gods. What distinguishes gods is their commandments. So, what does yours command."

"He commands everyone, including Golden Antelopes. I'll withdraw that last part if it causes a problem, because I don't really know."

"Right. Because your pope hasn't yet told you, one way or the other. What would you think if I told you the Goldie God likewise commands everyone? Including humans of whatever shade and color? Actually, that's a rhetorical question. You don't have to respond." He waved away her open mouth. "What I'm trying to get at is the main commandments. Our main commandments are to get rid of slippery rocks, dig wells and catchments for rainwater, pray toward the Golden stone, unfortunately on another tepui which will remain nameless, give alms to the poor, except we don't have poor anymore. We save alms by tossing poor antelopes off the tepui."

"Like you did to our suffering compatriots on the wrecked aircraft," said Mack.

"They were already croaked. You admitted that, when you were checking out the whackety thud. Remember?"

"I remember. You're right. I withdraw the accusation."

"Right. Now what are the commandments of your good and everywhere god, Ms. Ellen?"

"That's Mrs. I let it go plenty of times, but when you have predators circling the wagons, you can't be too careful."

"There's only one of me and I haven't been circling," said Mack.

"Not for wont of trying," sniffed Ellen. "Our commandments are ten."

"I thought that was Judaism, not Christianity," said the Judge Pope.

"There is some overlap."

"How can you tell which religion is right, whether it's Judaism or Christianity?"

"Well, I just know it."

"That's a pretty stupid response," said the judge Pope.

"Whose response are you calling stupid? How do you tell which of the antelope religions is right?"

"I am the Judge Pope."

351

"That's hardly an answer. The point is, your god is no better than my God." "How do you know your god exists?"

"This is getting out of hand," said Lucas through Mack's tinny mic. "Of course, that means I have something to say and this is what it is. 'Supposing a man-hater had desired to render the human race as unhappy as possible, what could he have invented for the purpose better than belief in an incomprehensible being about whom men can never be able to agree?' That sums it up pretty darn good."

"That's hooey," said Mack. "There's no men involved in the argument. It's Ellen against a Golden Antelope."

"That was shifty. Ellen and Courtney went tooth and nail a few minutes ago."

"We did not," said Ellen. "Besides, we weren't arguing about our gods. They're the same."

"You couldn't tell it by me," said the Judge Pope. "It sounded like they contradicted each other."

Mack said, "You're a fine one to talk. Gods only broadcast through popes and such. You have an entire species hanging on your every word, which supposedly comes direct from whatever god bosses you around. *She's* a lot different from the other antelope gods."

"There is no supposedly about it." The Judge Pope was miffed, his nose turning scarlet around the pin-pricks.

"Oh, yeah. And how does this transmission of information occur? Do you receive written documents admissible in evidence? Or the occasional email that could be electronically traced? Exactly how do these god-messages come winging their way?"

"Oh, ye of little faith. Answering such a question is so far beneath me as to be subterranean. I'll humor your disbelieving mind, though 'mind' is an obvious exaggeration. Like all good popes, of whom I'm the only true one, I meditate. I listen, I pray, I communicate with God."

"I have a riddle."

"I can't wait to hear it."

"What's the difference between a Judge Pope hearing god voices, a drunk seeing pink elephants, and a hippie hallucinating happy hookers?"

"That's disrespectful. Guards."

"I wondered what took you so long," said Btsht.

"Forget it." Mack crossed his arms like warding off vampires. "We don't have time to torture me again. You have a war to get on with, finding a substitute for Courtney, and then there's the ratings. Legionnaires seizing a poor weak human won't are going to help ratings— Yelp." Three vaguely familiar Legionnaires pinioned his arms at bad angles behind him. "I give up," said Mack. "I surrender my freedom of speech and—"

"And your big mouth," said the Judge Pope. "You must be respectful to God whether you believe in her or not. Ms. Ellen would agree."

"I agree." So succulently that Mack insides melted anew.

"I give up, and agree," said Mack weakly.

"Thank you," said the Judge Pope, receiving a warning frown from Btsht. "It is the judgment of this court that Mack burn in oil as a substitute for Courtney. You have one last chance to address the court before your demise."

"Thank you kindly. Anyone who'd believe in a god would believe anything. Thank you." He bowed.

"That's heretical. Does all your lot agree with that? We'll poll your fellows. Answer up. First, Peter Peter Pecker Eater."

"Oh, give it a rest." Peter rolled his eyes. "Anything is more interesting than the religious crap you keep batting around. I prefer cartwheels, holy weed, and especially babes. I can't wait to get home to the comely darlings. I vote with Mack on whatever he was talking about."

"Then you stand equally condemned. How about you, Mr. Madison."

"I'm sad to say, I've hit the hay, wake me up, another day. Let a laying dog obey, all I'll say is friggin' nay." He smiled like a doofus in drag.

"You've been influenced by evil companions. Whether that means you deserve boiling oil will be held in abeyance. Next is Mr. Roy."

Roy failed to move a muscle, staring into the middle distance.

"Mr. Roy," repeated the Judge Pope.

"Eh," started Roy. "You speakin' to me? Sorry. I'm under the weather and like, everything is going downhill." His hand gesture was grand, though a little ragged.

"I'll show you how vividly everything can go downhill. Do you agree with Mack or not? I won't repeat the question."

"Oh, whoa. Then I'll have to guess the question. It's like twenty questions with every last one plunging into a precipice. I don't know where to begin." He scratched his head with his left hand, seized with the inspiration of dancing around like he had a banana in the other hand.

"Real cute, but you owe me a response." The Judge Pope stared sternly at Roy.

"Oh my god. I've forgotten the question that you asked after the question I never knew about. I'm gonna have to start from scratch." He wrinkled up his face. "Did it have something to do with Mack?" Upon the Judge Pope's affirmative nod Roy said, "Then that settles it. If I know what's good for me, to avoid going further downhill, I vote the opposite." He laughed and bowed.

"You are too lucky."

"Well, hell. I had a fifty-fifty chance. Catch me after the show's over," tossing a joint at the Judge Pope, who instinctively caught it. "We'll do a little holy communion."

Under the baleful stare of Btsht, the Judge Pope dropped the joint like a hot coal. "Your luck is up, Mr. Roy. You will join Mr. Mack and Mr. Peter in boiling oil. That brings us to Mr. Barry."

"Yes, sir." Barry saluted like his hand was a precision dagger.

"As you were." Barry snapped to parade rest. "I take it you know the question."

"I do, sir, and I disagree with Mack on this issue. Not everyone who believes in a god would believe anything.

354

Though it may be true that almost anyone will believe anything anyway. Such as witchcraft and sorcery, especially if it fits their biases. Not that witchcraft and sorcery are in your repertoire, or any superstitions like that."

"Touché, and well put. No need to go deeper into metaphysics. You are spared, for the time being. You may join Mr. Madison and Mrs. Ellen."

Tinny clapping resounded from Mack's collar mic. "Bravo, Honorable Judge Pope. You rank with the various Inquisitors. Whether against or by Protestants, Jews, or Catholics. And yes, since you're tensely waiting, here's the quote. 'To deny the possibility, nay, actual existence of witchcraft and sorcery is at once flatly to contradict the revealed word of God in various passages of both the Old and New Testament.' I trust you won't take this too literally and condemn Barry as a result?"

"That Lucas fellow is a nuisance," said the Judge Pope.

"Not good, Lucas," said Mack. "I hope the Judge Pope didn't understand what you're talking about. But since he's not much into the Bible, witchcraft, or sorcery, it probably doesn't matter. I'm a condemned man. My life is fading before my eyes, like wind on water. I'm tearing up."

"Yeah, I can tell by the sniffle in your voice. You're feeling sorry for yourself."

"You'd feel sorry for myself, too, if you had the stench of boiling oil in your nostrils. I'm so close that the bubbles are spitting freckles and getting closer."

"Gee, you're observant," said the Judge Pope. "That's because you're in the harness. You don't always pay attention."

"I completely missed that," said Mack. "How did I get into the harness without noticing?"

"You were preoccupied and we put you in gently. We didn't want to disturb your last soliloquy with Mr. Lucas. We're not entirely uncivilized, you know."

"No, I didn't." Mack swung free as the hoist lifted him above the boiling oil.

"Oh, Mack," wailed Ellen.

"This could be worth it," said Mack.

"Oh Mack, oh Mack, it in you'll pack," said Madison. "The deck they stack, but you'll be back, or you're not Mack, and that's a fact."

"Thanks, Maddy old boy, but I have other things on my wee mind just now. Hey, Btsht. One last request."

"Oh, right. One last request. You may lower him."

The Legionnaire in charge took the order literally, lowering Mack so fast that his shoes touched the burbling oil. Mack jerked and twitched as Btsht ordered the lowering outside the boiling cauldron.

"Sorry, chief," said the Legionnaire.

"It's no skin off my nose," said Btsht.

"That's easy for you to say," said Mack as they levered him upright, black leather shoes charred a nasty gray. "That's skin off my toes."

"Last request, remember. Snap it up. We haven't all day."

"My last request, Honorable Big Guy Number One, Btsht, sir, is for us to resolve your conflict with the Ermies and Ivies."

"Well, I don't know. We grant last requests but they can't take all day. This might take more than I'm willing to invest, time-wise."

"That's too bad. It's my last request and I insist."

"Very well, but make it quick," said Btsht in a rush.

"Of course, I'll make it as quick as I can. First to lay the groundwork."

"I sense obfuscation," muttered the Judge Pope.

"You too?" said Btsht.

"I'm hurrying," said Mack. "Here's my suggestion. If you had the same religion it would ease things and lead to instant peace."

"Perhaps," said the Judge Pope, "but we don't have the same religion. So, there you have it. Our religions aren't related, though Radnicharra is a cousin twice removed from the Ermies' Famigusta. And a millennium ago the Ivies patriarch was in the line of succession for the predecessor thrice removed from Famigusta. But other than that, we're not anywhere close. We're about as different as they come. For example, our

356

commandments are different. We have the big five while the Ermies only have to confess, commune, and live forever, so they say. We've never seen them live forever. I hope I'm not keeping you from something."

"Oh, no. I'm anything but bored. Maybe you have the same god." Mack was frantic.

"Maybe. Maybe not. No one knows."

"That's not the problem, Mack," said Btsht. "You keep getting off track because you've never been on track. The real problem is the Ermies and Ivies welcoming the scurrilous human race to our tepuis. We can't handle crazy human tourists and we don't want to live in human zoos. We have an insoluble problem."

"If you're such hot shots at technology, why don't you make yourselves invisible? Then you wouldn't have to worry about discovery by our air force men in blue."

"We might have to do exactly that."

"Might, as in you would if you could, or if your scientists figure out how to make you invisible in the next hour or so. You're a bag of wind, Btsht, and you know it."

"Since you've finished, we proceed. Guards. Levitate the prisoner."

The cauldron burbled as the slack sucked out of the rope and Mack flipped upside down. Sweat poured down Mack's face, "Surely your religion has some connection with ethics. You wouldn't want to boil a poor human who never did you wrong? One who never carved up a golden idol, or the image of your sacred God? Your God will punish you for such an act and bar you from eternal life, or whatever it is you get when you croak. He, er, she would, wouldn't she?"

"Perfect," came Lucas's tinny tones as Mack spiraled skyward. "How do you do it, Mack? You must have read me mum's big book of quotes and retained them subconsciously, like myself. 'A man's ethical behavior should be based effectually on sympathy, education and social ties; no religious basis is necessary. Man would indeed be in a poor way if he had to be restrained by fear of punishment and hope of reward after death.' Maybe that'll get you off the hook."

357

"Thanks loads. The hook is sinking deep in my innards, piercing my very being."

"Is the harness a little tight?" asked the nice Legionnaire.

"Thanks for your concern but the discomfort will only be temporary. It won't last after boiling in oil."

The Legionnaire rubbed his chin with a horny paw. "You're probably right."

"I'm really upset about Lucas and his absurd quotes. The last one will do me in. I appealed to religious ethics and Lucas says religion has nothing to do with ethics."

Mack said to Lucas, "I hope you come up with a better idea fast. That one didn't work."

"That's a rational assessment," said Btsht. "Don't you agree, Judge Pope?"

"Oh, I surely do."

"Then we may proceed." Btsht flashed a thumb's down at the nice Legionnaire, who seemed almost doleful as he dropped Mack toward the splattering oil. The black cauldron swung to and fro on its tiny legs, slopping oil over the marble floor, staining it horrid shades of green and yellow.

"Woe is me," said Mack as the Legionnaire stopped him three inches above the scorching liquid. "This stuff is really really hot. Yoweeeeee," he added as the Legionnaire adjusted the rate of descent to three inches a minute.

"You have an entire minute before you fry," said the Judge Pope with relish.

Ellen said, "Oh, Mack," clasping a convex portion of her chest.

"Whoa," said Mack. "It's hot and getting hotter. My throat is clogging."

"It is a far, far better thing you do—" began Courtney. She slumped to her knees, clasped pudgy hands, and turned her shining face toward the heavens. "You're doing this for me in his name. Let this cup pass from Mack. I want it for myself." She wept.

"You're welcome to it," croaked Mack. "Come on, Ellen, give us a little kiss."

"Is that your last request?" Ellen rushed forward, fending off spitting oil with an upraised hand.

"Gosh, Mack," said Peter. "I didn't think it'd ever happen. At least not to you."

"Alack, alack, oh Mack come back," said Madison.

"You're sure as hell going downhill big time," said Roy. "Don't let us down, Mack. Defy the laws of thermodynamics."

18

Barry sat transfixed as Ellen braved the oil that spackled her sheltering hand. She bent to kiss Mack's terrified face and all hell broke loose. The top of the huge auditorium flew off and a dazzling light descended, chirping around the perimeter. It homed in and buried its burning snout between Btsht's eyes. Btsht didn't have time say a word before he split in two. His wide nose disintegrated, along with his face as he fell backward, tipping the pulpit over and taking the Judge Pope with him.

"Up and back and over and away," shouted Mack at the startled Legionnaire. The Legionnaire executed the order as if made by former Big Guy Number One, Btsht, decedent.

"Oh, Ellen." Mack swooped upward. "That was a wonderful gesture. I'll never forget your kiss."

Lucas yelled something over Mack's mic, which nearly disintegrated with feedback, wailing like the Mormon Tabernacle Choir missing a double high C.

Mack slapped the mic as his charred shoes hit the floor, flailing halfway across the room to return the kiss on Ellen's still pursed lips.

"Yuck." She jerked back. "What are you doing out of the harness, away from the burbling cauldron, safe and sound?"

"Sorry about that," said Mack.

Lucas yelled, "Our preemptive strike saved your paltry life."

"Your preemptive strike? You did that?" Mack was amazed. "You knocked off the Big Guy to save my paltry life. He was Big Guy Number One and I'm just a state employee."

"This isn't like you Mack. How come you're not gloating and dancing around like a banshee?"

"Because this means war. Our life expectancy isn't more than a couple of minutes now."

"You're not yourself, Mack. This means no war."

"How can it mean no war? You knocked off the Really Big Guy and the Goldies aren't going to take it lightly. I can tell they're not, because the General is riding down the stairs on a golden horse."

"Oh my god, I see that. It's plastered all over the telly. Is that horse real gold? Never mind. A CNN bulletin says the Yanks are coming. There's no reason for war because we're almost discovered. The Venezuelans gave permission for a US search after confirming that a spy satellite got a fix on the black box before the Goldies destroyed it."

"Oh, right. I'm sure CNN said that, about the Goldies destroying it."

"Well, not exactly. The position of the black box was pinpointed after the aircraft disappeared from radar screens and—"

"So, they've narrowed the search area to a thousand square miles. Get real Lucas. There's no way to stop this war, which is all my fault."

"I can't believe you're upset that we saved your miserable life."

"I'm not upset about that. I owe you, or I owe someone. You did well knocking off my former buddy Btsht, who was about to fry me. My face is half singed off, I won't have to shave for weeks and my eyeballs are fireballs. But it was worth it. Ellen gave me a kiss before my impending death."

"You'll never learn, Mack. Ellen's a devout Catholic and you're a newly devout heathen, and never the twain. You get my drift?"

"I wasn't looking for a lifetime companion."

"We'd better repair to our respective bomb shelters," said Lucas.

"You're right. The Goldie general is clearing the auditorium. Everyone's headed for the dungeon. It's supposed to fend off Ermie and Ivie smart bombs, but I have my doubts."

"You have doubts about everything."

"That's because everything is doubtful. The General has ordered a counter-attack and a launcher is firing a hundred missiles a second. Smoky tails are shooting over the auditorium. Aren't you getting flak over there or are the Goldies lousy shots?"

"We're locked down in a dungeon and nothing's happening yet. I'll bring you up to date on the Ivies and Reg's bunch."

"Oops. The Judge Pope is taking command. Hey, Honorable Judge Pope. Call the war off. The Yanks are coming and your ugly mug will be plastered all over the internet. You've no place to hide. So, stop this nonsense so we can live happily ever after."

The Judge Pope's golden lace was limp, his frock soiled, and his grand headpiece crumpled like a crumpet. He snarled. "This war is a religious necessity. The Ermies interrupted a sacrifice to God."

"I am sorry to be alive. But unless you stop it super quick, our air force men in blue will wipe the deck with the likes of you. That will prove your gold-plated god doesn't exist and you'll wake up dead."

"Oh, sure. Like you can wake up dead."

"Well, it happened in the Bible, so why not? But in either event, you gain nothing by waging war over Btsht's dead body."

"Don't be obtuse. We must avenge his honor. We'll win the war for Btsht, who gave his all."

"He gave his all to a sucker punch."

"Which is all the more reason to avenge his memory. His death is an inspiration to us all. Shoo along to the dungeon where you'll be secure."

"If the Ermie bombs are as smart as they've been so far, there's no place to hide."

"I can't believe you're worried about inferior Ermies. They're cannon fodder for our boys. Look at the General over there, firing off salvos, avenging the memory of our dearly departed leader—"

"The crap's getting a little thick over there," said Lucas. "Give the Judge Pope what for. Here's the ammunition.

'Possibly if a true estimate were made of the morality and religions of the world, we would find that the far greater part of mankind received even those opinions and ceremonies they would die for, rather from the fashions of their countries and the constant practice of those about them, than from any convictions of their reason.' That should fix his teetering trolley."

"Christ on a crutch, I'll give you that one," said Mack.

"That boy's a heretic," said the Judge Pope. "When we get him back here, he's a goner. Get going or we'll take you to the dungeon in a wheelbarrow, trophy humans in case of emergency." A super wheelbarrow big enough to hold twenty humans sat next to a brawny Legionnaire with epaulettes jutting a foot off his shoulders.

Kerboooooom. The pulpit imploded. The blast took out the first baliff and three court reporting machines, searing the Judge Pope's frock to burnt sienna. Mack and the rest ran to the wheelbarrow and sat perched on top. A squad of Legionnaires wrapped them in clear plastic wrap and trundled them out of the battle-scarred auditorium, bumpety-bump down the emerald road to the open doors of the dungeon. The doors swung shut behind the Judge Pope, the General, a legion of Legionnaires, and the new Big Guy Number One, the Honorable Judge Grdam.

"Ahem," said Judge Grdam as the wheelbarrow tipped over. Seven plastic-wrapped humans tumbled onto the metal floor of the dungeon, surrounded by three hundred Legionnaires.

"My god, what a bummer," mumbled Mack through little holes in the plastic wrap. He rolled around, trying to get to his feet.

The Honorable Big Guy Number One Judge Grdam pressed a mic to his lips, instructing the General. "Wipe 'em all out. Spare no one. No quarter asked and none given. Over," he shrieked.

The General's tenor squeal came back, "Yes sir, Honorable Big Guy Number One Grdam, sir. But we're suffering above average casualties. You left at the right time. Half our troops have been slaughtered."

"You mean—"

"That's exactly what I mean. Have you had casualties in the dungeon?" And the world as they knew it, ended.

The huge double doors imploded to reveal eighteen medium range warheads dancing outside. After the barest split second, they homed in on their smart targets. Mack rolled against the others, shifting their collective weight, tipping the gigantic wheelbarrow on top of them. After eighteen explosions wracked the immediate vicinity, Mack thrust a foot under the edge of the wheelbarrow and ejected himself into a smoke-choked dungeon.

"Cough, cough." Mack spit out plastic wrap as he rolled in a circle. "Hey, Mr. Legionnaire Extraordinaire, sir. Could you get us out of this plastic crap? Cough, cough." The Legionnaire failed to respond.

"I'd consider it a favor, which I'd be happy to mention to the air force men in blue when they come looking for scapegoat antelopes."

Still no response, which made Mack roll to the side of the Legionnaire with the long epaulets, "Whoa. Sorry fella. I didn't know you were dead. I'll try someone else."

Smoke coiled around the dungeon as Mack rolled to the left, finding himself where he'd always dreamed. Nose to nose and toes to toes with Ellen. Except she was out cold, unresponsive as a Catholic girl after confession.

"Oh dear, I must rescue the damsel in distress." But she wasn't really in distress, more like Sleeping Beauty. Her chest rose and fell with hypnotic regularity, though very slightly, due to the plastic wrap.

"Whoa. I am entranced." With herculean effort he tore his gaze from Ellen's chest, looking up to see a Legionnaire holding the wheelbarrow high above them, ready to destroy seven humans with one blow.

"Put the wheelbarrow down," bellowed the Honorable Judge Grdam. The renegade Legionnaire turned toward the Big Guy with the wheelbarrow high above his head.

"That's right. Slowly. No. Not on them, dodo. Over to the side. They're valuable. Yes, I know they're inferior aliens, but they're our ticket to safety. Don't do anything rash or you'll die in this dungeon. And I am the judge."

"Right," said the renegade Legionnaire. He threw the wheelbarrow against the wall, shattering it into flying shrapnel.

"Thank God for plastic wrap," said Mack. They looked like pincushions after a game of darts, metal bits sticking out of plastic wrap every which way.

"Loosen their bonds," ordered Judge Grdam.

The renegade Legionnaire suffered a bad case of surly lip but followed the order. He tugged the ends of the plastic wrap, unwrapping the humans like yoyos shot from a cannon. Peter, Madison, Ellen, Courtney, Mack, Roy, and Barry almost splattered as they hit the far wall.

Mack stumbled as he tried to stand up. "I am crunched."

"I don't think he likes you," said Judge Grdam, smiling at the Legionnaire.

"I thought if he hurt us you were going to lock him in the dungeon forever."

"Murdering you is one thing but banging you around is super fun." The last words Judge Grdam would ever utter, as a smart missile splattered him against the wall.

"We're losing reception," said Lucas's reedy Aussie twang. "The picture is flickering. We're getting hits in our safe room. I want to pass something on—"

"No, no," said Mack. "No more quotes."

"'We are mad, not only individually, but nationally. We check manslaughter and isolated murders; but what of war and the much-vaunted crime of slaughtering whole peoples?' That fits, eh?"

"The slaughtering of whole peoples, or antelopes, is patriotism, nationalism, and racism. The terms are interchangeable."

"You left out religion. Are you under the weather?"

"I am a little depressed. It's dark in the dungeon and we're jammed next to eighteen jelly loaves in a row. Judge Grdam and the big Legionnaire with extra-long epaulettes were killed by missiles, and I have a stomach ache. There's no Valium or Prozac in the first-aid kit."

"Peter or Roy might have something for what ails you."

"I don't want to addle my brains any further than they already are. And worse, I'm laying right next to Ellen and she's out cold."

"Lucky her."

"Thanks. And now— Oh, jeez, the haze is clearing and more smart missiles are dancing around—"

Ear-splitting explosions drowned out Mack. Afterwards, Mack said, "I don't know how many of us survived. Or if any Goldies are left. A Legionnaire I just talked to was disemboweled."

"Disemboweled sounds real bad," said Lucas.

"His guts are hanging out and there are flies everywhere. Where'd flies come from and how'd they get here so fast?"

"You don't sound too good, Mack."

"I'm snapping out of it. How's it over there? Are the Goldies firing on you guys?"

"They're wiping out Ermies like gnats, but we're fine, as far as I know. Nick and Mary have been gone for ages and everyone figures the worst. Benny went with a bunch of Ermies to see racing monkeys. I don't know where James and Billy K. are, but Ef is here. Reg's transmitter must have been confiscated as we haven't been in touch."

"Didn't your good buddy Badsr tell you what's going on?"

"Badsr's gone."

"Where'd he go? Is he hiding out?"

"First Goldie missile and he turned into a red jelly casserole."

"I like the fact the Big Guys are the first to eat it in a war. If our wars worked that way, we wouldn't have any."

"Boy ain't that the truth. But no Ermies are left, that we know of. I'm discombobulated."

"I know what you mean, but I'm sure glad they hit the bigwigs first, which I'd do if it were up to me."

"I didn't think you were the warmongering type," said Lucas.

"You know what I mean. If I *had* to run a war, the first thing I'd do is shoot the kingpins on the other side. Only makes sense. We say we're against war but look at German civilians last century. Cough. The smoke's so thick I can't see what's going on, continuous explosions. The walls must be absorbing the blasts or we'd all be dead."

"You don't really know much of anything."

"That's one thing we can agree upon. Except when your performance evaluation rolls around. Let's find out who's in charge and see if they'll call off the war. One of us might get hurt."

"Worth a shot," said Lucas. "The Ermie generals bought the farm right away. I'm dealing with the lower ranks."

"Gosh, I hope it isn't beneath you. I'm heading out after I tell everyone what we're doing. They might miss me, eh?" Lucas listened to Mack say, "Right. Yeah, I know. You got most of it. Sure. That's all we can do. Thanks, Ellen. I'll treasure that."

Lucas asked brightly, "Did you finally score?"

"Not exactly. She slapped me for talking to you instead of helping her and Courtney. Rows of casserole pans are lined up in the dungeon like Arlington without lids. We escaped and are finally above the smoke. The only antelopes left are Legionnaires, no Big Guy in sight. Whoops. More incoming missiles."

Lucas said, "We're all on the edge of the tepui next to the main missile battery. You need a badge to get in so I flashed my lottery ID. The antelope on the gate must be new." Lucas sounded shocked, "Christ. Not that new. The Goldies had his serial number. He was blasted in front of my eyes. There's no shrapnel. They implode and the debris transforms itself into a casserole pan. Yuck. He's still quivering." Lucas gagged.

"They're falling like ten pins over here, lines of antelopes moving up to replace them like automatic cannon fodder. Who said soldiers were made to be killed? I, of course, don't know who said it, but he or she said it better than that."

"Probably anyone would have said it better. This one fits pretty good. 'Theirs not to make reply, Theirs not to reason why, Theirs but to do or die.' Whataya think?"

"I agree. It fits good."

"You're mellowing out, buddy."

"I take it back. No one's in charge here and I only see casserole pans. Very large casserole pans for formerly large antelopes. Lucas, take a look at your casserole pans. Ours have insignia on them, lined up by rank. You should see how this works. Guy catches a missile and as soon as the casserole pan forms it slides around and fits into a slot according to rank. This last guy was a lieutenant, a pan with a little golden hoof on it. I'm following it around, which isn't easy. They slide like greased lightning. Whoosh. This one slid into place and locked. Lieutenants on both sides. I can't read the Goldie script, but they have silver and golden hooves, slippery rocks, little birds, and stars. Maybe subdivided by time in grade."

"By gum, you're right. Same thing with the Ermies. Of course, we have black casserole pans."

"Ours are golden. It's quite neighborly to code missiles to form the right color casserole pan. I'm working up the line to see if anyone's alive. Whoa. Here's a captain."

The Captain looked sharp, his trousers creased like all outdoors. He was feeding little slivers of celluloid into a missile launcher.

"Howdy, Captain. How're they hangin'?" said Mack.

"Hanging good, human person. I don't think we've been introduced."

The Legionnaire Captain wore twin golden hooves on shoulder epaulettes.

"I represent the diplomatic corps of the human species. We recently arrived on this tepui, which you may have heard from military scuttlebutt. I'm here to tell you that there's no reason to continue this stupid war. So, if you'd call it off, we humans would deem it a big favor. Thank you, sir."

"Request denied. I have my orders."

"And from whom do they come?"

The Captain sensed a trap, but for the life of him couldn't put a horny finger on it. "Um, from the General."

"This is only a suggestion, but let's troop the colors. Review the Goldie military establishment and do a reconnoiter."

"Like what?" The Captain was puzzled.

"You are likely," Mack rubbed his chin, "the new Number One Big Guy for the Goldie National Tepui, Inc. That means you have to make ultimate decisions. There are no generals, lieutenant generals, major generals, brigadier generals, bird Colonels, lieutenant colonels, or majors left in the Goldie armed forces."

"You're joking. I couldn't be Big Guy Number One. There are five or six thousand officers who outrank me. Plus, the entire government bureaucracy, which numbers in the gazillions."

"How many missiles do you fire every minute? I assume it's about the same as the Ermies and Ivies."

"That, sir, is a compound question and I object."

"Oh, no, Captain sir. You weren't a lawyer in real life, were you? Are you a product of the national guard, whatever it's called on this tepui?"

"Well, yes sir, I am. I have a sweet little practice to go back to when this little fracas is over."

"It could be over right now, soldier, if you deem it appropriate."

"But I have my orders. Oops. Getting a little behind here." The Captain extracted a celluloid strip from a pouch bulging with similar tabs. He fed it into the missile launcher that had stopped for the merest split second. It burped and re-embarked on its lethal mission, rat-a-tat-tatting missiles like mad.

"What are you down to on your little strips there, Captain?"

The Captain said, suspiciously, "What do you mean, down to?"

"Is that still a lieutenant's strip or are you down to sergeants yet?"

"Oh, I see what you mean." The Captain pulled out a pair of horn rim glasses and fitted them over his wide nose. "Now I really see what you mean." He grinned. "Yep. This is a sergeant strip. Probably hit privates pretty soon. But how did you know?"

"Let's take a walk, Captain. Back down the row of casserole pans."

369

The captain's look said he was a little busy. Mack rolled his eyes. "Pull the missile launcher behind you and you won't miss a beat. I'm sure you won't be charged with being AWOL."

"Yes, that could impact a civilian career."

"Yes, I know. We're working our way backward here. You know what these are?"

"Well, sure. These are the funerary depositories for our dear recently departed."

"Any idea why you aren't in one?"

At the Captain's blank look Mack said, "Take a look." The missile launcher continued faultlessly as the captain bent to peer through the bottom of his horn rims. He whipped them off a second later.

"Got to get new glasses. Eyes not as young as they used to be." He looked closer. "Right. They're all captains. I knew one of them. Of course, I was only called up this morning."

"Figured something like that. Otherwise the Ermies would have shot your number by now. Let's work our way back, a little faster. See these here?"

"That's not real good English, Mr. Ambassador. Are you sure you're duly accredited?"

"Well, of course." Mack was a little snippy, "But take a closer look. That messy mass is the General. I knew him well, a few minutes ago."

"But there are more trays behind his."

"He was outranked by the Big Guys, the Judge Pope, and a few others. There are seven trays before the General. Can you make out the inscriptions?"

The captain went to the first tray and stiffened to rigid attention. "That's Big Guy Number One Btsht. I never met him."

"He was a particular friend of mine," said Mack sadly. "Do you understand you're the Number One Big Guy, that no one outranks you? You can call this silly war off and go back to your lucrative practice of law."

"No way." The Captain jammed three more strips into the missile launcher. "We're kicking ass, down to buck privates now. Pretty soon we'll have wiped out the entire Ermie and Ivie tepuis. And to think I did it single-handed. I'll get a commendation."

"You, you—you—Captain. You can give yourself your own commendation. You're the ranking Goldie. Don't you understand?"

"Hey," said a voice out of the tinny wilderness. "He's right. The Ermies are down to buck privates and counting. Which brings me to a most topical quote, as you might have anticipated. 'War is Peace; Freedom is Slavery; Ignorance is Strength.' That sounds familiar."

"Well it should, you dolt. That's *Animal Farm*. Even an Aussie would recognize that."

"You're the dolt, Mack, because that's the first quote you've recognized."

"What's happened to the intellectual capacity of our youth?"

"You don't fit the youth category," said Lucas. "You're forty."

"I know you're a meager thirty-two. That you have no practical experience dealing with alien nations. So, I must get back to the Captain." Mack snapped his fingers. "Captain."

"Yes, sir, Mr. Ambassador," counting the sheaf of celluloid strips and paying no attention to Mack.

"Follow me to the dungeon to see if anyone's left." Mack was worried about Ellen, Madison, Peter, Roy, Barry, and Courtney, in approximately that order. At the Captain's hesitation Mack said, "Bring the missile launcher along."

"Well." The Captain hesitated.

"I doubt there's any ranking Goldies left. The dungeon doors were blown out."

"Then there's no reason to go." He tugged the missile launcher back to its former position.

"Actually, there is. I have to talk sense into you before the Ermie missiles get down to lawyers, though that might take a while. And then where will you be? Come along now."

Mack led the way down the emerald road with the Captain in hesitant steps behind, towing the launcher as it spit ten missiles a second. The Captain looked like a two-year-old

371

with a pull toy, deciding whether to follow Mom or stamp his foot in rebellion.

"Hey, guys. I'm back." Mack felt his way into the smoke-filled dungeon. The Captain furiously rubbed his eyes as the missile launcher bounced around like a blob of grease on a red-hot griddle.

"Over here," came a voice, sounded like Courtney.

"Hey, Court. What's up?" said Mack, feeling exuberant.

"Ellen's dying."

Mack's spirits plunged. "She's what?" he screamed, gritting his teeth.

"Dying, stupid. What part of dying don't you understand?" Courtney was exasperated.

"Oh my god. I'm coming. Where is she?" He wind-milled into the choking smoke, stumbling and sliding across the floor on his chest. The front of his uniform ripped as he skidded into the circle surrounding Ellen.

"What happened?" he demanded, jumping up, brushing the shredded uniform.

"It's all your fault." Courtney stood with hands on her hips. "You should have been here."

"But what happened?"

"They put us in protective custody. We were surrounded by Legionnaires who said they'd shield us. I didn't believe a word of it."

"So, what happened?"

"The Legionnaires exploded at the same time. Actually, they kind of collapsed. Like turning inside out, ending up in loaf-pan coffins. Quite large loaf pans. You could bake a moose in one."

"They imploded?" Mack stared at Ellen's pitiful figure. She was as white as a holy ghost, hands demurely at her sides, eyes closed, and her long black hair spread out like a fan. The bodice of her tattered blouse had been adjusted to conceal instead of reveal, barely rising and falling. Her fingers twitched as he looked down at her shapely legs. "Where's her foot?"

"I was getting to that." Courtney dripped rebuke.

Mack inched forward and grasped a waxy hand.

"One of the coffins— They weigh quite a lot."

"I know they weigh a lot."

"It formed on her foot and sort of bit it off. The coffin was sitting over there but it's left now, scooted down the row somewhere."

"Did you look inside? Try to find her foot?" He massaged her hand, which felt like a frozen candle. "Brrrr."

"It must have been under the Legionnaire's body. You know. The red jelly that quivers like—"

"You tried a tourniquet?"

"Biggest shoe string we could find."

"She'd already bled a lot?"

"She had." Courtney slapped Mack on the back, trying to buck him up. "I'm afraid she's a goner."

Ellen's hand gave a twitch and was still. Mack stood terror-stricken, dropping her hand, which clunked on the floor. Mack flinched like he'd been slapped, tears coursing down shaggy cheeks.

"For god's sake," objected Lucas. "You were never meant for each other. You only had a cheap case of the hots."

"She was really pretty and nice. I think I loved her."

"You couldn't have loved her. She was Catholic and married, and you're a newborn heathen. You two would have made Romeo and Juliet look like chump change. A relationship wouldn't have lasted twelve minutes."

"But what a twelve minutes. I know you're right, but what does that have to do with it? She was lovely and sometimes kind. I am so disappointed in her god. What good did he do her? What am I saying?"

"Who knows? Maybe she's schmoozing on the right hand of her god this very second. But think about this. 'It is absurd to call him a God of justice and goodness, who inflicts evil indiscriminately on the good and the wicked, upon the innocent and the guilty. It is idle to demand that the unfortunate should console themselves for their misfortunes in the very arms of the one who alone is the author of them.' I hope that helps."

"That sucks. She would have hated it. You're sullying the memory of a women I really liked a lot, probably loved."

"It's a good thing I'm not doing your performance evaluation. You're a disgrace to state service, wearing your libido on your sleeve."

"The human race is poorer by your existence," said Courtney. "Ellen was a married woman."

"Lay off the poor guy," said Peter. He and Roy awkwardly patted Mack on the back while Barry stood like a dunce, shocked at Ellen's demise.

Madison said, "I don't know what to say just now, but Courtney dear don't start a row. Mack has lost a dream I fear, for lovely Ellen was a dear, on occasion."

"What do you mean, 'on occasion'?" said Mack. "Her prickly moments were justified by the mere fact of my presence. Did you resign from the rhyming poets society?"

Madison shrugged as the floor shuddered and Courtney said, "The missiles have stopped and something weird is going on."

Mack yelled through billowing smoke, "Oh Captain, my Captain. Where art thou? Is something amiss? Have you decided to end the war? Where are you?" No answer.

"We should go look for him," said Peter.

"We have to take care of Ellen first," said Mack.

"How can we take care of her?" said Roy. "She's gone as far downhill as she can go."

"I hate to say it." Mack shook his head. "But we have to give her a Christian burial. Commemorate her memory. I want to make a speech."

"We'll take her remains back when we're rescued by the air force men in blue," said Barry. "I almost think they're going to show up."

"You have a point. The air force is on its way and she will return for proper burial. I'm glad that's settled. There no place on this tepui where we could dig far enough to bury anyone. And we shouldn't leave her here anyway."

"How do they bury the loaf pans?" said Peter.

"That's their problem. I'm going to find the Captain. The smoke is clearing since the missiles stopped firing."

"It's not just that," said Courtney. "It's the quietest I can remember."

"That's true." Mack looked sorrowfully at Ellen. "Courtney. Would you get her ready to go back with us?"

"I will," said Courtney.

"Come on guys. We're going after the Captain. See whether the war is over." The floor started cracking.

"It's coming from over there." Peter pointed at the line of loaf pans. "At the end, where the Big Number One Guy's pure golden thingamabob is." The smoke cleared and they could see Btsht's loaf pan glowing, an elephant-sized ingot of molten gold. With dignity it sank into the floor of the dungeon.

"What the hell—" Mack raced forward. "Look at this. It's melting the floor, which liquefies easily. Must be lead." He dug at the floor with a fingernail. "Yep, lead."

"Who cares what it is," said Roy. "It's making me go further downhill than I ever been."

They watched uneasily as the coffin lowered itself into the dungeon floor and disappeared. Lead flowed over the top as the next coffin in line glowed gold and sank.

"Catch the name on that one," said Mack. "We never knew who took over from Btsht."

"It's our good buddy, Judge Grdam. Our former warden has been released from his bonds." Barry was somber.

Mack shook his head. "I didn't believe him when he said he was next in line. I'm going upstairs, find the Captain. See whether the war's over and it's safe to come out. Anyone want to go with me? Roy, Peter, Barry? Okay, Madison. Come along."

"Thank ye, boss. I be cool, rap along, like a fool."

"Please, Madison. I'm not ready for rap."

"Mea culpa ding-a-ling, nor am I, I have to sing." Madison pasted on a goofy smile as they tiptoed out of the dungeon, the huge doors hanging awry.

"Right around the corner."

"Well if you'll look, I think you'll see, he ain't here, so where he be?"

"Oh, Christ. It shouldn't be hard to find him." Missiles began firing above their heads as Mack broke into a run with Madison right behind. They groped their way through black tarry smoke as missiles exploded left and right.

"Captain," yelled Mack. "Where are you? We can't see diddley."

"You can't be an ambassador. Your English is abominable," said the Captain.

"Whatever you say. Have you grown war weary yet, so we can call off the slaughter?"

"Don't be ridiculous." They could finally see the Captain through the haze, feeding celluloid strips into the missile launcher, lickety-split.

"Don't you be ridiculous. Whoever gave you the order is dead and buried under the dungeon floor. You can be your own antelope now."

"I have always been my own antelope," sneered the Captain. "Go away. I've sworn to uphold the dignity of the Golden Antelopes, which I'll do until my dying breath. We're really kicking butt now. I found fresh disks for the super maximum smart missile launcher. See that baby go."

"Who are you shooting at? You must have exterminated everyone in the Ermie and Ivie armies by now."

"Sure did. That's when I ran out of disks. But I searched the General's office, got the combination to the safe, and found stacks of these babies. See."

"They aren't labeled." Mack nosed through the piles.

"They're Ermie and Ivie civilians, starting with court personnel."

"Baliffs then?"

The Captain continued, "—court reporters, clerks, marshals, process servers. They were feather bedders anyway. Got rid of the entire legislative branch. Senators and representatives and interns and pages. Knocked off all the lobbyists." The Captain rubbed horny hands together. "Then the entire military industrial complex."

"I take it they've done the same so there are no Goldie equivalents left."

"Don't know. But you hit the old nail on the head. It's a good thing I was called up this morning. Otherwise the war would be over and the Goldie nation beaten into submission. But thank God for me, eh? Otherwise I couldn't have taken over and gotten things done. If I'd been in the army before, I might

376

have been killed." The Captain seemed shocked at the possibility. But it was difficult to read his wide face in the sooty smoke.

"Might have been, eh," snorted Mack. "So, you're murdering civilians since they're the only ones left. The Ermies will target Goldie lawyers any second now."

Madison said, "Slash your throat and make you terminal, you're a common wartime criminal."

"Are you threatening me?" roared the Captain. "There's no diplomatic immunity here. I can take your identification and feed it into the super maximum smart missile launcher. See how you like that."

"You've got no balls that I can see, take your gun and you would flee." Madison stuck out a fat pink tongue.

"Enough," said Mack as the Captain lunged for Madison. Madison ducked behind Mack, who was flattened by the Captain.

The missile launcher fell silent for want of disks as the Captain stooped to help Mack up. He mumbled, "Sorry about that. I didn't mean to create a diplomatic incident."

"Well, you came pretty darn close," said Mack, milking his miff. He held up a hand as the Captain rushed back to the missile launcher. "Before you create so much racket we can't think and so much smoke we can't see, let's take a minute to resolve this conflict. It's far worse for you than us. We've only lost one person and I mourn her dearly. But you've lost hundreds of thousands and your losses continue."

The incoming shells pounded rhythmically into the tepui, shaking it with each blow. "I'm falling down on the job." The Captain shoved a fresh batch of disks into the smoking missile launcher and it resumed its rain of death.

"The reason for the war has ended."

"I never heard what the reason was. Except we were attacked by the scurrilous Ermies and Ivies. They want to wipe us out and commit antelopeicide. Only scoundrels like the Ermies and Ivies would attack a peace-loving nation like ourselves."

"It was a simple misunderstanding. The Goldie Big Guys were frantic at being discovered by humans, while the

Ivies and Ermies thought it would happen sooner or later. So, the Ermies and Ivies decided to welcome our rescuers and come out of hiding. This difference of opinion flared from insults to open war when our air force men in blue headed this way. Thus, the reason for war has vanished, assuming there was one to begin with. The Goldies didn't want to go to war with the Ermies and Ivies any more than vice versa. Which means you can stop the war. In fact, I have the perfect method of communication. An open mic to the Ermie tepui, right here." Mack pointed to his tattered lapel.

The Captain raised a shaggy eyebrow. "Your rescuers are rather slow. If they were really coming, they'd be here by now."

"Certainly not. They left when the war started and that was only—What time is it? I've lost track but it wasn't more than an hour ago."

"Doesn't make any difference. As a member of the bar I have a finely honed sense of duty and patriotism. I will follow orders until no longer able. Besides, what you said doesn't make sense. You'd put us in zoos the second we're discovered."

"You're already discovered and the whole world will know about you in five more minutes. The air force men in blue will be accompanied by a CNN cameraman. You'll be on the front page of every newspaper on the planet. There's no reason to continue the war, so let's call it off right now. Use my lapel mic and call the Ermies and Ivies, urge a cease-fire. They'd like that as much as you would."

"Sorry," said the Captain. "I have no interest in stopping the war. And the Ermies and Ivies don't want to stop it either. Spiffy little trap you tried getting me into."

"You're not listening. The war began because your bosses were afraid of being discovered by us. But the whole world will know about you in a few seconds. So, stop it! If you don't stop now, you'll end up worse than in a zoo."

"Threats and logic have no effect on me." The Captain looked proud of himself as he shoved more disks into the rapidly puffing missile launcher.

"Squawk," shrieked Mack's mic as Lucas said, "You're striking out because you keep repeating yourself. 'Nothing is said nowadays that hasn't been said before.' You'd do better with a fresh argument."

"And what have you been doing for the peace effort? Have you talked sense into whoever's leading the Ermie side?"

"If there were anyone around to talk to, I'd try, but I haven't seen an Ermie for ages. And Ermie coffins have been burying themselves the same as the Goldies'. I don't know if there are survivors, who's running the show, or where Ermie missiles are firing from."

"What do you mean no one to talk to? Don't you have your group?"

"Yes. All of them: Benny, James, and Billy K., though Mary's doing right poorly, hanging on by a thread, and Nick is incoherent. They just got back. All the Ermies have disappeared. Maybe in hiding. Hey. One just ran past the door."

"Send someone after him and find out what's going on."

"Actually, James tried, but they're faster'n snot. We only know the war's still going on."

"Then come back to the Goldie tepui. If we were together, we could figure a way out."

"Good point. Why stick around here if they can rescue us from the same tepui. Of course, we don't exactly know to get back. I know where the pneumatic tubes are. But I don't know how they work."

Mack could hear Billy K. say, "I know how they work."

"Hey, Your Excellency," yelled the Captain. "What are you cooking up over there? You guys don't have visas. The Goldie government requires visas *before* arrival."

"You're the Goldie government," said Mack. "What's your personal policy on letting them come back?"

"It's not a very good idea." The Captain joyfully stuffed disks into the missile launcher, which was hopping around like on fire. "It's bad enough that you're here. We don't want more aliens on our noble Goldie tepui."

"You're a racist."

"So, what's new? Everyone prefers their own kind. If that's racism, then everyone's a racist. Besides, it's more like speciesism than racism. Humans eat other species after raising them."

At Mack's chagrined look the Captain said, "Racist liar, pants on fire."

Madison ducked behind Mack, waving his hands in a reggae beat. "That's not bad oh Captain, my Captain. Pretty soon you be able to rap them. Snap them horny fingernails when you search for holy grails. Your heritage is all gone phooey, no one left on this tepui. Where they gone do you suppose, maybe screwed by Ermie Hos. So, listen up—" The Captain swung the stainless-steel missile launcher at Madison's ample middle.

"I surrender, guess I better, otherwise I'll end as butter." Madison held his hands up as smart missiles spurted from the launcher, dipping and swerving to avoid Madison as they homed in on preprogramed targets.

Mack nudged the Captain in the ribs. "I have an idea."

"Watch it, buster. I'm ticklish."

"Right, but I have a great idea. What's the exchange rate between whatever your currency is and the Yankee dollar?"

"That's the dumbest question I ever heard. We don't have an exchange rate because we don't exchange. End of story."

"But Btsht hinted that you sometimes slip into Caracas incognito during Carnival. You might have changed a few shekels then."

"Never heard of it myself. But I'm just a country lawyer."

"Let's try this," said Mack. "What does a pound of your colorful fodder cost in whatever your currency is?"

"Colorful fodder?" The Captain was puzzled. "Oh, the stuff they fed you. I heard about that. It was all over antelopebook. It's fed to criminals and lunatics. We don't eat the stuff ourselves. We eat fresh fruits and veg, not other species like some do."

"You didn't answer the question." Mack felt queasy for no particular reason. "How much does an average meal cost in whatever your currency is? This is not an idle question and could make you tons of money."

"We don't have bank accounts and we don't have to pay for food." The Captain turned his back, slamming floppy disks into the super chromium missile launcher.

Mack gritted his teeth. "Surely you have coin, paper, or plastic that you use to buy items not provided by the government. What do you call that?"

"Filthy lucre." The Captain laughed. "We're not into capitalism."

"What do you use this filthy lucre for?"

The Captain shrugged. "We tithe to the Holy Goldie Church. Every Thursday at services, and fortnightly at 'Ohmigods,' a special celebration presided over by the Judge Pope. Or whatever he's called now."

"Right now, he's called 'dead and buried.' How many Goldie dollars do you contribute, say weekly, to the church?"

"Not dollars." The Captain held his big wide nose with horny fingers. "Goldie Getz, named after the mother of our country."

"I've been meaning to ask why there are no females on the Goldie tepui, yet your gods and the founder of your country are all females. What gives?"

The Captain had a sly look. "We're androgynous. You've only seen what you think are males, such as myself. But when we go home to our husbands, we're females. Naturally it's a sexist culture."

"We've gotten off track. How many Getz would it take to buy the Goldie tepui? I'm sure the US government would buy it to put a stop to this stupid war. And how many Getz would it cost to get visas for my compadres, who will be here shortly? We can combine the two amounts and stop the war when my friends arrive. Or would that be too much to ask?"

"Whoa." The Captain turned from the Gatling missile launcher. "Are you trying to bribe a government official? And exactly how much did you have in mind."

"Wise choice. Your economy is kaput and you're the entire government. How much do you want?"

The Captain's contemplation was interrupted by, "Yo Mama, baby. We're back. Great to see youse guys."

Mack did a double-take at his lapel mic before he realized it was Lucas in the flesh. Mack threw his arms open as Lucas jumped into them. "I am so happy to see you back. All of you." Mack hugged Lucas extra hard, letting him go and doing the same with Billy K., who said, "Real good to see you." Ef harrumphed like he was clearing his throat, and James did his famous hand-cutting-the-air trick. Benny practically whinnied, which left somber Nick. Nick hugged Mack with one arm while holding pasty Mary up with the other.

Mack kissed Mary on the cheek and her eyelids fluttered. Nick lowered her to the cold white floor of the auditorium, streaked gray by blow back from the super-duper missile launcher. Mack said, "The rest are downstairs. That's where Ellen's body rests—" He burst out crying. "I miss her a lot."

"No visas," said the Captain. "Your friends will have to go back where they came from."

"Think about it when you get time. I made you a fair offer but you never named a price."

"You may have started to make an offer but you never did."

"Okay, but include visas and an end to the war. A package deal."

"Hi sailor," said a big, big voice.

19

Mack couldn't believe Reg was walking toward him with the rest of his gang in tow. This required twice the hugs. Fats thanked his karma and Rudd said the Arizona Lottery completely botched everything. Betty and Molly bubbled over at seeing everyone again, while Arturo was the usual introvert.

The Captain said, "That doubles the number of visas. Costs are shooting up." He didn't miss feeding little plastic cards into the huge spitting bazooka for a single millisecond.

"We can't make a deal when you're busy with your toy," said Mack. "Shut the missiles down for a minute so we can work things out."

"No need. I'm way ahead in the war game. There are only a thousand cards left so that gives us a hundred seconds. What's your offer? And don't forget that in addition to let's see—hmmmm, thirteen visas, plus you want to buy the entire government."

"Right now, it's not a very big government."

"Maybe so, but it's all we've got and that's what it takes to stop the war."

"Watch this shyster," said Lucas before Mack could respond. "'A government big enough to give you everything you want is a government big enough to take from you everything you have.' I don't know who said it but it must fit, because it came to mind immediately."

"You never learn," said Mack. "He just said the government isn't very big. So, it can't give us everything we want. Or take away everything we have. Besides, we're trying to buy the damn thing. Not get something from it. So, your latest stupid quote doesn't fit."

Mack paused. "Sorry, Captain. My buddy here is a constant distraction. I hope we have some of the hundred seconds left because I'm prepared to offer you five thousand Yankee dollars for each visa. That totals sixty-five thousand big ones. I'll double that to buy the entire Goldie government, lock stock and barrel. You are released from government service and can return to your country law practice. Whataya say Captain, my Captain?"

"I don't know how much a thousand Yankee dollars are worth. Much less sixty-five or a hundred thirty thousand."

"That's why I was trying to find a Goldie equivalent. So, we can make a deal. But I have to make sure the cash is available before I can make a firm offer. Troops." Mack turned to the new arrivals. "Could you each contribute a share so we give a hundred thirty thousand bucks to the Captain? How much is that apiece?"

"Well." Lucas wrinkled his brow. "There's seventeen shares, counting Nick and Mary as one since Nick brought a spouse. So, all you have to do is divide seventeen into a hundred thirty thousand."

"Who has a calculator?" Mack looked at blank faces. He scratched his head a few times, mumbling to himself, "—and carry the two. Got it. It comes out to seven thousand six hundred forty-seven dollars each."

Lucas laughed. "As if anyone has change. So, round it off to seventy-six hundred and the Captain can make do."

"Got it." Mack gnashed his teeth in calculation. "Everyone has to kick in. Since the lottery gave you ten thousand each for spending money, that shouldn't be a problem. We'll be rescued in a few minutes and your contribution will guarantee that none of us are blown up and allow our air force men in blue to land without also being blown to smithereens."

At their blank looks Mack said, "Madison, run down and get the others. Please."

Madison said, "Gone am I, gone down the road. Stumbling emer'lds like a toad. But I'll fetch them, come what may. Kick their butts, back this way." He danced merrily out and was gone.

"He's a good man." Mack addressed the group. "Can you contribute part of your pocket money for the cause? Ensure our safety. Shut the guns off and get us home?" He added, "I'm sure the lottery will reimburse you when we get back."

"You mean we're not going to Rio after we're rescued?" said Rudd. "That's a crock. The lottery owes us a big trip. Not only is it a matter of contract, but they're honor-bound."

"We'll take that up with the lottery when we get back. I'll be your spokesperson. I promise."

The Captain was back slinging missiles, bored by the conversation. Mack said, "Come on my fellow Americans. Let's chip in and get our butts home."

"Good idea," said Reg. "I heartily recommend that my crew chip in seventy-six hundred apiece and here's mine to start."

"Thanks, Reg." Mack looked at Lucas expectantly.

"Sure," said Lucas. "We'll go along with that, too, and hopefully your group will follow suit."

"Thanks for the vote of confidence," as Mack's group came straggling in behind Madison, carrying Ellen's body above their heads.

Mack blanched. "Put her down, gently."

"Of course." Courtney helped lower Ellen onto the streaked floor. "We wrapped her up as best we could."

"Good job." Mack turned away so he couldn't see. "We're going to settle the war, buy the tepui and visas, and secure the area for the arrival of our rescuers. I've negotiated a price with the sole surviving member of the Goldie government."

"That's me," said the Captain proudly. "I think Mr. Mack is right. There's no one left but me. Otherwise, they would have relieved me of command a long time ago."

"Right. We're going to kick in seventy-six hundred apiece. What's the problem, Rudd?" Rudd had his obstinate look on.

Everyone turned and glared at Rudd to no effect whatsoever. "Anyway," said Mack. "If you could pony up, we'll get this thing settled."

"One point," said Ef. "Seventy-six hundred apiece from seventeen people is less than a hundred thirty thou. Are you taking a rake off?"

"Of course, not. I was about to approach the Captain with the exact amount but he's been busy."

"I'm not doing it for less than a hundred thirty thousand Yankee dollars," said the Captain. "Are you already starting to welch? Don't answer that because I have another question. What happens to the Goldie religion? Are you buying that too?"

"Of course not. I can't imagine what we'd do with it."

"It's kind of like the government. Selling the government and issuing all these visas might compromise our sacred religion. After all, that woman there is a heretic. She was convicted."

Mack stared back. "That's old history. The former Big Guy Honorable Btsht was going to pardon her. That would have been the end of it, but war broke out."

"So, he didn't pardon her and she still stands convicted of heresy, correct?"

"But he was going to pardon her. It was a done deal, pretty much."

"I'll butt in here," said Lucas, "with an utterly apropos quote."

Mack groaned but the Captain looked interested. "Who're you going to quote?"

"Well, I don't rightly know, but it's squarely on point. Maybe it will let us get to something more important."

The Captain scoffed. "Nothing's more important than avoiding the compromise of the Goldie religion. But you have one chance. Make it a good one."

"Indeed, I will. 'See skulking Truth to her old cavern fled, Mountains of casuistry heap'd o'er her head! Philosophy, that lean'd on Heaven before, Shrinks to her second cause, and is no more. Physic or metaphysic begs defense, and Metaphysic calls for aid on Sense! See Mystery to Mathematics fly! In vain! They gaze, turn giddy, rave, and die. Religion, blushing, veils her sacred fires, and unawares, Morality expires.' Pretty good, eh, Honorable Big Guy Number One Captain?"

The Captain was dazed, whether from his new title or the quote itself. "Well, yes, that might be— Funny quote you had there, Mr. Lucas. I may call you Mr. Lucas?"

"You are the Number One Big Guy. You can call me whatever you want."

"Thanks." The Captain ignored the silent missile launcher. "Are you saying—" he paused. "Saying that religion could be immoral? That's a pretty hefty accusation, don't you think?"

"He doesn't think," said Mack. "He quotes. Don't take offense because he can't help it. Quotes come rolling out of him like topsy."

"How much is a hundred thirty thousand Yankee dollars? What would that buy?"

"The whole tepui. Don't think of holding us up for more. That's all we have available, and actually, we might not have quite that much."

"I couldn't help overhearing that your group has a hundred seventy thousand in pocket change. A hundred seventy thousand has bigger ring to it, you know what I mean?"

"I do know what you mean. But I'll be lucky to squeeze a hundred thirty grand out of these tightwads. Look at their faces. That one over there, for example. You could torture him within an inch of his rotten miserable life and he wouldn't kick in a hundred dollars."

The Captain peered at Rudd. "I see what you mean. Tell you what. A hundred thirty thousand Yankee dollars sounds like a chunk of change. Besides, your friends are already here and I really don't want to send them back. I'm worried about where the rest of the Goldies are. It hasn't been this quiet since August when everyone was on vacation—" A boom went off exceptionally close, though not in their line of sight. "Quiet, except for the explosions. Oh my God, I forgot to feed the missile launcher. Go ahead and get the money together. I have to get back to work."

The Captain charged back to the super-duper chromium missile Gatling gun, fiddling with his pockets as he ran, extracting diskettes.

"Hey. Wait a minute," said Mack. "We've got a deal, so the war is over. Don't feed that gun." But it was too late. The gun was belching ten times a second.

The Captain turned around, bemused. "I got stuff going on here. Until you come up with cold cash, the war continues."

Kerboom, a dumb missile landed within their line of sight, smashing pulpits and raining toothpicks on their head.

"They aren't all smart bombs," said Mack. "So, to avoid annihilation we'd better get the money together. Come on, guys. Put your contributions in this little box. It's the top of a court reporting machine, abandoned by baliffs busy burying themselves."

"They were still burying themselves when Madison came after us," said Courtney. "It's a sad thing, not having Christian burials."

"They aren't, weren't, and never will be Christians." Mack crammed stacks of bills into the shell of the court reporting machine as Lucas pressed them flat and handed them over. "Besides, you said antelopes are mere animals. Christians don't bury animals with honors."

Courtney stamped a burly brogan. "I don't think they're animals anymore. They might have souls. Might be worth saving."

"They're not in the image of your Baptist god, but don't argue. We need to get off of this dratted tepui." Mack asked Lucas, "How much does that make?"

"Well, we got contributions from everyone but Ellen, and as predicted, from Rudd. I hope you didn't count Ellen in the total?"

"Why did you have to mention her?" Mack was freshly stricken. "And you did it twice!"

"Only to make sure you didn't screw up the calculation. Let's see. There's Courtney, of course, and the rest of your crew who survived—"

"Thanks, a whole lot."

"Barry, Peter, Roy, and Madison, which is five and my group makes ten and with Reg's bunch you have a total of sixteen. At seventy-six hundred each, counting Rudd, that's a hundred twenty-one thou. Without Rudd we're down to a hundred fourteen. You really miscounted."

"I forget to leave Ellen out of the count," said Mack. "My mistake. And of course, I shouldn't have included Rudd."

"Okay," said Rudd, as Reg pushed him forward, "Here's five hundred."

"Thanks a lot," said Mack. "I hope that didn't strain you."

"I'm still working on him," said Reg.

"Ahem," said Mack to the Captain. "We've been able to raise about a hundred seven thousand."

"You're welching," yelled the Captain over the infernal noise of the missile launcher. "You're not trying hard enough. You should be looking through the dead girl's purse."

Mack went ballistic, slamming the box of money on the floor and careening off the Captain's backside with both fists. The Captain swatted Mack a backhand that dropped Mack like a lead balloon. Mack jumped to his feet and grabbed the Captain's horny paw, sticking the tips into his mouth, blowing a note so shrill that the Captain ripped the horny hand from Mack's lips, slammed both paws over his ears, and swooned to the floor.

"So, you'll take the hundred seven grand, right?" Mack dropped the box of money on the Captain's heaving chest.

The Captain's eyes fluttered. "What did you say, Mr. Mack? Whatever it was, that's fine."

"Shut the missile launcher down."

"It's running the last disks." The Captain bounded up on tiny feet, the money box clasped to his chest as the gun hiccupped and went silent.

"Quiet as a dead rattler, hain't it?" said Billy K. "We should get on the horn. Call up them Ermies and get them to cut it out too."

"Hey, Cap'n," said Mack. "Why are missiles tearing up property? I thought they were smarter than that."

The Captain turned from tiptoeing out of the auditorium. "They're made and fired by Ermies, so there's no accounting for them." At their skeptical looks he said, "They've probably been buzzing around since the war began. Looking for someone who's already deceased, or nowhere to be found. They give up and settle for property damage." He backed out of the big room with the money box behind his back.

"Go get him," said Rudd. "He has our money and there was no reason to give it to him. The war's over and no one's left to deport us. Mack pulled another dumb move." Rudd paused, "Listen."

Except for the patter of their own feet, it was quiet as they ran after the rapidly disappearing Captain. The procession puffed up the emerald road where blown-out doors opened onto the surface of the tepui.

"Mr. Rudd is partly correct," said the Captain as they straggled into open air. "The war is over and you're not going to be deported. But I fulfilled my part of the contract. I earned every cent of this paltry hundred seven thou."

"They're coming," yelled Mack joyfully. "See up there in the wild blue yonder. It's our air force men in blue."

Everyone corkscrewed their necks, peering into the brilliant sky. Three contrails burned ribbons in the heavens, swooping toward them. Two jets barely skimmed the surface of the tepui as the third did a fancy side slip and dipsy-doodle, dodging boulders as big as buildings as it came skidding in. That same second a black missile caught the Captain full frontal. His earthly remains of quivering red jelly were deposited in a metal box, which about-faced and slid down the emerald road as the air force jet rolled to a stop in front of them.

The pilot flipped the canopy open and jumped down from the sleek jet. "Howdy, buckaroos," he said. "Whar is yore aircraft?"

"Weeelll, I reckon we misplaced it," said Mack.

"He's a captain too," said Barry.

"Funny coincidence, don't you think?" said Benny.

"That other captain disappeared really fast," said Betty Boop, twirling gingham skirts.

"I thought he was cute in an antelope kind of way," said Molly.

"We were kidnapped by aliens," said Fats.

"We have to get our money back," said Rudd, everyone nodding in unison.

The new captain said, "Mass hysteria. It'll pass."

"Well, no. I don't think it will," said Mack. "You see—It's a long story."

"Praise the Lord, hallelujah," said Courtney. "Though I kind of miss being fried in oil. It would have only been fitting."

"Praise the Lord, amen," said Reg.

"We are saved," said Ef. "Another day, another parcel of real estate to peddle. You're right, Courtney. Hallelujah." Ef grabbed Courtney's hands and danced a jig.

"Don't make light of it, you boob." Courtney snatched her hands back. "We've been saved by the one true God, who moves in mysterious ways. He didn't do it so you could clean up on Ussery Pass real estate."

"Got it," said Lucas. "Here we go. 'But inasmuch as He is the one true God, wholly incomprehensible and inaccessible to man's understanding, it is reasonable, indeed inevitable, that His justice also should be incomprehensible.' That pretty much sums it up."

"Nut cases," muttered the new captain. "Who's in charge here?"

"Didn't you see anything?" said Mack. "Weren't you paying attention?"

"What are you babbling on about? I just got here. I've had no time to see anything."

"When you were landing this lovely aircraft." Mack rubbed the shiny nose. "Didn't you see a missile swoop out of the sky and cream a rather large antelope, standing right about where we are now?"

The new captain peered at them like they were mad. "I've been busy. This isn't the most hospitable environment to land a multimillion-dollar aircraft. Just to rescue a bunch of civilians." At their gaping looks he added, "Sorry. Didn't mean to offend you."

"You certainly took your time getting here," said Rudd, pushing into the captain's face. "We've been here for days."

"Two and a half days. It took us that long to get permission to enter Venezuelan airspace. We did pretty darn good, considering the Micky Mouse red tape we had to go through. Made you all famous. I recognize ever last one of you.

Well, except you two," he said, indicating Lucas and Mack. "The rest have been on CNN for two days. 'Lottery Millionaires Disappear,' 'Rags to Glitches,' specials on each one of you. 'The People's Poet.' Right," said the Captain. He poked Madison in the stomach and flashed a worshipful grin. "Who could ever forget, 'A last sigh for a butterfly'?"

Madison beamed as the captain continued, "Or the valiant seventy-two-year-old widow. Before she won the lottery, she was already rich in land and cotton. Inherited from her recently deceased husband." He favored Courtney with a benevolent smile. "Your faith helped bring the group through. Am I right?" He faked a fast-draw, plugging Courtney between the eyes with his forefinger. "You rock, lady." Everyone gaped.

"The Tennessee cop." He pointed at Barry.

"The long-suffering Serbian Orthodox preacher," waving to Nick. "And his lovely wife." He did a double-take at Mary's pasty stare.

The Captain swiveled, pointing at Ef. "Now I remember you. You're the crackerjack real estate salesman." Then pointing at Reg, "The devout Catholic brother, retired from Wall Street at age thirty-eight. Of course, he donated his lottery winnings to the Church."

"You didn't," gasped Rudd. His ratty eyes begged Reg to say it wasn't so.

"And where's the beautiful housewife. She's the real star. I don't see her," said the Captain.

"She'll fly back with you," said Mack.

"Not with me. There's a cargo plane to take you back, though where it'll land I haven't a clue. I couldn't fit anyone in this little ole thang." He elbowed the fighter jet. "It's a single seater."

"Where'd your escorts go?"

"We triangulated the signal from the black box. And the special thermal indicator showed life on the surface of this desolate mesa. I don't know how the box got way down below with you on top, but we'll sort it out later. It's a miracle we found you at all."

"It's a miracle," said Courtney. "One minute I was condemned to boil in oil. The next I'm a celebrity, saved by the grace of God."

Mack said, "Our real savior was buying the Goldie government. But I give all the credit to our air force men in blue." He bowed to the Captain.

"Thanks for the complement to *your* air force. But what is a Goldie government? Our government is sure enough gold-plated but it ain't solid gold, yet." He laughed at the near witticism.

Courtney ignored the Captain. "Mack, you'll never learn. Oh, ye of little faith."

"Make that no faith at all. Faith is believing in something without a speck of evidence. Faith is belief based on sheer cantankerousness."

"Oh, yeah." Courtney squared up, hands clenched in front of her.

"Whoa, guys," said Lucas, slipping between them. "There's a middle ground. 'It is the final proof of God's omnipotence that he need not exist in order to save us.' If that doesn't satisfy Mack's skepticism and Courtney's dogmatism, nothing will."

"So, nothing will," said Mack. "We'll leave it at that. Okay, Courtney?"

She shrugged.

"Fair enough," said Reg. "Religion can once again recede into the background. We're headed back to secular-ville, and we're all rooting for Mary." Nick's eyes were woefully large as Reg said, "Face it, Courtney. We didn't do well here."

"We could have done better if they'd gone through with the execution." Courtney broke into song, "Just aboilin' in the oil, boiling in the oil. I'd 'ave been boilin' in the oil— Still, we have to thank the Lord. Thank you, Lord." She bowed her head.

"Black box," said Mack. "Air force men in blue. A god had nothing to do with it."

Courtney opened her eyes at the unholy interruption. "You get mighty feisty when you're almost home free. And you still need you mouth washed out with soap."

"We have our various viewpoints and never the twain shall meet," said Reg. "So, let it lie."

"The lie is all Mack's," said Courtney. "You know that as well as anyone."

Nick said, "Religion is a personal matter, sacred to each of us. No one should denigrate another's personal beliefs."

"Yeah," said Mack. "I'm always the bad guy. But if you can't question religious beliefs, then dangerous black cats and witches are off limits too. What's the difference between religion and superstition? Both are based on belief without the slightest evidence. Boogey men and shibboleths rustling in the night."

"On this earth we all must dwell. Otherwise it's Bambi-hell," said Madison.

"The kid's great," said the Captain, beaming, high-fiving Madison. "He really delivers."

"So does Pizza Hut," said Lucas. "We need more reconciliation and less delivery. With my uncanny ability to find a middle ground, here's your reconciliation. 'The great mystery is not that we should have been thrown down here at random between the profusion of matter and that of the stars; it is that from our very prison we should draw, from our own selves, images powerful enough to deny our nothingness.' Now that is cool."

"After the last few days, it's become difficult to deny our nothingness," said Mack. "But it won't convince Courtney of anything. She's personally acquainted with the guy who made more stars than we can count. Nothingness doesn't compute. Right, Courtney?"

"No mystery, no randomness, no problem," said Courtney. "I won't argue with the likes of you. When you know for sure, there's nothing to argue about."

"Sound like purt'inear all of us," said Billy K., giving the Captain a wink. "Everyone of us know it all, whether religion or most anything else. If you don't believe us, ask us."

"You should be happy," said the Captain, "instead of arguing stupid stuff about religion."

Mack shook his head. "We've just experienced religion up close and in our faces. Though we try to ignore it, it's

394

powerful stuff, sometimes lurking to ambush us in our beds. Unless we demystify it, face it head on, uncover its absurdities and weaknesses, we're indentured to religion. I prefer freedom."

"Mack has this new theory that he never makes clear," said Lucas. "I can sum it up. 'This would be the best of all possible worlds, if there were no religion in it.' I wish I knew who said this stuff. Of course, this last one's radical. Like John Lennon's *Imagine*. I don't suppose anyone of stature said it."

"I wrote a few keywords down." Mack waved a grimy notepad. "When we get back, we can plug them into a search engine and figure out who said what. Not that we care right now. Let's go see if there's anyone we want to say goodbye to while waiting for the cargo plane."

"What's that?" said the Captain. "Are there other survivors?"

"Not really," said Mack. "I just want to wander around for a few minutes. Visit places we explored the last few days. See if strange animals might be about. Some were sighted, you know. At times we felt like we were their guests."

"Maybe we shouldn't go poking around nooks and crannies," said Ef. "You never know what might be out there. Just be happy the way things turned out."

Mack frowned. "What turned out? The experience changed no one. Except me. Before all this I didn't care a hoot about religion. Now I do."

"Was your experience really that bad?" said the Captain. "Did you have enough food and water?"

"Yeah, we had plenty of food and water," said Lucas.

"It was quite posh," said Reg.

The Captain said, "You call rocks posh? Something weird is going on."

"Maybe. Maybe not," said Mack. "But Lucas and I will reconnoiter while you await the cargo plane. If we find anyone else, we'll let you know."

"We'll what?" Lucas waved his hands. "I don't think it's a good idea to go wandering around this dratted tepui, if you know what I mean." The others clustered in groups, talking excitedly about going home, ignoring Lucas and Mack.

"Over here," whispered Mack. "See that behind the big rock."

Lucas came with worry lines across his forehead. "See that?"

Mack snatched a particularly bent up object and dusted it off. A crunched-up court reporter's machine.

"Oh," said Lucas.

"Oh, indeed. And guess what. There's a lot more than a hundred seven grand." Mack flipped open the lid. The wad of money lay on top. Mack took it out and handed it to Lucas. "More importantly, see what's under it."

"Yeah. So? A bunch of paper. You prefer that to money?"

Mack lifted the paper and opened it up. "Take a look at the first page." Lucas glanced and did a double take. "A transcript in English. Well, that's interesting. But what good is it?"

"It includes your sacred quotes so I can pin them down. More importantly, it's a book about the world's first encounter with aliens. A definite best seller. There was a great old song called 'Take This Job and Shove It.' With this small box, I can do exactly that."

"What about me?"

"I promised you a sterling evaluation and you'll get it, assuming we get back. We can split the money."

"There's no reason to assume. We've been rescued and we're going back. Besides, they're my quotes. I should get a bigger cut."

"Oh, hell. You can have all the money. No, I'll keep ten grand to get me back to the States. In the meantime, let's head to the edge of the tepui. You weren't here when we explored it, but I have a surprise." Mack stuffed the transcript back in the battered box, laying the cash on top.

"But we have a ride home we don't want to miss. What if antelopes come out of hiding?"

"Don't worry about that. Anyway, I'm not going back on a plane with Ellen's body."

"You were serious about her?"

"Well, as serious as I've been for a while. She was fabulous, and religious, like my mom likes."

"She was a religious nut, and married. I told you I have a friend named Nancy who looks like Ellen. She's not a religious nut and she's single. But last year you worried about your mum meeting her."

"I've gotten over mom's religious persnicketies. I just want to get off this tepui. We stashed a healthy coil of rope over there and I believe you said you're into abseiling."

"I hate it when you have ideas. We should stay and catch the cargo plane, instead of taking off on our own. We have hearings next month, you for child support and me for immigration."

"Maybe we should stay. But there's no place big enough for a cargo plane to land. They'll have to drop food and water before the poor millionaires find a way off this damned tepui. We can be off and down the river in a few hours, with the loot intact. And a transcript worth its weight in Powerball tickets."

"I always like a bit of adventure. It inspires me."

"No. Please don't. First thing back, I'll get you a fresh copy of your mum's big book of quotes, if only you'll—"

"Too late. I exact a price for my company. 'There is no sure cure for birth and death save to enjoy the interval.' Finally, something you can agree on, eh?"

"Eh." Mack hurried off with Lucas on his heels, flipping the rope over the edge of the tepui, tying the end around a boulder.

Lucas said, "Pray we don't fall."

"Let's don't."

The End

If you liked this book, please leave a review.

Also by David Rich:

Sail the World? – An Absurdly True Story, Prequel to RV the World

Myths of the Tribe - When Religion and Ethics Diverge

Scribes of the Tribe - The Great Thinkers on Religion and Ethics

The ISIS Affair - Putting the Fun Back in Fundamentalism

RV the World, 2nd Ed. (excerpt below)

The following is the introduction to *RV the World*. The book includes an exploration of the tepui featured in Antelopes:

IN THE BEGINNING

THE MONKEY ON MY BACK: TO SEE IT ALL

For my part, I travel not to go anywhere, but to go. I travel for travel's sake. The great affair is to move; to feel the needs and hitches of our life more nearly; to come down off this feather-bed of civilization, and find the globe granite underfoot and strewn with cutting flints.

—Robert Louis Stevenson

My earliest vivid memory is of a photo from an old geography book: Vesuvius in full-color eruption spewing fluorescent orange magma, torching rich Romans in Pompeii. This hit me between the eyes. *Whoa.* I really had to see that in person. What six-year-old wouldn't?

I could never kick this early memory, which evolved into a dream of seeing the world, the whole lot of it. My earliest ambition was finding the world's most fabulous volcanoes, my curiosity spurred by schoolteacher parents with a passion for travel and geography. I inherited a travel addiction, doomed to see the entire world or die trying.

I nagged my long-suffering parents to drive down every road, reasoning that we might stumble across Vesuvius anywhere. Humoring me, they drove down lots of dirt roads, many ending on the edges of deep canyons in Colorado, New Mexico, Utah, and Arizona, the Four Corners area where I grew up. They'd brought it on themselves, infecting me with a travel-and-geography obsession, insisting in return for my see-the-end-of-every-road harassment that I learn context, all the states, their capitals, and the capital of every country on the planet. I was crushed to find Vesuvius nowhere near the Four Corners.

An outlet for itchy feet fortuitously appeared when I was teaching at the local law school. A student said, "Hey, come help me try out my new sailboat." That day one of Arizona's many lakes became a scene of high comedy. By 10 a.m. we finally got the pole up. I later learned it was called a mast. Though we scooted down the lake in half an hour, downwind, it took until sunset to sail back as we cursed gods whose proper names we didn't know—the gods of tacking, coming about, and shifting winds. I was indelibly hooked.

After a few months of torture on my friend's Hobie Cat, including six crazy days sailing down the Mexican coast from Puerto Penasco to Bahia Kino, I finally enrolled—along with my wife, Mary—in a learn-to-sail course at the Annapolis Sailing School in San Diego. Then I tackled the advanced sailing course, which theoretically qualified me to bareboat charter.

Suddenly I wanted to sail around the world. People said, "But you live in Arizona. There's no water, except a few ridiculous lakes." By then everyone knew I'd gone stark raving mad—including Mary, but she gradually contracted the insatiable wanderlust encouraged by my parents.

I captained seventeen charters in Greece, Turkey, Vancouver, Belize, and most of the Bahamas and Caribbean Islands. It was my responsibility to find a proper sailing vessel (best price), set up the charter, organize disorganized friends during bouts of personal disorganization, and then, once we arrived at the destination, find water, fuel, and a likely place to moor or anchor each night. I halfway learned to sail a dozen different sailboats while my accompanying friends coughed up three hundred dollars per person for the pleasure of crewing. Aren't friends fabulous?

The second most glorious day of my life was buying a dreamboat to sail around the world. I named her *Grendel*. Mary and I spent years flying on weekends from Phoenix to San Diego, putting every toy aboard, from mast steps to radar to a water maker. The big day arrived when, after saving every penny on a ten-year plan that stretched to eleven years, I sold everything and sailed *Grendel* out of San Diego Harbor.

It became abundantly clear that Dave and Mary sailing around the world was not exactly as it appeared in *Romancing the Stone* when Michael Douglas and Kathleen Turner sailed into the sunset. No, life on *Grendel* was more about *la problema del dia,* the problem of the day, especially for someone who'd flunked grade school shop and was the least mechanically minded in the history of the Montezuma County public school system in Cortez, Colorado. To sail around the world you not only need to know how to sail but also how to fix stuff—all the stuff, including mechanical and electrical— and you need the baksheesh to coax replacement parts through foreign customs.

Hollywood had done me a disservice—or perhaps, like those guys who count landing at an international airport as visiting a country, I was a dope. After a year we were still in Mexico, though far down the Pacific Coast. The Marquesas and Tuamotus islands were next on our itinerary, and as the specter of a thirty- to forty-day ocean crossing loomed closer, I faced up to my terminal ineptness with a multi-meter and a monkey wrench, and Mary admitted to hating unending oceans. A compulsive jogger, she found the deck was too small for laps. We turned north to San Diego, where I experienced my most glorious day, selling *Grendel.*

By no means was this the end of my dream of seeing the world but instead the true beginning. Living on a sailboat relegated us, two non-beach persons, to the coast, though 90 percent of what there is to see is inland. We found sailing the very best way to spend time fixing stuff in exotic ports, leaving little time for exploration.

We began international RVing in 1994. That year we flew to Germany and bought an RV with the proceeds from *Grendel*. We lived the next three years in forty countries, spending summers in the United Kingdom, Ireland, Norway, and Scandinavia and winters in Spain, Portugal, Morocco, Italy (where I finally saw Vesuvius not erupting), Greece, Turkey, Israel, Jordan, and Egypt, plus all the countries in between. Seventeen years later, though we have stopped full-time RVing, we're still RVing the world six months a year.

We've visited hundreds of scenic spots available overnight only by tent or RV. Among our favorite experiences have been overnighting within or next to:

The Horns of Hittite, where the Crusaders met their final demise above Lake Kinneret (aka the Sea of Galilee), where we were visited by a helicopter.

New Zealand's Mount Cook, framed by our RV's panoramic windows, and Milford Sound, which we had all to ourselves after the tour buses had gone home for the night.

A remote beach in New South Wales, where we were surrounded by kangaroos.

The world's most incredible ruins at ancient Petra, and definitely by ourselves in remote Wadi Rum, where Larry of Arabia hung out, both in Jordan.

Alice Springs in Australia's Northern Territory, where we watched a full eclipse of the moon atop our RV.

The wind-hewn canyons of the Negev Desert in Israel.

A French canal and an ancient French monastery in a primeval forest.

Hobart Bay and Cradle Mountain in Tasmania.

Purnululu National Park in the orange-and-black-striped mountains of the Bungle Bungles, and at the confluence of sandstone slot canyons in Karajini National Park, in Western Australia.

The waterfront in Ushuaia, Argentina, the southernmost city in the world, where we watched ships leave for Antarctica, and in Tierra Del Fuego National Park, outside Ushuaia, at the foot of the last of the Andes, on the Beagle Channel.

Vesuvius overlooking the bay and the lights of Naples.

The canals of Bruges, Amsterdam, and Venice. (Unfortunately, the Chinese government prohibits driving an RV to the canals of Suzhou).

Finland's many lakes, surrounded by reindeer.

The waterfront in Stockholm, where we camped for a week.

Lake Titicaca in Bolivia. Another Bolivian favorite is Mount Sajama (21,000 feet), where we camped at 15,000 feet next to hot springs a few kilometers from the border with Chile and a lake perfectly reflected twin Fuji-esque cones.

The week before I quit playing lawyer, several friends said they envied my plan. The brevity of life had been vividly illustrated to them. They, like me, had always treated life as if it went on forever. One guy's brother had been diagnosed with inoperable cancer, a month before his scheduled retirement. Another's father had prostate cancer, chose the operation, and died two weeks after retiring. Mary's boss had dreamed of buying an oceangoing fishing boat but kept putting it off. He needed to add to his retirement kitty. Just before we left he was diagnosed with a brain tumor and died a year later. Do it now, whatever it is you want to do. If we don't do it now, the odds are we never will. Perhaps along the way you'll find the world's most picturesque volcano.

www.ingramcontent.com/pod-product-compliance
Lightning Source LLC
Chambersburg PA
CBHW071004280626

47160CB00016B/2170